ICE MAGIC

1.75

Cold shocked his f̶͟ ... Anskiere's wards, Jaric gasped, then ... as chill bit into the tissue of his lungs. He called up fire to counter. But even as warmth answered his will, a starred pulse of light canceled his effort. Weather sorcery closed like a fist mailed with winter, smothering flame into darkness. Jaric staggered backward into the red heat of the cavern. Frost spiked his hair and tunic. His hands were numb, unresponsive and whitened as bread dough. Ivainson rubbed his fingers. Shivering in discomfort as circulation returned, he contemplated the wards, and knew fear. . . .

SHADOWFANE

Praise for
THE CYCLE OF FIRE . . .

"Outstanding . . . an excellent and absorbing tale."

—*Andre Norton*

"There's high magic here and, more importantly, real people and fine writing."

—*Lynn Abbey*

"A great natural storyteller!"

—*L. Sprague de Camp*

JANNY WURTS

BOOK THREE OF THE CYCLE OF FIRE

SHADOWFANE

ACE BOOKS, NEW YORK

This book is an Ace
original edition, and
has never been previously
published.

SHADOWFANE

An Ace Book/published by arrangement with
the author

PRINTING HISTORY
Ace edition/November 1988

ISBN: 0-441-76082-1

Ace Books are published by The Berkley Publishing Group,
200 Madison Avenue, New York, New York 10016.
The name "Ace" and the "A" logo
are trademarks belonging to
Charter Communications, Inc.
PRINTED IN THE UNITED STATES OF AMERICA

10 9 8 7 6 5 4 3 2 1

For Raymond E. Feist
true friend, talented author,
and
(my influence to the contrary)
an incurable enthusiast of jazz and the Chargers

Acknowledgments

The finish of a series requires a great deal of thanks to the many individuals who helped the author along the way. In particular my appreciation goes to the following individuals, for efforts that made all the difference:

Terri Windling, for seeing three books between the lines of two, and asking gently to make it happen;

Virginia Kidd, for her tireless efforts of negotiation; and Jonathan Matson and Abner Stein, for the same, but overseas;

Soni Gross and Fern Edison, whose contributions above and beyond the normal call helped make the start a success;

Peter Schneider, for off-the-cuff assistance with promotion;

My parents, who put up with a lot of unreasonable dreams;

My friend and former landlord, Daniel P. Mannix, who for eleven years gave me guidance and a roof under which to create;

Beth Fleisher, my editor, for sharing my passion for sailing and twisted plots;

Gene Mydlowski, art director, for belief in an author who happens also to paint;

Elaine Chubb, copy editor, whose unfailing devotion to detail is a mystery and a miracle all by itself.

Northsea

Wrecker's Bay

Clover's Warren

Felwaithe

Kierkforest

Murieton

Canyon Lake

Riftwater

Kisburn

Eastplain

Royal Palace

Mainstrait

Elrithfaer Tower

Merk's Point

Terin Sea

Elrinfaer

Telshire

Cael's Falls

Mhored Kara

Deshforest

Prologue

The seeress of the well in Gaire's Main woke gasping in the straw of the stables where she sheltered. She shivered, blind eyes milky in the moonlight that spilled from the loft. The visions that had broken her sleep racked her still, bringing terror beyond anything mortal. The seeress stirred ancient joints and rose. Clothed in scraps of knotted leather, she groped down the dusty ladder and made her way past stall and grain stores, then out into the waning autumn night.

Beyond the barn lay a crossroad and a trough awash with muddy puddles. The folk of Gaire's Main presently used the sacred spring as a watering place for beast and household; to them the seeress was a senile beggar woman given to strange outbursts and mumbling. But tonight no confusion blurred her movements. She knelt on the chill ground and scrabbled through pig droppings until she located the stone that founded the mystery of her craft.

The slab was black, laced with metallic streaks of gold, and rinsed clean by overflow from the spring. Tears brimmed from the seeress's lashless eyes as she laid her palms against the talisman. Energy welled from the contact. With a cry of agonized relief, she surrendered her burden of dreams to its current. . . .

In the wind-whipped darkness of an ocean roiled by the aftermath of a gale, a boat with tattered sails rolled hove to in the swell. There a black-haired man dressed in the cottons of a fisherman reached out to an injured Thienz-demon who clung to a drift of timber in the waves. Neither kindness nor compassion prompted the man's action; his spirit was not human, an evil sensed palpably across the fabric of the seeress's dream.

The rescued demon was not to survive its deliverance from the waves. As its toadlike fingers closed upon the man's wrist, the seeress sensed its agony, the burning sting of salt splashed into its gills. Poisoned beyond healing, the demon endured only long enough to deliver its death-dream, which held intact the death-dreams of others who had perished earlier, in a backlash of forces brought about by no natural means.

These memories the Thienz impressed directly into the mind of the human in the boat, for their significance to mankind's enemies offered proof that an artifact of paramount significance still existed. Untempered and entire, the death-dream of the Thienz seared like magma through the young man's awareness. When he screamed, the seeress screamed with him, and the well-stone beneath her hands relayed the dying demon's legacy to mankind's most ancient defender. . . .

On an islet far distant from Gaire's Main, the old woman's sending cut like the cry of a dying doe across a grove of enchanted twilight; there an entity known as the Vaere received her images with an understanding not given to mortal men. The news promised grimmest consequences. The dying Thienz had stumbled upon a secret centuries old. When that knowledge reached the demon compact at Shadowfane, its full import would be recognized. Then would the wardenship of the Vaere itself become threatened. Now the untried talents of the sorcerer's heir but recently come to sanctuary offered the only expedient. If Ivainson Jaric failed to master his father's talents, if he failed in the Cycle of Fire while the compact unriddled the mystery of the Vaere, mankind would suffer extinction at the hands of demon foes. . . .

The seeress broke contact with a quivering sigh; and silence ominous as the calm before cataclysm settled over the grove of the Vaere.

～❦ I ❦～

Riddle

Cold came early to the wastes beyond Felwaithe; frosts rimed the lichens and traced a madman's patterns on the bare rock of the hills. Here, far north of Keithland's border and the lands inhabited by men, a single lantern burned in a hall of bleak stone. Within its circle of light, Scait, Demon Lord of Shadowfane, sat upon a chair fashioned from the bones and the hides of human victims. He pared his thumb spurs to needlepoints with a penknife, while an immature Thienz ornamented with beads crouched at his feet, froglike limbs folded against its loins.

Scait flexed scaled wrists and paused in his sharpening. His upper lip curled over rows of sharklike teeth as he addressed his groveling underling. "What has occurred that Thienz elders send a hatchling to trouble my thoughts? Speak, tadpole! What tidings do you bring?"

The Thienz cowered against the icy stone floor. The sovereign of Shadowfane quite often killed out of temper, and this youngster brought ill news of the worst import. It flapped its gills in distress. "Most-mighty, I bring word of the boats sent into Keithland to capture Ivainson-Firelord's-heir-Jaric. Your servants have failed. Jaric has reached sanctuary on the Isle of the Vaere."

Scait hissed explosively. *"Seed-of his-father, accursed!* How did one wretched boy slip past five dozen Thienz elders?"

Beads chinked against stillness; the Thienz battled an overwhelming instinct to flee, yet the flash of displeasure in its master's sultry eyes did not metamorphose into blows. Its crest flattened in reluctance against its blunt head, the youngster pre-

3

pared to offer images of storm and death, and the wreckage of the fleet that had failed in its directive to take the gold-haired son of Ivain Firelord.

But the sovereign Lord of Shadowfane refused direct sharing. Instead he twisted the blade of his knife and pricked at the stuffed human thigh that comprised the throne arm. "I would know the particulars of Jaric's escape from one who is senior, and experienced. Fetch me Thienz-eldest, for no other will suffice."

The young demon bobbed hasty obeisance, then scuttled from the dais, its discharge of fear and relief a palpable stink in the air. Once clear of the steps, it spun and fled around the mirror pool set into the floor beyond. Scait watched with slitted eyes as it vanished into the gloom of the doorway; rage born of frustration bristled the long hackles at his neck. He had hoped to capture Jaric, enslave and manipulate his Firelord's potential for the ruin and sorrow of humanity. Now this recent failure by the Thienz invited terrible risk. Ivainson Jaric might survive the Cycle of Fire; then would humans gain another Vaere-trained sorcerer, one powerful enough to free Anskiere of Elrinfaer from his prison of ward-spelled ice. The paired threat of Stormwarden and Firelord would pose a serious inconvenience, if not a direct impediment, to the conquest planned by the demon compact at Shadowfane.

Scait paced, knife clenched between spurred fingers. He ground his teeth in agitation until the Thienz elder he had summoned presented itself before the dais.

Lest an underling of no consequence sense his distress, the Lord of Shadowfane smoothed his long hackles and sat. As the elder completed its obeisance, he scraped one spur across the bared edge of his knife and demanded, "How did Ivainson-Fire-lord's-heir-Jaric come to reach the Isle of the Vaere?"

The Thienz replied in words, the barest ruffle of its crest hinting defiance. "Ivain's-get-Jaric arranged the release of a weather ward of Anskiere's." Offered the clear, precise image of a storm-falcon's feather, and the blue-violet shimmer of sorcery that had released a ruinous gale across the southwest reaches, Scait bared his teeth.

The Thienz hastily continued. "Storm-death did not bring the bane of all Thienze-cousins sent hunting. Another hazard entirely prevented their closing with the prey." The Thienz closed tiny eyes and sent the death-dream salvaged from a failing survivor by Maelgrim Dark-dreamer. In precise, empathic images, the Lord of Shadowfane shared the last memories of three Thienz who had huddled in drenched misery aboard a boat many leagues to the south.

Only moments before death, they whimpered among them-selves, their shared thoughts riddled with terror. The storm that Ivain Firelord's heir had caused to be unleashed had bashed and capsized and drowned the crews of seven companion vessels. The Thienz who sailed aboard the last boat trembled, fearful their own doom would follow.

Scait hissed. The dagger dangled forgotten in his grip as the doomed creatures' vision filled his sensors. At one with the memories of the Thienz who had crouched afraid in that-boat-sent-to-apprehend-Jaric, he, too, beheld the roiling and spume-frothed crests of gale-whipped ocean.

Suddenly the air seemed to shimmer. Sky and swells rippled, blurred, and shifted into pearly mist; then fog in turn dissolved, transformed to a prismatic chaos of energy, all shattered bands of color and light. The display lasted only a moment before cruel fields of energy blistered the Thienz' bodies. They fell, crying curses, the agony of their dying accompanied by wood that popped and steamed, and canvas that burst sullenly into flame.

The dream ended. Scait's lids snapped open, unveiling irises hard as topaz. Needle rows of teeth gleamed as he framed words in speculation. "Tell me, lowly toad. What memory does that death-dream call to mind?"

Possessed of the eidetic recall common to all demons, the Thienz squirmed uneasily upon the carpet. "This death was the same as that dreamed by ancestor-among-the-stars who died, trapped by the expanding field of a time anomaly when a ship drive malfunctioned. But such interpretation is questionable. Keithland's humans have lost all memory of technology."

"Not entirely." Scait snapped his jaws closed. Delicately he stroked his dagger across the arm of his throne. "Veriset-Nav," he mused triumphantly. "This dream gives proof beyond doubt. The navigational guidance module must have survived the crash of star-probe-*Corinne-Dane*-accursed. We have only to find it, and recover the unit intact, and our exile from home-star will be ended."

The Thienz wailed, its crest flattened against its earless skull. "Lord-highest, you suggest the impossible. Where can we seek? *Corinne Dane*'s emergency systems capsule plunged into ocean, destroyed." The Thienz paused to whistle soulfully, its tune an expression of knowledge lost.

But Scait ignored its protests. Preoccupied, he arose from his chair. Wire ornaments jangled against scaled knuckles as he paced the dais.

Like an ill-sewn frog puppet, the Thienz twisted its blunt head to follow its master's steps. "Mightiest, Set-Nav is lost, still."

"Perhaps not." Scait jerked to a stop. He leered down at the Thienz. "I say all along that Set-Nav may have hidden behind a persona called the Vaere."

At this the Thienz rocked back on webbed feet, snorted, then burst into croaking peals of laughter. "Mightiest, O mightiest, you surely jest! We know the Vaere! Human superstition, brought forward from earliest, most barbaric remnants of old Earth culture." All in the compact knew that Tamlin originated in a tale conceived by primitive ballad singers; funny indeed, if mankind might be witless enough to mistake the most sophisticated technology its people ever created with a make-believe creature of faerie!

"Silence!" Scait's short hackles lifted in warning. "Be still, one-who-forgets."

The demon beneath the dais quivered at the insult. It rolled whiteless eyes as Scait leaned over and thrust the knife toward its chin. "Myth or not, facts are these: Tamlin of the Vaere reputedly trained our greatest foe, Anskiere, and also Ivain Firelord. And, one-who-forgets, remember that humans possess no senses to differentiate between the dream-state and reality experienced! Recall that *Corinne Dane*'s Set-Nav guidance unit came equipped with mind-link modules."

Such machines could induce a man to dream for years, and still preserve his body. The Thienze blinked, jolted to sober reflection. The time-differential field of the star drive neatly accounted for the unnatural aging that afflicted those mortals who received their sorcerer's training from the Vaere.

Scait shot to his feet, eyes ablaze with excitement. "Now, one-who-forgets, let scornful laughter pucker your tongue with the taste and the texture of excrement. For I think humankind does not know its sorcerers are guided to mastery by technology its people once possessed."

The Thienz whuffed its gills, silent, while Scait subsided back into his chair. Strangely, terribly, the Demon Lord's reasoning suggested truth. Man might have forgotten his vanquished empire among the stars; yet an electronic guidance system endowed with intelligence, self-repair, and the logic to master the bewildering mathematics of interstellar navigation would never lose its loyalty, or its mission. As killers and imprisoners of creatures with paranormal endowment, Stormwarden and Firelord might indeed continue the starprobe *Corinne Dane*'s original directive: to discover means of defending mankind against the psionic warfare of aliens.

Curled in idle malice upon his chair of human remains, Scait qualified the Thienz' thought. "Toad, you misjudge. Deliberately Set-Nav may have cloaked its identity as Tamlin, that the compact might overlook its existence."

The Thienz twisted the tiny fingers of its forelimbs and moaned, while in abrupt agitation the Demon Lord stabbed the dagger to the hilt into stuffed human upholstery. "O toad, the death-dream of your companion brings promise of triumph-and-trouble. We must unravel the riddle of Tamlin, for time is precious. Ivainson-cursed-sorcerer's-heir-Jaric escaped us. Now, surely as stars turn, a firelord could emerge to balk us. If so, we might face the hatching of the Morrigierj unprepared."

The Thienz stiffened. It raised, then lowered its webbed crest, and a tremble invaded its limbs. The memories-of-ancestors knew Morrigierj, that grand-master entity spawned each three thousand years to bind the collective powers of the Gierj into a single force; of all sentients sworn to the compact of Shadowfane, the mindless Gierjlings owned a latent capacity for destruction that intimidated even the strongest demon. With a squeak of apprehension, the Thienz fled the chamber; it slid with a scrape of claws around the doorjamb and scuttled like a dog down the stairwell.

Scait laughed at its flight. His threat had been a lie designed to intimidate; when the silly Thienz paused to think, it would recall that no grand hatching could occur without maturity of a Morrigierj spore. Since his predecessor's death at Anskiere's hand, the Demon Lord held power against the machinations of ambitious subordinates; at best, his supremacy at Shadowfane was precariously secured. With his current plot to defeat mankind thrown into setback, underlings must be kept cowed to discourage rivals; for challengers there would be, unless Scait found means to counter the threat posed by the possibility of a new firelord. The discovery of Set-Nav, though of paramount significance, was of secondary importance to politics and power within the compact.

Scait thought bitterly upon Jaric. Once he had glimpsed the boy's aura; demon-perceived clarity had sensed the ringing patterns of energy that mapped a gifted human's aptitude for mastery of Sathid-bonded forces. Never until then had any demon imagined that humans, even rare ones, might hold so much latent

affinity for power. Untrained, such individuals could easily be
enslaved and turned to the detriment of their own kind; the loss of
Jaric's talents stung doubly. Scait bristled his hackles in frustration. Humanity bred and proliferated like pest parasites. Except
for the wizards inhabiting the towers at Mhored Kara, most were
blind to the psychic energies of the mind. Perhaps among Keithland's teeming towns, other children born with such gifts were
overlooked.

Scait blinked and shifted in his chair. If such children existed,
they might be taken and exploited. Yet members of the compact
could not cross into Keithland to explore without drawing notice.
Subterfuge would be necessary.

The lantern suddenly flickered; in its failing light, Scait's teeth
flashed in a leer of wild excitement. There existed one for whom
such restrictions would not exist. Maelgrim Dark-dreamer's talents were already controlled by the compact; through him, a way
could be found to conduct such a search undetected. Excited now,
Scait reached in thought for the mind of the Thienz elder who had
recently departed his presence.

'Where is Maelgrim now?'

The image sent in reply was prompt, but clouded with a resentment most probably effected by the ruse concerning the Morrigierj; Scait chose forbearance in his lust for information. All of
Maelgrim's Thienz crew had perished of salt poisoning; alone in
a boat severely battered by the aftermath of the storm set loose by
Jaric, the Dark-dreamer currently struggled to patch tattered
canvas, that he might sail for Shadowfane and the north. Scait
clicked his spurs in irritation; his new plan must wait until the
boy-slave-human returned, a delay that might extend through
several months, since winter's inevitable gales would brew up
weather unfavorable for passage. Forced to patience, the Demon
Lord brooded upon the possibilities presented by rediscovery of
the Veriset-Nav computer. Hours passed. The lamp flickered out
and predawn gloom infused Shadowfane's empty hall. Spurred
fingers stroked the dagger left embedded in cured human flesh,
while, outside, wind wailed like a funeral dirge across the frost-
blasted fells.

Twenty-seven generations after the fall of the probe ship *Corinne Dane*, the navigational computer that had calculated courses
between stars analyzed its latest acquisition, a sorcerer's son who
aspired to undertake the Cycle of Fire. Small, lean, and callused
from the rigors of the storm that had delivered him to the fabled

isle, Jaric was remarkably like his sire, Ivain; except here and there lay clues to differences that extended beyond mere flesh.

The boy's sun-bleached hair and seafarer's tan seemed oddly misplaced under the red-lit glimmer of the control panels. His clothing had been meticulously mended with a sail needle, before being torn again. His rope belt was not tasseled, but perfectly end-spliced; only his bootlaces revealed haste or impatience, one being tied with sailors' knots, the other whipped into tangles that the mechanical arms of the robots unsnarled with difficulty. The body beneath the clothing proved bruised and abraded, the legacy of hardship and stress.

The father had chosen his path to mastery in far less agony of spirit; unlike his son, he had arrived upon the isle with a companion at his side, his passage uncontested by hunting packs of Thienz. Much hope or much setback might arise from Jaric's experience. Unaffected by sentiment, the guardian of mankind's future reviewed his candidacy for the Cycle of Fire with precise and passionless logic.

The boy under scrutiny remained unaware that the creature he knew as Tamlin of the Vaere was an entity fabricated by a sophisticated array of machinery. Taken into custody from the woodland clearing where he had succumbed to drugged sleep, and bundled by robots into a metal-walled chamber hidden beneath the soil, Ivainson Jaric presently rested within a life-support capsule that once had equipped the starship's flight deck.

Servo-mechanisms labored over his body, completing hookups that in the past had enabled human navigators to interface with the Veriset-Nav's complex circuitry. Like every human visitor before him, Jaric would experience only dreams during his stay upon the fabled isle.

The Vaere had kept its true form secret since the crash of *Corinne Dane*. Ejected intact from its parent ship, the unit retained power generators and drive field; but with Starhope fallen to enemies, a distress flare would draw attack rather than rescue. Set-Nav found itself shepherd to refugees incapable of defending its data from aliens who could reprogram its functions for their own use. Even as the germ plasms of earth-type flora and fauna had survived and altered the face of Keithland, so had the guidance computer changed, adapted, and evolved, cloaked in a guise of myth. Despite time and attrition, its primary directive remained. Set-Nav even yet sought means to end the predations of psionically endowed aliens that mankind now called demons.

In its latest, most effective offensive, Veriset-Nav trained psi-talented humans to mastery of a double Sathid-link that gained them direct control over the elements. Jaric was the latest candidate for a procedure fraught with danger.

Of countless human subjects, only Anskiere and Ivain had survived to achieve dual mastery; but their success had justified the deaths of their predecessors. Paired crystals had granted them power enough to eradicate some species of demons and imprison others. The task of freeing Keithland from threat had begun. But talent capable of training for such feats was sparse, ever difficult to obtain; Ivainson, whose life was already sought by demons, possessed potential both precious and rare.

A switch closed. Lights flickered green over the access console, tinting Jaric like a wax figure while programs designed for complex navigational mathematics exhaustively mapped his potential. The Vaere matched the crippling self-doubt of this boy's childhood against his determination to achieve a Firelord's inheritance. It tallied strength, weakness, and raw potential and completed its model with direct observations shared by the Dreamweaver, Taen. Information streamed into the data banks, then transmuted, meshed and interwoven to a sequence of intricate probability equations. Inflexibly logical, the Vaere calculated Jaric's potential to survive the dual mastery that comprised the Cycle of Fire.

The conclusion was disturbing. Never in Keithland history had the Vaere detected such raw potential for power in the mind of a man; yet the latent ability Jaric possessed proved coupled with a personality sensitive to the point of fragility, balanced upon a selfhood newly and precariously established. Considered alone, this analysis might have disqualified the boy from training; but now, with demons aware of the origins of the Vaere, the slimmest opportunity counted.

An access circuit closed. Alongside Jaric's statistics the Vaere added the composite analysis of Keithland, then an estimated projection of the Dark-dreamer's acquired power. The forecast proved bleak. Maelgrim's mastery derived from a Sathid already dominated by Thienz-demons; his talents would be like his sister's, but reversed. Where Taen wove dreams to heal and defend, her brother would spin visions to destroy. She could influence individuals; but with the combined might of Shadowfane's compact to back him, Maelgrim might instigate wholesale madness, corrupt governments, or incite soldiers to war against the very cities they were armed to protect. Before such an onslaught, even the defenses at Landfast might topple.

The Vaere sequenced scenarios of possible countermoves for days and nights without letup. At the end, only one held hope. Shadowfane's invasion might be deterred if the Stormwarden, Anskiere of Elrinfaer, were freed from the ice. That task required a firelord's skills. Time was too short to seek an alternate for the Cycle of Fire, even should a second candidate exist with Keithland's population.

Had the Vaere reacted as a mortal, such a quandary would have caused grief and trepidation; being a machine of passionless logic, it executed decisions within a millisecond. Jaric must be placed in jeopardy; after a brief training period, the boy must attempt Earthmastery. If he retained control after primary bonding, he must go on to attempt mastery of a second Sathid matrix, the most difficult challenge a sorcerer could attempt. He must endure and survive the Cycle of Fire. Should he fail, if the Sathid entities he must battle for dominance conquered his will, both he and Anskiere would perish. Then the defense of Keithland would rest upon a Dreamweaver's frail and inadequate resources.

Lights blinked and vanished, and the consoles went dark beside the amber glow of the life-support unit. Veriset-Nav initiated an entry command, and the circuitry that cross-linked the master navigator's capsule shifted status to active. Monitors winked to life, glowing blue over a boy framed in a nest of silvery wires. The heir of Ivain Firelord stirred in the depths of his sleep, even as the guidance systems from *Corinne Dane* induced the first of a series of dreams designed to prepare him for the trials of a sorcerer's mastery.

Unaware his senses were subject to illusion, Jaric believed that he roused to twilit silence in the grove of the Vaere. He opened his eyes to grass and flowers, and to the same enchanted clearing where he had earlier fallen asleep. A chill roughened his flesh. Nothing appeared to have changed, and that unsettled him. His hands still stung with abrasions from muscling *Callinde*'s helm against stormwinds. Both clothing and skin glittered with salt crystals, crusted by spray upon his person. Puzzled, for he had expected some sign of great magic, he blinked and pushed himself erect. The soil felt cool under his palms. Overhead, the trees arched in the silvery half-light like a congregation of leaf-bearded patriarchs. Irritated to discover that his body had stiffened during his rest on damp ground, the boy stretched, then froze with his arms half-raised. Tamlin of the Vaere sat perched on the low gray rock at the center of the grove.

An insouciant grin crinkled the tiny man's features. His beard tumbled in tangles over his fawn colored jacket. Beads and feathered bells sewn to the cuffs jingled merrily in rhythm with his booted feet, which swung idly above the tips of the flowers, and the pipe in his hand trailed smoke like braid through the air.

Jaric raked back mussed hair, wary of the lightless black eyes that watched his every move. "How long have you been here?"

"Always, and never." The Vaere made no effort to qualify his oblique statement, but bit down on his pipestem, drew, and puffed out a perfect smoke ring. "Are you going to ask why?"

Jaric tucked his knees within the circle of his arms and frowned. "Would you answer?"

Tamlin laughed. Feathers danced on his sleeves as he lowered his pipe, yet his mirth dispersed with the smoke ring. "I have no answers, only riddles. Do you still desire a firelord's mastery?"

Aware his integrity was under question, Jaric chose his reply with care. "I wish Keithland secure from demons." He rose, too nervous to keep still any longer.

"No difference, then, son of Ivain." The Vaere leaped from his perch and landed in grass that did not rustle; full height, he stood no higher than Jaric's hip. "To spare your people, you must conquer all weakness, then master the skills that were your father's. Are you prepared?"

"No." Jaric waited, tense down to his heels. Hemmed in by the eerie stillness of the grove, he shied from remembering the demons, and the fate that awaited the people and the woman he loved if he failed. "Is any man born prepared to suffer madness? I can do nothing more than try."

"You say!" Bells clinked briskly as Tamlin took a step forward. "You cannot survive the Cycle of Fire without first mastering the earth. For that, your resolve must be unassailable. *Is it?*"

Jaric swallowed. With a bitter heart, he pictured Taen Dreamweaver's smile, bright as the song of the woodlarks in Seitforest; he remembered the banners flying free over the towers of Landfast, and the Kielmark's wild anger when Cliffhaven stood threatened by armies with demon allies. These things he treasured, and longed to protect. But it had been the wild clans of Cael's Falls and their sacrifice of thirty-nine lives to preserve him from demon captivity that had irrevocably sealed his resolve to attempt the Cycle of Fire. Nothing short of death could deflect Jaric from his decision, though the passage to a firelord's mastery had worked upon Ivain a total annihilation of identity: a vicious, irreversible insanity that caused people across Keithland to fear him. Years after the morning he had ended his misery with a dagger thrust through his heart, Ivain Firelord was remembered with curses. The mention of his name caused folk of all stations to raise crossed wrists in the sign against evil brought on by sorcery.

Tamlin gestured and the pipe vanished instantly from his hand. He spoke as though he were privy to the boy's dark fears. "Son of Ivain, you will need more than determination. The Sathid crystal you must subjugate to gain Earthmastery will already be self-aware at the time it links with your consciousness. It will explore your innermost self, back to the time of birth, seeking weakness that can be turned to exploit you. How much of your past can you face without flinching?"

Though pressured where he was most vulnerable, Jaric refused to give ground. From the instant he reached the fabled isle, Tamlin seemed bent on intimidating him. The idea dawned that the Vaere's words might not be warnings but a ploy intended to provoke him.

"So!" Tamlin sprang aggressively onto the stone, his gaze turned terribly, piercingly direct. "Your mind is quick. But anger will not be enough to overcome what lies ahead. Shall I prove that?"

Without further warning the Vaere clapped his hands. A dissonant jangle of bells tangled with Jaric's shout as the ground dissolved from beneath his feet. His senses overturned, and he tumbled backward into a memory from his past.

↫ II ↬

Mastery of Earth

The fruit trees in Morbrith's walled orchard stood stripped of leaves, and branches rattled like bones in the grip of ice and wind. Yet the gardens Jaric recalled from childhood were not desolate, even in the harshest freeze of winter. The footprints of small boys rumpled the snow between the paths, and laughter rang through frosty air. Only Jaric, an assigned ward of the Smith's Guild, hung back from the rough play of his peers. On the morning of his fourth birthday, a big man who smelled of horses had taken him from the hearth of his latest foster-mother. From now on, he understood he would live in the loft over the forge with the rest of the guild apprentices. The other boys were older than Jaric by several years; in the cruel fashion of children, they resented the intruder in their midst.

"Why, he's nothing but a baby!" Garrey, the eldest, had mocked, and the rest followed his lead like a pack.

Cold air bit through Jaric's mittens. Longingly he watched the apprentices run and leap at tag-ball; earlier, Garrey had told him he was unwelcome to join their play. But the game fascinated a boy whose foster-mother had kept him separate from her own children, and whispered when she thought he would not hear that his presence brought ill luck to her house. Drawn by the laughter, the running, and the carefree scuffling of the young, Jaric edged closer. Unwittingly he crossed the boundary line of the game.

Garrey missed a difficult catch. A burly boy, but quick, he spun and dashed after the ball, only to encounter Jaric standing squarely in his path. He checked and slipped, and barreled heav-

14

ily into the younger child. Knocked to one knee, Jaric struggled to regain his feet. Garrey whirled before he could run.

Scowling, his red face speckled with snowflakes, the larger boy curled his lip in contempt. "Hey! Milk-nose!"

He did not turn from Jaric as the tag-ball glanced off the wall beyond. The rebound became soundlessly absorbed by a snow-drift as Garrey's companions closed in a semicircle around the slight, blond boy who had clumsily spoiled their play. Jaric backed one step, two, then stopped, cornered against the thorny stems of a rosebush.

"You're not wanted," said Garrey. He stripped off his gloves and raised crossed fists in the traditional sign against ill fortune. "Your own mother tried to kill you, don't you know? And after-ward, the father who spared your life got hung, condemned by the Earl's justice for her murder."

"No," whispered Jaric. "You lie, surely."

"Do I so? Then where's your mother, whore's get? And your father?" Garrey grinned, displaying gapped teeth where a horse had kicked him. His tone turned boastful. "I saw Kerain die. His face turned purple, and his eyes bled. Ask the Guildmaster." The older boy knocked Jaric to the ground with a savage shove. Other boys joined in, striking with fists and boots.

But Kerainson, whose upbringing had been charged to the Smith's Guild, hardly felt the blows that pummeled his body. A peer's thoughtless cruelty had revealed the truth behind the townsfolk's tendency to shun him. For the first time he had words to set to the dream that broke his sleep, week after restless week. The nightmare left him wailing in terror from a remembered flash of silver, followed by a man's bruising grip, and blood smell, and a terrible shout mingled with a woman's scream of anguish.

As Garrey's band of apprentices tumbled him over and over in the snow, Jaric felt the darkness of those nightmares return. He choked and bit his lip, but could not smother the scream that rose in his throat. Once that scream escaped, another followed, and another, until his senses reeled and drowned in reverberations of remembered fear.

That day in the past, the apprentices had pulled back. Alarmed, they fled the presence of the boy who screamed as if crazed in the snow. They ignored him when he recovered; and pursued by a horror no longer formless, the boy had repeatedly fallen ill rather than watch their play from the sidelines. Now a man grown, Jaric felt both memory and snow melt away into air.

His last cry rang without echo within the grove of the Vaere. Yet even as he separated past from present, the hands now callused from sword and sheet line remained clenched across his eyes.

Bells tinkled nearby. Jaric drew a shaking breath and forced his sweating fingers to loosen. When he looked up, Tamlin stood over him, his bearded features vague in the twilight.

"Ivainson Jaric, to achieve a sorcerer's powers, you must first master yourself. The training will go hard for you. I say again, are you prepared?"

Jaric swallowed. He spoke in a voice still husky from tears. "Yes."

Tamlin did not relent. "Would you return to the memory you just left, and suffer the pain of that experience ten times tenfold?"

Blond hair gleamed in the half-light as Jaric lifted his head. Brown eyes met black, the former angrily determined, the latter fathomlessly dark. For a moment human and Vaere poised, motionless. Then Jaric rose. He glared down at the fey form of his tormentor, his stance the unwitting image of Ivain's.

"Yes," he said softly. "Send me back to suffer if you must. Only don't turn me away empty-handed. Should you do that, all that I value will perish. To watch and be helpless would be worse than any torment a Sathid could devise."

"Very well, then." Tamlin gestured with a shimmering jingle of bells. "You have earned the chance to train." He paused, and a gleam of admonition lit his eyes. "But remember, self-defense will not avail if on the day of trial no weapon is ready to your hand."

Tamlin winked and promptly vanished. Left alone in the glade, Jaric barely grasped that he had gained the chance to attempt a sorcerer's mastery. Instead, chagrined, he wondered how Tamlin had learned of the sword he inevitably forgot to carry, to the repeated dismay of his instructors.

Lights flickered, patternless as stars across the consoles, as the Vaere sorted the data acquired during Jaric's first trial of will. If the early figures showed promise, they also outlined need for major work to come. To survive the Cycle of Fire, Jaric must bring his present-day resilience to bear upon the inadequacies of his childhood. Motivated, not by hope, but by the relentless reality of numbers, the Vaere sorted options and prepared for the future

Mechanical extensions trapped the small, squirming bodies of two earth-diggers from the soil beneath the forest floor. Barely a handspan across, the creatures lacked both eyesight and measurable intelligence; yet within their living bodies Set-Nav would create the seeds of a sorcerer's command of elements. Machinery hummed, and gears spun in frictionless silence. The earth-diggers squeaked protest as needles pierced their hides, inoculating each of them with a separate solution of Sathid matrix. Set-Nav placed the squalling animals in cages. The first would host its crystal until its flesh transformed to seed-matrix at the completion of the Sathid's cycle; when it was secondarily bonded to a human subject, memories stored from the matrix's previous existence would expand. From them Jaric must shape his Earthmaster's powers. If he succeeded, the remaining digger would be set aflame. Sathid matrix recovered from its ashes would initiate Jaric to the Cycle of Fire, if his courage did not fail him. For by the most conservative estimate, Set-Nav determined that Keithland had less than a year to offset the threat of Maelgrim. All too soon the dark dreams of demons would influence humanity toward destruction.

In Keithland the days shortened. Crops ripened to harvest, gathered in before the frosts that withered the stubble in the fields. Leaves cloaked the hillsides in colors until winter winds ripped them away; but while snowfall might silt the thickets elsewhere with drifts, time and season remained constant on the Isle of the Vaere. Grasses flowered soft as spring above the installation that housed Set-Nav. Securely dreaming inside his silver capsule, the boy who aspired to a firelord's mastery slowly completed his training. Through months of careful schooling, Tamlin taught him to reshape the nightmares of his childhood. The insecurities Jaric had known as an apprentice scribe were painstakingly unraveled, early uncertainty excised by the confidence of later achievements until recognition of his own self-worth underlay the boy's being like bedrock. For the first time in his life, Jaric could explore his past without feeling haunted by inadequacy.

Yet the freedom inspired by his accomplishment was not to last. The moment the odds of probability favored success, Set-Nav recovered the seed Sathid that had survived the first earth-digger's death and dissolved it in saline solution. Jaric felt no pain as the needle pierced his unconscious flesh. Even as an alien entity entered a vein in his wrist, he dreamed of a twilit grove; there a tiny man dressed in leather and bells delivered final instructions.

"Remember, your danger lies in the weakness within your-

self." Bells tinkled as the Vaere wagged his finger at the young
man who sat before him on the grass. He had been born slight,
this son of Ivain; blighted early by rejection and misunderstand-
ing, still he had grown to manhood. Now the hope of Keithland's
survival rested upon his shoulders. Forcefully, Tamlin resumed.

"Fear must be controlled at all times, or you will be lost,
forever subservient to the will of the Sathid. If you block the
matrix's first attempt at dominance, it will revert and turn its
previous memories of the soil against you. You are near then to
victory, but do not be careless. At that moment, you must seize
control and unriddle the mysteries of the earth. If you misstep
then, you shall perish."

Kneeling, Jaric fingered the petals of a flower that rested
against his knee. The softness of the bloom reminded him of
Taen's skin; thought of her woke a tremble deep in his gut. He
forced the memory away, only to recall the face of Mathieson
Keldric, the elderly fisherman whose boat had borne him safely
through seas and storms. Before Keldric and *Callinde* there had
been the forester who had taught him independence, a master
scribe who had given him literacy, and later, thirty-nine clansfolk
who had lost their lives to secure his safety. Jaric reviewed the
sacrifices made by the Kielmark, Brith, and sharp-tongued Corley; and lastly, he considered the Stormwarden, locked living in
his tomb of ice. Except for his geas of summoning, Anskiere had
forced no man's will, though his rescue depended upon sacrifice
of another.

"Boy," said Tamlin softly.

Jaric flinched, and the flower stem snapped between his
fingers. He glanced up, bleak with the realization that if he failed
his father's inheritance, he would be more fortunate than his
friends and fellows. Dead, he would not have to suffer through
the demise of Keithland.

Tamlin folded his arms, his hair and beard shining silver in the
gloom of the grove. "Boy, whatever your father's reputation, remember this: Ivain gave himself for the greater good. He preserved far more than he destroyed in the time he served Keithland
as Firelord."

But where Ivain had begun his trial of Earthmastery with a
shrug and a whistle on his lips, Jaric knelt in silence. He did not
look as Tamlin's form faded away into air. Left vulnerable and
alone, the boy felt a presence that was no part of himself stir
within his mind; already the Sathid germinated inside his body.
Since the matrix had previously mastered the flesh of the earth-

digger, it did not grope, but quickly established contact with its new partner. Though every instinct rebelled, Jaric forced himself to remain passive, even as his awareness of the clearing slipped away, replaced by scenes from early childhood.

The memories unreeled more vividly than any dream; *then* became *now*, and Jaric regressed to the time he was a babe cradled in his mother's lap. Under the expanded awareness of the Sathid-link, he experienced his surroundings with a clarity no infant could have achieved. His mother's heart beat rapidly beneath his ear; she had carried him in haste to a woodland dell, a place of frost-killed leaves and tangled vines beyond view of any dwelling. The hand poised against her breast gripped the haft of a sharpened knife.

Jaric watched, fascinated by the gleam of the steel. Too young to understand peril, he saw his mother's knuckles whiten. She murmured an appeal for forgiveness, and a curse against Ivain Firelord; then she raised the dagger and angled the point to murder the son on her knee.

A frantic shout cut the stillness. "No!"

Leaves crunched under a man's running feet. Jaric felt his mother jerk as if slapped. She struck with desperate strength, caught short as the grip of Smithson Kerain imprisoned her fine-boned wrist. Jostled and pinched against the man's leather breeches, her child wailed in fear.

But the man's voice cut through his cries. "Kor's mercy! Woman, are you mad? *That's our son. Why should you kill him?* Your father agreed we could marry!"

The woman gasped with exertion as she tried and failed to free her arm. "This brat's none of yours, Kerain. Fires, why did you come here? Nothing I say will make you understand."

With a lunge that bumped Jaric onto his stomach, his mother snatched up the knife left-handed. She stabbed at the child a second time, single-mindedly determined.

Caught off guard as the steel arced down, Kerain shouted and snatched at Jaric's garments. He yanked the howling infant out of death's reach, while the woman cursed with astonishing viciousness.

Hard fingers bit into Jaric's ribs, jerking him upright. He continued to wail while the smith shouted angrily. "My love, are you sick? What could you expect? Should I turn my back while you murder our child?"

But the woman seemed not to hear. She doubled over, gasping. Blood ran between her fingers. Only at that instant did Kerain discover that his betrothed had continued her stroke and plunged the knife into her own heart. He screamed himself then, his grief blending with the shrill cries of the child. Crushed against the man's shirt of sweaty linen, Jaric knew terror and the mingled smell of blood and damp earth. Not until many years later did he understand that the woman had taken her life with her own hand.

Established now within the framework of Jaric's mind, the Sathid deepened its hold. Voracious, insistent, it assimilated more memories, passing through the time of upheaval while Kerain stood trial for the murder of his betrothed. Jaric lived in the care of a crabbed old midwife, guarded always by the Earl of Morbrith's men at arms. The woman was deaf. She did not always notice the baby when he cried; and the guards filled long days and nights with endless games of dice.

Kerain was convicted and hanged. Fed a potion by the midwife, Jaric slept through the execution. He was too small to understand the condemned man's final bequest, that the orphan be named his own get and raised as ward of the Smith's Guild. For Jaric the result was a loveless succession of foster homes, then a bed in the chilly garret over the forge. Driven by the influence of the Sathid, he relived the slights of his peers, the fights, the humiliation, and the lonely nights spend with his face muffled in bedclothes lest the other boys rouse when he woke crying out from his nightmares. Again he endured the degrading moment when, at ten years of age, he still lacked the strength to heft ingots of unwrought iron from the traders' wagons to the forge. In disgust, the smiths sent him back to work the bellows. But the fumes of the coal fire made him cough; work that other youngsters managed easily taxed Jaric's health. Age brought no improvement. As a slight, pale twelve-year-old, he proved too timid to restrain the mares brought in from pasture to be shod.

"Fires above, but you're useless!" shouted the master smith. Exasperated, he threw his hammer down with a clang and glared at the lad who shrank in the dimmest corner of the forge. "What can I do but apply to the High Earl for compensation? The guild can't waste silver to feed a ninny. Kor, we've got all the wives and daughters we need to cook and sew shirts!"

All the next day, Jaric huddled on his cot; the Sathid analyzed his misery like a starved predator while, in the yard beneath the dormer, loud-voiced men appointed a delegation to appeal to the Earl. They called Jaric from the loft with impatience, and joked over his girlish ways as they hurried him through the town to the council hall. In a solemn room filled with hard chairs and officials, Jaric listened while the smiths presented their case. The phrases *"cursed since birth"* and *"not Kerain's get"* occurred frequently. The boy they referred to twisted slender fingers in his lap. He tried desperately not to weep, while the Earl listened, frowning, his wrists and collar resplendent with emerald clasps.

The Sathid savored Jaric's discomfort as the petition grew heated. But before the Earl made judgment, the stooped old scribe who kept records interceded in the boy's behalf.

Master Iveg had a quiet voice. A moment passed before anyone noticed his offer. Then clamor abruptly stilled, and the elderly scholar's words echoed through the tapestried chamber. "If Jaric is a burden to the smiths, let him apprentice as a copyist. I need help with the archives anyway. If the boy applies himself, his earnings can pay for his upkeep at the forge."

"Done," snapped the Earl, impatient to be away to his hawks.

His decree changed the life of Kerainson Jaric. By day, the boy studied letters and books. The silence of the library became his haven; each night he dreaded his return to the loft, and the jibes of the smiths' apprentices. With years his roommates grew brown and boisterous and burly, while he stayed slight and pale. At fifteen, the older boys' boasts rang through the alehouse. They arm-wrestled for the chance to kiss the barmaid; and the wench, who was buxom and shameless, turned from them to chaff Jaric for his slenderness. She coddled him, bringing bowls of hot milk for his coughs. Once she caught him peeping down the laces of her blouse. She pinched his cheek like a child's; but the box on the ears he deserved would have hurt less.

Two years later, Jaric's delicate stature had not changed, except that he learned to excel at his scholarly trade. Then, without warning, Anskiere's geas sundered the life he knew at Morbrith. The Sathid was taken aback. It saw its subject outgrow the debilitating insecurities of childhood. Jaric acquired self-reliance under the guidance of the forester, Telemark, and strength through restoring the timbers of *Callinde*'s neglected hull. Through the experiences and the year that followed, the matrix realized with growing frustration that Jaric had faced and overcome every trace of his former softness. Only one chink remained in the boy's integrity when Tamlin's training was complete: Jaric still feared his father's madness, and the awesome potential for destruction inherent in a sorcerer's powers. This a Sathid parasite might exploit to secure its goal of permanent self-awareness. Accustomed to dominance from its interval with the earth-digger, it shaped its snare cunningly and well.

The bond between crystal and human consciousness evolved toward completion. Like a sleeper wakened from drugged rest, Jaric stirred within the stillness of the grove. At once he experienced the vastly expanded awareness that accompanied the Sathid-link. His thoughts rang strange and resonant with energy; intuitive perception and latent talent had now transformed to tangible force. Jaric experimented and discovered he could channel this power at whim. The crystalline entity encouraged curiosity, urging the fledgling mage to explore his newfound abilities.

Jaric stood, struck motionless by wonder. Preternaturally aware of the grass and soil under his feet, he blinked and realized he viewed the trees through altered vision. His eyes perceived the life force in the lofty gray trunks; each leaf was limned by a faint halo of light. If he listened, the boy could hear the plants around him, their growth and flowering a deep, subliminal buzz. The novelty overwhelmed him. At first he failed to realize that the living essence of the grove was also answerable to his will.

A moment later, a tree leaned to one side *simply because he wished to see beyond it.* Revelation struck with a rush that turned him dizzy. Stunned to find he could command the living forest, Jaric sat abruptly. *How could he marshal such power?* Touched by self-doubt, his imagination supplied visions of withered branches and trunks drained to sapless husks. The boy chafed his hands on his forearms in distress, until a presence within his mind jostled recognition that he could preserve with equal facility. Wards could reverse the effects of age and storm, even avert the depredations of the axe.

Soothed, Jaric failed to distinguish that the reassurance arose from an entity not part of himself. Unaware that the Sathid manipulated him, he found himself imagining ways to curb fate, perhaps defend the Dreamweaver he loved from the brother who threatened her life. Yet even as he planned, his fears betrayed him. Jaric recalled the ruins of Tierl Enneth with vivid and appalling clarity. Hemmed in by walls of crumbled stone, he stood exposed while unburied skulls accused him with empty, beseeching eye sockets. Fleshless mouths seemed to wail in anguish, reminding that Anskiere of Elrinfaer had taken oath to protect, then unleashed destruction when a witch enslaved by demons usurped his powers.

Jaric bowed his head. His hands whitened in his lap as he tried to shut the image out. But the Sathid tightened its net of terror over his mind. Every sorcerer trained by the Vaere represented a threat, a magnet for disaster and a target for demon conquest. The Sathid supplied grisly detail; Jaric saw his gifts raised against the sanctuaries at Landfast, his own hands drenched with the blood of the innocent slain. He cried out in purest despair, unaware of the enemy that sapped his defenses.

The Sathid felt him weaken; in a bid for swift and final victory, it seized the one thing Jaric prized above all else, and set that in jeopardy. Helplessly the boy watched as the wards he had raised to safeguard Taen twisted out of control. Power exploded with the fury of a cyclone and bashed her bones through rags of torn flesh.

"No!" Jaric clenched his fingers into fists. His mind seductively insisted that he could avoid such ruin if he chose to relinquish control; Taen could be kept safe if he yielded his mastery to wisdom. But the plurality of the concept rang false. Warned alert, Jaric corrected the Sathid's misapprehension. He realigned reason with a human fact he had nearly been lulled into forgetting: *no power on Keithland or beyond could induce him to betray the Dreamweaver of Imrill Kand*, for he loved Taen beyond life.

The Sathid drew back, uncertain; it knew little of love. Few clues existed to inform it of the nature of its error, for Jaric's past had been cruelly solitary. For a fractional instant, the matrix hesitated in its attack.

The reprieve gave the boy space to realize that the images of torment were none of his own. Now aware that the matrix challenged him for dominance, Jaric responded with anger.

The crystal counterattacked, cut him with reminders that Ivain's fine intentions had soured into unbridled wickedness. Like his father before him, so might the son ravage and betray. Jaric choked on denial. Driven to his knees by visions of Elrinfaer, of people and lands blasted by the depredations of the Mharg, he strove to hold firm. But the Sathid sensed uncertainty; it pressured him ever closer to despair. Battered into retreat, the boy backed his resistance with advice Telemark the forester had offered when he had confronted a seemingly impossible problem in the depths of a winter storm.

"Remember that no man can handle more than one step at a time. The most troublesome difficulty must be broken down into small tasks, each one easily mastered." On the night those words were spoken, Jaric had surpassed his former limits. He had saved the life of his friend. Later, perhaps, he might not manage power with total infallibility; but to the end of conscious will he could

ensure he never harmed his own, even if his only means of defense was to yield up his life as prevention.

The Sathid queried the sincerity of its victim's resolve, and abruptly found itself cornered. Jaric's immediate past held record of an incident when the boy had risked his neck to the Kielmark's sword, all for the sake of a principle. A limit existed beyond which he could not be forced, and the crystalline entity had unwittingly transgressed that point when it had first suggested threat to Taen. Now only one resource remained; to subdue the will of its host entity, the Sathid must re-create fear drawn from the earth-digger it had dominated first, then pitch the result in assault against the human mind.

The shift in tactics caught Jaric unprepared. Without warning, he plunged into dampness and dark. Smells of roots and soil filled his nostrils. Suddenly a shower of pebbles and loose dirt rattled down around his shoulders; a falling slide of dirt mired feet, then legs, then hands. Jaric struggled to free himself, to no avail. Unlike the digger, he had no claws to tunnel. Earth compacted his chest, then avalanched in a smothering mass over his nose and face as, with demoralizing accuracy, the Sathid re-created the digger's memory of a tunnel collapse.

Jaric repressed the instinct to panic. Tamlin had warned of this last, desperate trick of the Sathid's. Only wits and the paranormal perception of the link would help him now. Survival depended upon Jaric's ability to unriddle the secrets of earth before suffocation overcame him.

Ivainson ignored the bodily clamor for air. He turned his new awareness toward the soil that imprisoned his body; humus, pebbles, clay, and moisture, he assessed the content of the earth. Even as he groped for means to shift its mass, the Sathid goaded his nerves. Fear shattered his calm. *He could not breathe! He would die here, entombed forever in an unmarked grave.* Sweat slicked Jaric's flesh. He expended precious moments restoring equilibrium, then drove his perception into the dirt once again. This time he sought energy, a life force similar to the aura the trees possessed, which he might tap to save himself.

Yet the earth proved stubbornly inert. Sand and stones had never lived; except for the stirring of occasional insects and worms, particles of soil were comprised largely of dead things, or organisms too tiny to matter. Jaric checked in dismay. Unsure where to search next, he resisted the raking pains in his chest. He must not give in, or his will would be lost forever. *Somehow,*

*Ivain Firelord had untangled the secrets of earth and had won
free before death overwhelmed him.*

Dizziness wrung Jaric's senses. Again he drew solace from
Telemark's advice; strengthened, he resumed with dogged and
desperate concentration, and studied each separate particle. Stone
seemed least promising of all; yet Ivain Firelord had been known
to step through solid granite on a whim. Harried by a wave of
faintness, Jaric attacked the problem. He hammered at dark, un-
yielding matter until his head ached with effort.

'*You are losing,*' the Sathid interjected, '*Shortly, your flesh
will succumb from lack of breath. Before you perish, my victory
shall be complete.*'

'*No.*' Jaric resisted an impulse to curse. His head whirled unpleasantly, and his equilibrium was utterly disoriented. Only seconds remained for his bid to preserve free will.

'*You struggle for nothing,*' goaded the Sathid.

Jaric did not retort. Teetering on the edge of delirium, he
strove to unravel the power within the earth. One instant he grappled with the particles that comprised the soil; the next, giddiness
overbalanced his touch. The thrust of his thoughts slammed hard
against the flinty surface of a pebble. Jaric had no reflexes left to
brace and avoid impact. But the rock yielded. His astonished
perception melted into stone with the ease of a fall into water.
Here at last lay energy enough to move mountains, strung in
symmetrical, glittering strands that awed the spirit with beauty.
Inside each fleck of sand, each rock, each boulder, abided the
strength of the earth. Like the Stormwarden's sources of weather
and wave, an Earthmaster's dominion could never be exhausted.
Jaric had only to apply his will to release the ties that defined the
pebble's structure. The rush of freed forces would be more than
ample for him to escape his prison of mud.

The process should have come fluid as thought. But smothered to the brink of unconsciousness, Jaric fought for clarity of
mind. His lungs burned. Control eluded him; the energy strands
within the stone slipped his grasp like broken chains of pearls.
Even as he strove, and failed, pain lanced his body. His lungs felt
wrapped in hot wire. And the waiting Sathid invaded, intending
to secure control as he foundered.

Jaric recoiled. Stung into rage, he lashed back, forgetful of
thoughts left joined within the structure of the stone. Lattices of
matter splintered; energy roared forth with the coruscating fury of
explosion. Stunned by a shimmering flash of light, Jaric cried

out. He tumbled, twisting, onto green turf, then wept as a sweet rush of air filled his lungs.

Agonized and gasping, Keithland's newest sorcerer lay prone within the twilight of the grove. He waited, expecting the matrix to stir in his mind. Yet no whisper of dissent arose. He had battled the Sathid into submission. But its quiescence was only temporary; while Jaric rejoiced in his victory, a small digger screamed and died in an agony of flames. The Vaere recovered seed Sathid from the ashes. On the day the young master attempted the Cycle of Fire, the crystal he had subjugated would rouse to bond with the second. The paired Sathid would then seek domination with an exponential increase in power. Not even Set-Nav could prepare the heir of Ivain for such a trial. As they sought dual mastery, Tamlin had watched even the fittest aspirants die.

~~~ III ~~~

Return

Winter knifed across the barrens north of Felwaithe; wind sang mournfully over bare rock and winnowed the snowfall into ranges of sculptured drifts. This was a land of harshest desolation, but nowhere was the ice more bleak than on the crag where rose the demon fortress of Shadowfane. Snow did not settle there, but was packed by gales into hardened gray sheets, glazed shiny under the pale midseason sun. On just such a bitter day, a man clad in tattered sailcloth picked his way up the frozen slope. He moved cautiously, for the footing was treacherous, and the soles of his boots sorely worn.

Thienz sentries spotted him long before he reached the final ascent to the gates. Gabbling excitedly, they sent an underling to inform their senior. Yet this once, the presence of a human so far beyond the inhabited bounds of Keithland raised no consternation. The arrival of this particular man had been expected.

The Thienz senior instructed the messenger to return to its post with the sentries. Then, with a whuff of its gills, it scuttled quickly to inform Lord Scait that Maelgrim Dark-dreamer had returned from the south reaches of Keithland.

The sovereign of Shadowfane received the Thienz elder while still immersed in his bath cauldron. His eyes lit with keen anticipation, yellow as sparks through the steam that wreathed his scaled head. Since good news usually had a settling effect upon the Demon Lord, the Thienz elder stretched once and crouched, content to bask in the warmth and moisture; but this once it misjudged.

27

Scait waved away the spiny, six-legged attendants that scuttled busily about the chamber, stoking peat on the fires that kept his bath water boiling. To the bead-ornamented Thienz elder he said, "Send the Dark-dreamer to the main hall at once. Have him await me there."

The Thienz hesitated, reluctant to leave its comforts.

'*Go now!*' Scait snapped, his sending barbed with threat. As the Thienz started up and scrabbled off on its errand, the Lord of Shadowfane doused his narrow head one final time and stepped briskly from the cauldron. Droplets splashed from his scales, and struck with a hiss of instantaneous evaporation against the heated stone by the fire pit. Impervious to burns, the Demon Lord fluffed his hackles dry. As an afterthought, he sent thought-image after the retreating Thienz. '*See the human's needs are met, toad. I will not love the delay if he faints in my presence from hunger or chill.*'

The chambers comprising Shadowfane's interior were interlinked by a mazelike warren of corridors. Stairwells bent and spiraled between levels with the random twists of kinked thread. Human logic could decipher no pattern to aid in the memory of its array, yet the eidetic recall of demons mastered such complexity without effort. Scait hurried from his bath chamber to the central hall on the upper level. He paused only to cuff at the black forms of Gierjlings whose entwined, sleeping bodies blocked his path. Lacking any overlord to animate them to purpose, the creatures were mindless as vegetables. They blinked eyes the lightless gray of grave mist, and moved chittering from underfoot. Scait kicked the tardy ones aside. Unlike other demons, the Gierj were active and successful breeders; Keithland's climate gave their females and their fertility no difficulties. Lately there seemed to be even more of them underfoot than usual. Scait made mental note to inquire of the Watcher-of-Gierj whether their numbers were on the increase. Then, excited by the prospect of beginning his grand plan, and concerned lest one of his rivals should speak to the Dark-dreamer ahead of him, the overlord of Shadowfane's compact hastened with a faint scrape of spurs through the diamond-shaped lintels that opened into the central hall.

The one who had once been Marlson Emien, brother to Taen Dreamweaver, sat on the stone by the mirror pool chewing on smoked fish. His birth name no longer held meaning for him, if indeed he recalled his life with a human family at all. Since the day he had been renamed by demons, the mind of Maelgrim Dark-dreamer had become a warped snarl of hatred and passions, controlled by a Thienz-dominated Sathid-bond. He might retain the shape of a man, but his thoughts and his desires were Shadowfane's.

Since his return, his clothing of ill-sewn sailcloth had been discarded for a tunic of woven wool. No other amenity had been granted by the Thienz who had escorted him in. The fine cloth caught and clung against his unwashed skin, mottled still with the ravages of frostbite and cold. Maelgrim's black hair hung lank with tangles, and a three-month growth of beard matted his chin. Still, though his body had been starved and depleted by the abuses of weather, the awareness within was not dull. Maelgrim looked up at Scait's entrance, his ice-blue eyes unblinking as a fanatic's. In silence he prostrated himself before his overlord.

Scait noted the sincerity of the obeisance with keen satisfaction. Here at least was one pawn who could never betray his loyalty. Snarling at thoughts of other factions who might, the Demon Lord leaped onto the dais. He seated himself with a predator's grace upon his throne, and since in this case he need not intimidate to maintain supremacy, he allowed his servant to rise.

Maelgrim straightened, half-squatting on his heels. He lifted a fleshless hand and resumed gnawing his meal. The fish head he spat into the mirror pool, a transgression Scait forgave. The Dark-dreamer was more than a pet. He was a weapon exquisitely crafted for carving out vengeance upon the human inhabitants of Keithland.

Scait established his opening in words, that his finer concentration be available to sample Maelgrim's inner thoughts. "You have been long in returning."

The Dark-dreamer answered around a mouthful. "Winter in the north latitudes doesn't favor passage, far less with a boat whose sails are ripped to shreds."

Scait's mental probe sampled the truth of the words, and Maelgrim stiffened, very still with the awareness of his overlord's scrutiny. He waited, eyes fixed blankly on the morsel of fish in his grasp, while the master's presence explored; the weather had been terrible, storm after storm battering down upon an already sprung and leaking sloop. Only a fisherman's upbringing had permitted him to bring the boat safely in at all. Maelgrim had done well to achieve landfall at Northsea, but for resentful reasons of his own he had not hurried once he gained shore. As Scait rummaged through his memories to divine the reason, the

Dark-dreamer flashed thought across the link. *'Thienz could have killed him at Elrinfaer, and didn't. Why not?'*

Awareness interlinked with the human's, Scait required no guesswork to answer. "The Firelord's heir possessed rare potential, and talents that might have been exploited for the benefit of Shadowfane's compact."

"But now he is free!" Maelgrim's hand clenched angrily, crushing the carcass of the fish. "Like my sister who was beguiled, and even as his father before him, he has gone to the Isle of the Vaere to be trained."

Scait's hiss of irritation caught Maelgrim's protest short. "Alive, Ivainson Jaric could have been compelled to betray Keithland. Now, with his Firelord's potential lost to us, your own talent as Dark-dreamer becomes of paramount importance." The Lord of Demons paused and rubbed scaled hands together. The plan he had devised surely would wring admiration from even his bitterest rivals. All in the compact were aware that the wizards at Mhored Kara conscripted paranormally gifted children for training. That they culled their apprentices from families in the towns and villages of the southern kingdoms and the Free Isles' Alliance was also known fact, but what of the north? Parents there might breed equal numbers of exceptional offspring; except in the backlands, perhaps these children passed unnoticed. With keenest anticipation, the current ruler of the compact intended to correct this oversight.

Scait extended a spurred hand toward the human crouched at the foot of the dais. "Maelgrim, by my command you will engage your powers as Dark-dreamer. Seek among men, and the children of men, for ones born with talent that any who go for training with the Vaere must possess. Find these gifted ones, and call them hither to Shadowfane. I shall reward them generously, and see that they receive instruction befitting their talents."

Maelgrim swallowed a bite of crushed fish, then licked at the oil on his fingers. Black hair veiled his eyes as he pressed his forehead to the stone before the dais. "Your will, mightiest Lord, but humbly I offer warning. The plan you suggest has flaws."

Displeased, Scait cupped his chin in flinty claws. "Name them."

"Human parents differ from those of demons." Here Maelgrim abandoned language and engaged his Dark-dreamer's skills to impart his concept intact. Humans lacked the treasures of eidetic memory; to them, the past, and the histories of the dead that were of such vital significance to demonkind, came second to the young whose future had yet to be written.

"My kind will fight the loss of their children, mighty Lord. They will send armies to claim back their young." A gleam of calculating hatred spiked Maelgrim's words of conclusion. "After the first shock of surprise, the humans will organize. They will guard the children of Keithland beyond reach of my probes and my lures, for the Vaere-trained Dreamweaver who was my sister is capable of unraveling this grand plan. She is bound to defend Keithland from the designs of demonkind, else break her oath of service to the Vaere."

Scait growled low in his throat, for Maelgrim was wiser in the ways of mankind than any demon at Shadowfane. A canny ruler must heed the human's counsel and look beyond for means to turn detriment to advantage. Scait pondered a moment, yellow eyes closed to slits. Then he straightened with a leer of satisfaction. To Maelgrim he commanded, "You shall study the ways of power, and be granted control in mind-meld with the Thienz, that you can draw force from their link to augment your own. When you have mastered these skills, come to me, and we will plot. For I think that humans might be distracted from noticing those few among their young that we summon. The Dreamweaver is only one girl. She may be lured, and captured, and perhaps forced to Sathid domination as well."

The one who had been born her brother licked lips that glistened with fish oil. He smiled and fawned on the floor in abject gratitude. Twisted in ways no human could imagine, Maelgrim relished the assignment of creating his sister's demise. Taen's downfall would be all the sweeter if the Stormwarden were to be rescued by Keithland's new Firelord, only to discover his other protégé lost in thrall to the enemy.

"Your will, mightiest Lord." Maelgrim arose with joyful, overweening malice and tossed the remains of his meal into the mirror pool. As he departed, Scait caught a last glimpse of his eyes: frost-blue, and alight with hatred like a weapon's polished edge. The boy Emien had been manipulated into absolute subservience quite satisfactorily, except that his eating habits were irritating in the extreme.

Distastefully, Scait Demon Lord regarded the half-chewed fish tail that drifted, spreading an oil slick on the surface of the water. The next rival who crossed him would find itself wading to scoop out the garbage. This settled, Scait's thoughts ranged futureward, and preoccupied speculation gave way to desire fierce as greed.

The finding and enslavement of gifted human children must proceed without setbacks. Once Shadowfane had developed a collection of such changelings, they could be set loose for the destruction and the extermination of mankind. Then would Scait's sovereignty be secured beyond question. The way would be clear for the compact to reclaim Veriset-Nav from the ocean and summon rescue from their homeworlds in triumph.

Winter was all but spent on the day the peace was disturbed in Keithland. High in the tors of Imrill Kand, the sister Maelgrim Dark-dreamer plotted to ruin sat amid the cropped grass of a goat pasture, soggy skirts gathered about her knees. Her cloak was pinned tight at her neck; hair black as her brother's coiled damply over her shoulders, and her slim woman's hands twisted restlessly in her lap. Though the sleet that fell at dawn had ceased, the morning remained unbearably bleak. Fog curled off dirtied patches of snow, and last season's grass lay flattened and brown against soil still rutted with ice. Taen Dreamweaver shivered. Sick with horror, she covered her eyes and tried to subdue the grief in her heart. Always, she had known this moment would come, but never had she guessed that its impact might cut her so deeply.

Ivainson Jaric might have offered comfort. But he was beyond reach on the Isle of the Vaere, training for his final ordeal, the Cycle of Fire that had driven his father to madness. If he survived, he would emerge forever changed, and no succor would he then owe to anyone. Taen lowered her hands. She stuffed reddened fingers into the cuffs of her shirt, an oversized garment of unbleached linen and silver-tipped laces she had won in a bet with a pirate captain. The fabric was dry but offered no warmth. This day the brother lost to Shadowfane had turned his demon-inspired malice against Keithland, and though Jaric's sacrifice might someday put an end to such atrocity, the sting brought on by the loss of his company only this moment struck home. The bare, ice-rimmed tor became more than a landscape ravaged by winter; some of its bleakness turned inward and invaded Taen's spirit.

Aching and weary already from long hours of husbanding power, she forced her sorrow aside. No good could be gained from brooding. Tough as the fisherfolk who had bred and raised her, the young woman mustered her Dreamweaver's awareness once more. Shortly the call she shaped sped southeast, to the straits and the isle of Cliffhaven.

The subject of Taen's search was never a hard man to locate even when obscured by a crowd. The incisive force of his thoughts struck easily through the interference patterns cast by others in his presence. By nature, the Lord of Pirates was quick to sense change, and even swifter to act. From the instant the Dreamweaver made contact, the Kielmark disregarded the presence of the two captains he had summoned into conference in his chart room. Arrested in mid-sentence, he fell silent, the maps and the pins he had been using to discuss strategy abandoned under his huge, square-fingered hands. In less than the space of a heartbeat, he slammed back his chair.

His captains knew better than to interrupt when his moods came suddenly upon him. They sat, carefully motionless, as their master arose and tossed a cloak of maroon wool over his muscled frame. Then, without a word or a look back, the Kielmark kicked open the postern and stepped out into the sea breeze that whipped across the battlements overlooking the harbor.

Taen locked her dream-sense in and framed him there, brawny and wolf-quick on his feet, his dark, curled hair crushed flat by wind and his great fists clenched at his sides. Deftly as the Dreamweaver engaged his attention, he started like a wild animal.

"Taen?" The sovereign Lord of Cliffhaven glanced over his shoulder, at a fortress that remained deserted under gray clouds and ice. No child wearing a woman's form walked the battlements to meet him, with eyes that saw far too much, and clothes that seemed always overlarge for her slim frame. The Kielmark shed his wariness with forced deliberation. Certain now that the call had come from within, he waited with cutting impatience for the Dreamweaver's message to resume.

'Trouble has arrived, and far sooner than expected,' Taen sent. The clang of goat bells on the tor faded into distance as she centered her focus upon the ruler of Cliffhaven.

The Kielmark sprang tense. "What trouble?" Even as he spoke, Taen sensed his reflexive review of men, warships, and the current offensive capability of his island fortress.

'Maelgrim has begun to try his powers.' The Dreamweaver clarified with images gathered that morning from the northern borders of Hallowild, knowing as she spun memory into dream-form that the impact would inflame the Kielmark's caustic restlessness to action.

The Lord of Cliffhaven recoiled slightly as her dream-link embraced his mind. Strong fingers bit down on the crenellation as his view of the ocean wavered, overlaid by the crude planks of a farmsteader's cottage. Sheep grazed in the dooryard. Hedges of matted thorn enclosed a snow-bound patch of garden, but there all semblance of normality ended. Blood pooled around the base of the stump the steader used to split firewood. Sodden bundles of cloth lay sprawled to one side, and with a sickened lurch of his gut, the Kielmark saw that the lumps beneath the rags had once been human. Something had driven an honest man to dismember his wife and children with an axe, and leave the corpses steaming on the ice for scavengers to pick.

The Kielmark's hackles rose. "Kordane's Fires, why?" The alarm underlying his tension struck with the force of a whiplash.

Taen instinctively tightened her protective screens. *'Dreams, dark dreams spun by Maelgrim.'* She qualified with a memory gleaned from a tinker she had found mumbling and crazed in the gloom of the steader's root cellar.

Taen shaped no more than a fragment. Yet that one glimpse was enough to make a man shudder like an insect pinned on a needle. The Kielmark started back in horror. His skin rose into gooseflesh while his awareness danced to measures of insanity. Even thirdhand, the creeping, poisonous web Maelgrim cast over his victim's minds made the spirit curdle in despair.

Taen banished the nightmare. The Kielmark stood granite-still against the bite of the wind, his blue eyes unfocused and his thoughts turned morbidly inward; she stung him alert with facts. *'When the tinker came out and saw the corpses, he ran to the barn and slashed his wrists with a scythe.'* She paused, waiting, while the sovereign on the battlements of a fortress many leagues distant steadied his shaken nerves. *'Lord, I showed you only a fraction of the force Maelgrim has brought to bear. This evil cannot be battled from a distance. I must go to Hallowild, and quickly.'*

The Kielmark looked up. The reflexive, splintering transition into fury that so often intimidated his captains drove him to swift decision. "You'll have ships. I'll place Deison Corley in command. But you'll wait to leave until he gives you escort, am I clear?"

Taen protested. *'Folk will die while I delay!'*

The Kielmark's anger went cold. "Show me the steader who can replace your talents, girl. Wait. Corley will sail with the tide. I promise you, no captain in Keithland can wring more speed from the wind than he."

The precaution was sensible; Keithland's defenses were spread perilously thin already, with the Stormwarden still trapped within the ice. Taen conceded the Kielmark's point; she would await the arrival of Deison Corley's fleet, though the constraint of delay was a bitter one.

The Dreamweaver released contact, and sensed, through the dissolution of the link, the Kielmark's great shout that brought a familiar chestnut-haired captain bounding from the warmth of the chart room. He received his master's orders, while on another isle to the north a vista of fog-bound tors swam slowly back into focus around the Dreamweaver.

After the Kielmark's explosive vitality, the chime of the goat bells seemed strangely thin and unreal. Taen sneezed at the drop of water she found trembling on the tip of her nose. Moisture seeped through her clothing; during her interval in trance, the sky had begun to spit sleet. Yet even the hostilities of the weather could not make her return to shelter in the village beside the shore. Instead she gathered herself yet again and bent her Dream-weaver's perception southwestward. Tamlin of the Vaere must be informed of the ill tidings from Felwaithe.

Taen was unsurprised when her first attempt showed nothing but a view of white-capped sea. The fabled isle was difficult to locate, even on days when she was not depleted with exhaustion and cold. Tamlin named himself master of riddles. His powers extended across both space and time, and, seemingly at whim, he caused his isle to undergo slight shifts in location. Only when he made contact with those rare few he chose to train was he found inhabiting the present.

Taen adjusted the energy at her command and successfully completed the transition into the shadowy, altered dream-image that reflected the past. Now she perceived an islet, a crescent spit of land hammered by breakers. The shoreline was jagged and storm-whipped, jumbled with stunted trees all twisted by gales and tide. Taen laced her powers into the physical presence of the land, then shaped an image wrought of dream over all. Tumbled sands and jagged rocks became a beach of smooth and creamy white. Grasses softened the dunes. Scrub trees filled out into a forest of stately cedars, tall, green, and unbent by wind. Taen wrought change until the untidy spit of land stood transformed, a place of bewitched perfection set like a jewel on the face of the sea; for by shifting that same isle beyond reach of ocean storms and out of phase with the seasons for longer than the memory of men, the Vaere had made it so.

Taen settled her dream-sense, until soil and rock and shoreline lay in balance with her image of Tamlin's isle. Then, with delicate care, she moved her awareness futureward until land and dream-vision converged into solid reality. The spicy scent of cedars filled her nostrils. She knew sunlight as gentle as spring, and soft breezes sighing through dune grass where sand swallows dipped and cried. Yet although Taen knew she had located the true Isle of the Vaere, at once she sensed something vital amiss. Precisely what was lacking eluded her, until she sought the grove within the forest where dwelt the network of energies that comprised the presence of Tamlin. No resonance of power met her dream-sense. She encountered only dark, and space, and the soundless emptiness of void. The enchanted grove had vanished from the face of Keithland as thoroughly as if it had never existed.

Though dismayed, Taen Dreamweaver did not give way to alarm. The mysteries of the Vaere were riddles within riddles, and knowledge beyond the pale of mortal men. Though no little man in feathers and bells materialized to tell her, Taen placed only one interpretation upon the emptiness she found at the isle's center. Ivainson Jaric had begun his last trial of mastery, the Cycle of Fire itself. Tamlin of the Vaere had withdrawn to oversee his ordeal and, through the time of passage, could not be recalled by any means a mortal might command. There was no remedy for the fact that the timing could not be worse, that the guardian of mankind had withdrawn beyond reach when his guidance was needed most sorely.

Troubled, Taen released the bindings of her call. The enchanted isle faded from her dream-sense, restoring her awareness to cutting cold and the strident cries of curlews. The Dreamweaver of Imrill Kand dispelled the last of her trance and stared out over the harbor beyond the tor. With the fishing fleet out plying their nets, the waters spread gray, empty except for one derelict dory left at anchor, and the mastless hulk of a sloop. As near as a fortnight hence, the bay would echo with the crack of spars and canvas; black brigantines manned by battle-trained crews would shear around the headland, the Kielmark's red wolf banner flying from masthead and halyard. Aching with worry for Jaric, and impatient to be away, Taen could do nothing but count the minutes until she could board and sail to Felwaithe. For with Jaric irrevocably committed to the Cycle of Fire, and the Stormwarden of Elrinfaer imprisoned in ice until a firelord's mastery could free him, Taen alone remained to resist Maelgrim Darkdreamer and the forefront of the demon assault.

* * *

Warmth came unseasonably late to the latitudes of Keithland, and the ocean tossed, coldly veiled in spindrift. Corley and the *Moonless*'s five companion vessels sailed briskly, sped by the storms that habitually raked the Corine Sea before equinox. Ice still scabbed the tors by the time the small fleet hove into view off Imrill Kand.

A young cousin ran from the fishers' wharf to the cottage off Rat's Alley with the news. He found the Dreamweaver taking leave of her mother, her meager store of clothing already bundled and waiting by the door. Taen had followed the Kielmark's brigantines by sorcery, and the time of their arrival was known to her long before the masts breasted the horizon. Though the enchantress spoke her thanks, and Marl's widow offered warm bread in return for his favor, the boy refused hospitality and left. Just before the door swung closed, Taen saw him raise crossed wrists in the timeworn sign against evils brought on by enchantment.

She turned a wry grin toward her mother. "Well, you won't be sorry to see an end to that nonsense. Do you suppose the wool seller's niece will stop sending you skeins with knots to tangle my spells?"

Marl's widow grunted and shoved another billet of wood into the stove. "Won't be mattering much then. Not with you gone to sea, and unable to keep on tearing good cloaks in the briar. Now I'll only have your uncle's socks to darn. Doubt he'd be noticing knots, anyhow, with his calluses thick enought to sole boots. Kor, but it would be a blessing if he washed his feet more than once in a fortnight. His woolens would rot less, for one thing."

Even through the chatter, Taen could sense her mother's distress. Carefully unmentioned between them hung the name of Marlson Emien, the son that Taen must sail north to oppose. Prolonging the moment she must leave for that purpose could do nothing to ease the heartache. The Dreamweaver caught her cloak from the bench and reached to gather up her bundle.

Her hand blundered into her mother's stout bulk, and the next instant she found herself buried in a smothering embrace. "Don't you go cozening any more gifts from pirate captains' mates," said the widow in a strangely altered voice.

Taen's protest emerged muffled by an apron that smelled of woodsmoke and, faintly, cleaned fish. She pulled back from her mother in affront. "Corley's nobody's mate, but a captain and an officer of the Kielmark's. A shirt won on a bet doesn't mean he's in love with me. I understand from his crew that he has a collection of very lovely ladies that he visits at carefully measured intervals. All of them take money for their charms, and none of them have hair that smells of fish!"

But today Marl's widow did not respond with the dour, barbed wit Taen had known throughout childhood. Instead she raised a careworn hand and smoothed a black strand of hair that had escaped her daughter's braid. "It's a husband you should be seeking, not some ill-turned adventure against Kor's Accursed that could leave you dead, or much worse."

Silence fell in the tiny kitchen, heavy and dense and somehow untouched by the workaday bickering of children in Rat's Alley. Taen sighed, picked up her bundle, and paused by the door.

Her mother stood with her back turned, regret for her words and her faltering courage evident in her stiff pose. Taen blinked back sudden tears. "I'll be back to marry when children can be born into Keithland without nightmares waiting to kill them."

Marl's widow nodded, reached for a pot, and banged it angrily down on the stove. "Just come back, girl," she whispered. But Taen had already gone, and latched the door silently behind her.

Winter's chill hung damp on the air, and the wind blew brisk off the sea. Once past the shelter of Rat's Alley, Taen ran, fighting the tug of her cloak, her bundle bouncing off knees still scabbed from the briars she had hiked through in her outings across the tors. Ahead, across the market square hung with the drab tents of drying fishnets, she saw the masts and sails of the brigantines, tanbark-red against cloud-silvered sky. Already, tiny forms swarmed into the rigging, crewmen sent aloft to shorten sail. As Taen reached the docks, the lead vessel rounded with mechanical precision, backed sail, and dropped anchor with a splash like a faint plume of smoke. Even as her hook bit into the harbor bed, a longboat lowered from the davits. Oarsmen clambered aboard the instant the keel kissed water, and looms flashed and bit with the trained and deadly timing that marked the Kielmark's crews; none showed better discipline than the company under the command of Deison Corley, Taen decided. The longboat clove toward the wharf with near-uncanny speed.

Taen boarded the instant the boat reached the dock. The strong hands of the coxswain caught her bundle from her, and his call to resume stroke was obeyed with such promptness that Taen unbalanced and slammed rump first into the bow seat.

"Kor, man, be easy or ye'll bruise the goods." The nearer of the starboard oarsmen capped his complaint with a gap-toothed grin at the Dreamweaver. Without missing stroke, he added, "Welcome back, girlie. In the forecastle we've a pack o' cards that ain't too soggy yet. Got a game promised after the change in the watch."

Taen caught her cloak hood before the wind scooped it from her head. "I'll be there, but only if I can beg a stake of beans from the cook."

"No bother," said the oarsman with a wink. "Some kind soul saved yer stash."

"You?" Taen flushed in a manner that made even the roughest scoundrel in the boat draw back in appreciation. "If you saved beans at all, it was to keep the wind in your sails."

"Lively!" snapped the coxswain, as the crewman drew breath to defend his dignity. "Dress oars, you fish-brained jacks, yer captain's watching."

The looms rose dripping from the sea, and the longboat drifted smartly into the lee of the Kielmark's brigantine, *Moonless*. Taen reached out to catch the waiting rope, only to have it snatched from her hands by the oarsman she had just finished teasing. Another man caught her strongly from behind. "Goods most certainly wasn't bruised," he observed.

Taen tried to retaliate with a punch, but lost the chance as she was propelled strongly upward. Forced to abandon her reprisal and grab for the strakes, or risk a fall into the heaving sea beneath, she climbed. The next moment her bundle of belongings sailed boisterously over her shoulder, and the bearded, weather-beaten face of Deison Corley appeared at the rail.

A large man with chestnut hair only just beginning to gray, the captain caught her spare clothes. With the reflexes of a trained swordsman, he slung them aside into the grasp of a sailor. "Keep the tar on your mitts, not the dresses," he cautioned, then reached out and caught the Dreamweaver's hand, half lifting her as she clambered aboard. Taen seemed even slighter than he remembered, her eyes enormous under the patterned border of her hood. Yet the wait and the worry had not sapped her spirit.

"You look as if a bellyful of sour apples left you griped," the girl observed. "Or do you wear that dumbfounded expression because you lost your whetstone overboard?"

Corley tugged the Dreamweaver off balance into his chest, his sea-roughened hands in no way clumsy as he flipped the hood over her eyes and bundled her into his embrace. "I always pack spares." His chestnut beard split to reveal a grin. "And a lucky thing, too, for I see I may be needing my flints to blunt the edge from your tongue."

Taen pinched him blindly in the arm and pulled free. She did

not resist when *Moonless*'s steward hustled her off to the dry
warmth of the stern cabin. Beneath the captain's gruff humor, she
had sensed the question he tactfully refrained from asking; the
perception left her aching, for where Ivainson Jaric was concerned, she had no reassurance to offer at all.

ᕙᐤ IV ᕙᐤ

Light Falcon

Moonless raised anchor. Accompanied by her entourage, she scudded past Imrill Kand's headland without waiting for the tide to turn. The crossing to the shores of Hallowild was tempestuous and prolonged by contrary winds. Captain Corley kept to the quarterdeck except for brief intervals to snatch rest. But for fierce bouts of cards with the sailhands, Taen remained isolated. Daily she retired to the stern cabin and plied her talents to track the emergence of the Dark-dreamer's influence. Her findings were unremittingly bleak, a systematic destruction of lives and sanity that so far afflicted the country folk toward the north borders of Morbrith. The particulars Taen kept to herself, as well as the fact that Maelgrim's influence was predictably spreading southward. Corley could not drive his command any faster, and ill tidings could do nothing but blunt the spirits of his hardworking crew.

At last, in the weeks before spring planting, the Kielmark's fleet of six made landfall. Taen stood at the rail while the brigantines anchored in the waters off the traders' docks that lined the banks downriver from Corlin Town. The estuary of the Redwater was clear of ice, but a freak late snowfall stung the faces of the sailhands as they stripped the canvas from the yards. Since all but a maintenance crew would march north as the Dreamweaver's escort, the small fleet might remain in the harbor for weeks yet to come.

Corley spotted Taen between rounds of inspection, her blue cloak being the brightest color on board after weeks of gray swells. "Why not join the supply party?" he yelled across the deck. "The outing would do you good, and you can help the men with the bargaining."

"For horses? I'm better practiced at cleaning fish." But outraged sensibilities could not quite quell Taen's smile. Her Dreamweaver's perception had revealed the motive behind the captain's request: he wanted a woman along to allay the suspicion invariably aroused by companies under Cliffhaven's banner. She agreed to the plan for reasons of her own. For a short time, the sounds and sights of a strange town might divert her, enable her to cease brooding over the fate of Ivainson Jaric, and the cruelty of the brother sworn over to demons.

The longboat dispatched to Corlin carried no device, and the men on board rowed with weapons and swords bundled out of sight beneath their cloaks. Still, Taen saw laborers and teamsters pause to stare as the boat passed the landings and warehouses of the trade port. The oarsmen's rapacious efficiency trademarked a fighting command, and six black brigantines flying the wolf in the estuary had not escaped remark. The Duke's officer of the port questioned them tactfully upon landing. He wore gold chains by the dozen, and a cloak bordered with peacock feathers; under the weight of all his finery, he sweated more than the situation seemed to warrant.

"We're just here to buy horses," said Corley's boatswain. Hatless in the cold, his single hoop earring emphasizing the fact that he had once lost half his scalp to a sword cut, he gestured toward Taen with his elbow. "Would I be lyin' in front of a woman, sir?"

"You'd lie in front of your mother, so," grumbled the official. But he granted them leave to moor the longboat.

As the Kielmark's shore party plowed into the press before the gates, the boatswain grinned at the Dreamweaver and confided, "I think the man knew we'd've bashed his birdie brains out if he refused." The pirate officer sounded self-righteously cheerful.

But Taen proved more interested in the city than in acknowledging seaman's boasts. Corlin stood at the edge of Seitforest and the backland domains of the north. Fortified by square walls of brick, trade prospered there despite roving bands of outlaws that preyed upon passing caravans; the marketplace in the commons bustled with merchants, craft tents, beggars, and a vigilant squad of men at arms, for Corlin's Duke was a man dedicated to security. Since the streets were safe and prosperous, Corley had encouraged Taen to browse and listen for rumors from the remote frontiers of Hallowild.

A girl raised in the austere society of Imrill Kand needed little

excuse to explore. By day, Corlin's central square offered a maze
of temporary stalls. The Dreamweaver wandered, enthralled, past
merchants selling bread and beads and cloth. She stopped to hear
street minstrels and watch a dancer with a monkey that leaped to
catch coins. At the mouth of Craftsman's Alley, Taen found birds
in wicker cages and tools new from the forge. Jostled by a ped-
dler selling wine, she half tripped over a drag-sleigh piled with
cured pelts. The hand she thrust out for balance sank to the wrist
in rare fur. Mottled black and silver, a cloak sewn of ice-otter
pelts would be prized like the jewels of a duchess.

Taen clenched her fingers in silky hair, remembering: Jaric
had set traps for such beasts the year he had sheltered in Seitforest.

"That's hardly a perfect specimen," said a mild-mannered
voice. "Would the lady care to see a better one?"

Taen looked up. At her side stood a leather-clad forester,
streaked black hair tumbled over his shoulders. His face had
weathered into permanent lines of patience, but his eyes were
light, intent, and fierce as a hawk's.

Slammed by recognition, Taen felt words stop in her throat.
She knew this man. Here stood the forester who had remade
Jaric's self-reliance, a process the Dreamweaver had shared
through a winter in close rapport. The shock of meeting Telemark
in the flesh overwhelmed her. Desperately she longed to speak of
Jaric, to unburden her concern upon the forester's staunch sympathy. But to reveal Ivainson's trial in the grove of the Vaere to this
man would shatter a peace of mind so deep that the notion itself
was a cruelty. Miserably, Taen kept her silence.

"Lady?" Strong fingers supported her shoulder. "Are you ill?
Do you need help?"

The touch was sure, familiar to the point of heartbreak; for
thus had Telemark steadied Jaric through a period of painful con-
valescence. Taen bit back an urge to weep and found herself
overcome. Her mind sought after Jaric in a rush of uncontrollable
need.

Power surged inside her, far too cataclysmic to bridle. With-
out warning, her awareness exploded across space and time.
After months of empty silence, Taen achieved contact with
Jaric's consciousness.

Flame raged across the link, blistering flesh with pain that had
no voice and no outlet; feeding on nerve and muscle and bone,
Sathid-born hatred consumed the living body of the man who
suffered the Cycle of Fire. In agony, Jaric resisted. Torment

stripped away his humanity, left nothing but instinct to survive. He recognized no presence beyond the enemy, and the reflexive vehemence of his defense flung the Dreamweaver's contact outward into darkness.

Reality returned with a disorienting jerk. Restored to the bustle of Corlin market, Taen found herself weeping in the sturdy arms of the forester.

Telemark shifted his grip, his trap-scarred knuckles warm through the folds of her cloak. "Girl, are you ill?"

"No." His shirt smelled of balsam and woodsmoke, just as Jaric remembered. Bravely Taen composed herself. "I'm sorry. By accident you reminded me of someone I know and love."

She disentangled herself from Telemark's embrace, then fled before he could question her further. The crowd hid her from view; but for a long while afterward Taen sensed the forester staring after her with a frown of puzzled concern.

By early afternoon the boatswain and his three henchmen had driven a milling mass of horses out of Corlin market. They made rendezvous with Corley and the main company from the ships just beyond the gates. Between the shouting and the sorting of mounts and men, Taen's silence passed unnoticed; numbed by Jaric's predicament, she mounted with little of the trepidation that riding usually inspired. Beside her, the boatswain reported to his captain.

City gossip had included no mention of Maelgrim's blighted dreams, yet the lack of news was no basis for encouragement. With roads still mired with snow-melt, word would travel slowly until caravans resumed trade to the north.

"The High Earl was imprisoned for heresy, though." The boatswain stowed his bulk with surprising grace in the saddle of a rangy chestnut.

"Oh?" Corley chose a gray that nipped at his seat as he turned to mount. Unperturbed, he slapped its muzzle and vaulted astride. "When did that happen?"

"Summer before last." The boatswain spat. "Kor's brotherhood governs Morbrith in the Earl's stead. Farmers griped over the tax shares. Claimed that bloody simpering initiates counted the oats in the sheep pats to pad out their tallies."

Corley grinned, settling easy as the gray sidled beneath his weight. "Fires. I wouldn't have wanted to be the man in charge of inspecting the grain tax, then."

The boatswain howled with laughter. "Farmers would've

bagged sheep leavings, surely. But they dared not, unless they wanted to see their Earl staked out for the fire."

Corley looked thoughtful for a moment. Then he summed up his opinion of priests in an epithet, and motioned his company forward. The last men mounted, and with startling speed the stamping, snorting mass of beasts sorted out into columns. Taen reined her mare in behind the lead company of men at arms. She did not join in the laughter as the sailors' contempt of the saddle found expression in a spate of coarse jokes. While Jaric suffered in his struggle to master the Cycle of Fire, she could do nothing but go forward to defend the borders; and unless he won free very soon and came north to free Anskiere, even that effort would prove futile.

Snow shifted to cold rain as the Kielmark's contingent left the road and pressed on into the hill country north of Corlin. Here the terrain was rocky, dense with forest unrelieved by way stations or hostels; the only inhabitants were the occasional isolated farmsteader, or wandering tribes of clansmen. At night the men slung their ship's hammocks from trees, or slept on boggy soil. Bowhunting for deer kept their marksmanship sharp, and Corley's vigilance ensured that mail stayed polished, and swordblades maintained a killing edge. That six armed companies had been dispatched to protect a single enchantress was a necessity no man questioned. The Kielmark's orders were never gainsaid, and the ways of demons could be unpredictably savage as spring storms.

Yet Maelgrim once had been human, and his actions did not entirely lack pattern. He preferred to strike at night. Taen did not try to oppose him at once, but watched, well shielded, until Corley's company had traveled close enough for her talents to have maximum effect.

Seated by lanternlight in the confines of her tent, she wiped damp palms on the cotton robe she preferred to her daytime garb of riding leathers, then bent her mind into trance. Cautiously she cast her awareness over the land. The north country of Morbrith was a patchwork of wilderness interspersed with the tilled fields and orchards of steaders. Apple branches rattled in winds still edged with winter, the buds of blossom and leaf tightly furled against the cold. Taen deepened her net. The discipline of Tamlin's teaching enabled her to sense the life force of the earth, to share awareness of every natural rhythm, from beasts in hibernation to the sleeping presence of the steaders' families. She merged with the essence of their dreams and waited with coiled patience for the first, spoiling disharmony that signaled Maelgrim's attack.

This night he chose a child, a small boy with auburn hair who slept under quilts sewn by his sister and grandmother. Taen narrowed her focus, warned as the victim twitched with the first stirrings of nightmare. He dreamed that his bedclothes came alive and pinned his small limbs helplessly to the mattress.

Only a Dreamweaver's sensitivity could perceive the unnatural lattice of energies gathered about the boy's form. Taen balanced her own resources. Before his rest could be shattered with images of blood and terror and every crawling fear that Maelgrim wrought to unhinge the spirit, the Dreamweaver shot a bar of light across the child's mind, a shield to repel intrusion.

A startled pulse of force answered her effort, daunting for its intensity. At first contact, Maelgrim's strength proved more powerful than her worst anticipation. Frightened at how sorely she might be tested, Taen Dreamweaver held firm. Strangely, the counterattack she expected did not follow. Maelgrim paused in his weaving, his web work of destruction drifting incomplete above the wards she had set to protect the little boy. Rather than batter her defenses with energies to reclaim his victim, the Darkdreamer sent words across the link. *'Sister! Have the Vaere made you timid? I had expected to encounter you sooner.'*

The message held overtones of challenge, an exuberant anticipation of battle joined that made Taen's flesh creep. She strengthened her protection about the child. Then, her own shields tightly shuttered, she extended a query into her brother's mind in an effort to explore his motives. Maelgrim sensed her touch. He responded with a crackling flare of force that stung her back, but not before she divined his intent. Shadowfane's human minion intended to draw her north, and weaken her, and afterward claim her person and her powers for exploitation by demons.

Revelation of such betrayal caused a sharp ache of sorrow; still, Taen did not lose equilibrium. This moment had been inevitable since the recovery of the Keys to Elrinfaer. That day the man she knew as her brother had been forever lost. The Dreamweaver checked to be certain the momentary disruption had left her guard over the little boy's mind intact. Then, chilled by the potency of her enemy's rejection, she forgave the Kielmark's tyrannical concern for her safety. The escort he had assigned in his obsession was no less than grave necessity. Without his men at arms to safeguard her through the hours she must spend in dream-trance, the Dreamweaver would have been forced to abandon her defense of the north.

An echo of laughter cut short her thought. *'Do you think men with steel can protect you?'*

Taen drew a shaky breath. The spite that rang through the Dark-dreamer's words pained like a wound to the heart. Yet, in another manner, the nature of his cruelties only stiffened her resolve. Some aspects of her brother's character had not changed. Behind Maelgrim's malice she detected impatience, and bitter annoyance. The men at arms were an unexpected complication. Before Maelgrim could take her, he would have to contend with swords in the hands of the most tenacious fighters in Keithland.

The Dark-dreamer returned her assessment with mockery. *'And do you think I will find killing the Kielmark's few soldiers very difficult?'*

Taen started, shocked that he could so easily broach her awareness.

Maelgrim indulged in a moment of poisonous amusement. *'There are other ways to defeat steel.'* Then, with no warning, without even the briefest pretext of contention, he ripped aside the Dreamweaver's wards and pinched out the life of the child.

'No!' Taen recoiled in horror, that defeat should happen that fast, that easily, and with such terrible, irreversible finality. The little boy's fingers remained entwined in his pillow. His hair spilled in tangles across his brow as if he still slept, but his eyes would never open to see the morning.

'I could destroy the Kielmark's men at arms as easily,' warned the Dark-dreamer; and Taen saw that he might. All along he had been feinting, toying with the lives of steaders and clansmen. Never until now had he unveiled the full extent of his strength.

Yet the arrogance that drove him to flaunt his superior power itself was his greatest weakness.

"You can try." Knowing he would read her words, Taen seized the advantage. She struck while satisfaction left him unguarded, and in one bold move sounded and discovered her adversary's link with the Thienz-demons. Their collective mind augmented Maelgrim's will, granted him means to overwhelm her wards and kill.

The loss of the child was bitter. Taen let herself weep, but refused to be trapped by despair. The Dark-dreamer might break her wards over distance this first time. Now that she knew of the demons, she could alter her tactics to compensate; the abominations of the Thienz might be deflected. Within the confines of the campsite she could safeguard the minds of Corley's men. At least while the effects of Maelgrim's early training matured, to the limit of her Vaere-trained resources she would fight.

'You do that,' the Dark-dreamer invited. Hatred rang through his words. *'Hard or easy, slowly or not, the victory at the end shall be mine.'*

Taen offered no reply. Brashly stubborn as her fisherman father, she waited without moving until the abrasive evil of her brother's presence faded and departed.

The Dreamweaver roused sluggishly from trance. Drenched with sweat, and gasping from the aftermath of tears and emotional stress, she reoriented to her surroundings with a shock like pain.

The air in the tent was close, sour with the scent of mildewed canvas. Taen's robe clung unpleasantly to her skin. She wrestled off the damp cotton and sat shivering.

This night a child under her protection had died. The loss was insufferable. The Dreamweaver unstuck a lock of hair from her forehead, hammered a fist into her thigh, and uttered the favorite obscenity of Imrill Kand's most coarse-tempered fishwife. Then, feeling not one whit better, she hurled herself into trance and lashed a stinging hedge of wards about the cottage that sheltered the murdered child. She could do nothing more for the boy. But he had parents, and the young sister and the grandmother who had sewn his quilts. If Taen kept watch, she could ensure that the child's family survived to grieve.

But the night passed without incident. No trace of Maelgrim's presence returned to try her. When at last the sunrise spilled motes of light through the trees to speckle the tent canvas, Taen dispelled her wards. She rubbed tired eyes and lay down beside the blankets that were folded, unused, by her knee. Without enthusiasm she contemplated her riding leathers and hairbrush, and the daily trial of rising to wash in a creek surrounded by ruffians who inventively sought excuses to interrupt her. Though friendly, their persistence seemed suddenly too much. Taen squeezed her eyes closed. Weariness overcame her, and she drifted into sleep across her crumpled robe.

Her peace was not to last. Half an hour later the Dreamweaver was roused by a raucous whistle, followed immediately by the slackening of a guy line. The post that supported the ridgepole of her tent toppled unceremoniously across her knees.

"Shall we pack you in with the cooking pots, then," gibed the boisterous voice of a sailor.

Taen batted collapsing walls of canvas out of her face and returned an epithet.

"Hoo, she's alive, then," observed her tormentor. But he stilled his tongue, fast, at an irritable reprimand from Corley.

The next moment the captain himself raised the tent flap and peered through the gloom within. "Taen? It's daylight. We've got to move camp." Only when his eyes adjusted did he note the raw pain in her eyes, and the mouth set with unbreakable determination. Corley's manner turned briskly direct. "What happened?"

With the canvas propped awkwardly over her head and shoulders, Taen told him everything, not sparing Maelgrim's threats against the six companies under the captain's command.

Corley considered her keenly as she finished. "You've chosen to fight, yes?"

Taen nodded. Abruptly recalled to the fact that she had thrown off her overrobe, she flushed bright pink and groped over the ridgepole for her leathers.

The Kielmark's most trusted captain dropped the tent flap without apology for his intrusion. "You'll have our full support," he said bluntly. Taen chose not to delay as he called rapid orders to his sailhands, but burrowed in panic under slack canvas to locate her tunic and boots. Her haste proved unnecessary. No man came to tease or to pack her tent until after she emerged, fully clothed.

The company moved north, and the wind grew blustery. Flat clouds lifted to admit sunlight, and in time the warmth of an overdue spring softened the frost from the ground. But while the men became suntanned and robust, Taen grew careworn, withdrawn, and pale.

By day she dream-wove defenses, intricate patterns of energy bound into wards to protect the men at arms whose ready vigilance kept her safe from assault by demons. By night she engaged in deep trance. With painstaking care she reviewed the scattered inhabitants of Keithland's north wilderness, from newborn babes in untamed circles of clansmen, to the work-weary minds of steaders. The predations of Maelgrim Dark-dreamer continued, relentlessly. In time, through repeated failure, the Dreamweaver who opposed him came to understand his Thienzclever tricks: traps that sprung and struck her blind, or false feints that eroded her strength. Plainly, Maelgrim intended to exhaust her, then slash around her wards and take command. But the Vaere never chose the fainthearted for the training meted out to so few. As long as resource remained, Taen fought. She gained experience, and a few victories, and snatched rest in catnaps while the men made camp and cut firewood.

Corley woke her each evening an hour after sundown, and stayed through her meal of hot barley cakes, sausage, and soup. "You can hardly keep on like this," he remarked when for the second day she pushed her bowl aside, barely touched.

Taen looked at him. Her eyes seemed the only thing alive in her elfin face. "I must. No one in Keithland can help these people. If I stop, the peril will spread."

Corley stifled an urge to argue; the fact the girl was right did nothing to ease his frustration. Abruptly he lost enthusiasm for the contest at darts started among the men by the fireside. He stamped off instead to inspect the picket lines, while the Dreamweaver settled yet again to ply her talents through the night.

Maelgrim and his Thienz never opposed her directly. Catlike, they preferred to toy with her, harrying her resources with snares and false threats. Then, in the depths of the dark when her concentration waned from weariness, they would choose an isolated camp or farmstead, and smash the defenses so laboriously strengthened each night.

Taen always sensed the destruction of her wards. Sweating in the throes of trance, she knew an answering flare of pain as her energies unraveled into chaos. Such times she rallied what resources remained and strove to block the evil dreams that Maelgrim wove about the minds of his victims. Power ebbed and flooded, pulled like tidal surge between opposing factions. Sometimes Maelgrim fashioned nightmares for the collective presence of a family; other nights he attacked a child, or someone's cherished elder, and broke their minds like twigs before an avalanche of terror.

Taen lacked the resources to rout such nightmares directly. Maelgrim could draw endlessly upon the reserves of his Thienz; through their support, he could outlast her endurance, sour her efforts with despair. At best Taen slowed his work, blurred his focus, and dissipated the potency of his imagery; occasionally her intervention enabled his stronger victims to survive. Far more often, conflict ended with the loss of a life. Grapevines might flower with spring, and sunshine return each morning, but the backlands of northern Hallowild became cursed with terror and madness.

In the chill gray hour before dawn, Corley returned to Taen's side. Invariably he found her shivering in the extremity of exhaustion, yet never would he let her see the depth of his concern. Each morning he affirmed her faith in life with carefully tempered banter. Toward the fourth week, when the release of laughter began to fail, he gathered her up and held her until she slept like a child in the hollow of his shoulder. Then he wrapped her slack form in blankets, settled her in a horse litter, and yelled for the camp to pack up. Risk increased so near the borders of the fells. The best defense was to keep moving, that demons could engineer no ambush upon his position.

Constantly shifting camp, the company traversed the orchards of northern Morbrith. Taen's exhaustion deepened. The day came when she did not waken until the column rested at noon. Frowning, irritable, she kicked free of her blankets and waspishly upbraided Corley for not rousing her sooner.

Dismounted to loosen his gelding's girth, the captain unwisely neglected to watch his back. "Fires, witch, you didn't miss a damn thing."

"The boatswain says differently," accused the Dreamweaver.

Corley rolled his eyes. "That man lies to his soup at night. Will you let be? All we saw was a priest who groused that Cliffhaven's rabble appeared to be trampling territory belonging to Morbrith apples."

Taen's annoyance changed to interest. "What did you do to him?"

The gray snapped. Too late, Corley delivered a ringing slap on its muzzle. "Sent him galloping back to the Brotherhood with arrows sticking through his cowl. Now go eat. I don't want to answer to the Kielmark if you waste away to bones."

Taen departed, leaving the captain cursing the gray, who had inconsiderately ripped his last pair of leggings; suddenly the Dreamweaver's exhaustion became excuse enough to camp early. Irritable at the last, Corley stripped to skin and knife sheaths and tore into the baggage looking for awl and spare thongs. Men at arms gathered around him like vultures. They speculated heatedly over the number and anatomical location of the insect bites their captain was sure to suffer, and presently debate gave rise to an exchange of spirited wagers. But the betting lost impetus when the man who listed sums and odds got assigned to waxing bowstrings. Grumbling and irrepressible, the Kielmark's company settled for the night.

Taen completed her defense wards and rolled in a blanket to nap. Although her bones ached with weariness, rest eluded her.

The fields of her Dreamweaver's awareness remained tuned and wary; even the chirp of spring peepers added to her restlessness. She shifted in her blankets, eyes open to the twilight that seeped through her tent flap. By nightfall, Maelgrim Dark-dreamer would choose another victim and strike. His strength grew steadily with the passage of time, while her own resources dwindled, overtaxed by exhaustion. Very soon she would be unable to cope. The day would come when nothing remained but to tell the Kielmark's stalwart captains to order a retreat to the south.

Hopes of Jaric and the Cycle of Fire only fueled her despair. Surely no man of his sensitivity could weather the agonies she had sensed in Corlin market; one bitter moment, Taen had glimpsed understanding of Ivain's crazed malice. That Keithland's need required such suffering of the son was cause for deepest grief. Weary to the heart, the Dreamweaver felt the burden of Jaric's sacrifice as a sorrow more tragic than death.

Daylight seeped from the sky. The inside of the tent darkened to blackness unrelieved by any star. Taen lay sleepless, listening to the wind. At any moment the Dark-dreamer would tumble her wards.

Yet this time the attack came with none of the usual warning. Energy slashed Taen's thoughts with the splintering force of a lightning bolt. Slammed into dirt as she flung herself clear of her blankets, the girl recoiled in defense. Barriers bristled reflexively across her mind before she realized this intrusion held no trace of Maelgrim's malice. Raw energy continued to prickle across her skin. Confused, the Dreamweaver probed with her talents.

Light stabbed her eyes. Dazzled nearly to blindness, Taen squinted. Etched in painful glare, she beheld a bird of prey ringed with fire. The image echoed the configuration of Anskiere's stormfalcon, and sudden revelation caught her breath in a sob.

"Jaric!"

Her cry opened contact. Swept into thundering torrents of power, Taen screamed aloud. Her spirit was wrenched across an abyss of time and space, to meld with another that inhabited a flaming crucible of agony. Racked by torment that burned the spirit to a febrile spark of consciousness, Taen beheld the branching nexus of choice presently confronting Ivainson Jaric on the Isle of the Vaere.

One path led to darkness and oblivion; but the death at the end was illusion. Sathid would conquer before life was extinguished. Although suffering battered his thoughts to shapes unimaginably severe, Jaric rejected self-immolation. Neither did he reason as mortal man might; as Taen shared his passage, she perceived the defense that hopeless suffering drove him to consider. Like Ivain before him, Jaric understood that life might continue if mortal emotion were canceled. Fire could be endured, pain overcome, the unthinkable ignored, *if he let himself feel nothing at all, not joy, not compassion, not love*. He would yield his humanity. But in turn the Sathid would lose all his vulnerabilities to exploit; it must surrender to his will and reward him with power beyond measure.

Thus had Ivain conquered the Cycle of Fire; pressured to the limit of endurance, Jaric fought but found no alternative. Stripped of pride and grace, at the last he appealed to the peer he cherished for forgiveness, since the madness he must inherit to survive could not help but cause her sorrow.

Taen's control crumbled away, and the falcon's graceful form splintered through a lens of tears.

"Jaric, don't!" Protest was futile. She felt Ivainson's fiery presence begin to withdraw, even as she spoke. Grief prompted her to act.

Once, when Anskiere's geas had forced Jaric to untenable suffering, Taen had used dream-sense to weave him a haven; now experience gained in conflict with Maelgrim made her adept at turning nightmares and suffering aside. Swiftly, surely, the Dreamweaver fashioned a shelter for Jaric's beleaguered mind. She shaped peace where the Sathid could not reach, numbed the hurt of burned and lacerated nerves. Her work took immediate effect. Jaric yielded gratefully to exhaustion. Punished beyond thought, he slipped into deepest sleep, while the Sathid striving for conquest hammered vainly against Taen's bastion of wards.

The Dreamweaver realized then that Jaric's humanity did not have to be lost. With her help, he might recover equilibrium, even escape the madness inherent in the Cycle of Fire. Excited to hope, Taen forgot caution. Her discipline slackened for one preoccupied instant; and the crystals paired to Jaric gathered force, then turned poisonously against the source of interference.

The attack caught Taen woefully unprepared. Her Sathid-based powers as Dreamweaver resonated in sympathetic response; in an instant, her own crystal could cross-link and join the raging conflict with Jaric. Taen knew fear like the plunge of a knife. Should such a melding occur, the combined strength of the Sathid would expand in exponential proportions; battered by a ninefold increase in force, Dreamweaver and Firelord's heir would find their wills pinched out like candle flame.

Taen struggled to restore separation and balance. Immediately she sensed she would fail. Ivainson could not help; with his matrix-based powers still in dispute, he had no control to apply. And since the dream-link that bound him to the Dreamweaver skewed through time as well as space, the energies were tenuous and difficult to maintain. No enchantress who commanded the resources of a single crystal could hope to repel attack by wild Sathid within so fragile a framework. Power stabbed Taen's defenses. She countered, barely in time. Her bond-crystal quivered, half-wakened to rebellion, as backlash deflected like sparks.

Disaster awaited if she lingered through a second such shock. No choice remained except to release contact with Jaric, cleanly and at once. But the cruelty of that expedient marred judgment. Taen hesitated, and the untamed Sathid struck again.

Energy whirled her off center. Flayed by a vortex intense as a cyclone, the Dreamweaver screamed. In desperation she collapsed the wards protecting Jaric. Fire tore him awake with a heartrending cry of agony. He all but lost his grip upon life as mingled awareness revealed the extent of Taen's peril. Overwhelmed by fear for her, he reached for the only available recourse. Only the madness of Ivain would enable him to bridle his Sathid before the Dreamweaver he loved suffered harm.

"Jaric, no!" Taen's cry crackled across widening veils of distance. "Jaric, hold firm. I will disengage. If I journey to the Isle of the Vaere, I believe I can help you with safety. Wait for me . . . fish-brains, please wait. . . ."

⌁ V ⌁

Deliverance

The contact dimmed and snapped. Taen roused, shuddering, and broke into stormy tears. Returned to darkness and her blankets in northern Hallowild, she blinked eyes stinging yet with the light-falcon's afterimage. No means existed to determine whether Jaric had heeded her plea. Her dream-sense roiled like current disturbed by tide, and she needed every shred of concentration to settle her half-roused Sathid. The upheaval slowly subsided. Restored to emotional balance, Taen started as mail jangled suddenly beyond the tent flap. A swordblade slashed the ties. Canvas gaped open to reveal a flood of torchlight and men at arms, with Corley in the lead in his steel cap and armor.

"What's happened?" The captain's tone held no inflection, as if he anticipated killing. With a shock Taen realized the sentry on duty had heard her outcry and gone on to muster camp in expectation of attack.

She answered quickly to disarm the tension. "I had a vision, but not from Shadowfane. Jaric struggles to master the Cycle of Fire. If I journey at once to the Isle of the Vaere, quite possibly I can spare him the madness that destroyed Ivain."

Corley passed his lantern to the nearest man at arms. His eyes gleamed hard and dark as shield studs as he sheathed his sword. "If we go, the north will be left defenseless against the Dark-dreamer."

Taen met his expression, her features white with empathy. She well understood the consequences of her suggestion, and her

55

honesty was painful to observe. "I cannot stay Maelgrim once his command of Thienz-linked power matures."

The tent flickered into shadow as wind winnowed the lantern flame. The man holding the light shifted uneasily.

Only Corley stood like a rock, the beads of reflection on his helm so still they might have been nailed in place. "I think no option exists. Whether you misjudge or not, we risk Morbrith. But if Jaric fails, all hope is lost for Keithland."

Relief broke Taen's composure; seeming suddenly, poignantly frail, she bent and buried her face in her hands. Jolted by recollection that her chronological age did not match her maturity, Corley disbanded his swordsmen with curt orders to break camp. Speed and protection were the only comforts he could offer the Dreamweaver under his care; but for beleaguered Morbrith, dependent on priesthood and prayers, he intended a last brave gesture.

Corley stooped and gently raised Taen's chin. Tears dampened his knuckles, twisting at his heart, but still he managed a lopsided grin. "Dress for the saddle, little witch. We've a task to finish before *Moonless* strains her stays for the sake of Ivainson Firelord."

Bits chinked in the darkness, counterpointed by the grimmer chime of mail and weaponry. The Kielmark's sailhands turned soldier mounted with none of their usual cursing as they began their southward march through Morbrith. To Taen, riding behind Corley's gray, the freshening beauty of spring seemed displaced by wrongness sensed elsewhere. Here moonlight might silver the apple blossoms like lace against star-strewn skies; but northward the Dark-dreamer remained free to dismember the minds of children at will, and the man with potential to check him writhed in agonies of flame on the Isle of the Vaere to the south. Though surrounded by fresh new life, Taen could not escape her burden of care.

The company seemed to reflect her mood. Scouts rode out at the alert, as if threatened by hostile territory, and the brisk pace set by the vanguard soon mingled the pungency of horse sweat with the fragrance of the orchards. Taen sat uneasily to the rhythm of her mare's stride. Dulled by concern, she failed at first to notice that Corley's second-in-command, captain of *Shearfish*, had reined up, blocking the head of the column.

Slit-eyed and large, the man bristled with belligerence even in the best of tempers. Usually he restrained his moods enough to avoid challenging his commander, but tonight's tension appeared to have upset his judgment. "You're going to Corlin by road. Man, are you crazy?"

Corley regarded his subordinate with fixed lack of expression. "The road is the fastest route to the port. Now, if that horse isn't lame, you'd better make it trot."

The officer pressed on heedlessly. "Fires, you'd ride through Morbrith? Priests'll be onto you like wasps."

"I know." A subtle change in the captain's manner made Taen start with chills.

The officer also saw; he swore and kicked his mount into stride alongside Corley's. "Priests hate the Kielmark. You know that." Jostled as his horse ducked the teeth of the gray, the man resumed without minding his superior's warning. "You ride past Morbrith keep, you'll start a battle. Road won't take you anywhere quick then."

"So," Corley said equably. He did nothing apparent but flick his reins. Yet his gray sidled violently and bashed the insubordinate officer's mount into a tree. Taen saw metal flash in the moonlight. There followed an abbreviated thunk; and the officer reined up short, the handle of Corley's belt knife quivering in bark beneath his chin.

For a moment the two men glared at each other, breathing hard. Then Corley spat. "Since when has any captain of the Kielmark's taken orders from Kordane's Brotherhood? Get back into line."

Only then did Taen notice that a second knife waited, gripped in a hand held steady to throw. The officer's lips curled back from his teeth in an animal display of anger; but he spun his horse and abruptly rejoined his company.

At the head of the column, Corley twisted in his saddle. As he jerked his blade from the tree trunk, Taen glimpsed his expression; witnessed firsthand, the force of personality required to maintain discipline among a band of renegades made her gut wrench. She might have sympathized with the priests, except that the preternatural alertness of the men who rode beside her suggested danger. Very likely the officer's complaint was just. Still, the Kielmark's first captain proceeded southeast, straight for Morbrith keep.

The company traveled through the night without incident. Moonlight yielded to pearly dawn, and the orchards thinned to farmland mantled in mist. Taen rode with her reins slackened on the mare's neck. She said nothing of the wards broken by Maelgrim, or the family of hillfolk stripped of human reason and slaughtered in her absence. Saddle-weary and wan, the Dream-weaver barely reacted when Corley's mount jostled to a halt ahead of her.

"Hold hard, Taen." The captain caught her horse's bridle and jerked it to a stop. "We've a scout coming in."

In her preoccupation Taen had not seen the horseman who approached at a gallop. He called out as soon as he reached hailing distance.

"Morbrith's mustered. Three companies march, not two miles ahead." Dirt scattered over wet grass as the scout reined in his winded mount. "They're fully armed, maybe two hundred mounted lancers, as many bowmen, and two divisions of pike-men."

Corley sat still, eyes narrowed to slits; then his fist tightened. The gray shook its head with a dissonant jangle of bit rings. "They set after us yesterday, then, and won't expect us this far south. Tell me what banners they carry."

"Stars and fireburst of the priesthood. The High Earl's stan-dard flies underneath." The scout hesitated, then added, "If they don't expect us, they look uncommon keen."

"So." Corley sounded unimpressed. A madcap glint lit his eyes, and he turned aside to face the Dreamweaver. "Taen, would you dream-send a message to an army, if I asked you?"

Struck by suspicion, she glared at the Kielmark's captain. "You planned this! Didn't you?"

Corley grinned. "Provoked it, rather. I can't leave a domain threatened by demons to rot under incompetent leadership. If the priests wanted Morbrith, they should've burned the High Earl while they had the chance."

"That's an excuse, you bloodthirsty maniac." But the captain's spirited daring left Taen much heartened. She agreed to lend her talents to his plan.

There followed an interval through which Corley issued a rapid string of orders. The company re-formed with the ease that stamped every enterprise beneath Cliffhaven's command. Men cleared weapons from their sheaths, and faced their shields at the ready. They did not curse, but moved as machines perfectly tuned; even the clink of armor and weapons became subdued. When the flag bearer unfurled the Kielmark's red wolf standard, a whistle like the reedy call of a gull signaled the advance. The men moved silent as ghosts through thinning cobwebs of mist.

The air smelled of grass and dew and plowed earth; birdsong

rang from the treetops. Riding through a world spangled gold by early sunlight, Taen felt exhilarated and uncertain all at once. She might be surrounded by the most competent fighters on Keithland, yet fact remained: an army outnumbering Cliffhaven's force four to one barred her way to the Isle of the Vaere.

Corley worked on unperturbed. He positioned his men in a copse that flanked the verge of a dirt lane. Then he, the flag bearer, and a picked team from *Moonless* arrayed themselves across the gap. Taen could see them plainly from her position at the edge of the wood. But archers stationed scarcely twenty paces off blended invisibly among the trees.

The lane stretched empty to the south, a ribbon of packed earth dividing a plowed expanse of cropland. The fields were newly turned, deep and moist, and impossibly peaceful for a site that might soon see a battle staged. Tentatively Taen extended her dream-sense. At once her sensitivity encountered overwhelming numbers of men: mounted lancers with bodies weighed down with steel; garrison soldiers well trained at arms but soft on foot, their heels sore and blistered from a march forced on them by priests; after them came archers, some still blinking sleep from their eyes. Taen sampled the mood of the men from Morbrith and found them hungry, disgruntled, and surly over the fact that their own green standard hung beneath the starfield and fireburst of Kordane's initiates. Corley's assessment of the host sent against them was dead accurate. Carefully the Dreamweaver set about shaping the call he had asked of her, even as the troops rode into view.

Lance heads splintered the morning light, tightly clumped as tatting needles jabbed through silver lace. The reason for Corley's deployment immediately became apparent. The front riders from Morbrith crowded the narrow way to avoid miring their mounts in the soft earth of the field. War-horses bunched and jostled, squeezing mailed legs and scabbards one upon another, and bumping painfully against the lighter riding horses that conveyed the commanding priests. Kor's Brotherhood protested. Like a swirl in a log-jammed current, they pressed ahead to ease their battered knees.

In the shadow of the copse, Taen saw Corley's teeth flash in a grin. Then a leaf flicked close by; one of the Kielmark's archers nocked a shaft to his bowstring. With lethal steadiness, he drew, released, and the morning stillness became shattered by a wailing scream as a whistle arrow sprang aloft.

The lancers' destriers were war-trained, and not an animal

among them flicked an ear at the head-splitting racket. But the Earl's palfreys shied and spun and reared, flapping blue robes, and spilling two priests off into freshly turned earth.

"Behold, the Great Fall," shouted Corley from the lane. The priests still in their saddles looked up. In outrage they spotted the small force awaiting them under the Kielmark's wolf banner. Then the whistle arrow bit into ground, leaving memory of the captain's mocking profanity ringing across silence.

The priests still in their saddles gesticulated like a conclave of angry puppets, while the ones who had fallen caught their horses and remounted. Someone shouted a command. The starburst standard wavered and thrust straight. Lance tips, pikes, and helms roiled as the men at arms behind gathered to charge. The actual moment of threat seemed utterly unreal. Taen swallowed, biting lips gone white as her cheeks. She shut her eyes, forced her mind to focus, and stabbed the full force of her Dreamweaver's powers straight into the gathered army.

'All men loyal to Morbrith stand firm! Desist from attack at the edge of the trees. Let Cliffhaven strike only those who usurp the rule of their High Earl.'

The call touched the men at the instant they spurred their horses. Hooves gouged the turf, gathered into the thunder of full stride. But in the act of charging, the oncoming line broke, forced to separate to avoid its disordered knot of priests. The men on the flanks trailed raggedly behind as their horses plunged off the road, to labor over the grabbing soil of plowed ground. Taen sensed answering movement around her. The Kielmark's archers nocked broadheads to their bows while the war host hammered down on their position. Posed as bait in the lane, Corley clamped his thighs to his saddle and unsheathed his blade to signal his concealed men to kill.

In panic, Taen sent to the war host again. *'For the love of your Earl, halt now!'*

For a moment, nothing changed. Then somebody in Morbrith's front lines whooped like a boy and reined in. Around him, leveled rows of lance tips shuddered, and raised, and a cheer burst forth from the men. War-horses slid on their hocks, and like drops sprayed from a pool, six blue-robed priests suddenly galloped undefended toward the wood.

"Strike your mark!" yelled Corley.

The archers in the trees released. A storm of shafts darkened the air, struck flesh with a sickening smatter of sound. Bristled like pincushions, the mounts of the priests staggered out of stride and fell screaming. Kor's initiates spilled like rags into the road. They scrambled to pick themselves up, while in disciplined silence, Corley's chosen company swooped out of cover to claim their prey.

As they closed, the head priest reached his feet. Mud-scuffed and bleeding from a scraped cheek, he straightened his silver-bordered tabard, glared at the naked steel that surrounded him, then lifted his bearded chin to meet the Kielmark's captain. Others of his order were herded into a bunch while a pair of scar-faced sailhands manhandled one who was slow to his feet. The man cried out, possibly injured. But his captors showed him no pity.

"You commit an atrocity," accused the High Priest. Lank, almost shriveled with age, his voice carried thinly over the tumult. The boisterous noise of the Morbrith men quieted as he spoke. "Since when do armed companies of criminals trespass upon the lawful domains of Keithland? Landfast will punish your boldness."

"Fires!" Grinning as his blasphemy caused the priest to flinch, Corley resumed in a tone gone dangerously mild. "Since when have the Kielmark's captains wasted time taking heed of religion?"

From her vantage point among the trees, Taen saw two of the High Priest's companions tense. One edged closer to his master, hands fluttering nervously at his waist.

"Don't move!" snapped Corley. "D'you think the Lord of Cliffhaven gives a bent half-copper for your lives?"

Mention of the Kielmark made the High Priest blanch; he lost any inclination to speak. At present, the ships carrying temple gold from Kisburn to Landfast passed through Mainstrait untouched except for tax. But a word from the Lord of Pirates would cause those vessels to be boarded, plundered, and sunk. Much revenue might be lost.

Corley sat, reins pinched under crossed hands on his saddle horn. "Here's what you are going to do for the Kielmark," he began. "For a start—" And suddenly, without warning, he jerked straight.

Steel flickered between his fingers. A blade scribed a line through sunlight, and Taen saw the nearest of the priests crumple over with a scream. He pitched to the ground, blood flooding in a stream over the fists pressed tight to his abdomen. The Dreamweaver recoiled, sickened. Corley was always accurate with his knives; without visible provocation he had struck a man down, his intent not to kill, but to torture.

Taen barely felt the arms that steadied her in the saddle. "Don't look," said *Moonless's* steward in her ear.

But shutting her eyes did nothing to block the screams that ripped across the wood. Corley's voice rose like a scourge above the noise. "I said, *don't touch him.* Do you all want a steel decoration in your guts?"

Taen shivered, weeping. Her dream-call had brought an unarmed man to suffer. She sat stunned, as slivering cries of anguish subsided to retching whimpers no whit more bearable. Corley continued without break, his icy phrases directing his captains and Morbrith's army to the completion of his plan.

"You, muster the men from the ships *Ballad, Scythe,* and *Sea Lance.* Take this priest at sword point to the Sanctuary tower. Free the High Earl and accompany him home to defend his keep. Make the Brotherhood understand that Cliffhaven will level the temple if even one initiate attempts interference. The other two ships' companies will escort the Morbrith army back. The rest of the Brotherhood go with them, as hostages. I don't care if you slit their holy hides to achieve it, but make the temple garrison there open the gates. Since the Brotherhood's services from that time on will be unnecessary, you will all stay on and aid the Earl with his defenses."

Men shuffled, and silence fell suddenly, as the wounded man ceased outcry.

"Murderer!" shrieked the High Priest. "Fires consume your wicked flesh!"

His passion drew Taen's attention. Despite the steward's protest, she looked in time to see the High Priest's lunge hammered short by the closed fist of a seaman. On the ground the wounded brother lay still, a second knife transfixed through his throat. Corley spurred his horse callously over the corpse. *"Moonless's* company, to me. We've a crossing to complete, and quickly."

Sticks snapped as the Kielmark's first captain reined his gray through the muddle of men at arms. He entered the woods in time to see Taen pull free of the steward's arms, her face pinched white with shock.

He stared at her, taken aback. Then his eyes turned bright with anger. "Oh, Fires, get her moving," he snapped to his servant. Then he jerked his head at *Moonless's* mate. The rest of *Moon-*

less's company formed up promptly and began their brutal ride across Morbrith.

Within the hour the horses jogged lathered with sweat; breath labored in their lungs, and foam spattered from their bits. Still Corley drove onward. Taen clung to her mare until her mind swam with exhaustion. The sun shone hot on her head, adding dizziness to fatigue. Her knees rubbed raw on the saddle. Even her fingers blistered. Of Morbrith's broad fields and gray stone keep she remembered little; progress became marked by the change in the ground, hoofbeats shifting from the deadened thud of dirt to the jarring clang of packed roadway. The company stopped to change mounts at a post station. Shortly afterward a sailor caught the Dreamweaver swaying in the saddle. He said no word to his captain, but watched her without slackening pace. When her hands slipped from the reins, he reached out and caught her as she fell. Taen finished the ride half-conscious in his arms.

At noon the riders swept into the crossroads settlement of Gaire's Main. The site had once been sacred to the hill tribes, but the spring where the clansmen convened for rites now filled a brick trough for watering livestock. Sleepy stone cottages roofed in thatch lined the thoroughfare. Hens scattered squawking through the dust as the horsemen reined up in the square; doors banged and shutters slammed in the lane beyond as villagers fled hastily into their homes. Their fear made Corley grimace in annoyance; his horses all stumbled, and the men who rode them were tired, hungry, and thirsty to the point where an insult might knock them down.

The captain halted his gray in the yard before a rambling two-story tavern. He signaled the men to dismount, then crossed to the doorway in three stiff strides. The latch proved to be bolted. Out of temper, Corley whirled and caught the signboard that swung creaking from the gable. One yank snapped its rusted chain, and his follow-through battered the nearest shutter and splintered the hasp. The window crashed open. A frying pan flew out, fended off with a clang by Corley's mailed fist.

He sprang and wedged the shutter back with his sword hilt. "Kor's Fires, woman! I'm not here to rape your wenches. My men pay silver for meat and rest. But by damn, deny them, and I'll let them kick in your walls for sport!"

Chain rattled. The door creaked, then widened, and a raw-boned blonde in frowsy skirts stepped out, hands braced on her

hips. She surveyed the company of men and horses crowded un-
tidily across the spring yard.

Then, with sharp calculation, she regarded the burly captain
who had dented her best piece of kitchenware. "Inside, and welcome, then. But damages will be added to your tally, starting
with my busted sign and shutter."

Corley refused to haggle. Having spotted one seaman still
mounted with Taen lying limp in his arms, he turned on his heel
and splashed his way through the mud beside the spring. The
tavern mistress watched with hard eyes as he exchanged low
words with the sailhand. Then, without fuss, he lifted the girl
down himself.

Black hair tumbled free of the Dreamweaver's hood as Corley
strode back to the tavern. "Open your door," he said briskly.

The girl's extreme pallor convinced the woman to abandon
argument. She shook out her apron, stamped across the threshold, and bawled for her daughter to fetch a flask of spirits from
the cellars. Then, as the old stablemaster and his single lad ventured from their hiding place in the grain stores, she motioned
Corley and his following into the tap.

Minutes later, Taen aroused to the sharp taste of plum brandy.
Tired, aching, and disoriented, she opened stinging eyes and discovered that she slouched on a chair in a low-beamed room
crammed with men. Someone knelt by her with a flask. Weaponry chinked as he bent closer. Shocked back to memory, Taen
recognized Corley, still clad for battle in his mail and helm. The
same hand that had knifed the priest reached down to help her sit
straight. She cringed back reflexively.

"Kor!" Corley's blasphemy came out a whisper. He shot to his
feet, and brandy spattered his wrist like blood.

Taen ached to speak, but words would not pass her lips. As
she hesitated, the captain turned his back. For a moment he stood
as if he would say something. Then, abruptly, he strode off.

Soon afterward, *Moonless*'s steward arrived at the Dreamweaver's side. He clutched the brandy flask anxiously against his
chest, but one glance convinced him that drink would not ease
the distraught girl. The servant abandoned the spirits on the nearest trestle and glanced quickly over his shoulder. Corley was not
in sight.

"Step outdoors for a moment with me. The air might do you
good." The steward caught Taen's shoulder, pulling her firmly to
her feet. She quivered under his fingers as he steered her past the

hearth, around tables of men wolfing stew, and out through the wide plank door.

Midday sun warmed the inn yard; overflow from the spring trickled soothingly over the lip of the trough. Nearby the aged stablemaster and a freckle-faced lad hustled to and fro, watering horses. The steward searched for a quiet spot and finally found a log bench against one wing of the inn. He seated Taen, then settled himself on the grass at her feet.

On shipboard he was known as a gray-haired, unimposing man, by turns appreciated for efficiency and cursed for his motherly sense of propriety. But today his fingers jabbed nervously at the grass and he spoke with hesitation. "Lady, I'm going to tell you things my captain will not. He's got pride like the devil, enough so he'd lay me across a hatch grating to be flogged if he knew I'd interfered."

"Don't." Mention of further violence caused Taen to tense in distress.

The steward reached out and caught her hand. "I must."

Taen shuddered. She pulled free in protest, but did not turn away as the steward continued.

"You couldn't see from the wood. But that priest got knifed because he disregarded the captain's warning. The Brotherhood often communicate with hand signals. Corley caught the wretch trying to provoke a plot with his fellows. Had no one cowed them, forcefully and at once, that small batch of priests could've brewed trouble clear to Landfast."

"But why? Corley tortured that man before he killed him. What could justify such brutality?" Taen chewed at a broken thumbnail, and started as she tore it to the quick.

The steward answered gently. "Ending dissent could, at the cost of one life rather than many. The road was fastest, and any delay threatens Jaric. Had you forgotten?"

"No." Taen pressed her stinging finger against her leathers and waited, sensing the steward would add more.

"Corley's mother was a Morbrith lady's handmaid. While he was a lad, a hilltribe's chief stole her away during summerfair. In bitterness the father ruined himself with drink. The High Earl saw the boy got leavings from his own board so he'd have enough to eat. The mother returned years later with a hillman's get, a girl-child who spoke clan dialect and never learned civilized words. Corley fought himself bloody, defending his sister from abuse. But one day he caught three boys at rape. The scuffle that re-

sulted left the Morbrith heir badly cut. Rather than shame his
benefactor at trial, Corley shipped out with a trader. He ended
serving the Kielmark."

Here the steward paused. He checked to be certain Taen still
listened. "Corley once said his High Lord was a hard man, but
just. In arranging the Earl's freedom, I think our captain cleared
what he saw as a debt."

Taen stared at the ground. Despite her Dreamweaver's perception, she had never probed Corley's mind throughout her time on
Moonless. What had shocked her most that morning was the
chilly calculation that inspired the man to violence; unlike the
Kielmark's, this captain's temperament did not skirt the edge of
madness.

"I suppose I owe him an apology." She looked up, but noticed
the steward had left her. Probably he hoped she would think and
forgive his captain on her own; the courtesy left her relieved. At
least she would not be pressured to confront the matter at the
extreme end of her resources.

Taen sighed. Too tired to move, she curled against the warm
boards of the inn and slept. Afternoon passed; the shadows gradually lengthened and trees striped patches of shadow against the
gray timbers of the wall. At the usual hour, the blind, senile
woman who served as priestess of the well crawled from her
nook in the loft. Though decades had passed since hillfolk cele-
brated rites at her spring, she still wore the knotted leather garments of the clans. Her shuffling step carried her past the bench
where the Dreamweaver lay asleep. For a moment the woman's
milky eyes turned aside. A prickle of warning stirred within her;
she strained to interpret, but lost the thread of prophecy in the
vagueness of advanced age. Muttering and shaking straw-tangled
hair, the priestess moved on to the kitchen stoop, where the inn
mistress's daughter waited with her daily mug of milk.

Taen slept until Corley's mate came to fetch her at sundown.
She barely had time to eat supper before the men saddled horses
in the stableyard. The trip to Corlin resumed with stops through
the night to change mounts; Corley steered himself clear of the
Dreamweaver's presence throughout.

The company reached the ferry over the Redwater by dawn.
With the least possible delay, the captain left the horses in the
care of a drover, then bribed the bargemaster on duty with gold.
Stranded caravans and merchants hollered imprecations from the

bank, while the men loaded gear, and a Dreamweaver who slept soundly in blankets; they completed the trip down the estuary afloat. *Moonless* put to sea before Taen awoke. By then the shores of Hallowild had disappeared astern. The brigantine drove with the wind on her quarter, toward Jaric and the Isle of the Vaere.

~~VI~~

Demon Council

Lanterns shuttered with scarlet glass cast baleful, bloody light over the rock hall of Shadowfane. Demons all the sizes and shapes of nightmare stirred restlessly in the gallery, while, dark against darker shadow, a newly spawned Karas shape-changer lay puddled like slime on the floor behind the mirror pool. Presiding from the dais above, Lord Scait sat his throne of human trophies, spiny hands poised on stuffed knees. None in the chamber made a sound, though alliances within Shadowfane were uneasy; the sighted and the eyeless alike strained forward, attention fixed on the human who knelt at Scait's feet.

"Rise." The Lord of Shadowfane blinked, scaled lids momentarily eclipsing evil yellow eyes. "Speak the tidings you came to deliver."

The one known as Maelgrim touched his forehead to the floor. "Your will, Lord Mightiest." Wire bracelets chimed at his wrists as he straightened. Extended periods spent in mind-link with the Thienz had left him painfully thin. Black hair fell uncut to his shoulders, and a tunic of dyed linen clothed his wiry frame, belted at the hips with a sash of woven gold.

A rustle crossed the assembly, scratchy as wind through dry leaves. Maelgrim raised his face toward the throne. His eyes shone ice-pale, accentuated by bony sockets. When he spoke, he mixed images with words no human would comprehend. "She has gone, this Dreamweaver sent by the Vaere. The might of Shadowfane could have killed her easily. By your command, such was not done. Now she has sailed for the Isle of the Vaere with the ship *Moonless* and the red-haired captain of the Kielmark's." The creature who had once been human paused, his expression twisted with frustration. "Lord, by your command, two most troublesome enemies are granted liberty to escape the net I wove. Why should this be?"

This news roused consternation from the gathering. Murmurs arose, sullen in overtone, underlaid by whispers of complaint. Scait's favorites exchanged uneasy glances, while numerous cadres of rivals expectantly licked pointed teeth.

Their stirrings and rustlings caused Scait to clash his jaws, and the long hackles trembled at his neck. "Silence!" He surveyed the room, his glare baleful red in the lanternlight. As the assembly subsided to stillness, he focused once again upon Maelgrim. "Your insolence is inappropriate, spawn-of-a-mewling-human. More important matters lie at stake than the death of your sister-accursed. Listen well. Learn patience, for the Dreamweaver and her captain go free only to dance to a grander plan. Be content, Dark-dreamer. You shall have what you desire, and sooner than you presently think."

The Lord of Shadowfane croaked with a demonic equivalent of laughter, then arose from his throne of human remains. He spoke loudly that all might hear. "O my kindred, my brothers, the Kielmark's captain has divided his force. Half of them convey to Ivain's heir, Jaric, the Dreamweaver who might have unraveled my plan. The rest remain, abandoned to their fates in Morbrith domain. These ones and all they stay to defend now lie vulnerable to exploitation. Listen and know! Maelgrim's search has located human children with the talent we require. These will be taken alive and brought to Shadowfane. Once their enslavement to a Thienz-dominated Sathid is complete, their talents will be turned to the ruin of humanity. Then shall the descendants of *Corinne Dane* suffer revenge for our centuries of exile!"

Beneath the dais, Scait's circle of favorites nodded among themselves. A quiver rippled the jellylike surface of the Karas, and Thienz hummed softly in mind-meld. Here and there, dark as clotted ink between the feet of the larger demons, the furred forms of Gierjlings twitched in communal sleep. But the boldest of Scait's rivals were not satisfied.

The nearest leaped up with a guttural growl of displeasure. Swift as the lash of a whip, Scait interrupted before she could speak. *'Be still, or earn bloodshed, for I have not forgotten the Set-Nav unit from* Corinne Dane *accursed!'*

The rival bristled her short hackles. She poised on the verge of

challenge, but the colleagues at her side chose not to support her
defiance. They wished to hear of Scait's plot, and alone she was
no match for the Lord enthroned on the dais. Left without recourse, she subsided as hushed anticipation settled over the assembly.

As if no disturbance had occurred, Scait outlined the re-
mainder of his intentions. By the time he finished, even the most
bloodthirsty rivals were forced to reluctant admiration; the plan to
storm Keithland and reclaim the lost Veriset-Nav computer was a
masterwork. Corley had unwittingly played straight into the
Dark-dreamer's hands; and even the Kielmark's formidable discipline became a tool for Shadowfane's machinations.

Jabber arose from the packed ranks of the assembly. Young
Thienz clustered about their elders to share in subtlety and speculation. Gierjlings sensed the rising excitement and stirred from
sleep, their opened, reasonless eyes glowing violet in the
shadows. Now only the most vicious of the rivals considered
dissent. The plan for humanity's destruction seemed brilliantly
conceived.

The brigantines left at Corlin might indeed be purloined. They
could ply south to recover Set-Nav with no human to dispute
their passage, for did not vessels under the Kielmark's banner
fare at will within Keithland? No king, no councilman of the
Alliance, and no priest of Kordane's Brotherhood interfered with
captains who flew the red wolf banner. To risk the Pirate Lord's
displeasure was to set a stranglehold upon commerce, and
humans did not place their gold in jeopardy. This every demon
understood.

But snags remained: neither did the Kielmark's officers brook
interference. Their loyalty was tight as old roots, impossible to
bend or loosen. Memories-of-ancestors confirmed such beyond
question: demons had died screaming upon Cliffhaven. To meddle with the King-wolf-pirate was to risk much, or so the rivals
determined. Some of them gnashed their teeth. One female,
Scait-egg-sister, went further and dared raise an objection. "Lord,
your proposal is flawed-dangerous, a plan for the wise to spurn.
Kielmark-accursed has a taste for mad-vengeance, and his chestnut-haired captain is like him."

Scait disdained to raise his hackles against a sibling. With a
lazy hiss, he gestured toward the newly hatched shape-changer
that glistened like jelly at his feet. "But we have a Karas to
replace this captain," he admonished. "Through the crews left
vulnerable at Morbrith, we shall gain access to *Moonless,* and

through *Moonless*'s master, shape-changed to a likeness of Dei-son-Corley-killer-of-brethren, the Kielmark shall meet his death. So shall my grand plan triumph."

The Lord of Shadowfane waved a spurred forearm. In the corner farthest from the dais, a black knot of flesh stirred and unraveled into the separate forms of a mature circle of Gierj-lings. Six sets of eyes glimmered like sparks in the gloom.

Scait turned eyes the disturbed gold of turbid oil upon the boy from Imrill Kand. "Maelgrim Dark-dreamer, at last you may claim the greatest gift of your inheritance. Accept these Gierj-lings and school yourself to merge with their minds. When you are able to embrace their powers fully, you are to wreak the bondage of Shadowfane upon the souls of Morbrith and with them the Kielmark's crewmen. That is my command."

In the deepest hour of night four days after *Moonless*'s depar-ture, the Kielmark's four captains left stationed in Hallowild left their beds, though no circumstance had arisen to waken them. In separate but simultaneous movement, they dressed, and armed, and abruptly rousted their ships' companies to depart from Mor-brith keep. The men obeyed with spiritless efficiency. By torch-light they saddled and mounted. A puzzled captain of the Earl's guard watched them ride out in cheerless silence. Once past the gates, they spurred south on the road toward Corlin.

The early hours before daylight saw their arrival at the cross-roads settlement of Gaire's Main. There, while villagers shrank behind locked doors, the men at arms paused to water tired horses.

Disturbed by the chink of metal, the ancient priestess of the well stirred in the loft above the stableyard. The strange, prick-ling sensation that accompanied her gift of clairvoyance brought her fully and instantly awake. Stiff-jointed, but clear of mind, she rose from the straw and crept to the trapdoor. Night wind carried the scents of horses and man-sweat; yet the creatures who moved among the animals below were not as they should be. The priest-ess blinked blind eyes. As a maiden she had undergone training and a painful initiation to gain the enhanced perception of a clan priestess. Her altered mind sensed a wrongness about these horsemen who swaggered in the stableyard below.

Troubled, the clanswoman scratched her belly through a rent in the skins that clothed her. Slowly, muttering all the while, she made her way to the ladder and crept into the shadowed darkness of the stable. None noticed as she shuffled to the doorway by the grain bins.

Close at hand, the sense of wrongness became overpowering. Horses stamped and men cursed; the company had remounted, ready to resume their ride. But over the clank of weapons, stirrups, and mail, the priestess sensed a ringing overtone that bordered the edges of pain. Never in life had she known such a presence of evil. Her duty was plain. Trembling, the crone stepped into the yard to challenge.

Her voice rang girlishly clear. "Behold! Trespassers enter Keithland. They ride as humans, yet they are shells, emptied of spirit and possessed by demons. True men, be not deceived. Know ye stand in the company of Kor's Accursed!"

"Fires!" Corley's first captain slammed his mount with his heels and jerked around to face her. "Woman, as you value life, be silent."

"Demon." The priestess stabbed a bony finger in his direction. "Death cannot change the truth!"

The captain gripped his sword hilt. "Since when do the Kielmark's officers take orders from old women?" He smiled with icy mockery; and still smiling, drew steel and cut the blind priestess down.

She fell against the water trough with a coughing cry. Blood flooded hot over her hands. Yet purpose made her fight for strength. Sinking to her knees, she groped through the mud and the run-off from the spring. Her palms touched the sacred surface of the well-stone. Energy surged from the contact. Dying, the priestess melded with the mystery within and sent warning.

South, in the underground installation on the Isle of the Vaere, a monitor light flashed on the communications panel. Circuitry activated to receive an incoming signal that twisted across time and through space; the message originated from a dying priestess in Gaire's Main. Though the culture of the hilltribes was patterned after primitive ritual magic, the clairvoyance of their priestesses in fact disguised a network of Set-Nav's comlink; thus had the remotest wilds of Keithland been watched continually for intrusion, transmissions sent by means of talisman stones no demon yet thought to examine for technological artifacts.

Even as the clan priestess breathed her last, Set-Nav merged her fragmented warning with data in the memory banks. Numbers flashed through probability equations, and the monitors glittered amber with distress lights. Keithland's existing defenses were critically inadequate to offset Shadowfane's latest offensive. Set-Nav had no means to sequence secondary alternatives. Jaric's Firemastery lay yet in jeopardy. Although he clung stubbornly to sanity, his strength ebbed with each passing day; even if he embraced Ivain's philosophy at once, his resilience had worn to the point where the paired Sathid might still overthrow his will. The Dreamweaver perhaps could save him. But Set-Nav sorted facts, and by extrapolation perceived impending danger to Taen.

Power surged to transmit the priestess's warning. Far to the north, a century and a quarter out of phase, Taen Dreamweaver started awake in her berth aboard *Moonless*.

Jostled against the lee boards by the rising toss of the sea, the girl lay in darkness, straining to catch a silvery jangle of bells. Yet she heard only the thud and hiss of waves against the hull, and wind thrumming through the rigging. No trace remained of Tamlin of the Vaere except the warning left echoing in her mind.

Taen shivered and sat up. Her cabin seemed suddenly ominous with threat. The darkness oppressed her without remedy. The lamp in its gimbaled bracket was empty of oil, the reservoir dry since the evening before. With *Moonless* pitching uncomfortably to weather, the girl had stayed in rather than cross spray-drenched decks to find the steward.

Yet deep in her heart, Taen knew that weather was only an excuse; she had avoided the kindly old servant since leaving Gaire's Main. Her self-consciousness stemmed from the fact that she had yet to muster the nerve to make her peace with *Moonless*'s captain. While crew and brigantine drove south under straining yards of canvas, Corley kept to the quarterdeck. Storms invariably made the captain moody and unreasonable about interruptions. But now the Dreamweaver had no choice. Tamlin's warning forced her to confront him without delay.

Taen slipped from her blankets into dank, chill air. More than cold raised gooseflesh on her skin as she tugged a linen shift over her head. Too hurried to fight the pitch and toss of the deck and dig out heavy clothing, she slipped the latch, then clawed her way against the elements to the quarterdeck.

Topside, the brigantine seemed frail as a sliver slammed through a black expanse of spindrift and sea. Wave crests foamed across the waist, carved into geysers by the ratlines; after each successive flooding, spray showered back in sheets between taut curves of canvas. In the puddled glow of the binnacle, two men labored to hold the brigantine on course, lanternlight glazing their fingers orange as they strained against the drag of the double-spoked wheel. The nearer one worked with his hood thrown back. Through tangled chestnut hair, Taen recognized *Moonless*'s captain. She called out and worked her way aft, over planking sleek with seawater.

Corley lifted his head. Startled to see the Dreamweaver on deck, he mistimed his pull. The wheel kicked under his hands. He lost a spoke, swore, and threw his weight against the helm as a headsail banged forward. *Moonless* heeled, overcanvassed, and unforgiving under a murderous burden of wind. Two strong men could barely maintain her course.

Corley shouted to the officer on watch. "Call the boatswain away from the pumps. He's needed on deck. And tell him to roust the second mate to replace him below."

Somewhere in the darkness, a crewman answered. With less than a minute's delay, the boatswain arrived, panting, to relieve his captain of the wheel.

Corley stepped aside, a bulking, windblown shadow with water dripping silver from his beard. He lingered over the compass. Then, satisfied *Moonless* was secure on her heading, he turned and met the Dreamweaver with eyes that were bright and inquiring and alert as a predator's.

Killer's eyes, Taen thought; she shivered involuntarily.

Corley misinterpreted. "You're chilled." Swiftly he shed his cloak. Before the Dreamweaver could decline, his hands bundled her in salt-drenched wool that soaked her own garment to the skin. Yet she endured the damp rather than suffer the captain's touch again.

Moonless tossed. Balanced on his feet with catlike ease, Corley spared her the need to speak first. "What brings you out? Not the shaggy mug of my helmsman, surely."

His humor raised no smile. "I have tidings from the Vaere," said Taen. "We are pursued out of Hallowild. I was told to warn you. Beware of the demon-possessed."

Corley frowned. He did not move, even when a shower of windblown spray plastered his shirt to his back. Suddenly he gestured with decision. "Come below. We'll talk."

Given any choice, Taen would have declined. But strained emotions did not blight her common sense; she knew the captain's request concerned the men left stationed at Morbrith. For their sake, she permitted Corley to hustle her through the hatch and into the dry comfort of his stern cabin.

A lantern burned over the starboard sea chest. In wildly flickering light, Taen observed that the sheets were turned down on

Corley's berth. Evidently the steward cherished hopes that his captain would snatch time to undress and sleep. But as always, such solicitude proved futile. Corley flung off his drenched tunic and tossed it carelessly across the linen. Then he gestured for Taen to sit on the locker nearest the coal stove.

The Dreamweaver did not remove his dripping cloak. Though the spare orderliness of the captain's quarters had always before reassured her, she had lost any inclination to abandon her reserve. "The Vaere gave me no particulars. I know only what I told you on deck."

Voices in the cabin drew the steward, who ducked his head in the door. Corley dispatched the servant to the galley to fetch mulled wine, then seated himself before the streaked panes of the stern window. He scrubbed the salt from his brow with his knuckles and again looked at the Dreamweaver. "I need your help to contact my captains at Hallowild. They may be better informed of the danger we face. If not, they deserve warning. Our peril might become theirs as well."

Taen bent her head, expression hidden by a fallen veil of hair. She sat so still that Corley thought for a moment she had refused his request.

He tried gently to reason with her. "If you can't act for my men, then do so for the safety of Morbrith's folk."

But Taen did not hear. Already she had blanked her physical senses and slipped deep into trance. She extended her focus across leagues of wind-torn ocean to the far shores of Hallowild. To her dream-sense, the town of Corlin appeared as clustered sparks of light, each person a jewel shining against velvet dark. Other glimmers lay scattered across the expanse beyond: post stations, farmsteaders, and foresters plying livelihoods in solitude. Taen refined her probe, centering upon the estuary of the Redwater where five brigantines rode at anchor, commanded by the captain of Cliffhaven's vessel *Ballad*.

Although the river was jammed with the customary traders, no spark matched the abrasive presence of *Ballad*'s master. Taen hesitated, perplexed. On the chance the man was off board, perhaps enjoying a drink or a wench in one of Corlin's three taverns, she swept the harbor again, seeking the *Ballad*'s boatswain. That search failed also. Alarmed now, Taen turned north to Morbrith where the Kielmark's other companies remained to defend the keep.

The backland hills lay studded with familiar compass-ring formations that marked a clansmen's camp; northwest held only darkness. Puzzled, Taen hesitated. Beyond the sparkling cross that was Gaire's Main, the living folk of Morbrith should have glimmered like a constellation of stars. No light remained. Shadow seemed to have fallen over keep and farmstead and wildlands. Touched by fear, the Dreamweaver intensified her search. Through the lengthening days of spring she had guarded twice ten thousand people from the predations of the Dark-dreamer; surely Shadowfane could not have obliterated so many in so short a span of time!

Yet Morbrith domain stayed dark, as if a veil of mourning had been drawn across the land. Not the High Earl in his hall, nor the surly temper of Corley's first-in-command, nor a single man of Cliffhaven's defense force remained. Reckless with disbelief, the Dreamweaver delved deeper. She strained the limits of her strength seeking life, to no avail. *Nothing;* blackness absorbed her effort. Her senses sank into endless, numbing cold. Shock and grief drove her to sound that well of oblivion; but as Taen extended her senses, evil moved at its heart. She jerked back in alarm. Aware of her, the presence that occupied Morbrith keep reached out in challenge. Though its essence was recognizably part of Maelgrim Dark-dreamer, another more alien resonance suffused the pattern of his being. This overtone was *other,* and terrifying in a manner no word could describe. The Dreamweaver dared not delve deeper over distance. If the people of an entire domain could fall to the Dark-dreamer's strange and amplified influence, hope for Keithland now relied upon *Moonless* and Ivainson Jaric.

Taen broke contact, restored to the toss of stormy seas and the clink of mugs as the steward served spiced wine in the stern cabin. She clenched bloodless fingers in the wool that cloaked her shoulders. Feeling helpless and desperate and alone, she sought means to voice a horror that defied credibility. Shadowfane had struck. Morbrith was no more; every competent, roughmannered seaman who had remained to defend the High Earl was now lost to the living. Taen tried to speak, but anguish and disbelief stifled the breath in her lungs.

"Taen?" Warned of something brutally wrong, Corley dismissed the steward, and said, "Girl, you look ill. What's happened?"

The Dreamweaver could do nothing at all except break the news. "Morbrith has fallen to Kor's Accursed. Not a man, woman, or child escaped." She shivered, forced herself to qualify though her voice broke. "I don't know how! But your men are gone, even *Shearfish*'s master and crew. I found no trace of the companies you stationed to aid the High Earl's defense."

An interval loud with waves and creaking timber answered her terrible words. The only movement in the cabin was the rising curl of steam from the one mug the steward had managed to pour. Jolted by the captain's profound stillness, Taen at last looked up. The blanket bunched in her trembling fingers. Where she had braced herself in expectation of curses and violence, Corley had done very little more than surge to his feet.

His face was open as few ever saw it, a naked expression of horror and pain and disbelief. As Taen watched, the creases around his eyes clenched. The grief that rocked him was deep, and private, and woundingly intense. Incongruity struck her like a slap. That a cold-handed killer could own such depth of compassion became impossible to countenance.

Unable to reconcile the emotion with the man, Taen gasped and quivered and at last gave way to tears. "Corley, they're gone, all gone. Even *Ballad*'s awful cook, who put all that pepper in the beans."

The captain's stunned moment of suspension broke. He reached her in a stride, caught her heaving shoulders in his hands, and stroked her hair. "Easy. Easy."

His control seemed restored, his shock and his loss instantly masked to master the needs of the moment; but no one with a Dreamweaver's sensitivities could ignore the truth: the man behind the facade still wept inwardly for the death of the crews under his command, as well as the mother left behind years past at Morbrith. Taen felt a hard something give inside. The distrust that had festered since the incident with the priests found release in racking sobs. The Dreamweaver buried her distress in dry linen that smelled of soap and the herbs the steward used to sweeten the sea chests. Yet horror did not abate. Deison Corley might be forgiven his cruelties; the firm play of muscles beneath her cheek might steady her, but no human comfort could ease her sorrow. Not even for the sake of Ivainson Jaric could Taen forgive herself for abandoning Morbrith to the mercy of the Darkdreamer.

Corley shook her gently. "Ease up, little witch. You've pitched yourself alone against an enemy too great for all of us. Don't feel craven for stepping back." His tone assumed a hint of iron. "Once Jaric gains his mastery, we'll have the means to fight."

Yet the captain's confidence was forced. Morbrith had fallen, quickly, inexplicably, and finally, claiming the only relation who recognized him and five companies of the Kielmark's best men. Grimly Corley wondered when the pursuit promised by Tamlin's warning would overtake his single ship; even if he contrived to escape the fate that had befallen the High Earl, how long before Ivainson Jaric broke under agonies beyond the means of any human mind to endure?

That question would not find answer in darkness on the open sea. As soon as Taen had calmed somewhat, Corley settled her by the stove and belatedly offered mulled wine. White-faced, fighting to control her sorrow, she badly needed the restorative. Although she accepted the cup, she did not drink.

Instead she clenched her fingers as if her hands were cold. "The Kielmark will have to be told."

Corley expelled an inaudible sigh of relief. He had always known the girl had pluck. For the first time he realized how dependably he could count on her good sense. "You might want to finish your wine first."

Taen shook her head. "No." The faintest amusement brightened her tone. "Unless the Kielmark has miraculously learned temperance, I rather think I'll need the drink afterward."

She hooked her mug in a bracket to warm upon the stove, then bowed her head in dream-trance once more. Her powers answered with reluctance. Weary in a manner that had little to do with the lateness of the hour, she gathered her awareness in hand. The scent of sweet wine and spices and the salt-smell of Corley's sodden woolens faded slowly from perception as she cast her call outward, over leagues of storm-tossed ocean toward the Kielmark's stronghold on Cliffhaven.

Corley poured no wine for himself, but paced the cabin while he waited for her to rouse. He compensated without effort against the roll of the deck as *Moonless* thrashed through the swells. Gusts blew savage blasts of rain against the stern windows. Streaks of wet ran down the glass, gilt against the darkness beyond. Corley gazed into the storm with unseeing eyes and noticed very little until the steward appeared at the companionway with a quiet inquiry after Taen. The captain paused then, abruptly aware that the Dreamweaver had lingered too long in trance.

His concern transformed to alarm. The girl lay motionless by the stove, black hair drying in tangles over her shoulders. Her borrowed cloak had slipped aside, the one wrist visible beyond the edge too still to seem alive. Between one stride and the next, Corley knelt at the Dreamweaver's side.

Taen stirred almost immediately. Conscious of the captain's presence even before she had reoriented to the stern cabin aboard *Moonless,* she opened eyes gone bleak with dismay. "I couldn't get through."

Corley reined back an overpowering urge to question; his impatience could only add to the girl's alarm. Against all instinct he waited, and in her own time Taen qualified. She touched his mind directly with her dream-sense, and Corley shared firsthand the dense, almost suffocating darkness blocking her attempt to reach the Kielmark.

He spoke the instant her touch released his mind. "Do you think the event is related?"

Taen knew he referred to the disappearance of his men and the strange darkness over Morbrith. "We dare not assume otherwise." Her hands twisted the cloak's damp fabric over and over, while Corley assessed the implications of leaving the Kielmark uninformed.

But Taen already thought ahead of him on that count. "Cliffhaven must be told. With Tamlin of the Vaere unavailable for advice, no choice remains but to work through the wizards of Mhored Kara."

The girl's resilience astonished. Still on his knees, Corley started back, his hand out of habit clenched on the hilt of his most convenient knife. "You risk much," he said incredulously. "There's no love lost between the college of sorcery and the Kielmark."

"Meaning they fight like weasels." Taen was not intimidated when Corley drew his blade and tested the edge with his finger.

"One of the conjurers Anskiere destroyed on Imrill Kand was the Lord of Mhored Kara's son." The captain flipped the blade neatly and made a cutting motion in the air. "Why do you think the Kielmark's so touchy on the subject of sorcery? Aside from the upset arranged by the witch Tathagres, we've been expecting arcane retaliation in some form for the better part of a year."

"Yet your master cannot guard Mainstrait against a threat he knows nothing about." Taen reached out and with a touch stilled Corley's knife hand in the air. "Some problems can't be solved with steel. You'll need to trust my judgment."

The captain disengaged and returned the bleakest of smiles. "My boatswain says you're a crafty hand at cards. That's a fair blessing, girl. Because against the wizards of Mhored Kara, you'll need every trick you have, and a dozen others only the devil could arrange." The knife flashed once as Corley turned the blade and rammed it into the sheath at his wrist. Worry hidden behind brusqueness, he added, "Good luck, little witch. If you get through, and if the Kielmark neglects to thank you properly for the service, I'll personally thrash him at quarterstaffs the next time we dock at Cliffhaven."

Taen grinned. "You'll try." And she ducked as Corley grabbed for her. "Don't expect me to watch you get bruised."

"There's faith." The captain grimaced sourly and rose, half-thrown to his feet as *Moonless* yawed over a swell. The wind had freshened. The scream of the gusts through the rigging penetrated even the cabins below decks. By now the watch would be changing. Anxious to return to his command, Corley yelled for the steward to bring his spare cloak. Then, too impatient to wait, he stamped through the companionway into the storm. Let the servant pursue him to the quarterdeck. The Kielmark's first captain had great courage, but not so much that he could stay and watch as a Dreamweaver too young for her burdens rallied her remaining resources and plunged once again into trance.

～VII～

Cycle of Fire

The settlement of Mhored Kara lay on the coast east of Elrinfaer, to the south of the merchant city of Telshire. Taen had never traveled those shores, but during off-watch hours Corley's sailhands had told her tales. The wizards' towers perched on the very tip of a peninsula, black and notched, or black and pointed like rows of soldiers' spears. The structures had few windows. On dark nights strange lights burned from slits cut in the seaward walls, sometimes green, othertimes red. The phenomenon was not without precedent, for Vaerish sorceries commonly generated illumination; but as described by the sailors, the spells of Mhored Kara were scintillant and hurtful to the eye.

Taen considered her task with trepidation. For centuries the conclave had provided conjurers for the courts of Felwaithe and Kisburn. Only once had the Dreamweaver encountered their work. As a child she had seen three such sorcerers set the enchanted fetters that blocked Anskiere's command of wave and weather. The strongest of the three, who once served as Grand Conjurer to Kisburn's King, had gone on to strip the Stormwarden of protection, by murdering the birds fashioned of weather wards for defense. Taen recalled the sorcerer's hands, streaked and dripping with blood as they stabbed and stabbed again with the knife. Even the memory made her feel ill.

She had been untrained then, utterly ignorant of her Dreamweaver's potential. Newly wise to the ways of power, she lacked the understanding to determine how a Vaere-trained sorcerer in the fullness of his mastery could be subdued by lesser wizards from the south. Perhaps against three, Anskiere could not save himself; far more likely he had surrendered willingly for some obscure purpose of his own. Whatever the reason, that Kisburn's conjurers had constrained his powers was a real and chilling fact. Taen gathered herself in trance, coldly aware that she courted danger.

Caution was necessary also because the location of Mhored Kara was unfamiliar to her; to find the wizards' towers she had only a compass direction plotted off Corley's charts, and imperfect images garnered from the recollections of sailors. She began quickly, lest her resolve become daunted by uncertainties.

The lash of the seas and the work and creak of *Moonless* dimmed in the Dreamweaver's ears as she unreeled her awareness over Elrinfaer. She crossed acres wasted by Mharg-demons in the generation before she was born, league upon league of desolation where life had yet to recover. Her mind traversed a landscape of treeless rock, of earth ripped by wind into sand and dust devils. Deserted cottages caught drifts of soil in the stones of tumbled chimneys. The pastures that once nourished livestock grew no fodder, but baked and cracked like desert bottomlands deprived of any shade. Not even bones remained of the folk who had once tilled fields and pruned lush acres of orchards. The sky overhead was empty of clouds or birds; beneath the golden glare of sunrise, sorrow seemed instilled in the stripped bones of the hills.

Taen pressed south and east, to the far side of the tors of Telshire. There bare earth gave way to stunted weeds, then grasses tasseled with seed. Spring was well along in the lower latitudes. Wild apple trees showed hard green knots of new fruit. Beyond rose the deep, dark pines of the Deshforest, all shadows and interlaced branches fragrant with the scent of resin. None dwelt here but wandering clans of hilltribes and the occasional isolated trapper. Farther still, the forest wilds fell behind. Taen traversed scrublands pale with reed marshes, and chains of brackish pools that smelled of kelp. As she neared the sea, the vegetation changed to saw grass and beach plum, which clothed the high dunes of the south peninsula. There at last she found the towers of Mhored Kara, dull black against dawn sky, and narrow as swords; slate roofs caught the light like silvered lead. None of the wheeling gulls that scavenged the shoreline circled near, or roosted there.

Taen damped her powers to a spark and guarded her presence under ward. The wizards might not be sensitive to the resonance of Vaerish sorcery, but only a fool would presume so. With apprehension and no small degree of misgiving, she narrowed her focus upon the tallest and slenderest of the spires and searched its salt-scoured stone for an opening.

She entered through a rune-carved arch nestling beneath the eaves. The interior beyond was dusty and dim. Her questing dream-sense encountered trestles scattered with books and the burnt-down stubs of candles. The strange paraphernalia of magic stood crammed between shelves of phials, philters, and collections of stoppered jars with faded labels. The bones of tiny animals moldered within, or birds preserved in brine. Unpleasantly reminded of Anskiere's slaughtered wards, Taen pressed on. Her awareness funneled down a spiral stairway dark with mirrors that did not reflect their surroundings. She sensed these for a trap and did not probe within; dream-sense warned her of mazes that twisted and turned in endless convolutions designed to ensnare the mind. For the first time, fear made her hesitate. What sort of intruder inspired the Mhored Karan wizards to build such cruel traps?

Yet news of the blight upon Morbrith allowed no space for faintheartedness. Taen forced herself onward. One level lower, she found storerooms filled with casks and boxes fastened with wire. The air had a musty smell, like fur locked too long in old trunks. By now aware that she had entered by way of the attics, Taen dropped lower still. Three levels down, she encountered gray-robed boys with shaved heads who meditated in cubicles of silence and shadow. A moment's pause revealed these to be novices, and not the ones she sought. Taen passed on, through a bare hall where the wind blew through slits in the wall. From there she descended yet another spiral stair and quite suddenly came upon the sound of voices.

In a chamber spread with wine-colored rugs, five sorcerers sat in a circle discussing the merits of an aspirant recently arrived from Telshire. Two wore black, two wore red, and the last, robed richly in purple and gold, was a wiry ancient with peaked brows and bleak eyes. His cheeks were tattooed with sigils of power, and each of his fingers, even his spatulate thumbs, was heavily ringed with silver. Taen extended her dream-sense. After the shallowest of scans, she singled the elder out as one great in the ways of power. He had an aura set into discipline like a watercourse channeled through rock, and his titles were Magelord of the Conclave, and Master of Mhored Kara.

He sensed the presence of the Dreamweaver at once. His cold eyes lifted, and he stiffened very slightly on his cushions. At his movement the black-robed wizard to his left murmured inquiry and was silenced by a wave of the old one's hand. Silver rings flashed briefly by candlelight. The gesture that followed was in some way arcane, for Taen felt a charge of force sting the outer barrier of her wards.

She deflected the thrust without difficulty, though the energy was configured differently from anything she had previously encountered. Whether the spell was shaped in defense or query, Taen chose not to fathom. Rather than wait for a second attack, she manifested a detailed illusion of her presence in the chamber at Mhored Kara.

Her form appeared between one breath and the next, robed in the pearlescent, shimmering gray given only to a Vaere-trained Dreamweaver. Her black hair was caught into a coil of wire, and her flesh gave off a tangible, living warmth. Her eyes, blue and direct as sky, were focused solely upon the Magelord of the Conclave. "Do you always greet visitors with hostile spells, Your Eminence?"

"Only those who arrive unasked, and by sorcery." The ancient's voice was dry as wind through dead leaves. He spoke as if to empty air, and to Taen's astonishment, the other four sorcerers in the chamber recoiled upon their cushions as if startled. The nearest of the red robes raised his hands. A spindle of light bloomed between his palms, but died out immediately as his Master snapped his fingers for him to desist. The underling subsided with a sullen look, while his Magelord answered Taen's puzzlement directly.

"My fellows of the conclave neither hear you speak nor see you." The old one qualified with ancient, embittered malice. "My conjurers see only what is real, Lady. Within these walls, you do not exist."

Taen absorbed this in furious thought and gained her first insight into the powers of Mhored Kara's conclave. They were unquestionably men of talent, but molded by tenets far different from those of any Vaerish master. Where the powers of Sathid bonding took inherent talent and by resonance expanded an inborn trait into something greater, the wizards of Mhored Kara learned to reach inward, to grapple and twist reality to the dictates of mortal will. Taen studied the ancient and his four confederates more closely, and concluded that such manipulation of natural order came at punishing cost. Pitiless decades of training left the wizards emaciated, humorless, and baleful as crows. Their tireless and exacting analysis of reality might strip and banish Sathid-born conjury as dream; led to extreme, these wizards might even enter the mind and sunder rapport between Sathid master and crystal. But in directly applicable force, Vaerish powers were as beyond them as sky over earth. Taen perceived the workings of how Anskiere's gifts had come to be bound by such constraints; what she might never understand was why the Stormwarden had permitted Kisburn's conjurers the opening to let his imprisonment happen.

The Magelord's manner sharpened suddenly. Perhaps he realized that Taen unraveled the secrets of his conclave in the dream-space of her silence, for he clenched his hands with a dissonant clash of rings. "Why do you send to the one place in Keithland where illusions such as yours are not welcome?"

Taen detected threat behind the words. Although in theory the Magelord's spells could not set her at risk, she chose not to test that chance. The Master of Mhored Kara certainly could be dangerous, cruel as he was within, and emotionally steeped in spite against all things he could not influence.

"I bring tidings," Taen said directly. "Keithland is imperiled." Without further opening, she translated the image of Morbrith, and all that its darkness signified, directly into the old mage's mind.

He hissed, his dark eyes wide with affront. Spindles of light snapped forth from the palms of all his underlings, the red-robed ones and the black. Taen felt a blow hammer her shields. The image she had constructed in the chamber shattered like a smashed mirror. She let it go without contention, and instead reshaped the core of her energy into a presence wrought of sound whose existence not even the underlings could deny. *'For the sake of Keithland and the reality you value, send warning and word of Morbrith's fall to the Kielmark on Cliffhaven.'*

The Magelord countered in rasping irritation. "The conclave has sworn no oath of protection to the Vaere! And the Kielmark deserves no favors. Do not forget that he once granted sanctuary to one who later killed two of our own."

Taen noticed the elder's queer reluctance to mention the Stormwarden by name. She probed on impulse, and perceived in the Magelord an apprehension that bordered upon outright fear. Anskiere's potential for redress against the wizards who had interfered with him did not sit well with the conclave at Mhored Kara. Though the idea of vengeance from the Vaere-trained was a misapprehension, Taen amplified their false belief to a cutting edge and pried at the wizards' reluctance. *'Do you wish to answer to Anskiere of Elrinfaer for release of the Frostwargs? To claim injury for Kisburn's conjurers is to assume culpability for their crimes.'*

The Magelord glared at the air. His ringed hands worked as if he longed to reach out and throttle the voice wrought of dreams. "What of the ice cliffs?" he rasped. "Your Stormwarden is prisoner still."

In answer, Taen sent him an image of Jaric, whose resemblance to his father, Ivain, at times could be uncanny. *'The Firelord left an heir, Eminence. He completes his passage to mastery even now on the Isle of the Vaere.'*

Though the Master of Mhored Kara would never concede defeat, the spite reflected in his obsidian eyes assured Taen better than promises that she had won his acquiescence. The conclave would inform Cliffhaven. And wily and snappish as a wolf, the Kielmark could be depended upon to inflame the rulers of Keithland's multiple, bickering governments until each and every one of them took action.

Corley checked his cabin later, to find Taen settled and asleep beneath the steward's watchful eye. Informed by the servant that her demand upon the conclave at Mhored Kara had been successful, he returned at once to his quarterdeck. Though the wind had risen, he issued no orders to shorten sail. Instead he posted a second lookout in the crosstrees and doubled the watch on deck. All night he stood by the helmsman, strained and tense and watching for dangers he had no words to describe. When dawn broke over the ragged crests of the waves, he called all hands and broke news of the evil that had overtaken their companions in the north.

After their captain's summons, *Moonless*'s company became haunted by insecurity. The sailhands glanced over their shoulders as they went about their duties; the smallest of unusual noises made them start. Banter and swearing ceased altogether. When the gale lifted, the men toiled in the rigging without hot food to sustain them, for Corley kept the galley fire out rather than risk having smoke reveal their position to the enemy.

Moonless made fast passage, sped by the fresh winds of spring. But the fact that the weather held fair and the horizon remained empty day after day did nothing to lift the spirits of her crewmen. Gaunt and wary, and driven by a captain with hunted eyes, they finally hove the brigantine to in the empty ocean southwest of the Free Isles' Alliance.

"I sail on alone," said Taen to the Kielmark's first captain.

Clad in a Dreamweaver's robes of silver-gray, she stood by the mainmast pinrail, her hands clenched as if she expected argument. "You can loan me the jolly boat."

Corley folded bare arms across his chest. The straps of his knife sheaths crisscrossed both wrists, cutting into his tanned skin. "Only you know where you're going, little witch. If you'll accept no escort to the Isle of the Vaere, at least know this. *Moonless* won't leave these waters until you and Jaric return."

Taen took a quick breath. "There's danger."

"Where is there not?" Corley grinned as if the threats of Shadowfane and the perils of the Vaere were of no consequence. "Besides, I want my jolly boat back. In one piece, mind. No chips or dings in the keel."

"Done." Taen tried valiantly to smile. The gesture made her seem poignantly vulnerable and young. "Well, do I have to launch the tub myself?"

"Maybe." The captain called two sailhands away from splicing a replacement stay and regarded the Dreamweaver intently. "You know my mate's fallen permanently in love with you. I'd bet my best dagger he'd rather take that jolly boat and scrape barnacles off *Moonless*'s rudder than see you row off without him."

"I'm flattered." The Dreamweaver pulled a sarcastic face, then ruined the effect by blushing. "Tell him to scrape barnacles anyway. If you wait for me, we all might need to leave in a panic."

Corley sobered instantly. "I'll chance that." Then, as if the sight of her caused him pain, he spun on his heel and shouted to the sailhands. "Get aft and lower that jolly boat. Lively!"

Men sprang to obey. Barely had they freed the tackles before Corley pushed the nearer sailor aside and busied both hands on the lines. His tongue turned sharp as his knives, and after the briefest possible interval the boat struck the sea with a smack. Before the ripples scattered, Taen found herself loaded and cast off. She seated herself jauntily on the jolly boat's seat, threaded oars, and glanced one last time at *Moonless*'s quarterdeck.

Corley stood with his back turned, hands braced on the binnacle. He refused to come aft to watch her off. If he glanced around once he would see how frail she looked, alone on the empty sea; then he could never bring himself to let her go.

"Keep your bearings, captain," Taen called. She turned her hands to the oars and wondered why her words made Corley flinch. Never before had she seen him uncertain; almost, she would rather have watched him killing priests.

The slanting light of afternoon touched the wave crests like chipped quartz, and flying fish scattered in shimmering arches before the bow of *Moonless*'s jolly boat. Taen rested her oars and rubbed a blistered palm on her knee. Well practiced at rowing as the daughter of a fisherman, she had made good progress in her slight craft. The brigantine had diminished astern until tanbark sails showed as a speck against flawless ocean; ahead, no life stirred but the strafing flight of shearwaters. Yet that emptiness itself was deceptive. Taen knew by her dream-sense that she neared the Isle of the Vaere.

She extended her perception, and once again the minute vibrations that could be neither seen nor felt by the flesh touched her dream-sense. The fabled isle lay very near. Careless of her blisters, the Dreamweaver lifted the oars. She rowed one stroke, two, three; a wave lifted the keel and coasted the jolly boat forward. Suddenly the vibrations peaked, the dissonance against her inner awareness clearing to a single sweet tone. Taen jabbed the oars deep, scattering spray as the wave rolled past. Before the current could drift her off location, she shaped a dream-call to alert Tamlin of her presence.

Sky, sunlight, and shearwaters vanished without transition into mist. Wind slapped the water, and wave crests frayed into sudden foam. Taen shipped the jolly boat's oars. Through a whipping tangle of hair she saw a flicker like heat lightning rend the air. A booming report followed, but the Dreamweaver did not hear. The ocean around the jolly boat underwent an abrupt change. The gale died to a breeze, and she drifted amid a roiled patch of water. Elsewhere the sea lay preternaturally calm. Slate-gray clouds extended to an empty horizon; *Moonless*'s sails no longer showed astern. But off the jolly boat's bow stretched beaches unmarred by tide wrack. No storm had ever hammered the dune line beyond, nor the cedar forests of terrible beauty that lifted majestically skyward. Taen had visited the Isle of the Vaere before, yet her breath caught in wonder all the same. The unspoiled splendor of the place could bewitch the most jaded of eyes.

Then, with a thrill of joy, the Dreamweaver noticed something less than perfect upon that enchanted shoreline. On the sands at the sea's edge rested an ungainly wooden fishing boat, the name *Callinde* carved on her thwart. Anxious for Jaric, Taen Dreamweaver slammed oars into rowlocks and hurled her craft toward shore.

Bells jangled the instant the jolly boat grounded. Taen twisted around in time to see Tamlin stride down the side of a dune. His cap lay askew, and the white beard strewn across his shoulders tangled with fringes of feathers and beads in his haste.

"You won't listen. That's trouble." The tiny creature stamped his foot in anger. Taen looked on without surprise as his boot left no impression in the sand. "You promised help to Jaric. Did you guess you risk your life, and his as well?"

Taen jammed the oars one by one beneath the jolly boat's stern seat, then stepped, barefoot, into the shallows. An ebbing wavelet chuckled over her ankles, sucking the sand from under her soles. "I had to come."

"So." Tamlin cocked his head and frowned keenly. His black eyes seemed to bore holes through her flesh; no approval showed on his shriveled, walnut features. "So," he said again, then slapped his thigh in conclusion. "You love him, yes?"

Taen caught her breath, then released a gasp. She blinked, sat on the jolly boat's thwart, and stared unseeing at her sandy toes. "I never thought of him that way." But the instant Tamlin had broached the subject, she realized she must.

Troubled by emotions she barely dared to confront, Taen turned her Dreamweaver's perception inward to reexamine the past. While the jolly boat heaved beneath her on the surge of an incoming wavelet, she recalled Jaric as she had encountered him first, tying supplies on a drag-sleigh in the snowy yard of a forester's cabin. He had been younger then, troubled and uncertain, and frightened of the future. Taen had felt pity at the time, not love. Later, she had restored the memory he had lost, used her talents to force his destiny; then she had acted upon the orders of the Vaere, for the sake of Keithland and the brother imperiled by Kor's Accursed. Taen frowned, oblivious to the sunlight that broke through the clouds and warmed her back. She had gone on to deliver Jaric to the merciless terms of Anskiere's geas. Love did not effect such betrayals.

Neither did love abandon a man to a lonely crossing in an open boat, without comfort. Taen swallowed, fighting an irrational urge to weep. Unbidden, a memory sprang complete in her mind. Once she had stood on cold stone in the Kielmark's dungeon and waited while Jaric rubbed at wrists scraped raw by steel fetters. At the time, Tamlin's directive had been clear: force Ivainson to the completion of Anskiere's geas. Yet Taen had not intervened. Instead she had left the decision to Jaric himself. Closer to him than anyone in Keithland, she had known he had the fortitude not to flee. She had cared for his integrity enough to free him; and afterward she had defied the Vaere, defending Cliffhaven from demon assault, all for the safety of Ivainson Jaric.

Taen drew an unsteady breath. She attempted to picture another man in Jaric's place, and felt misery. She tried to imagine a future without him, and could not; plainly, foolishly, she realized all along she had been thinking as a child, not the Vaere-trained enchantress who now was a woman grown.

"Yes." Taen's reply to the Vaere was filled with wonder and discovery. "I love him." And recognizing as she spoke that Jaric might well regard the fact as a nuisance, Taen swore until she exhausted every profanity learned from Corley's sailhands and the fishwives of Imrill Kand. When next the Dreamweaver sought Tamlin, he stared stubbornly out to sea.

The jolly boat bumped and ground against the sand. Moved by habit, Taen kicked the craft into slightly deeper water. Poised uncomfortably on the thwart, she waited through a tactful interval until the Vaere spoke again.

Fey creature though he was, Tamlin understood human nature quite clearly. "For Keithland's sake, you must succeed."

Taen stood. Afraid of what her mentor might add, she heaved the jolly boat onto the beach with a coarse grating of pebbles. "Then allow me to try at once."

Bells jingled. The Vaere vanished and reappeared, standing on the bow with his head level with hers. Breeze still blew strongly off the sea, but his feathers hung motionless. His wizened features seemed wistful and sad and hopeful all at once. "Fortune speed you, child. Be brave and finish what you began."

Taen shivered. She tried to break the creature's gaze, but the Vaere spoke sharply. "Listen! Stay here. Do not enter the grove. Engage your Dreamweaver's powers in behalf of Ivainson Jaric. Then stand firm. If your man survives to win his mastery, he will return to *Callinde* and find you."

The air rippled as if disturbed by heatwaves. Then, with a faint sigh of bells, Tamlin disappeared.

Taen regarded sunlit boards where the Vaere had stood, as if she might read the riddle of his existence in the grain of the wood. The creature would not return; with growing apprehension, the Dreamweaver pondered how much had been left unsaid. Her peril was no less for Tamlin's silence.

Fear shadowed Taen's resolve. Her Sathid might easily rouse and link with the dual matrix Jaric fought to subdue. If that happened, both of them would be killed. They might die quickly, even painlessly under the merciful touch of the Vaere; but die they certainly would, for Tamlin had once revealed that no man who undertook mastery of three crystals ever escaped domination. The few attempts had turned out monsters, beings so malevolently warped that, for the safety of Keithland, the Vaere had destroyed life rather than let them survive.

Decision bore heavily upon the Dreamweaver. To act at all was to assume responsibility for a loved one's life. Each instant of deliberation extended Jaric's pain; that suffering must eventually drive him to madness became insupportable. Taen could never endure such an outcome. To watch as he lived and breathed, unable to comfort or share emotion, was to lose him in a manner more final even than death. Taen dug her toes in hot sand, but in the end she could not keep still. She abandoned the jolly boat where it lay and crossed the sand spit to *Callinde*.

The boat had not been left trim. Jaric had brailed the mainsail neatly to the yardarm, but jib and spanker lay heaped in the bow, a negligence he never would have tolerated by choice. A halyard dangled loose in the breeze. An incomplete splice marred one end; Taen rested a hand on the prow and wondered what mishap had parted so stout a line. The boat reminded her poignantly of Jaric, laughing and strong with his hair tangled from wind; together they had sailed this same craft to Cliffhaven with the Keys to Elrinfaer in hand. Taen bit back an urge to call his name aloud. Courage returned. Life or death, suddenly she realized she had no choice but share his passage to mastery. Keithland and her own heart would be as a wasteland without his presence.

Taen raised her knee over *Callinde*'s thwart. She clambered aboard. Sand from her toes pattered over floorboards soiled with swallow droppings. The dirt would have annoyed old Mathieson; grinning at recollection of the aged man's swearing, the Dreamweaver sat on the folded mass of the spanker and stared over the mast. Blue sky shone like enamel between torn streamers of cloud. For an instant she imagined she might never behold such beauty again. Then, with the sturdy self-reliance of her fisherman forbears, the girl closed her eyes and gathered her talent.

Heat and pain and searing brilliance: Taen felt herself immersed in fire. Body and mind, she shared the suffering that riddled Jaric's flesh. Strangely, his will seemed absent. Through a bottomless well of torment she searched, yet found only the echoes of contentment generated by Sathid entities that judged their conquest assured. But the conflict was not finished. Somewhere, somehow, Jaric resisted still, for pain flared and sparked over his nerves with an intensity that dismembered thought.

Taen fought to sustain her purpose. Though able to banish torment in an instant, she dared not grant Jaric the reprieve she had offered once before; should she try, his paired Sathid would recognize outside intervention and attack. This time her only chance was to work through the beleaguered consciousness of the victim himself. Though the agony inherent in the Cycle of Fire dizzied her almost to delirium, Taen shaped her presence into a call of compassion. Then, softly, tortuously, with many a hesitation and misstep, she began to trace the network comprising the mind of Ivainson Jaric.

The process caused her to know him better than ever before. Underneath the Sathid's litany of conquest, she experienced the despair of an infant deprived of mother and father. The taunts of boyhood apprentices became slights against herself; and later, on the wind-whipped deck of a fishing boat, she shared a betrayal she herself had helped complete, when the weight of a sorcerer's inheritance fell full force upon the shoulders of a boy ill equipped to cope. Pained by his suffering, Taen continued her search, through the heartbreak, and the hardship, and rare moments of happiness. She explored Jaric's growth all the way to adulthood, but still encountered no spark of the consciousness that made the man.

At a loss, Taen drew back; bereft, almost beaten, she fought to preserve hope, even as the predatory litany of Jaric's Sathid battered her dream-sense ragged. At any moment the crystals might conquer, destroy this mortal who, against the severest odds, had mustered courage to strive after powers he had never desired. Desperate to avert the inevitable, Taen ransacked memories like an eavesdropper. By accident she stumbled across a sliver of remembrance so well protected that she had overlooked it entirely until now. Jaric had sailed to the Isle of the Vaere for Keithland; *and also for love of the black-haired daughter of an Imrill Kand fisherman.*

Taen knew pain then, sharper than the physical torment of flame. Never could she endure the ruin of one who treasured her more than life itself. Heedless of discomfort, she hurled herself into the very heart of the conflagration. There she found Jaric. Like a limpet in a tide pool, he clung to the most precious memory he possessed. Once he had stood in *Moonless*'s aft cabin,

struck dumb by recognition and loss; now, against the insupportable anguish of the Cycle of Fire, Taen saw that he defended the
last of his integrity with the memory of herself, asleep in trance
against the fine-grained wood of Corley's chart table.

The discovery nearly unbalanced her. Dangerous as the bared
edge of a razor, the Sathid prepared to press their final attack. No
margin for error remained. Taen engaged her Dreamweaver's
powers with utmost care. She did not force or possess, but
blended with Jaric's awareness; tenderly she reshaped the memory he held in his inward eye. Adding dream-vision to his image,
she caused the girl at the table to lift her head and smile; along
with awareness of her presence, Taen gifted him with hope, and
compassion, and light. She met the gaze of the boy in the dreaming mind of the man; there followed a moment of recognition as
deep as the sea's depths, endlessly wide as night sky.

The Sathid felt Jaric stir with renewed life. Vengefully strong,
they redoubled their onslaught of pain. But even as fires flared to
unendurable torment, Taen acted. She reached through the network of Jaric's consciousness and blocked all sensation of hurt.

His relief was immediate, but exhaustion left him limp. He
lacked the vitality to respond. Taen wept in dismay. The Sathid
also felt Jaric falter; they chiseled at his defenses with ferocious
energy. The Dreamweaver understood that the instant he broke,
her presence would be discovered. The matrixes would then
strike to engage her own crystal, and defeat for them both would
be final. Enraged by the threat of such loss, Taen could not bring
herself to retreat.

Suddenly a voice reached through her dismay. *'Fishwife. Will
you never learn to be patient?'*

Taen smothered a flash of hope. Perhaps Jaric's passivity was
feigned, a ruse intended to throw the Sathid off guard while he
marshaled resources for his final step into mastery. Afraid for
him, but steady, Taen watched while Jaric extended his awareness into the raging heart of the conflagration. Defended against
pain, he now could merge with the living flame, unlock its structure even as he had unriddled the pebble that granted him Earthmastery. Taen sensed a stab of malevolence; Jaric and his enemy
Sathid blurred into a single entity. Then, in a split-second transition, he claimed his sorcerer's heritage and tapped the force of
the fire itself.

Energy raged raw across the contact. Taen felt herself savaged
by a light that brightened and blistered and waxed impossible to
endure. Jaric became lost to her, walled off by ringing roulades

of power. No mind could encompass his presence. Taen felt her dream-sense falter. Ivainson the man burned, then blazed, then exploded into brilliance more terrible than Keithland's sun. The Sathid presence recoiled in alarm. Jaric pursued. Vengeful as sword steel, he struck. Searing illumination sundered the web of contact Taen had drawn about his person. Even as Keithland's newest sorcerer achieved the Cycle of Fire, her own awareness winnowed like blown sparks and went dark.

～VIII～

Gierj Circle

Alone in a sapphire expanse of ocean and sky, the Kielmark's brigantine *Moonless* changed tack precisely according to schedule. The helmsman turned the rudder hard alee. As the shadow of the spanker scythed across the quarterdeck, Corley paused with his hands gripped fast to the rail and gazed astern, toward the elusive Isle of the Vaere. The seas were mild, and the wind brisk. Canvas banged taut against sheet lines and boltropes. As crewmen trimmed the staysails, the brigantine lifted into a heel, the foam of her wake fanned like lace across sapphire waters; the weather was so clear that the horizon beyond seemed trimmed by a knife.

"Nor' nor'east, an' steady as she goes," called the quartermaster. *Moonless* cleaved like an axe through the swells, her crewmen trained to the keenest edge of fitness.

Still, her captain regarded the sea with brooding eyes. No pursuit had arisen yet from Shadowfane; but the slightest error in navigation might set his vessel too far south, within the influence of the fey caprice of the Vaere. Despite five days of easy sailing, the manner of Taen's departure made Corley fret. Watching through the ship's glass, he had seen *Moonless*'s jolly boat swallowed by fog arising out of nowhere. There had followed a shimmer like sheet lightning and a muffled boom; then the mist dispersed, ragged as torn gauze, with only the limitless blue of the water remaining. Corley shivered at the memory. The Dreamweaver and her tiny craft had disappeared as thoroughly as if they never existed.

Though the ocean presently showed no trace of the uncanny Isle of the Vaere, not a crewman aboard could look astern without qualms. The stress of unseen threat altered established patterns in *Moonless*'s routine. Sailors ceased grousing over the cook's mistakes in the galley; the mate took his sun sights at noon and quietly gnawed his nails down to the cuticle. Even the steward made himself scarce. All the while Corley paced the quarterdeck, his steps quick and tigerish, and his temper short.

"Deck there!" The lookout's hail from the crosstrees made the captain start at the rail. "Ships to windward!"

"How many?" Corley reached instinctively for knife and whetstone while the boatswain ordered a man aloft with a ship's glass.

"Two, sir." The lookout paused, leaned out, and caught the ship's glass from the sailor in the rigging. "Possibly more. But nothin' shows above the horizon yet but masts."

"Whose colors?" Corley sheathed his knife. With whetstone still in hand, he rocked impatiently on the balls of his toes, as if at any moment impatience might drive him to leap for the ratlines himself.

The lookout hooked a bronzed elbow around the shrouds and balanced against the lift and surge of the sea. Sunlight flashed on brass fittings as he focused his glass. Then, with a delighted whoop, he answered. "Kielmark's red wolf, cap'n! Damn me if our own *Shearfish* don't lead the lot."

Corley directed a tense glance at the compass. Then he swore with an emphasis he employed only before battle, unaware that hands in the waist left off mending canvas to stare. "Weather in their favor, and I'd bet silvers to a dog's fleas the other four sail behind her."

Headsails banged forward. Corley rounded angrily on the quartermaster, whose attention had strayed from the binnacle. "Steer small, you! Want to set us smack into the tricks o' the Vaere?" Without pause to draw breath, the captain shouted at the boatswain. "All hands on deck!"

His order tangled with another call from the lookout. "Five vessels, sir, flyin' Cliffhaven's colors. Dreamweaver steered us wrong, plain as the Fires o' judgment. Seems what ships we left in Hallowild all got clear."

Cheers arose from the men in the waist, enthusiastically repeated by newcomers rousted from the forecastle. Every man grinned in expectation of rendezvous and celebration, except

Corley. He spun from the helm with an explosive snarl of annoyance.

"Caulk yer gullets!" As the shouts lost gusto and died, the captain lowered his voice. But his tone made the hair prickle at the nape of his crewmen's necks. "I want this vessel trim and armed for battle, *now*. Move sharp! This may be the last engagement *Moonless* ever fights. We're five to one, and downwind, with a wee fey isle full of snares to leeward."

The sailhands shuffled callused feet. One among them muttered an astonished protest. Corley heard, and gestured for the boatswain to cull the offender from his fellows. A mutinous silence developed as the officer carried out the command.

"D'ye think I jest?" Corley ran stiffened fingers through his hair, his manner suddenly tired. "Those ships may be ours, but not the men. Do you understand? At best, *Shearfish* and the rest are traitors, for no man loyal to the Kielmark would leave his post of duty. Morbrith fell to demons. *Any one of ours would have died beside the High Earl.*"

With his crewmen stiffly, uncomfortably attentive, Corley shrugged as if harried by stinging flies. "I don't like taking arms against our own ships. But if we don't see the battle of our lives before sunset, I'll take the whipping due the man presently in care of the boatswain. Now arm this vessel! Man the pumps and wet down all sails and rigging."

The sailhands disbursed. There followed an interval of tense activity. While the first watch splashed seawater from stem to stern and spread wet sand on the decks, the second watch rolled oil casks into the waist and wedged them beneath the pinrails. They wheeled out arbalests, stripped their covers of oiled hide, and lashed them to bolt rings in the deck. Other men fetched lint and rags from the hold. The boatswain doled out bows, fire arrows, and weaponry, while Corley directed action from the quarterdeck. The lookout reported regularly from the crosstrees, as five vessels flying the red wolf of Cliffhaven bore down upon *Moonless*'s position, hastened by following wind.

Masts, then yardarms, then hulls became visible from the deck. Corley pocketed his whetstone and snatched his ship's glass from the steward. Glued to the quarterdeck rail, he searched the approaching fleet for discrepancy to prove the vessels unfriendly. His effort yielded nothing. From *Shearfish* in the lead to the trailing vessel, *Ballad*, Corley found only the clean-cut seamanship indicative of Cliffhaven's finest. Even the coding of the signal ensigns was correct. Sweating, frustrated, and acutely aware of discontent among the men who strung bows and oiled weapons in the waist, Corley almost missed the change, even as he saw it: *Ballad* sailed without anchors.

A chill roughened his flesh. "Lookout! Check *Ballad* and see whether you find anything amiss with her rigging."

Corley waited, taut with nerves. *Moonless* tossed under his feet, cavorting like a maid in the spray as the fleet closed the distance between.

The lookout's shout began with a blasphemy. "Kor! The fittings are missing from the masts, and by damn if the martingale chains aren't made of blackened brass. I can see by the scratches, fer Fires' sake!"

Corley's apprehension transformed to outright alarm. Only once had he seen a vessel altered in such a fashion; that ship had spearheaded the assault upon Cliffhaven one year past. She had carried the witch Tathagres and her allies, a sextet of Gierj-demons whose ruinous powers of destruction could be thwarted only by the presence of steel.

"By my grandmother's ass bone, we have trouble now." Corley swore, then prepared to lift his voice and inform his crew.

Words never passed his lips. A force cut into his mind, over-ran his intent with the trampling force of an avalanche. Air jammed in his lungs. He could not speak. Nor could he force his limbs to move, except as something alien and *other* commanded. His head whirled dizzily and his eyes lost power to see. Corley recoiled, struggling. For a second he felt the rail press solidly against his ribs. He gasped, forced a whisper past his throat. But the presence within his mind flung him back, helpless as a beetle drowning in oil. He thrashed inwardly, to no avail. Imprisoned within his own mind, Corley heard someone speak. Fearfully, horribly, he recognized the voice as his own, commanding *Moonless*'s crewmen to clear the decks of weapons and sand, and run up flags to welcome Cliffhaven's fleet.

The captain fought in a frenzy of anguish. He longed for one loyal man to notice the significance of *Ballad*'s missing anchors and stab a knife in his back. But the diabolical discipline of the Kielmark's command itself prevented insurrection; or else the sailhands worked under demon possession as well. Corley raged, even as the enemy smothered his awareness in darkness. The captain knew nothing more, while Maelgrim Dark-dreamer extended his hold through the borrowed powers of Gierj and claimed *Moonless* intact for Shadowfane.

* * *

Taen woke to a warmth like noon sunlight and the touch of someone's hand on her shoulder. She stirred, brushed an arm across her face, and felt the fingers withdraw from her person. Still disoriented from dream-trance, she opened her eyes to discover sundown already past. The crumpled sail where she lay was dusted silver with dew. *Callinde*'s thwart framed a starry expanse of sky, and both heat and a glow like candle flame emanated from a point just past her head. Taen frowned. The breeze off the sea flew briskly enough to extinguish anything but a shuttered lantern.

Even as the Dreamweaver raised herself on one elbow for a better look, the illumination began to fade. Before it died entirely, she glimpsed a man with hair the color of wheat at midsummer. He wore a red tunic trimmed with gold, and his eyes, dark as chestnuts, were strange and ancient as time.

"You were chilled," said Jaric out of the darkness.

Taen pushed herself to her knees, startled by cloth that fell with a slither around her calves. She touched, and felt fine velvet and silk; a Firelord's cloak had been tossed over her while she slept. The man who owned the garment sat intense and still, his presence as fathomless as sky.

Taen bit her lip. The Ivainson seated on *Callinde*'s aft sail locker both *was* and *was not* the boy she had known on board *Moonless*. Wrung by sudden uncertainty, the Dreamweaver drew a careful breath. "I thought you'd burned me like a charcoalman's sticks." She drew another breath, this one less than controlled. "Great Fall, *do you know what we've done?*"

Callinde's lines tapped the mast through a comfortless silence. Jaric did not reply. Roused to concern, Taen probed with her dream-sense. She discovered him afraid that if he reached for her, she would vanish away like the Vaere, leaving him in solitude on a desolate shore.

Her trembling transformed to laughter. "Fish-brains! You're Keithland's first sane Firelord, and still you haven't a featherweight of good sense." With that, the Dreamweaver surged forward and caught Ivainson around the neck. Half-grinning, half-weeping, she dragged him down into her nest of soggy sails.

Jaric stiffened with surprise. Then, as her cheek nestled into his shoulder and her tears fell hot on his throat, he caught her close in his arms. "Will you always arrive in time to haul me out of trouble by the heels?" But he did not wait for her answer; instead he threaded both hands in black hair, bent his head, and stopped her lips with his kiss.

The Firelord's cloak tumbled unheeded to the deck. Taen traced her fingers along the line of Jaric's collarbone. Gone to the Vaere as a child of ten, she had never known a man. Aside from the premature development that resulted from her mastery, in years and experience she was still very near to a child; but contact with elders on Imrill Kand had influenced the sensitivity that later gave rise to her Dreamweaver's powers. In some things the girl possessed an understanding far beyond her age. Taen snagged laces of braided gold and deftly began to untie them. "Did I hear you say I was cold? That's a lie."

Her reward was Jaric's quick laugh. "Shrew. I'll change that to no sense of propriety. Will you marry me on Imrill Kand?"

Taen freed the last tie and squirmed to reach his belt. "No." Hands busy, she kissed his chin. "I won't wait that long. Corley can marry us at sea." Sharply she tugged at his buckle.

Jaric twisted and caught her wrists. "Wait." He raised her and settled her comfortably against his side. "You can rush the wedding all you like, but not this. I love you. All Keithland can wait while I tell you so."

Gently he touched her face, her neck, her shoulders. Then he kissed her, softly as mist clinging to a flower. His hands moved, and he kissed her again. Taen felt the heat in his blood. In his restraint, she discovered something finer than the joyless appetites of the men from Imrill Kand. Tension, nervousness, and all fear inside her loosened. Jaric was here, now, for her, and she would never lose him. Warm fingers slipped the clothing from her shoulders. As the stars wheeled over the Isle of the Vaere, a Dreamweaver's robes of silver-gray joined the Firelord's cloak and tunic on the deck. By dawn, two lovers lay tangled asleep in the sails, heated by a tender glow of happiness.

Taen woke, this time to sunshine that was real. She lay with her head in Jaric's lap. By minute movements of his muscles, she realized he had roused ahead of her and busied himself with a chore. She opened her eyes, found him weaving a splice with his marlinspike, and promptly pinched his flank. "Haven't you anything better to do?"

"I didn't want to waken you." Jaric jammed his marlinspike through the plies in the rope and caught her teasing fingers.

But Taen's other hand remained at liberty, and with that she explored his person with provocative delight. She discovered him naked of clothing. Sitting up to admire the view, she saw that his skin had turned fair as ivory during his stay in the grove of the

Vaere. "Kor's mercy, stay sitting in the sun and you'll ripen like a turnip."

"So." Jaric grinned. "You're right." He dropped the halyard he had been mending, caught her laughing in his arms, and lifted her strongly.

"Jaric!"

But Taen shouted too late. Her man stepped solidly over the rail and ran with her into the sea. They stayed there most of the morning, cradled in each other's arms amid the swell of the waves. Only when both had loved to exhaustion did Jaric remember his unmended halyard. *Callinde* could not sail to weather with no headsail; back on board in the heat of the day with duty on his mind, Jaric sought a linen shirt to protect his back from the sun. But, clad like a sea queen in nothing but a wet and extravagant fall of hair, Taen sat squarely on the locker that contained his clothes.

"You'll spoil the fun," she teased.

Jaric laughed. Soaked himself, and caked with sand to the shins, he tried to protest. "I smell like a fish."

"Not to another fish." Taen uncoiled from her perch and piled full force into his middle. Both overbalanced into a loose mass of sailcloth.

Sundown found the two of them curled beneath the patched canvas of the headsail, asleep. *Callinde*'s lines slapped gently against the mast, repaired and ready for sailing. But Keithland waited one more night for the Firelord, while Jaric told his Dreamweaver that he loved her.

When he wished to be alone, Maelgrim Dark-dreamer preferred the cavern that riddled the rock beneath Shadowfane. There, surrounded by the sullen drip of subterranean springs, he could light oil lamps, or sit in darkness as he pleased, for his demon overlords entered caves with reluctance; their influence could not pierce solid rock. Places below ground made them feel their vulnerability, but Maelgrim did not share that discomfort. Above him rose the crag of Shadowfane, with walls and fortifications enough to ensure his safety. While the passage leading to the dungeon remained open, he had solitude, and a channel through which to implement his mastery.

At present, clad in wire ornaments and a loose-fitting tunic and hose, Maelgrim sat between a pair of unlit lanterns. Darkness helped him assimilate the focus of the Gierj-demons given him by

Scait. Although the creatures possessed neither intelligence nor self-awareness, a precise melding of minds enabled them to generate more raw force than a Vaere-trained enchanter. Manipulating a circle of six, Maelgrim had possessed five companies of the Kielmark's men at arms, and obliterated the inhabitants of Morbrith; with twelve, he boasted he could overrun Landfast. But Scait demanded otherwise. Cliffhaven was to be defeated first, and to that end, six Gierj had set sail on the decks of the Kielmark's brigantine *Ballad*.

From his nook in the caverns of Shadowfane, Maelgrim directed their song of power. One by one he extinguished the lives of additional crewmen captured in the south reaches of the Corine Sea. Aboard *Moonless,* their bodies lived on, but animated by an extension of Maelgrim's will made manifest by Gierj. The Dark-dreamer smiled in the shadows. Then he rested and dreamed, violent, bloody scenes of himself as Keithland's overlord.

When he woke, he resumed his trance. Far south, in the chilly hour before sunrise, Gierj stirred from sleep on the decks of *Ballad*. As the creatures opened their eyes, six sets of images inundated Maelgrim's mind: varied views of leaden swells hatched by stays and ratlines, of sanded decking, and a sky pricked by paling stars. The Gierjlings' multiple viewpoint still made him queasy. But demon masters had promised that his body would change to accommodate; over time, he would cease feeling disoriented by the impressions of separate eyes, and by vision that perceived more than a man's.

A shadow moved across *Ballad*'s waist. Secure in his cave, the Dark-dreamer translated images and identified the crewman who had once been first mate. The body might walk, talk, and act as a man, except now he was puppet to a master seated in Shadowfane.

Maelgrim shaped a mental command. Power flared through the Gierj-link like a spark touched into flame, and the mate called out to a sailor by the rail. "You there! Fetch Captain Corley on deck!"

The sailhand seemed unsurprised by an order to manhandle a superior. As stripped of spirit as *Ballad*'s officers, he hastened down the companionway to bring the Kielmark's first captain topside.

Maelgrim waited. Taut with anticipation, malleable to his every mood, the Gierj transmitted his restlessness. Claws scraped planking on the quarterdeck, and even the man on watch at the helm tapped his fingers against the oaken spoke of the wheel.

Gierj-images showed the sailhand's return in kaleidoscopic duplication. He prodded a second man ahead of him, one whose movement seemed drugged and slow. Demon perception revealed a greenish shimmer of light surrounding his body; that aura offered the only means to distinguish the living from the dead in thrall to the Gierj-link.

In the cave, wire clinked over the ceaseless drip of spring water; Maelgrim wrapped his forearms around his knees and studied his prisoner in multiple detail. *Moonless's* captain wore the same clothes he had at the time of his capture. But fine linen lay crumpled across his shoulders, and his tunic showed water-stains from the bilge. Ensnared by the Dark-dreamer's influence, his wide cinnamon eyes stayed fixed as polished stone. Maelgrim smiled in the darkness of his lair. Horribly, uncannily, Corley's lips echoed his overlord's expression, even as the sailor's dead hands prodded him up the companionway to the quarterdeck.

The captain stopped beside the mizzenmast. Maelgrim's view tumbled dizzily into change as, with wiry, insectlike movements, the Gierjlings surrounded their captive. The link stabilized, showing multiple views of Corley, silhouetted against a silvered predawn horizon, backed by the red glare of the binnacle lantern, and as a tall shadow with salt-matted hair looming against the mizzenmast shrouds. Maelgrim savored the moment well. Here at last stood the captain who had carried the false flag of surrender, luring Tathagres and eight demon allies into a trap of double intrigue that had foiled the compact's conquest of Cliffhaven. For that, Scait had commanded that a shape-changer impersonate *Moonless's* master and later assassinate the Kielmark. The process would destroy the original captive. Gloating like a spider with a fly, Maelgrim Dark-dreamer vowed to see Corley die screaming.

The unimpressed shape-changer imported from Shadowfane quickly scented its victim. Slimy and featureless as a slug, it slithered from its tub in the galley and wormed across the open deck. Atop the companionway, it subsided, a grayish puddle of flesh nestled between coils of rope. Everything stood ready. Carefully, triumphantly, Maelgrim Dark-dreamer eased the constraints upon Corley's mind; awareness returned for the first time since *Moonless's* capture.

The captain blinked, shook his head once, and frowned, for the helmsman was no crewman from his own command. Next he noticed demons ringing his feet: Gierj, lean and furtive as weasels, with eyes glowing lambent as a ghost ship's lanterns; at that moment Corley remembered. He stood, not on his own brigantine *Moonless*, but on the quarterdeck of *Ballad*. Both vessels now were prizes under Shadowfane's command. A spasm of anguish crossed the captain's face.

'*You live at my mercy,*' Maelgrim Dark-dreamer whispered through the Gierj-link.

Corley's head jerked up. He looked wildly around, but saw no speaker. He reached for the knives at his wrists, but found only empty sheaths. Belatedly he recalled that no steel could remain on his person in the presence of Gierj; then Maelgrim bound his limbs from movement. Corley fought, straining until the veins stood out on his neck. In a white heat of rage he never noticed that his enemy played him like a hooked fish. While he struggled, a Karas shape-changer's jellied mass quivered and slowly began to take form within a bight of rope to one side.

Through the Gierj-link, Maelgrim watched his victim's shirt become patched with sweat. The captain's hands locked into rigid claws, and breath escaped his throat in heaving gasps. The thing in the rope coils acquired two nostrils, and air began to sigh through them in unison. Corley heard. He attempted to turn his head, and with a sneer of contempt the Dark-dreamer allowed his captive that liberty. Maelgrim's lips parted with laughter as the captain jerked back in horror.

The Karas shape-changer now resembled a lump of softened wax, gray-white and gross except for two eyeballs of vivid, cinnamon brown. Even as Corley flinched, his reaction spurred growth. A smeared line opened beneath the creature's nostrils. Folds appeared, firmed, and shaped a recognizable pair of lips. Toothless and tongueless, the mouth was the mirror image of Corley's.

'*You see now,*' Maelgrim taunted through the link. '*You exist this moment expressly to serve Shadowfane.*'

Corley's features twisted. "Never!" But even as he protested, the thing at his feet puckered and flowed and changed. Tissue slimy as raw egg white filmed over, firmed, and developed a peppering of hair follicles. Within moments, it grew a beard textured chestnut and gray, strand for strand a counterpart of the captain's. The lips, fully fleshed, now worked; they mimed the original with chilling perfection.

'*Enjoy yourself,*' said the Dark-dreamer. '*Few men ever witness a shape-changer's metamorphosis.*'

Clued that his struggles might key the creature's alteration, Corley forced himself to relax. It he stayed passive, the loathsome creature's development might be arrested. Hope was probably in vain. Still, the captain closed his eyes. He did not think, but concentrated on sensations, from the lift of *Ballad*'s deck beneath his feet to the clean scents of sea and wet wood, overlaid by a sour tang of tarred rope. Aft, a pot clanged in the galley; as if the day were ordinary, the cook lit his fire and sliced sausage for sailhands about to come off watch. The unbroken adherence to routine raised a chill on Corley's flesh, aggravated by the step of the quartermaster, arrived to relieve the night helmsman. Sunrise brightened the east, tipping wave crests with sequin highlights; but the Kielmark's first captain felt cold to the heart. He stood still, listening to the wind, while Gierj coiled sinuously around his feet. Their limbs interwove until they resembled a ring of braided yarn, dotted with eyes glowing greenish as sparks from a drugged candle.

Corley concentrated on the immediate. Ballad sailed to a following breeze. An unoiled block squeaked with each roll, and one of her headsails luffed lightly. On *Moonless,* such lapses would earn the mate on watch a sharp reprimand.

'*Such is the difference between the Kielmark's senior captain, and their underlings,*' Maelgrim interjected, as if trying to prompt conversation through the Gierj-link.

Corley ignored the intrusion, following only the splash of spray off the bow. He ached; keeping still required an alarming amount of muscle tension. With his attention immersed in the rolling wash of the wake, the captain subdued the macabre need to see whether the shape-changer had evolved any further. Still, no effort of will could prevent him from noticing sounds not normal to a ship working on a broad reach. Something flopped on the deck by the pinrail, like a fish, but not.

Corley felt his skin raise into gooseflesh. He stood sweating until the Dark-dreamer jabbed through the Gierj-link and compelled him to look.

The captain opened his eyes to unmitigated horror. A half-completed replica of himself lay beyond the ring of Gierj. Hands, feet, face, and forearms, it matched his every detail, even to scars of former battles and the calluses of everyday living. But beyond wrist and neck and ankle, where clothing covered his body, the thing was formless jelly. One hand twitched and touched a deck fitting. Two fingers bent grotesquely, jointless as worm flesh, for as yet neither bone nor muscle supported the structure underneath.

Corley's stomach heaved; and even his revulsion triggered

growth. The abomination quivered and firmed, its abdomen acquiring the semblance of a rib cage. Sweat traced Corley's spine. The feeling of moisture trickling over his anatomy detailed the beginnings of an indentation on the shape-changer's back, made visible as it flopped across the deck. Sickened by the mirroring twitch of his nemesis, Corley averted his face.

Maelgrim's laughter echoed across the link. *'Ah, captain, you begin to understand the nature of Shadowfane's miracles.'* Bored with passive observation, the Dark-dreamer reached through the Gierj. He forced his victim to watch while the unfinished shape-changer scrabbled clumsily upright, then advanced on wobbling feet. It crossed inside the ring of demons and stopped at the captain's side.

Driven to tears of frustration, Corley beheld eyes, a complete face, identical to his own. "Why?" he gasped, revolted as the thing echoed with a slurred attempt at speech.

The Dark-dreamer reveled in the captain's discomfort. In reply, he had the quartermaster turn from the helm and speak in words of his choosing. "Can't you guess, my captain? The shape-changer will replace you, and sail *Moonless* to Cliffhaven. The Kielmark will never guess his first captain disguises as a demon, until too late. Your replica will run a knife through his heart."

The words struck Corley like the killing thrust of a sword. Through trust in his closest friend, the Kielmark would be betrayed. In anguish, the captain whispered, "No! Fires take you, not while I live!"

Maelgrim laughed through the mouths of *Ballad*'s crewmen, then made them chant in eerie unison. "But you won't live, my flag-bearing turncoat. Karas shape-changers devour their victims after metamorphosis to fix their final form. And through Gierj-power I shall keep you alive, while the Karas chews through your vitals one bite at a time."

Corley said nothing. White-faced, trembling with despair, he stared unseeing at the sea while the shape-changer pawed and fumbled, ineptly removing his clothing. Its touch proved corrosive; each brush of its fingers raised welts, sharp and painful as hornet stings. Try as he might, the captain could not contain his reaction. His muscles flinched and shivered in agony, each cord and tendon defined beneath his skin. As he suffered, his structure became faithfully recorded by the Karas, down to the smallest bulging vein, and the last bead of sweat.

Breeches, shirt, and knife sheaths lay in a tumbled pile on the deck when the Dark-dreamer made Corley dance. Up, down, around, he sprang in dizzying gyrations that forced the fullest range of extension from his body. The Karas followed suit, its contours molding ever closer to the brawny frame of the captain. Gasping, wretched, and sick with exhaustion and harrowed dignity, Corley knew that now not even his mother would recognize him from his demon counterpart. He wished himself dead; had the Dark-dreamer of Shadowfane relinquished control for an instant, the captain would have sought immediate means to end his life.

The Karas bent with mannerisms identical to Corley's and donned knife sheaths, then breeches and shirt. It ran its fingers through chestnut hair, adjusted a wrist strap, and laughed.

'*Once it tastes your flesh, its form becomes permanent.*' Maelgrim allowed satisfaction to seep across the link. '*Your skills, your memories, even your innermost secrets will all be inherited intact.*'

With a look of wry humor still on its face, the Karas reached for its counterpart's wrist. But the instant before contact, a burst of light shattered the horizon. The Gierj started up in alarm, eyes flaring like flame as the sun vanished into mist. Maelgrim's smile faded, and even the Karas paused. A shimmer like sheet lightning rent the sky. Thunder pealed, rattling timbers in the deck, and wind sprang out of nowhere, backwinding *Ballad*'s sails with a violence that snapped a stay.

Ballad's captain sprang half-dressed and shouting from the stern. "Quartermaster, bear up! All hands on deck to shorten sail!"

Yet the confused weather cleared before men could stumble from the forecastle. Fog dissolved into clear air, and breezes resumed from the west. South, where the horizon had bordered empty sky, an islet notched the sea. The shoreline glittered white in sunlight, sands ground fine as bleached flour, and mantled by a royal crown of cedars.

The Gierj twittered nervously. The linking bond of their attention faltered. Irritably, Maelgrim bound them tighter. Through their eyes, he beheld the elusive Isle of the Vaere where his sister had vanished after Anskiere stole her loyalty.

The Karas stared also. Its pose was an effortless replica of Corley's, but its allegiance was to Scait and Shadowfane as it murmured in excited discovery, "Set-Nav. Veriset-Nav for sure."

Suddenly a dull square of red unfurled above the beachhead. Maelgrim quivered like a hound on hot scent and focused his

Gierj. Multiple images showed him the frail silhouette of a fishing craft, her crew busily setting sail. The caverns beneath Shadowfane's dungeons rang with his harsh laugh, for there sailed *Callinde,* towing *Moonless*'s jolly boat; Jaric was not at her helm. Through the perception of his Gierj, the Dark-dreamer found the sister he longed to murder sitting defenseless at the small craft's steering oar.

The Karas whirled with Corley's crisp air of authority. "Call Scait," it commanded. "We must take Set-Nav. Its powers of communication can call allies from the stars. From them, the compact shall gain weapons and machines enough to desecrate all of Keithland. Then, when vengeance is complete, our exile upon this accursed planet may come to an end."

But Maelgrim did not respond, obsessed as he was by a glimpse of black hair against the white of *Callinde*'s wake. Duty warred with emotion; and the cruel conditioning of his mastery overturned both. "First I will smash the Dreamweaver." He lashed out through the link, sending the Gierj scrambling to form a circle unencumbered by shape-changers or men. The demons coalesced like ink and began the warbling whistle that focused their full range of power.

"No!" The Karas's muscles knotted. It seized the nearest demon, jerked it from the circle, and snarled to the Gierj-master who manipulated his minions from Shadowfane, "Desist! The girl may be defended. You must call Scait!"

Yet Maelgrim would brook no interference. Taen was alone, he had checked; she had grown powerful, strangely powerful, but before his might she was helpless. *He could slay her easily with the Gierj at his command.* The Dark-dreamer engaged his will. On *Ballad,* the Gierj hissed. Fanged jaws slashed at the Karas's forearm and forced it into retreat. Only then did it notice that, with Maelgrim's attention diverted, the Kielmark's first captain had managed to throw himself halfway over the rail.

"Look to your prisoner!" shouted the shape-changer.

The Dark-dreamer disregarded its urgency. In another moment his circle of demon underlings would generate the power to strike his sister down. Nettled by the Karas's interference, Maelgrim laughed over the rising song of the Gierj. He permitted Captain Corley his leap into the sea, knowing the Karas must pursue, or forfeit the pattern of its change.

⌒⌒ IX ⌒⌒

Counterstrike

The whistle of the Gierj ascended the scale, gaining volume until the very sky seemed to ring with harmonics.

Taen tightened her hands on *Callinde*'s steering oar. The sound beat against her ears, keen and deadly as a razor's edge; the demon circle would reach pitch at any second. The instant their powers peaked, Maelgrim Dark-dreamer would crush her defenses easily as a child might mash an ant.

Wind hooked *Callinde*'s spanker. Her hull heeled and drove bucking through a swell. Foam burst off the bow like a spray of thrown diamonds, but Taen had no attention to spare for beauty. She sailed by touch, eyes clenched shut while the Gierj-whistle jabbed like a lance into her dream-sense. The note keened abruptly to a crescendo. The darkness behind Taen's eyes buckled, then shattered into sparks before an onslaught of unbearable power. The steering oar slipped from her grasp. *Callinde* rounded to weather with a shattering bang of sails, her lapstrake planking exposed broadside to the demon fleet.

Taen threw back her head and drew a shuddering breath. "Now!" she cried. Before Maelgrim broke her mind, she released the veil of concealment she had cast about Ivainson Jaric.

Fire exploded from *Callinde*'s prow. The conflagration gained intensity until the waves themselves seemed aflame. A boiling, snapping inferno smothered the face of the sea. Caught like lint in a cauldron of hell, six of the Kielmark's brigantines crisped to ash in an instant. The Gierj-chant cut off as if strangled. Maelgrim's attack broke with it. Taen sagged exhausted against *Cal-*

linde's thwart, while her brother's thoughts echoed across the dying thread of the link that connected to him at Shadowfane. *He had lost his circle of Gierj, spoiled the chance to capture Set-Nav; now he must face Scait with ill news. Keithland had gained a new Firelord. . . .*

The contact subsided into fury, then dissolved. Taen roused to the thunder of luffing sails and a snaking mess of slacked lines. She lifted shaking arms, caught the steering oar, and muscled *Callinde* back on course, away from the Isle of the Vaere. Ahead, the horizon lay marred by smoke. Where tanbark sails had caught clean wind only moments before, charred beams wallowed amid ash-smeared waves.

"They're gone." Taen glanced to the bow where the Firelord knelt, staring fixedly at the hands held clenched against his chest.

Jaric flinched at the sound of her voice. He raised tortured eyes and said softly, "Already it begins."

Taen knew he referred to the killing, and the fact that his first use of mastery had been an act of destruction. She bit her lip, shaken herself by the swift and terrible ruin brought down upon a fleet that had included Corley's own *Moonless*. "They were all dead, puppets of demons." Cut by echoes of Jaric's pain, the Dreamweaver sounded more brisk than she intended. "To leave such men alive would be more cruel, surely!"

Jaric rose. His hair caught like fire with sunlight as he strode aft, eased the sheet lines, and took the steering oar from Taen's grasp. She trembled, uncontrollably.

Sickened himself, the son of Ivain caught her and pulled her close. "I know the burning was necessary," he murmured into her hair. He paused, while *Callinde* rocked gently under freed canvas. "But I don't have to like the violence. Otherwise, like my father, someday I might grow to enjoy such brute power too much."

Taen pressed against him, drawing comfort from his lean strength. Her eyes stung with tears not entirely due to the smoke. After a time, Jaric leaned around her, yanked mainsheets and jib taut, and swung the steering oar to restore *Callinde*'s course. His one free hand knotted fiercely in Taen's hair, then released.

"Little witch, I need you for one thing more." Ivainson sounded tired, even reluctant, to ask. "Check and make certain no demon-possessed remain. For Shadowfane must never gain access to the Isle of the Vaere."

Taen drew her knees up and curled against him on the stern seat. With her ear to Jaric's side, she heard his heartbeat and knew: he had been shocked as she, to emerge from the protection of the Vaere and discover Cliffhaven's six ships under Mael-grim's control. Neither of them could bear to mention names, or count the friends whose bodies had been consigned to flame.

Callinde drove steadily northward, into waters where splinters and burned cordage dirtied the crests of the waves. Subdued by sorrow and loss, Taen tuned her inner awareness and scanned the waters for sign of life. At first her dream-sense encountered only mindless flickers, schools of scavenging fish come to feed on remains. Then she caught something else, faint, almost missed: a remembered flash of steel by starlight.

The Dreamweaver shot upright with a gasp. "Corley!" She turned widened, hopeful eyes toward Jaric, then broke into a shout of relief. "Over there!" She pointed. "Deison Corley is alive."

The Firelord needed no urging. He sprang, whipped the sheets taut in the blocks, and threw his weight against the steering oar. The compass needle swung with maddening sluggishness, north, north-northeast, to east. *Callinde* changed tack, heeled, then set-tled, small as a chip on her new course. The jolly boat nosed at her stern rope like a puppy just broken to leash.

"Fetch the ship's glass from the port locker. Is the captain in pain?" At Taen's nod, Jaric continued briskly. "Then we'll need spare line. Maybe the storm sail, too, unless you think we can haul him over the jolly boat's thwart without adding to his in-jury."

Taen's shift flapped about her knees as she flung open lockers and delved after canvas and rope. The ship's glass she eliminated; dream-sense could locate a swimmer more efficiently than eye-sight, and time counted dearly. The pattern of energy she knew as the Kielmark's first captain was dim, and failing steadily. But *Callinde* closed the distance quickly; without question, Corley was alive, and very close by.

"There!" Jaric adjusted course and pointed. Ahead, dark against the crest of a swell, a man's head broke the surface of the sea. Taen saw him clearly before a drifting pall of smoke obliter-ated the view.

"Take the helm." Transformed by hope, Jaric snatched rope and spare sailcloth from Taen's hands. As she took the steering oar, he caught the jolly boat's tow line and yanked it inboard with hurried jerks of his arms. "Steer upwind, and heave to, can you? As we pass, I'll cast off and pick him up."

Taen nodded. Closer, through thinning wisps of steam, she

sighted Corley swimming strongly down the face of a wave. He
had seen *Callinde,* and his teeth flashed a smile of welcome that
did not mesh with the pattern touched by her dream-sense. Taen
frowned. The captain who pulled himself through the sea with
such sure overhand strokes seemed too vital for one whose skin
stung with abrasions, and whose lungs labored, cramped from
lack of air.

Callinde heeled under a gust.

"Steady on the helm!" shouted Jaric. He leaped into the jolly
boat and whipped the towline off the cleat. Suddenly afraid for
him, Taen called out, "Be careful!"

But, preoccupied with the friend in the water, Jaric seemed
not to hear. He bent immediately, threaded oars, and muscled his
boat stern first into the waves. The jolly boat seemed a toy
skewed crazily on the shoulder of the swell; smaller still seemed
the man in the sea, an insect on the face of creation. As Jaric
swung alongside and shipped his looms, Taen heard him shout
encouragement.

"Kor's grace, man, be quick. Knives rust to scrap in the sea,
don't you remember telling me?"

Corley's laugh boomed reassuringly back across the water.
"No fuss. I jettisoned the knives. Had to. Ballast would've
swamped me." He caught the jolly boat's transom with wet
fingers, and only then did the Dreamweaver notice the shadowy
wrongness that suffused his flesh.

Premonition made her shiver. Taen had seen such a phenomenon only once before, in the form of a demon shape-changer
planted in King Kisburn's court to sow discord.

She shouted, frantic, "Jaric!" But wind snatched her words.
The thing that looked like the captain caught the hand of his
rescuer and heaved himself, dripping, from the sea. *His wrists,
his hands, his very skin was unmarked, while the pattern Taen's
dream-sense knew as Corley stung with painful cuts.* "Jaric, he's
Shadowfane's!"

Yet even as the Dreamweaver called warning, the fists of a
Karas shape-changer clamped over Ivainson's throat. Jaric lashed
out in defense. Fire flared, bristled with terrible, spitting snaps
down the creature's arms.

The Karas screamed with Corley's voice. Crazed by an agony
of grief, Jaric reacted in madness. Flame shot skyward. Light
glared like molten metal over the waves, and the captain's form
became momentarily incandescent, reduced to ash in an instant.

Still the flame continued, searing the air with a shriek like hot steel hitting water.

Jaric shouted, his words a blasphemy against Kor's mercy. Then as if his knees had failed him, he folded against the jolly boat's thwart. Fire died while he wept. For a moment, Taen feared to touch him, his thoughts ranged so far beyond reason. Shaking, tearful with reaction herself, she steadied her dream-sense. The moment she tuned her powers, she encountered Corley again, reduced to a flicker, an echo, submerged beneath the waves. No time remained for finesse. Taen shaped a dream-call that bordered the edge of compulsion, and sent her find directly into Jaric's mind.

Then tears blurred her eyesight completely. She heard but did not see the splash as Ivainson dove. By the time her vision cleared, the jolly boat drifted empty, one oar canted crookedly against the bow seat. Wind puckered the swells, and *Callinde*'s sails flapped. Taen steadied the steering oar and waited an interminable interval until Jaric broke the surface, burdened by something heavy and limp. He kicked awkwardly and caught the jolly boat's rope.

Taen glimpsed a snarl of chestnut hair; this time there could be no mistake. Jaric had recovered the true Corley from the sea, for this victim matched the mangled pattern picked up by her dream-sense. Demon captivity had been cruel. The captain was injured and very near death from drowning. Jaric ran rope beneath Corley's shoulders and secured him to the jolly boat's transom. As he rowed and boarded *Callinde,* Taen raced and freed a spare halyard.

With all possible speed, Dreamweaver and Firelord hoisted the helpless man aboard *Callinde.* The crisscrossed marks of his knife sheaths showed white against Corley's tan; no scrap of clothing remained to hide skin torn everywhere with abrasions and burns. Something, horribly, had gnawed off one finger at the knuckle. Blood from the stump threaded streamers through the puddled water on the deck.

"Karas," said Taen faintly. "Shape-changers eat portions of their victims to permanently maintain form."

Jaric reined in the fury her words inspired. He spoke in a deadened voice and kept to immediate needs. "There's a tin of healer's salve in the starboard locker, and we can tear my dry shirts for bandages."

But the true extent of the damage did not become apparent

until Corley's hurts were dressed and he lay wrapped in blankets by the mainmast.

Taen knelt at the captain's side when his bruised brown eyes flickered open. "We're taking you back to Cliffhaven," she offered. But her words were received without comfort. All that remained of *Moonless* and her fleet of five brigantines was one man, and a jolly boat dragging astern. Corley turned his face miserably to the thwart. To him survival offered no joy but a burden nearly impossible to endure.

Taen touched the captain's shoulder and gently pressed his mind into sleep. Grief leaked through the contact, born of loss, but also something more: Corley was inwardly wounded beyond her power to console. He had prided himself for loyalty; the youthful sense of honor that drove him to leave Morbrith rather than shame the High Earl's son had matured to service and friendship now granted to the Kielmark. But on the decks of *Ballad*, Dark-dreamer and Karas had proven that faith could be corrupted into a weapon designed for murder; neither sword steel, integrity, nor death itself held power to avert a betrayal of everything Corley held dear.

Discouraged and sad, Taen rose and joined Jaric at the helm. The hope gained when Ivainson achieved his Firemastery seemed suddenly withered, blown to dust like seedlings killed in a drought. Shadowfane's reach was longer and more powerful than ever she could have imagined; Maelgrim's conquest of Morbrith and subsequent possession of Corley's command required powers that defied credibility. If his Gierj-circle was replaced, what damage might Keithland suffer before *Callinde* reached Cliffhaven to free Anskiere?

Troubled by Taen's stillness, Jaric threaded an arm around her waist and drew her close. "Don't fret, little witch. You've done enough, and more than enough."

Taen shook her head. Troubled by the memory of her brother's last thoughts, she spoke unthinkingly aloud. "Whatever did Maelgrim mean by Set-Nav, anyway?"

A wave jostled *Callinde* off course. Jaric reached to shift his grip and ended banging his knuckles against the shaft of the steering oar. "Tell me where you heard that." He turned and faced her, at once a stranger with the terrible, edged presence of a Vaere-trained Firelord.

Thrown off balance by the depths in him, Taen drew back. "When you flamed the Gierj, Maelgrim cursed the loss of a thing named Set-Nav. In some manner, his reference referred to the Isle of the Vaere. What do you think he meant?"

Jaric sat motionless. Through dream-sense, Taen determined that the term "Set-Nav" was familiar to him, and connected to a strange scrap of information found in Landfast's libraries. Then Jaric's expression turned harsh as chipped agate, and his mind became closed to her. He started to say something, paused, and instead arose to tighten the headsail halyard.

"Jaric!" Taen caught the abandoned steering oar and muscled *Callinde* back on course. "Whatever could Maelgrim mean?"

Ivainson replied with his attention trained keenly on the set of the jib. "I don't know."

He told the truth. Though Taen pressed after the reason for his unsettled response, Jaric refused to elaborate. A part of his mind would brook no interference; like the Stormwarden, Ivainson Firelord now owned mysteries even a Vaere-trained Dreamweaver could not encompass.

The sail north to Cliffhaven required six weeks. Taen soon found that the death of Maelgrim's Gierj had lifted the block preventing contact with Cliffhaven. She dream-sent only once, to ascertain that the conclave at Mhored Kara had honored her request and relayed the news of Morbrith's fall. Evidently it had, for the Kielmark was in a black temper, savagely intolerant of intrusion. Rather than exhaust herself needlessly trying to calm him enough to receive dream-image, Taen obtained her information through Captain Tamic, the Kielmark's next in command during Corley's absence.

The second captain was a burly man, given to boisterous phrases and rougher judgment. Taen he treated with respect, mostly because she had stopped his tongue with a spell the first time he tried to insult her. Forced speechlessness did not wear well with Captain Tamic. He greeted the Dreamweaver's sending from the south reaches with a curse, but related the state of affairs on Cliffhaven with the malicious abandon of a gossip.

"Oh, aye, yer tamed pack o' wizards sent word. Came in the form of a wee box carved with runes, dumped in with the tribute off a trader bark from Telshire."

'A box?' Taen queried.

She sensed Tamic's brows lift in reproof. "Aye, a box, wench. As sorcerers go, the conclave's lot aren't stupid. If the Magelord or one of his minions dared the straits, Kielmark'd dice him up like stew meat. For what his conjurers did to Anskiere, you understand, and probably a bit on general principle. Hates sorcery of any sort, does the Pirate King, since it litters up his domain with powers he can't control."

'*And the box?*' prompted the Dreamweaver.

"Kor." Tamic paused. Carefully he excised from his reply those obscenities which might earn him the Dreamweaver's reprisal. "That box had a message in it, all wrought of spells. Bad news by my guess, because the Kielmark hammered the table with his sword and gouged up a helluva splinter. Now there's activity in the harbor like sticks astirring through bee nests."

'*Morbrith fell to Shadowfane,*' Taen returned, '*that's why your Lord is distressed. When he's finished yelling, tell him I sail north on* Callinde *with the newly invested Firelord. Corley's with us.*' She kept her sending terse, mostly as an excuse to end contact. Even disaster could not upset her judgment enough to deliver word of the fleet lost to the Gierj with the Kielmark in a killing fury. As she released her dream-sense, Tamic's humor transformed from sharp concern to wonder, that the small, diffident boy he had once dragged off the north shore in a storm had gone on to complete the Cycle of Fire.

Callinde sailed on through the Free Isles. Twice Jaric made landfall for supplies, at Westisle and Skane's Edge. Corley helped with the loading, but refused to show his face to the villagers. That none would know him as the Kielmark's captain, he worked muffled in Jaric's spare storm cloak despite the warmth of high summer. Only Taen understood why.

"He fears to be used as a tool against Cliffhaven," she confided to Jaric, who cursed in exasperation and worried the captain might collapse from the heat. That the Firelord's anger was rooted in grief helped nothing. Each day it seemed more certain that Maelgrim and Shadowfane had broken the spirit of a friend.

Back at sea, Jaric flung open the locker nearest the helm, retrieved *Callinde*'s last rigging knife and whetstone, and presented them to the captain. "You can fashion a sheath from the leather I bought to make sandals," he offered. "Only stop moping in port like a priest losing faith at a heresy trial."

Corley accepted the gift, but did not sharpen the blade. Hour after hour his hands hung limp in his lap, except when *Callinde* required sails changed, or navigation, or repairs to worn rigging. Wind blew from the west, then the north, and slowly, shifted back due south. Following a stop at Innishari for water and food, fair weather alternated with two storms and a gale. The air grew sharp at night. Close to the first of autumn the sturdy craft neared the latitude of Cliffhaven.

Twelve leagues offshore, with the watchtower not yet visible on the horizon, Taen entered dream-trance and contacted the Kielmark for the last time before *Callinde* reached port. She had informed him long since of Morbrith's fall, and the fleet lost to Shadowfane; but not until now could she bear to reveal the ruinous change in Corley.

Seated in his library at the time, the Lord of Cliffhaven received her tidings with uncharacteristic equanimity. Taen suspected a more explosive reaction, perhaps held in check beneath his calm; but since he cut contact with more than his customary curtness she had no chance to read deeper. Though *Callinde* returned with a Firelord and hope for Anskiere, Taen roused feeling dispirited.

She retired to the bow rather than disturb Jaric, who tended *Callinde*'s steering oar with apprehensive thoughts of the ice cliffs, and the fact he must soon unravel the wards there with the same powers his father had used to betray the Stormwarden's peace.

Corley leaned against the mainmast with his shirt laces open at his throat. He seemed asleep; Taen knew by her dream-sense he was not. She huddled against the prow, troubled by doubts of her own. How would Anskiere judge her brother, when he wakened to find Morbrith lost, and Marlson Emien the cause? The Dreamweaver brooded, while the bow wave crumpled into froth beneath the keel and day wore on to afternoon.

Jaric's shout broke her reverie. *"Corley, no!"*

Taen spun in alarm, just as Ivainson sprang from the helm. He piled into the captain. *Callinde* veered sharply to weather; the shadow of the mainsail swung aft, and the Dreamweaver glimpsed a flash of sunlight on steel. Corley strove to sink the rigging knife into his chest. Only the straining hands of Ivainson Firelord prevented the blade from striking home.

"Taen, help," gasped Jaric. Corley's sweat slicked his palms, and his hold slipped. The blade dipped, quivering, and nicked into skin.

The Dreamweaver gathered power and slammed hard into the captain's mind. His limbs sagged with paralysis, and the knife tumbled, clanging, into the bilge. Jaric caught the unconscious man and eased him awkwardly to the floorboards.

"Kor's mercy!" Taen reached the captain. Corley breathed as if asleep, except that beads of crimson seeped through his shirt front. Taen bent and tugged the linen from his shoulders. Only when she proved the wound was a scratch did she start to quiver with shock. "What would make him desperate now, after all these weeks?"

Jaric did not answer. Instead he delved into an opened locker for the ship's glass, balanced himself against the roll of the swell, and scanned the eastern horizon.

Presently Taen saw his mouth flinch into a line. "Here's why." Ivainson lowered the glass with what seemed like annoyance. "There's a sloop out there on a broad reach, with one man aboard. Corley guessed who before I did. The Kielmark sails *Troessa* to meet us."

Untended, *Callinde* jibed with a thunderous bang of sails. Jaric leapt to slacken lines. Only when he had finished did Taen realize his curtness was rooted in distress. Corley lay sprawled on the floorboards, strong hands outflung and empty and his face untroubled in sleep. He might have been napping; except his friends remembered he never quite abandoned tension, even during rest.

"You did your work well, little witch." Jaric knelt, recovered the rigging knife, then wedged it out of sight behind a water cask. "He'll not wake if we move him? Then let's get him up."

Built light and lean to carry dispatches, *Troessa* raced down upon the ungainly *Callinde* with what seemed uncanny speed. Taen had barely made Corley comfortable in the bow when the small sloop rounded to weather. She drifted on *Callinde*'s windward side, sails slatting loose in the breeze. Jaric sprang and caught the line thrown by her helmsman.

The Kielmark paced with impatience while his craft was made fast to a cleat. Ebony hair ruffled against sky as, with astonishing agility for a man burdened with broadsword, boots, and crossbelts jingling with throwing knives, the sovereign Lord of Cliffhaven leapt the gap between boats. He landed sure-footedly on the thwart. *Callinde* rocked sharply, canvas flung into a jibe. Forced to duck the swing of the headsail, Taen sensed rather than saw the Kielmark check. Eyes pale as ice chips fixed on Corley's bloody shirt.

"Kor's Fires, what's happened to him?" Enormous in *Callinde*'s cramped cockpit, the Kielmark reached for his steel.

"That's a scratch!" Taen supplied hastily. "Corley's alive, and well, but not stable. He tried to take his life when *Troessa* breasted the horizon." She engaged her dream-sense and tried vainly to soften the impact of the news.

The Kielmark tensed at her touch. The ruby torque flashed at his neck as he whirled around, knuckles whitened on his sword hilt. Should he follow through with his draw, he could not help but slash stays and bring down the mast; but temper left him wild enough to strike without thought for consequences. "Take *Troessa* and see to your Stormwarden, enchantress. I'll look after my captain."

The Kielmark turned on his heel. Charged with threat like a thunderhead, he reached Corley in the bow, plainly intending to move him. When Jaric hastened to help, Taen restrained him with a dream-touch.

'*Don't. His Lordship is dangerously upset.*' She caught Jaric's wrist and held on as the Kielmark lifted Corley in his massive arms. Contact seemed to reassure him; the mad edge softened from his temper as he bore his captain aft.

The King of Renegades settled Corley in the stern seat, then positioned himself by the steering oar. "How long will he sleep?" he demanded of Taen.

"Well past nightfall, unless you wish otherwise." As the Kielmark's mood eased, the Dreamweaver sensed that his temper stemmed from more than Corley's straits. The tension probably rooted in the conjurer's message concerning Morbrith, but now was a poor moment to press the issue. Again urging restraint upon Jaric, Taen waited by the mast.

The Kielmark threw off baldric and crossbelts. Stripped to boots and leggings stamped with silver, he spoke with his gaze trained on Corley's still features. "Jaric, you must free Anskiere directly. If the wind holds, *Troessa* should bear you to the ice cliffs before sundown." He paused, raked sweat-damp hair from his temples, and looked up. "Every sovereign ruler of Keithland and all the council members of the Alliance await you at Cliffhaven. Return there when you can."

"Councilmen of the Alliance!" Jaric broke in. "How did you ever pry them out of Landfast?"

The Kielmark's teeth flashed in an expression not quite a smile. "I sent ships and men at arms to collect the first two. Then one day their conjurers told them that Morbrith's citizens had dropped in their tracks like carrion. After that, their eminences came flying like sparrows chased in by a gale." Pointedly not looking at the Dreamweaver, he leaned forward, caught the trailing end of the jib sheet and hauled in the sail. "Go now. Time is critical."

Canvas filled with wind, and *Callinde* bore off. Jaric squeezed

Taen's hand, released her, and stepped around the mast. He flipped *Troessa*'s line from the cleat. Tanned from seafaring, and clothed in a sailor's linen tunic, he hardly appeared the master of a firelord's powers as he leaped lightly onto the gunwale. But when the Dreamweaver hurried to join him, he paused, poised like a cat. "You sail with *Callinde*."

Taen stiffened to argue. "Where you go, I go also."

"No," said Jaric. "Not with frostwargs unleashed." He spoke quietly. But his voice carried an edge that made the Kielmark start at the steering oar. Ivainson was a lad no longer. On *Callinde*'s rail stood a sorcerer charged with ringing nets of power. His hair might be sun-bleached, his hands worn with sailing; but fire would blaze at his command, and the ordinary brown of his eyes reflected mysteries deep as earth.

"Stay," said Ivainson Jaric to Taen. His tone gentled. "I'll return with Anskiere, and meet you at the fortress."

He sprang into *Troessa* and cast off. Taen did not try to follow, but hung on the thwart as the sloop caught the wind and bore off northeast.

The Kielmark hardened the sheets. As *Callinde* steadied on course for the harbor, he looked up and noticed the Dreamweaver's expression. "Enchantress," he called grimly from the helm, "quit fretting. I'll be sending a patrol to the north strand with horses. You can go and meet your man. But first you'll help sail this bucket to shore. Are we agreed?"

"Horses!" Taen returned a brave but weary smile. "I sail a boat with far better grace than ever I sat a saddle."

Jaric landed *Troessa* at sunset. Slanting light tipped the topmost crags of the ice cliffs with rose and gilt; below, breakers crashed and threw smoking streamers of spray, tinged ice blue in shadow. As always, Anskiere's prison overwhelmed the eye with beauty. But the Firelord charged with the Stormwarden's deliverance felt no confidence as he beached his small sloop on the strand. He had no experience battling demons, and scant knowledge of the frostwargs he must subdue; far more than a sorcerer's survival rested on his success.

The air blew chill off the heights. Jaric shivered in his thin tunic and squared his shoulders to climb. Ice and rock had contained the frostwargs since Tathagres' sorcerers had provoked their escape; presumably fire would control them. Ivainson set his hands to the rock. Contact with the land proved a revelation after lengthy weeks at sea; stone and soil seemed alive, responsive to his Earthmastery. Unlike his previous climbs, the cliff face welcomed his presence, yielding footholds and fissures to his inner awareness. Jaric smiled with self-revelation; on a whim he could mold the rock face into stairs to ease his ascent. But caution and his own reluctance to wield power caused him to climb without enchantments. Later, against the frostwargs, he might need every available resource.

Twilight dyed the sea indigo beneath a violet arch of sky. Dwarfed by cascades of ice, Jaric set foot on the uppermost tier of the ledge. With closed eyes he extended his senses and mapped the tunnels carved by Ivain to contain the frostwargs. Sealed off by the cold, the entrance angled steeply beneath the headland. Passages bored deep into rock, linked by chains of caverns and buttresses of chiseled stone. The upper levels were choked with spellbound ice; below, closed in fetid darkness, lurked the frostwargs. Though the creatures preferred live prey, they could also draw sustenance from soil and rock. They did not breathe; water could not drown them, nor would flame consume their shells. Only extreme heat could cause them temporarily to shift form.

Surrounded by the smells of sea and tide wrack and the sour cries of gulls, Jaric laced his fingers together. He honed his will to a pinpoint of force, stepped forward, and sank straight down into rock. The stone flowed around him, thick and turgid as quicksand. Though his eyes were utterly blind, his Earthmaster's vision saw vistas: quartz like jagged veins of frost, crystals, and rust-dark ores, and a thousand textures of mineral. Down Jaric plunged, past level upon level encompassed by Anskiere's wards. With his heart pounding from tension, he emerged at last on a ledge just below the ceiling in the cavern confining the frostwargs.

A strident whistle slashed his ears. Jaric's skin tightened with gooseflesh. The calls of frostwargs grew nearer, threaded by a scraping and scrabbling of claws. Then the creatures scented the presence of prey and burst into a full-throated ululation.

Sweating, Jaric snapped a flame out of air. It flickered from his fingertips, weak red in the oxygen-poor atmosphere of the cavern. In baleful, bloody light, the Firelord sought his enemy. Ivain had floored the cave with a forest of sword-thin crystals; a thousand edges of reflection stabbed Jaric's eyes. Creatures scuttled between on segmented legs. Their carapaces were jointed like insects, ending in arched tails tipped with spikes. Eyes glowed violet in the dimness, speckling highlights over terrible,

curved mandibles and razor sets of foreclaws that gnashed air
with tireless ferocity. Stabbed by dread, Jaric saw frostwargs hur-
tle across the cavern and continue, *straight up rock walls toward
his feet*.

He had no moment to think. The demons moved with terrifying speed. Claws snicked scant inches from his flesh, even as he
set his hands to rock and transformed earth energy into fire. Light
and unbearable heat exploded over the cavern. Shells clicked on
rock, and whistles blended into dissonance. Pressed against
stone, Jaric struck, and struck again. Sparks flared in his hair and
clothes; cinders bit into his skin but he barely noticed pain. Over
and over he discharged power, until the whistles faded and died
amid a roaring avalanche of flame.

At length, weak-kneed and weary, Jaric permitted the fires to
dwindle. The cavern below lay awash in golden light, details
mantled under steam which drifted from the ice at the far side.
Jaric searched carefully, but saw no trace of movement. Scattered
amid the topaz sparkle of crystals he found black, spiny spheres,
each one a dormant frostwarg. No sooner had the Firelord identified the objects, when the nearer ones began to change form.
Smoky shell shifted texture, turned mottled in patterns of mustard
and ink.

Appalled to discover how swiftly the horrors could recover,
Jaric acted instantly. His Earthmaster's vision sounded the depths
of the shaft, and encountered a circular pit at the bottom. *Ivain
had not carved deep enough*. Shaping powers of fire and stone,
Keithland's new Firelord shattered the roof of the cavern, then
ignited the rubble and smothered the frostwargs' seed-forms in
seething magma. The air shimmered with heat. Fumes roiled up,
stinging his eyes. Jaric raised his hands and struck deeper. Energies crackled across rock. A chasm opened in the floor, spurting
lava like a sword wound. Jaric gathered himself and struck again.
Ivain's crystals melted and ran, while the base of the cavern softened, slithered, then collapsed with a roar over the brink, bearing
the shells of the frostwargs deep beneath the earth. The lava
would finally solidify, shackling the demons in stone until such
time as the mountain itself crumbled away.

⌒⌒X⌒⌒

Ice Wards

The cavern of the frostwargs smoldered like a counterpart of hell. Awash in ruddy light, Jaric crouched with his head in his hands, eyes stung to tears by fumes thrown off from the magma. Coughing poisoned air, and sapped by exhaustion, he struggled unsteadily to his feet. Although he had raised heat enough to sear solid stone to vapor, the ice imprisoning Anskiere remained imperviously shrouded in fog. Without stirring from the ledge, Jaric sensed that the weather wards that preserved the barrier held firm. The Stormwarden was prisoner still.

Though confrontation with the frostwargs had left him taxed and shaken, Jaric descended through a defile. The force of his defenses had plowed the cavern floor into a tortured maze of rubble; lava puddled and spilled through the rifts, radiating sultry highlights over pinnacles and arches of slagged stone. Jaric picked his way cautiously between, his skin flushed ruddy by the fires of his handiwork. Heat charred the soles from his boots as he walked; compelled to pause and engage mastery to prevent burns, he yearned sharply for his days with the trapper and the snow-bound silence of Seitforest. But Keithland's need would not wait for daydreams. Jaric moved on, his ears tortured by the hiss of calderas and the crack and boom of settling rock. The groan of the ravaged earth inflamed his inner senses like pain. Unable to escape the proof that he had inherited the destructive stamp of his sire, the Firelord reached the mist that cloaked the ice wall. Sad-

dened, and weary beyond thought, he stepped forward without
taking precautions.

Cold shocked his flesh. Clamped in the grip of Anskiere's
wards, Jaric gasped, then cried aloud as chill bit into the tissue of
his lungs. He called up fire to counter. But even as warmth answered his will, a starred pulse of light canceled his effort.
Weather sorcery closed like a fist mailed with winter, smothering
flame into darkness. Jaric staggered backward into the red heat of
the cavern. Frost spiked his hair and tunic. His hands were numb,
unresponsive and whitened as bread dough. Ivainson rubbed his
fingers. Shivering in discomfort as circulation returned, he contemplated the wards, and knew fear.

Never had he imagined the Stormwarden's defenses might be
so strong.

Determined, Jaric called forth a tendril of flame. Without
touching the mist, he teased the wards with lesser powers until
their structure radiated light; glittering ribbons of energy shot
through quartz-blue bastions of ice. The consummate skill of the
creator made Ivainson stumble in awe, for Anskiere had laid
down unimaginably potent defenses with the intricate geometry
of snowflakes; the new prison for frostwargs seemed clumsy and
rough by comparison.

At first Jaric despaired of finding weakness. But as he surveyed the wall, one portion of the pattern seemed dimmed, as if
time and attrition had deteriorated the original spell. Ivainson
refined his focus to a pinpoint, stepped up power, and rammed a
cracking torrent of force against the gap.

Sparks flew. Lines of fire struck ice, and craze marks spread
outward with a twang like harpstrings snapping under tension.
Then vision became dazzled by a tearing burst of light. Jaric shut
his eyes. He braced himself hard against the backlash, as energy
shed by the wards roared like a holocaust around him. But the
ordeal of Firemastery had once been as terrible; he held firm,
until the last of his strength ebbed from him and exhaustion unbound his control.

Fire sputtered and died. Tear-blind and tired and swaying on
his feet, Jaric surveyed the result of his effort. The disturbed
glimmer of the wards revealed the barest indentation, floored
with chunked ice, and churning with mist. Tentatively the Firelord extended his hand. Cold enclosed his flesh like a glove, but
without its earlier, killing penetration. Anskiere's barrier was
breached. But a long, arduous trial remained before help could

reach the sorcerer. Stressed to the edge of collapse, Jaric set his
shoulders against a warm cranny of rock. Though his heart ached
and his hands stung with burns, he would rest, then try again.

The effects of the Dreamweaver's stay-spell did not release
Deison Corley until well past nightfall on the day that *Callinde*
made port. Bound at wrist and ankle with cord, he wakened
sprawled on a moonlit expanse of carpet. Surrounded by smells
of parchment, oil, and leather, and the sharper pungency of horse
bridles left slung across the back of a brocade chair, he recognized the clutter of the Kielmark's personal study. The King of
Pirates was absent; but the bonds, when Corley twisted, proved
cruelly secure. *Moonless*'s former captain shut his eyes then,
overcome by failure. He had wished to avoid a return to Cliffhaven.

An hour passed in misery, while the moon swung in the sky.
The rectangle of light on the rug thinned to a sliver. Hooves
clattered from the courtyard; shouts and a clangor of arms heralded the midnight change of the guard. But the clockwork routine of Cliffhaven's fortifications no longer carried the
reassurance of home. Through the boisterous noise of the patrols,
Corley heard the sound he dreaded most. The door latch lifted,
and a soft, booted tread crossed the carpet.

Always the Kielmark moved with astonishing grace for a man
of his bulk. He lit no light. Neither did he stop where Corley
could see him, but spoke from behind in a voice pitched low with
anger. "When a captain under my command loses six of my
ships, and every living crewman aboard them, I expect him to
return and deliver a report. *What in Keithland gave you the idea
you could act otherwise?*"

Corley said nothing. On the carpet, the sliver of light narrowed to a needle, then winked out as the lintel of the window
eclipsed the moon. The room plunged into dark. Listless and
dead inside, the captain heard but did not react to the incisive
imprecations the Kielmark uttered against him.

"By Kor, you're not listening," said the Lord of Pirates. He
lashed out with a kick that tumbled the captain's body across the
rug. "I've killed men for less."

Corley blinked. He lay limp as the Kielmark followed with
stinging accusations, and then blows. Pain failed to rouse the
captain's attention; but eventually he noticed that the hard, emo-
tionless phrases were impersonal no longer.

"What of the sister you lost honor defending at Morbrith?" The Kielmark spat in the hearth. "Maybe she deserved what she got, or were you the one whose pleasure was interrupted in the dark?"

Corley jerked against his bonds.

The Kielmark laughed, very low in his throat. "Tell me, was it *your* brat the girl went back to the hilltribes to hide? What else could be expected of a man who loses his command to demons, *and then runs!*"

Anger claimed Corley. He yanked, suddenly wild to free his hands. The insults continued. The captain forgot that his tormentor was both friend and sovereign lord. Goaded to reasonless fury, he responded to a voice disembodied by darkness, soft footsteps that came and went, and hands that wantonly inflicted pain. Then suddenly, Corley felt steel lick his ankle. The restraining rope fell away. Savage with temper, he rolled to his feet. Another tug at his wrists freed his hands.

"Come fight," invited a whisper in the dark. "We've a score to settle, over *Moonless* and six companies of men."

Steel gleamed in shadow, then vanished. Disturbed air grazed Corley's cheek as a knife whickered past his skin. The weapon thunked into the settle, but the captain had already moved, springing off his toes to grapple his enemy in the night-black confines of the room.

His hands met air, then the hard edge of the table. A fist hammered into his side before Corley could recover balance. He staggered into a chair. Bit rings jangled. As his attacker lunged to throw him, the captain hooked a headstall. Harness whipped in an arc and connected; reins lashed flesh and wound taut, snaring his opponent. Corley pounced, answered by a grunt as he rammed solidly into muscle. Bits and buckles chinked as he grappled for a hold, missed, and received a second chop in the ribs. Then a hand caught his wrist and closed him in a wrestler's hold.

Corley countered with a move intentionally painful. Rewarded by a gasp, he pressed his advantage, freed his hand, and tried a throw. But a booted foot kicked his ankle from under him. Metal clanked faintly in reproof as the captain twisted, caught bridle leather and shirt with both hands, and dragged his adversary down with him.

The fighters struck floor with a force that left them winded. Entwined and struggling, neither seemed ready to retire. Carpet rucked under their exertions. Locked in single-minded conflict, they rolled the length and breadth of the chamber, while furnishings careened and toppled in their wake, glass ornaments and pearl veneer dashed to splinters against the tile.

Corley panted. Bleeding from a dozen small gashes, he closed his fingers over his enemy's throat and tried to throttle his windpipe. But an animal heave of muscles hurled him up, back, and over. His shin smashed a fire iron, and a knee gouged his stomach. Breathless, dizzied, he recalled the settle, and the knife left imbedded in its oaken rail. He flung sideways, heard knuckles smack the hearthstone where his head had rested only the moment before. Then two strong legs clamped his thigh and dragged him down. Corley stretched and caught a billet of wood from the grate. He hammered until the hold loosened. His enemy snared his makeshift bludgeon and wrenched it painfully away; but not before the captain closed his hand over the knife hilt.

A curse sounded in darkness; his enemy realized he was armed. Corley showed his teeth in a savage grin of triumph; and the stakes turned from vicious to desperate. Tables crashed, and chests overturned. Broken furnishings alternately served as shield and encumbrance to a murderous thrust of steel. In time, Corley felt himself entangled in the same bridles he had hurled before in self-defense. He cut himself loose and drove forward. Darkness and luck favored his lunge. The captain's fist closed in a mat of curly hair. One lightning reaction brought the knife down. Inflamed by a reasonless lust to kill, Corley pressed steel and knuckles against the cords of his victim's throat.

Yet even as he cut, the Kielmark's ruby torque grated under his hand. Deison Corley remembered: *he fought a friend whose life was dear to him as a brother*. Horror plunged ice through his heart. Wrenched by a queer, coughing cry, the captain snatched back his hand. He flung the knife into the grate, then braced his body for retaliation that never came. The man under his hands breathed in and out, short shallow breaths of exertion; neither blows nor speech arose in retribution.

Wrung by reaction, Corley drew back, until no contact remained between himself and his Lord by the hearth. Damp with sweat and the blood of minor abrasions, the captain sat and haltingly began to recount the loss of five brigantines and the flagship under his command. His voice steadied as he progressed. Helped by darkness, and the fact that the Kielmark made no attempt to interrupt, Corley finished his report with ringing bitterness.

"Lord, had Shadowfane's plot succeeded, I would have"—He

paused, then forced the words—"caused your murder. Luck alone spared us both. The Dark-dreamer's powers have no equal in Keithland. At any time, Kor's Accursed might claim my flesh as a weapon. Knowing that, did you think I'd risk Cliffhaven by coming back?"

A bit chimed in the shadows. The Kielmark stirred; he sighed under the combined effects of discomfort and amusement, then said unequivocally, "Yes. Because Cliffhaven is your home. And more than any other's in this warren of brigands, your loyalty is beyond question." The King of Pirates heaved to his feet. "Kor's grace! Have I got to stick my neck under your blade twice to convince you? In your right mind, or not, hot blood, or cold, you just proved you can't strike me down." The Kielmark ended with a snort of arrogant irony. "And if Shadowfane's demons send your husk or any shape-changed replica as assassin, they do so at their peril. Had you forgotten? *My captains never die una-venged.*"

A striker snapped in the dark. Flame rose from the candle stub in a nearby wall sconce. Shirtless, blood-streaked, and clad in ripped leggings, the Lord of Cliffhaven turned from the light and extended his hand. "Now get up. We have work ahead."

Corley noted the marks of his handiwork upon his sovereign's flesh. Then, embarrassed, he surveyed the shambled wreck of the study. "You planned this."

A grunt answered his accusation. The Kielmark bent stiffly, unlatched a chest by the far wall, and drew forth studded cross-belts and a set of beautifully crafted throwing knives. "Take these. Then find a whetstone. We have every crowned head in Keithland and the whole clutch of Alliance councilmen waiting in the great hall. That means a lot of nitpicking and a very lengthy council of war. Are you capable?"

Corley rose and accepted the gift. He drew one of the daggers and tested the blade with the finger adjacent to the stub left man-gled by the Karas. "Dull," he said thoughtfully, then curled a swollen lip. "Next time I should remember that my sister's a hill chief's get. She settles her own scores, I've no doubt, with stud-ded bracelets and weapons tempered in horse piss."

The Kielmark laughed with full-throated enthusiasm. "Fine woman. Next time you duck orders, I'll ask her to thrash you." Still smiling, he shoved Corley toward the door.

Disturbed in the depths of stasis, Anskiere dreamed, first of Elrinfaer's fair city, and then of storms and nightmare, and the terrible destruction wrought by the Mharg. Ivain's mad laughter echoed amid tumbled towers; then a fire-dance of sorcery slashed the dark. The Stormwarden's sleep thinned and broke. He had no chance to waken gradually. Roused to wet boots and a watery trickle of slush, he sensed disharmony like pain in his mind. A meddler had broached his wards. Flame had seared the patterning, torn gaping holes in a structure raised to confine frostwargs. Only one sorcerer in Keithland was capable of such feats.

"Ivain!" Anskiere's anguished whisper dissolved, pattering echoes amid the sullen drip of water. Stung by ancient pain, the Stormwarden shook melted ice from his hair. He reached for his staff, determined to mend the damage to his defenses. If frostwargs had escaped, he vowed he would silence the laughter of Elrinfaer's betrayer forever.

The tunnels that led downward were still blocked, yet the barrier had lost its glassy hardness; Anskiere touched ice gone rotten with thaw. He worked his mastery without thought for stiffened joints or muscles long unused to movement. Hair coiled damp against his shoulders. Icicles snapped beneath his tread as he cleared the passage with deft decision. Yet though he listened, he heard no whistle of frostwargs; just the whisper of his breath and the shift of frost-shackled rock. Only a thin sheet of ice sealed the entrance to the lower caverns. Keenly alert for danger, Anskiere dissolved the last barrier and looked out.

The mouth of the tunnel opened into a fiery glare of light. Squinting between drifts of fog, the Stormwarden glimpsed a cataclysmic vista of melted rock. He stepped forward, footfalls splashing through pooled water and floating shards of ice. Even in the wintry depths of the tunnel, the heat reddened his face. No frostwargs charged ravening to meet him, but their absence did not reassure. Fearful the creatures might already be released, Anskiere hurried his steps, then checked to discover a figure kneeling in his path.

The man's tunic was charred almost to rags. Spark-singed hair fringed his knuckles, which were clenched, obscuring his face; but his identity was never in question, for the skin of both wrists was abraded with the burns that were the trademarks of a Firelord's power.

Anskiere stiffened with a flash of antagonism. A halo of force flared active around the staff poised in his hands, and the slush underfoot hardened to frost with a crack like shattering crystal.

Light touched the Firelord where he knelt. With a sharp breath of surprise he raised his head to see the scarecrow figure of the

Stormwarden standing over him in the passage. "Your Grace!" Startled, and showing signs of advanced exhaustion, he offered the courtesy due a prince. "I have brought you the Keys to Elrin-faer."

Anskiere stared, ambivalent, into eyes that were deep and brown, yet lucid. The brightening aura of his staff lit hair that was not red but blond as grain at high summer. Memory returned. With a gasp, the Stormwarden separated past from present. "Jaric?"

The one who had once been a scribe's apprentice rose, grown now to a man and a sorcerer. He swayed unsteadily on his feet. But perception sharpened by Sathid-bond had already caught the spasm of distrust that flawed the Stormwarden's voice. "You think me crazed as Ivain," Jaric accused.

Anskiere declined answer. "What became of the frostwargs?"

Ivainson gestured toward the sultry glow at his back. "They are bound in fire and rock. With your help, I believe they could be permanently secured."

Still the Stormwarden did not speak. Wounded by his silence, and afraid to guess at its cause, Jaric lifted a hand to his neck. He snapped the thong that hung there with a swift jerk and extended a small leather pouch. "There will never be another betrayal like Elrinfaer."

"You cannot promise that. Time is measured in ages, and blood might tell." Anskiere accepted the pouch and found it un-accountably heavy. He flicked the drawstring open. Inside lay the basalt block that secured the wards over the Mharg-demons at Elrinfaer, and also something more. With careful fingers the Stormwarden lifted two weighty, smoke-colored jewels, faceted on a six-point axis, and cold as the arctic to his touch. He knew at once what he held. Jaric had given him the Sathid crystals that were the foundation of his mastery, presumably as a token of trust.

Anskiere closed his hand. The stones clicked like dice as he flicked droplets of water from his cuffs. "Why?"

Jaric's expression revealed a flash of rare anger. "Because I'm not my father." His voice quieted almost to a whisper. "I know no other way to convince you. With my powers under your control, perhaps you'll find your peace."

Anskiere dimmed the light of his staff. Cloaked in ambiguous shadow, he studied Ivainson's profile, lined blood-red in the glare from the cavern. Though resemblance to the sire was marked, details differed; this nose was straighter, the mouth less full. Jaric stood shorter by a full three fingers. Such discrepancies gradually eased the antipathy Anskiere felt upon encountering another Firelord in the flesh. Still, he avoided revealing the depth of the uncertainties left seeded by Ivain; nor did he mention the crystals given over with the Keys to Elrinfaer. "You are more powerful than your father," the Stormwarden remarked at last.

"That I doubt." Jaric rubbed blistered wrists and grimaced. "Your ice wards were too strong for me."

"No." Anskiere twisted his staff. The looped brass top caught light like sparks on a spindle. "You lack nothing but experience. Force flows through you like a river constantly passing. If you choose, you can refine your craft, and bind what energy you don't use to an object. Such reserves can be freed at need to craft a mightier ward." Roughness eased from Anskiere's tone. "But the particulars of a sorcerer's lore can wait. Ivain's debt is canceled. At last you are free of obligation."

Jaric made a small movement in the darkness. "Free? Neither of us is free, Your Grace. Kor's Accursed grew bold in your absence. Taen's brother, Emien, has gone the way of Merya Tathagres. He is now a servant of demons. In concert with a circle of Gierj, his dark dreams have conquered Morbrith."

Anskiere bent his head. Silver hair fanned over the fingers laced around his staff. Pain inflected Jaric's statement, a bitterness akin to his own scarred memories of Elrinfaer; unhappily the Stormwarden recalled: Morbrith keep had once been Jaric's home.

Puddled water rippled as the Firelord shifted position. "The Kielmark awaits at the fortress. He's gathered every crowned head in Keithland, and also the eminent of the Alliance for a council of war."

"We had better go, then." The Stormwarden searched the son of his former antagonist and found only solid sincerity. "Your treatment of the frostwargs must hold, temporarily. A breach in the borders won't wait."

Anskiere lifted his staff. The blue-violet radiance of his weather mastery flared over the tunnel that led to the surface as, straight-shouldered, and clad in threads of tattered velvet and gold, he began the ascent. Jaric followed. Neither sorcerer spoke of the fact that the Stormwarden retained the Sathid crystals which underlay the powers of a firelord, as token of a trust dearly bought.

* * *

Torchlight and the pinpoint gleam of wax candles lit the great hall at Cliffhaven, though the hour was well past midnight. Clad formally in robes and myrtle circlet, Taen Dreamweaver perched on the dais to the left of the Kielmark's chair while a crowd dressed in brocades and livery milled restlessly below. Royalty, the elect of the Alliance, and an assembly of town mayors, complete with servants and attendants, squabbled over seating for the council called by the Kielmark. His unreasonable choice of timing had cut sleep and tempers short. More than one delegate examined the furnishings with displeasure, recognizing prized gifts claimed as tribute, or items pirated from vessels that had attempted to run the straits without acknowledging Cliffhaven's sovereignty.

Taen smiled as the mayor-elect of Telshire squeezed into a cushioned chair too delicate for his enormous girth. Close by, the youngest crowned head in Keithland vanished between two pages, a secretary in hot pursuit; King Kisburn's untimely death had left an heir of eight, and royal advisors had their collective hands full playing nursemaid. Fifteen council members of the Alliance clustered, stiff-backed and disapproving, before a doorway guarded by the Kielmark's sentries. Beside their weaponed presence, the dignitaries seemed palsied and gray. Never had Keithland's vulnerabilities been more evident than in the diversity of rulers gathered to formulate the defense, Taen reflected. Their bickering and disorganization might easily last until dawn.

The sovereign Lord of Cliffhaven entered, shirtless but resplendent in white breeches, sea boots, and a magnificent silver-hilted broadsword. Rubies sparkled above his bronzed and muscular chest as he strode to the dais, his senior captain in full dress uniform on his right. The buzz of conversation faltered, then renewed with a note of defiance as the Kielmark reached his leopard-hide chair. He rested crossed wrists on the back, and his voice boomed out as if he stood on a ships's deck. "Kor's grace, some of the furnishings are interesting, even familiar, I admit, but *sit down, all of you, at once.*"

As if the words were a signal, the sentries at the door dressed weapons. The sharp, metallic clang stilled the crowd in the chamber; faces turned forward with resentment.

The Kielmark surveyed the officials and the royalty gathered in his hall. "That's better." With the passionless interest of a king wolf, he sat himself; and the sentries by the doorway sheathed steel to chilly silence.

Corley took the chair to the right. Bruises from a recent fight discolored the skin over his collar. But the death wish that had troubled him earlier now seemed utterly banished; as the Kielmark opened council, his senior captain calmly took up whetstone and knife. The Dreamweaver closed her eyes with relief.

"I called you here for the purpose of defending Keithland against Kor's Accursed." The sovereign of Cliffhaven paused and fingered his sword; and immediately the Alliance representative from Skane's Edge disrupted order. Bald, middle-aged, and overdressed in a robe festooned with ribbon, the man sprang to his feet.

"Pirate! How dare you preside over honest men? Is it true a Firelord has returned to Keithland soil? Your kitchen scullion said a son of Ivain took shelter on Cliffhaven only yesterday."

Uproar swept the chamber. Ivain's cruel exploits were remembered with resentment and fear, and news of an heir to the Cycle of Fire abruptly overturned propriety.

Yet the Kielmark ruled a lawless following. Within his halls he managed insolence with strength, brutality, or wolfish cleverness, whichever suited the moment best. Neither royalty nor the august peerage of the Free Isles merited exception. Before debate could organize to rebellion, the King of Pirates unsheathed his sword and bashed the flat of the blade across his chair.

"Silence!" The effect proved sufficient to intimidate. The councilman sat swiftly, and the noise subsided. The Kielmark rested his sword point against the floor and addressed the troublemaker in tones of blistering scorn. "Do you rule by the gossip of servants, *Eminence?* The scullion you bribed suffered a whipping for his indiscretion." Aware of a few sullen murmurs, the Lord of Cliffhaven inclined his head toward the captain seated to his right. "Corley, deliver your report."

Moonless's former captain rose and, with a poise impossible an hour before, related the demise of his fleet of six. By the time he spoke of his experience with the Karas shape-changer, the assembly sat strained and disturbed. Corley ended, finally, to thick silence.

The Kielmark now had their attention. He sheathed his great weapon, and one by one called upon the rulers of Keithland to evaluate the status of their domains. Other than prowling bands of Thienz, most had little to contribute; skeptical expressions crept back until the Queen of Hallowild announced that her northern domain of Morbrith had fallen to the Dark-dreamer's influence. In a voice tremulous with sorrow, she told of fields and towns littered with corpses, and of caravans that ventured through Gaire's Main never to return. The Kielmark incisively pointed out that the timing of the deaths coincided with Jaric's destruction of the Gierj.

Corley sat with his whetstone clenched in whitened knuckles; and Taen wept, for the folk she once had defended were now bones rotting in the sun. Even the irascible King of Felwaithe sat silent in his chair; his lands lay closest to Shadowfane, and only the inscrutable caprice of Kor's Accursed seemed to have spared his subjects from ruin.

The Kielmark stirred, eyes gone cold as chipped ice. "Plainly the demons challenge our borders once again. Landfast itself may be threatened. Any man who thinks our survival is not in peril may abdicate, now. Keithland has no leeway to spare for dissent."

A murmur swept the chamber, ominous as the grind of storm surf over rock. Though every ruler present bridled at the Kielmark's assumption of authority, none dared arise in complaint. Forced to alliance by a common cause, Keithland's council tallied resources and argued strategies of attack and defense until well after dawn. Taen listened in silent distress. Her Dreamweaver's perception grasped the truth: neither weapons nor the bulwark of faith in Kor's canons could match the Dark-dreamer and his circle of Gierj.

Daylight spilled cold, gray light through the arches when the clatter of hooves echoed up from the courtyard. Corley stilled his whetstone and knife. The Kielmark lifted his chin from his fist, eyes narrowed with speculation, as the great double doors burst open.

Two men entered, both of them ragged. The taller wore the remains of a blue velvet tunic; tangled silver hair streamed over the wool of a sentry's borrowed cloak. His lean features were hooked into a frown, and he carried a sorcerer's staff capped with looped brass. As he strode past the guards, a hush settled over the council. The pale eyes, sure step, and stern countenance of Anskiere of Elrinfaer were known the breadth of Keithland.

The silence grew strained at the appearance of the Stormwarden's companion, a slight, blond man in singed linen whose eyes no man could endure without discomfort. But to the woman in Dreamweaver's robes on the dais, the sight of Ivainson Firelord brought joy.

"Jaric!" Taen left her chair running. Her myrtle circlet whirled to the floor as she hurtled the length of the hall into his embrace.

Keithland's newest sorcerer spun her around. Oblivious to

propriety and the presence of royalty, he kissed her; and his exuberance shattered order within the council. Kings and council members rose, some in awe, others shouting imprecations. But louder than the din rose the Kielmark's rich laughter, and the voice of the King of Felwaithe.

"Hail Stormwarden! Hail, heir to the Firelord! Let Shadowfane rue this hour, and Keithland rejoice. For the victory!"

"For the victory!" echoed the elderly Queen of Hallowild, while, with a predatory smile, the Kielmark beckoned Stormwarden and Firelord to join him on the dais. To the right of the leopard chair, Corley smiled grimly. Plans to wrest Morbrith from the Dark-dreamer could now begin in earnest.

∽∾XI∽∾

Crisis

The click of beads echoed across the mirror pool at Shadowfane as the Thienz bowed obsequiously, forelimbs clutched to its chest. *'Lord-mightiest, I bring news.'*

Scait regarded the creature, his eyes already slitted with annoyance; earlier he had learned that two of the human children taken captive had died in training. A third had weakened to the point where it would not survive, and the advisors had begged to open it for dissection. Scait forbade them, though they grumbled; with only five human young left to be enslaved through a cross-linked Sathid, the Demon Lord gestured irritably for the Thienz to continue.

Beads clicked; the Thienz was young, an immature adult. It squirmed with reluctance, which meant that its message would be unwelcome. *'Exalted, the watcher sends word of a discovery,'* it blurted in a rush. *'Gierjlings have gathered. They have chosen a lair in the caves beneath Shadowfane. A spore to form the Morri-gierj is already spawned and growing apace.'*

Scait gouged spurred thumbs deep into the stuffing of his throne, while at his feet the Thienz cowered and shivered. No news could have been worse.

This setback made other difficulties pale to insignificance. The master plot to conquer Keithland hinged upon expendable human pawns to focus the Gierjlings' killing powers; but a Morri-gierj was the creatures' rightful overlord. This advent of a spawning was centuries premature, and a perilous upset, for the naturally focused forces of the Gierjlings were mightier by far than the combined powers of the compact. Shadowfane itself might be threatened. Scait snarled at the Thienz. *'You are certain of this?'*

The messenger bobbed, exuding a stink of nervous sweat. *'Mightiest, the Watcher-of-Gierj itself sent me.'*

'I come at once.' Human hide tore beneath Scait's claws as he thrust himself abruptly to his feet.

The Thienz scrambled to complete its bow, then scuttled off like a whipped dog. Normally the Demon Lord sent underlings upon those errands to the catacombs beneath Shadowfane. But with all hopes, even continued survival, ultimately dependent upon conquest of Keithland, the possible development of a Morrigierj became a priority concern. Inwardly as distressed as the Thienz, Scait strode from the hall without pause to call a lackey to replace the rent limb of his throne arm. While the Thienz scrabbled clear of its master's feet, the Demon Lord descended the spiral stair that gave access to the lower levels of the fortress. From there he traversed a mazelike chain of corridors that altered, in subterranean depths, from pillared construction and hexagonal brick to the uneven contours of a cave. Dampness streaked walls stained rust red with mineral deposits. The enclosing confines of rock seemed suffocating, a barrier impervious to the finely developed psychic sensors of most demons. Scait hissed uneasily. He blinked glowing eyes in the gloom and chose his path with caution. At length, on the heels of the Thienz, he arrived at the chamber the Gierjlings had chosen for their lair.

The underling scrabbled aside and fled. The Demon Lord it had escorted ducked through an archway into darkness studded with the yellow-green glimmer of eyes. Gierj were there, numbering hundreds or maybe even thousands, jumbled one upon another like a mat of living fungus.

Jostled by wiry, furred bodies, Scait snapped his teeth in displeasure. The creatures eddied away with a clicking of claws and an occasional whine of protest. Presently the Demon Lord gained an unobstructed view of the spore, a stonelike sphere nested in a depression in the floor, black and dull, and protected by a shell of insurmountable hardness. Scait already knew that no force possessed by the compact was capable of destroying it; memories-of-ancestors ascertained this fact beyond doubt. The only way to kill a Morrigierj spore was to launch it into the heart of a star. Lacking ships, such remedy was impossible; but space communication and transport might not prove beyond reach, should *Corinne Dane*'s Veriset navigational module be recovered.

Scait blinked, and opened his retinas to their widest aperture. Normally a spore should take a decade to mature, but past data offered no reassurance. Keithland's magnetic fields must be differently tuned from those of the home star where Gierj had evolved. Plainly, the natural rhythms of the cycle were upset. The spore that Scait regarded should not have been spawned for another two thousand years.

'*Other things than nature might stir the Gierj to a spawning.*' The sending originated from a hulking form that shuffled down the corridor beyond the Gierj-lair.

Scait stiffened, irritated that his guard had been breached. Only one being in Shadowfane would dare his anger; that one was very old, and far too wise to offer reckless challenge.

The Watcher-of-Gierj sent again with a note of driest acerbity. '*Your rivals will claim that misuse of the Gierjlings given over to Maelgrim served to hasten the breeding cycle. Whatever the cause, Lord-exalted, this spore in all probability will hatch prematurely.*'

Scait required no warning of the Morrigierj's pending development. His eyes had fully adjusted to the dimness. Now that his sensors had acclimated to the unaccustomed restrictions of stone, he, too, felt the flare of primal awareness that stirred beneath the spore's surface. Spider-limbed Gierjlings rustled restlessly in the dark. Their zombie eyes burned balefully while the Demon Lord sorted ramifications.

"The compact is thwarted, now." The shuffling step drew nearer. Presently the nasal voice of the Watcher sounded from the doorway immediately behind. "Morrigierj will upset all plans."

Scait spun around as the creature's domed hulk crowded through the arch. Hunched and armored like a scavenger beetle, it picked at the carcass of a fish. Cartilage crunched delicately as it cleared its mandibles and qualified. "Even fully bonded-to-Sathid, your talented litter of humans dare not contest the sovereignty of the Morrigierj. Most-jealous-of-masters, its vengeance would surely be bloody."

Scait's lip curled and bared rows of sharpened teeth. "What will that matter? Take Set-Nav, and we can escape this planet. Then let the retribution of the Morrigierj fall and wreak death upon mankind."

The watcher crunched a last bite of fish. "But Set-Nav's location is not known to us. The Sanctuary Towers at Landfast no doubt hold the key. Except they are guarded by priests, and the most secure of arcane defenses. The captive manlings bonded to

Sathid will never mature in time to spearhead your assault against
Keithland."

The Demon Lord shrugged with malevolent displeasure. The
Watcher was the last of its kind; it had no ambition for power. If
he slew it in a fit of defensive rage, its skills could not be replaced. "I will grant Maelgrim Dark-dreamer a Gierj circle of
sixty, and permission to enslave all of humanity."

"Gierj power on that scale will ruin the boy's health quickly,"
scoffed the Watcher. "That he would be dead long before Land-
fasts's securities could be broached is a foregone conclusion." It
blinked tiny, wise eyes and waited, but its overlord whirled and
strode from the chamber, kicking Gierj from his path with more
than his usual viciousness. The Watcher sighed with resignation.
Patiently it combed fish oil from its quills, while the Gierj closed
like a living blanket around the black spheroid of their spore.

Keithland mustered for war. On Cliffhaven, where armory and
warehouses were stocked with weapons for every contingency,
the Kielmark ordered the forges lit to benefit those domains less
well prepared. The clangor of his armorers' mallets rang night
and day over the fortress, while ships came and went in the harbor, delivering dispatches and transporting men. The vessels
sailed always with fair wind and full sails. Recovered from his
prison of ice, Anskiere of Elrinfaer served as weather warden.
Between time, he began instructing the Firelord to refine control
of his mastery. The Kielmark observed Jaric's progress with narrowed eyes, then immersed himself in strategy and planning.
Even the defenses of Vaere-trained sorcerers had limitations.
Force of arms must not be neglected in preparation for battle
against Shadowfane.

The south-shore kingdoms and the Alliance archipelagoes
proved woefully under equipped; Kisburn's troops were still depleted from an ill-fated alliance with Tathagres, which left the
northshore garrisons maintained by Hallowild and Felwaithe. The
Kielmark detailed captains to evaluate them; then, clad in the
white breeches he had not taken time to change since the council
two days past, he sent for Deison Corley.

The first captain was slow to arrive at the study. His smudged
hands and tunic showed that summons had reached him at the
waterfront, where he labored with the dock workers to black
down the rigging of the brigantine commissioned for his command. Both sleeves bore stains at the wrists from the tanner's oil
that softened a new set of knife sheaths.

The Kielmark analyzed such details at a glance; judging his captain well recovered from the incident with the Karas, he made a decision and spoke. "The sorcerers and the Dreamweaver sail for Morbrith with the turn of the tide."

Corley crossed the carpet, sat, and stared at his boot cuffs as if the leather desperately wanted mending. He showed no surprise. "Then you'll order me north to Cover's Warren, to muster the patrol fleet and guard Felwaithe?"

"No. Tamic's doing that." The Kielmark watched, muscles coiled like a snake's, as his first captain shot up straight with a screech of chair legs. For a moment blue eyes locked with ones of cinnamon brown.

Then Corley said, "Why?" A stranger would not have noticed his hurt, that his Lord had sent another, perhaps steadier man, where once he would have gone himself.

"Because I'd never trust Tamic to keep order in this den of outlaws." The Kielmark rested his fists on the table; rubies flashed like blood at his neck as he leaned forward. "We'd have mutiny and murder within the hour *Ladywolf* sailed."

Corley blinked and slowly turned white as the name of the brigantine registered. *Ladywolf* was the Kielmark's personal command. "You'll be going yourself, then, with Taen and the rest?" His brows peaked in disbelief. Through fifteen years of service he had never known the Lord of Cliffhaven to leave his island fortress.

"Who else could keep Alliance councilmen, Kor's priests, and a flighty mess of royalty in agreement enough to lead an army?" The Kielmark gestured in exasperation. "I have to go. I'm the only one who can threaten both trade and their treasuries. D'you know any better way of keeping humanity in accord?"

Corley grinned. A little color returned to his face. "You're Keithland's most likely candidate for a fine, solid citizen, right enough."

"Fires," snapped the Kielmark, for once intolerant of his first captain's sarcasm. "Slack the discipline while I'm gone, and I'll flay your hide from your heels up." As if reluctant to continue, he stopped, straightened, and twisted his jeweled torque from his neck. He cast the circlet onto the boards, and gold clanged sourly between his fist and his first captain's hand. "If any man questions your right to command, that's my token."

Corley swallowed, speechless. Light came and went like flame in the heart of the rubies as the Kielmark leaned across the window. He hooked his baldric from the marble arms of the cherub, then tossed his great sword over his back. Neither man spoke as he crossed the chamber; but both understood that the torque on the table was as close as this sovereign would come to naming a successor.

"Watch your back, friend," Corley whispered at last.

The Kielmark paused by the doorway, wary as always, but smiling. "Speak for yourself," he said roughly. Then he strode without farewell into the candleless gloom of the hall.

Ladywolf raised anchor within the hour. Jaric stood at her rail, hands laced over the cross guard of his own sword, newly reclaimed from the armory where it had lain since the last time Corley made port with *Moonless*. From the deck by his side, Taen regarded the weapon with trepidation. Traditionally, Vaere-trained sorcerers disdained to carry steel; but when Anskiere began training to refine this Firelord's talents, Ivainson claimed the blade for his focus. Neither reason nor propriety could induce him to revert to the usual staff. The newest sorcerer sworn to service by the Vaere owned an obstinacy that even a Dream-weaver who loved him dared not cross.

Taen's preoccupied silence passed unnoticed as the Kielmark shouted orders to his boatswain; feet thumped on planking, and crewmen surged up the ratlines to make sail. By itself, Jaric's dissent was a mere defiance of form; but when Stormwarden and Firelord were together, the Dreamweaver noticed each one guarded his thoughts. That uneasiness troubled her; for, to combat the demons of Shadowfane, the two sorcerers must work mind within mind, attuned in flawless rapport.

The boatswain shouted. Canvas cascaded from the yards with a crack and a slither of boltropes. Poised to work his mastery on the foredeck, the Stormwarden of Elrinfaer lifted his head, his eyes the gray of rain beneath an overcast. He wore a sailor's tunic of plain, bleached linen, knotted at the waist with a sash worked in silver. But simple clothes could never mask the magnitude of his powers. His touch with the wind seemed effortless, deft with a proficiency born through decades of experience.

Jaric watched the sails clap smartly into curves overhead, the mild, wistful expression Taen associated with admiration on his face. As the *Ladywolf* shuddered and steadied into a heel, he smiled, his hair tumbled by the eddies off the headsails. "Anskiere's control is matchless. If I tried something comparable, like lighting the galley fire with sorcery, I'd probably crisp everything to the waterline."

"You'll improve." Taen leaned hard into her man's shoulder, heartened by his enthusiasm for his new craft. But her contentment faltered as the Stormwarden glanced aside and noticed the Firelord watching him. Dark brows lowered almost to a frown; then, without greeting or encouragement, Anskiere strode aft.

Ivainson's exhilaration withered, and Taen felt tension harden the muscles of his forearm. "What happened at the ice cliffs?" she demanded impulsively. "Why should the Prince of Elrinfaer distrust you?"

Jaric considered his sword, as if inanimate Corlin steel might answer her query for him. His eyes turned deep, uncipherably intense, and he spoke at last with bitterness. "Anskiere believes that one day I will betray my own kind as my father did." Suddenly restless, he drew back, as if the very air might burn him. Taen clung to the rail. She did not follow as Jaric left her side. The quality of the Firelord's silence suggested that he had tried his utmost, in some manner even abandoned pride; still he had failed to assure Anskiere of Elrinfaer that his inheritance included no portion of his sire's mad malice.

Night fell, cloudy and fitful with gusts, over the Corine Sea. Despite the prevailing weather, the sky above *Ladywolf*'s masthead remained star-strewn and clear; her sails curved to the steady winds of a broad reach. On deck, the Kielmark remained braced against the rail long after the gleam of Cliffhaven's light tower vanished astern. His brigantine fared alone upon the sea. The bulk of the fleet stayed behind to defend Mainstrait; except for the picked company of men on board, the campaign to recapture Morbrith depended upon garrison troops to be levied from Corlin. The Duke at least maintained proper discipline, if the proficiency of his men at arms fell short of Cliffhaven's exacting standards. The Lord of Renegades frowned at the sparkle of phosphorescence churned up by the wake. Since no action could be taken until his vessel reached shore, he brooded; stable conditions left his crewmen idle, and himself more time than he liked for thought.

One fair day melted into the next. *Ladywolf* logged league after league at a steady twelve knots, but for Jaric the crossing did not lack challenge. Striving to master the nuances of a sorcerer's craft, he secluded himself in the chart room from morning till dark with the icy weight of his sword balanced across his knees. The weapon was the gift of Telemark the forester, granted on the eve that a boy had left Seitforest for his destiny as Firelord's heir. More than once the blade had drawn blood; never had it slain, but the armorer who had done the forging well knew his trade. From keen edge to the blue-black gloss of temper, the steel was fashioned expressly to maim. Jaric strove to change its nature. Yet day after exhausting day, success eluded him. A fortnight of effort had yielded no progress at all.

The Firelord sat back against the chart locker and sighed in frustration. Sunset had long since faded. Light from the deck lantern gilded the salt-crusted panes of the stern window, and shadow swathed the corners like velvet. The wear and creak of seagoing wood seemed abnormally loud, until Jaric recalled that the sailhands would be crowded in the galley at this hour. He should have been hungry, but supper did not interest him. Although the weight of the blade bore grooves in his thighs, quitting never entered his mind. He had not chosen the weapon for its deadly potential, as Anskiere believed. To marry power with a blade designed for killing might instead remind that the heritage of a Firelord tended ever toward terror and destruction. Jaric set his hands to the sword. Determined to complete what he had started, he closed his eyes in concentration.

He tuned his Earthmaster's perception to the blade. Like stone, or soil, or the symmetrical crystals of a mineral, the metal was composed of brightness; pinpoint eddies of energy interlocked and delicately balanced. Jaric embraced the pattern with his mind. Then he drew a filament of flame from his Sathid bond. With the care of a man unraveling spider silk, he endeavored to weave that energy, warp into weft through the steel. Sweat dampened the hair at his temples. To thread dissimilar powers through a structure of such delicacy taxed every resource he possessed; each attempt since dawn had ended the same way. Strain sustained for too long marred his control. Jaric cried out in dismay, even as energies strayed, jostling the symmetry of the metal fractionally out of alignment. The blade in his lap glared red, then white, disrupted by fire that licked and twisted to break free.

The Firelord stilled his inner mind. Heat beat unpleasantly against his flesh. The stresses of confined sorcery hammered his nerves like pain. He licked dry lips, tried to push back the fear that curled through his gut. This time his spell had progressed too far for retreat. Tired, and discouraged by knowledge that Anskiere could weave storm into a feather inside a fraction of an instant; he forced himself steady. No recourse remained but to correct his mistake.

"You're nearly there," said a voice at his shoulder. Cool hands slipped over Jaric's hot ones. A presence filled his mind like wavelets soaking gently into sand. "Try this." A prompt within his awareness flicked the fire-thread in another direction.

Jaric accepted the pointer; and like water breaking silver through a log jam, his spell unsnarled, lacing scarlet ribbons of energy through the steel. The process seemed utterly natural. Ivainson marveled, wondering why he had not worked in harmony with the metal's innate pattern earlier. Excitedly he continued the configuration, until the swordblade rang along its length with stored force; Jaric joined the ends of the energy complete and looked up, to lanternlight and the still presence of Anskiere of Elrinfaer. The sorcerer's eyes were gray and clear and kindly, and he smiled.

"I think I understand now." The Firelord lifted the weapon from his lap; its reddened glow touched his upturned features, underlighting his jaw to more angular contours, and lending his brows a pronounced arch. His gold hair gleamed copper with highlights. Through the touch still in his mind, Jaric shared the Stormwarden's viewpoint; for a split second, he beheld in himself the mirror image of his father, Ivain.

Anskiere flinched back. Sorcery answered by reflex, and his half-raised hands sparked blue. A whirlwind ripped into being, sharp with the bite of ozone. Charts flapped helter-skelter across the table, and the lantern pitched on gimbaled mounts, flame extinguished in the draft.

"No!" Bashed backward into the bulkhead, Jaric dropped the sword. "Ivain is *dead!*" His shout tangled with a belling clang as steel struck the deck at his feet.

The violence of Anskiere's reaction died away. Air winnowed, then stilled, and charts ruffled to rest. Beyond speech, the Stormwarden sat and bowed his head over sleeves of stainless white.

"I do understand." Jaric raised himself awkwardly. "Through Llondelei imaging I shared your grief at Elrinfaer's loss." His voice turned edged with anguish. "But how will we ever conquer demons? You can't trust, and I cannot be other than myself."

Anskiere looked up, a tired half smile restored to his face. "We shall manage, I think. Look." And he pointed to the sword, which lay forgotten in the dark.

Steel forged by Corlin's armorer was ordinary no longer, but shining with the orange-red halo that marked the primary ward of a Firelord's staff. Two more auras soon would accompany that foundation, one a secondary level of power, and the third a protection against tampering by strangers. Like braiding, Jaric grasped the concept; intuitively he knew he could master the remaining sorceries more easily than the first.

Yet as he lifted the weapon, he damped the light of his accomplishment like guilt. "What good is skill if you won't believe in me?"

Cloth rustled; Anskiere touched Ivainson's shoulder in darkness and sighed. "I must learn how to forget the past. For in all ways that matter, Jaric, you are son to the friend I loved like a brother, before the Cycle of Fire overturned his humanity."

Ivainson completed the defense wards on his sword in the heat of an Indian summer calm. The Corine Sea lay leaden and smooth, but Anskiere's winds held true; *Ladywolf* neared the shores of Hallowild late the following day. Trouble met her even before land appeared above the horizon.

The sun shone like a disc of tarnished gold through billowing veils of smoke. Sailhands gathered at the rail, while the King of Pirates himself climbed aloft to investigate.

Sweating in the heat, and clad in little but a sword belt and a matched pair of wristbands, the Kielmark swung down the ratlines. He passed his ship's glass to Anskiere, who waited on the deck, and said tersely, "By the heading, I'd guess Seitforest is ablaze. The weevil in the oatmeal is, why?"

Anskiere accepted the glass, but made no move to focus. "Not lightning," he said presently. "The nearest thunderhead lies three hundred leagues due north. Nor could someone's cooking fire ignite the forest by wind. The air is dead still in that region. Taen might inform you better."

The Dreamweaver was below decks, apparently asleep; the Kielmark ordered his steward to wake her, and also summon Jaric from the chart room. Then he turned cold eyes to the Stormwarden. "Make a gale and drive this vessel into Corlin. She'll blow out sails for certain, but the damned sticks'll take it."

But Taen Dreamweaver was not sleeping. When the Kielmark's steward reached the stern cabin, he found her berth empty. The enchantress was settled cross-legged on a sea chest, her eyes wide open and unseeing in the depths of trance. As leery of sorcery as his master, the man hesitated in the companionway;

the creak of a hinge betrayed him. Taen started slightly. She blinked and shivered. As if she were dazed, her gaze focused slowly upon the servant poised to enter her cabin.

The next instant she shoved to her feet, urgent with alarm. "Where's the Kielmark?" she said quickly. "Send him here, with both of the sorcerers. Peril has come to Hallowild."

The steward spun and all but collided with his master, who chafed at delay and impetuously sought Taen himself. The servant recoiled, then wisely ducked clear before the Kielmark shoved him bodily from the companionway.

"Seitforest burns," the Lord of Cliffhaven snapped directly. "Can you tell why, girl?"

Taen met the Kielmark's impatience with a poise like edged steel. "The Dark-dreamer brings us war like none fought in Keithland before." She abandoned language; the unspeakable could be explained more efficiently through her talents. Dream-image sheared into the Kielmark's mind. He recoiled with a curse and a gasp as through the influence of sorcery he beheld Shadow-fane's new army. The sight carried horror beyond all imagining.

Bull-mad with outrage, the King of Pirates roared out his orders before the vision was fully spent. Though called from below decks, his crewmen heard and obeyed his commands with alacrity. The brigantine came alive as men ran full tilt up the rigging. Canvas cracked from the yardarms, snapped into curves by the winds raised by sorcery. *Ladywolf* sheared into a violent heel and tossed Taen headlong from the trunk. The Kielmark's great fist caught her before she slammed into him. He righted her with a brusqueness that allowed no space for apology. "Fetch the Firelord. We'll be ashore before nightfall, and both of you must be ready to land."

Sunset came smudged by smoke pall. Though waters elsewhere lay polished under calm *Ladywolf* sheared into the estuary of the Redwater with her stuns'ls and flying jib flogged into tatters. Anskiere's winds dispersed, leaving canvas and snarled lines hanging limp as shreds on a scarecrow. While crewmen dropped anchor, a barge bearing ranking men at arms and the Duke's first commander approached from the quayside. As the craft pulled alongside, the officer confirmed Taen's initial dream-search in a voice inflected by fear.

Morbrith's dead had risen. Half-rotted corpses from the fields and towns took up swords, then marched in grisly ranks to pillage

and desecrate and wreak ruin on domains to the south. Fire might
stop them. To that end, panicky farmsteaders led by a priest had
set Seitforest ablaze, then prayed vainly for a breeze to arise and
spare their fields.

Their faith availed nothing, the officer concluded drily. Divine
Fires cared nothing for farmers, and south winds never blew during droughts. The army of the dead advanced and slaughtered
refugees without hindrance until the Duke's men at arms organ-
ized resistance.

The Kielmark demanded particulars, even as Firelord, Stormwarden, and Dreamweaver joined him at the rail.

The weather had been still, and seasonally dry; Seitforest
blazed past saving, even if every able man had not been busy
defending the borderlands. Worried for the trapper who had sheltered him as a boy, Jaric interrupted. "How much woodland has
burned?"

The first commander shrugged, his dress tunic darkened with
sweat. "Who can say? Last messenger thought seven square
leagues, but that was a guess, and hours old by now."

The Kielmark snapped a question. "How many men fight, and
how many of the garrison remain in Corlin?"

"The Duke rode out with all but three companies." Stung by a
frown of disapproval, the first commander qualified waspishly.
"Would you leave a town threatened by siege undefended? The
Dark-dreamer's army advances far south of Gaire's Main by now.
Corlin could be under attack by dawn."

"Belay that!" The Kielmark called a sailhand to uncleat the
barge's painter. Then, ignoring the honorific due Corlin's ranking
officer, he gave orders. "Take the sorcerers ashore and find
horses for them. My men will follow by longboat and muster
what troops remain. There had better be horses in the town somewhere, because I intend to march every available swordsman who
can ride against Maelgrim without delay."

Signaled by the boatswain, Taen started down the side battens,
while a stiff-faced first commander retorted with hysterical disbelief. "What! You give me two sorcerers and an enchantress, then
propose to strip Corlin defenseless? We fight an army of *corpses*,
man! Weapons can't kill what's already dead."

The Kielmark folded massive forearms. His cold, angry gaze
saw Jaric over the rail, then flicked back to the officer in the
barge. "You fight a human aberration and a demon circle of

Gierj. Shut the gates for a siege, and I tell you, everyone within
will die and join the Dark-dreamer's legions."

A tense moment passed while Anskiere followed the others
into the barge. The instant the Stormwarden set foot on the
thwart, the King of Pirates barked an order. The sailhand who
waited with the painter promptly cast off. Current swirled; caught
standing as the barge wheeled downstream, the officer lost his
balance. He flailed backward, tripped over the coxswain's
ankles, and toppled into the laps of his oarsmen. Confusion resulted. By the time looms could be threaded into rowlocks to
steady the ungainly craft, argument and decorum were irretriev-
ably lost.

Separated by a widening expanse of water, Corlin's first commander fumed helplessly as the Kielmark dispatched crew to
launch longboats. Cliffhaven's sailhands obeyed with formidable
speed. Blocks squealed and lines came unlashed without fouling
or wasted motion. The first boat smacked into the harbor within a
minute and a half, and oarsmen scrambled aboard. Somewhere in
the interim they had armed themselves for war. Their timing as
they threaded looms and initiated stroke against the tide was irk-
somely flawless. They would reach the town docks, all of them,
before the ungainly barge of state could recover headway.

The first commander of Corlin banged a frustrated fist against
the stern seat, while his own rowers strained awkwardly at their
benches. An officer, however senior, did not countermand his
Duke; and the Queen herself had delegated authority to this pirate
and his pack of trained cutthroats. Left no graceful recourse, the
disgruntled first commander saw two sorcerers and an enchantress delivered to the south shore landing and speedily mounted on
horses.

Though the animals were fresh, they suffered in the still air.
Their coats shone dark with sweat in the torch-lit yard by the
ferry dock. The jangle of bits and swords and mail made them
prance as the men at arms appointed as escort prepared to ride.

"Where will you go?" demanded the first commander. He
spoke through his nose, as if the air had a taint that disagreed
with him.

Anskiere replied with little more courtesy than the Kielmark.
"To Seitforest, and thence to the battlefield."

The officer reverted to outrage. "Kor's grace, sorcerer, are
trees and squirrels of more account than the living people of
Hallowild?" But his question was lost in dust and noise as the

Stormwarden's party thundered away from the docks. Taen had no chance to reassure the man that Jaric and Anskiere between them had formulated a plan; her own mount bolted to keep pace with the others. Caught flat-footed by the landing, the soldiers on escort detail clambered belatedly into saddles to give chase.

∿∿ XII ∿∿

Hallowild

Night fell; hidden in darkness, the track above Corlin ferry lay soft in the hollows, gouged by livestock and caravans to ruts where puddles were slow to dry. The horses cantered through air that smelled of crushed clover and mud and river reed. Southwest, beyond the streaming flame of the outriders' torches, Seitforest stood rimmed with fire and smoke. The swirl of the Redwater bounded the trail to the north, snagged into ghost-fingered foam where current curled over submerged rocks.

Taen clung by reflex to a bay gelding, her customary distrust of horses eclipsed by dream-trance. Immersed in nets of power, her mind ranged through woodland seeking a man who in autumn should be found wearing soft leather and a jingling clip of bird snares. While Seitforest burned, no semblance of seasonal rhythms remained to guide her search. The trails where the forester normally fared were overrun by panicstricken wildlife. Blazing thickets and smoke-smothered dells yielded no trace of human awareness. At last, on the verge of despair, Taen sampled the mind of a sparrow; through its ears she heard the sharp ring of an axe. She pinpointed the sound and immediately encountered a presence intent as a hawk's. With a cry of relief, the Dreamweaver broke trance and set heels to her horse.

The bay tossed its nose in protest, then lengthened stride to match pace with the Firelord's mount. Taen raised her voice in answer to Jaric's concern. "Telemark is unharmed. You'll find him cutting a slash in attempt to check the fire." Dream-image showed him a lantern-lit draw, thick with smoke and the scent of crushed fern; there the forester labored with shovel and axe in a solitary effort to avert disaster.

Ivainson knew the place. He also saw that the forefront of the blaze raged scarcely half a league distant. Trees exploded violently into flame, fanning deadly flurries of sparks. No mortal endeavor could spare Seitforest from ruin. Telemark worked on out of stubbornness, for the trap runs and the cabin that were all he loved in life. Obligated by friendship and a deep sense of debt, Jaric took immediate action. Trusting Taen to explain to Anskiere, he whipped up his mount and plunged toward the wood at a gallop.

An outrider reined from the column to follow. "Stay here!" commanded the Stormwarden. "You'll only get in his way."

The officer in attendance shouted protest. Anskiere of Elrinfaer did not trouble to answer, but instead woke the light in his staff.

Every horse in the company shied. Riders fought to stay astride, while the night around them grew charged with the sense of impending storm. Breezes heavily scented with rain licked the grasses, bowing their tasseled heads to the earth. The weather wards brightened steadily until Anskiere's tall form stood rinsed in violet glare. Around him, two score hard-bitten men at arms trembled in raw terror, while clouds whipped over the treetops, and the still, hot air of calm broke under influence of sorcery.

While other men of Hallowild battled to rout the Darkdreamer's horde of animated human remains, the forester, Telemark, sent his axe ringing into the trunk of a silver beech. Green wood resisted; the steel rebounded with force, chewing off the thinnest of chips. Telemark blinked tear-blurred eyes. Slowed by smoke and the sting of split blisters, he hefted his axe for another stroke, then paused as a rustle disturbed the undergrowth beyond the ground cleared by his efforts.

A man emerged from the trees, well proportioned and dressed for the saddle. As he strode closer, lanternlight revealed gold hair, a tunic of imported design that had fared badly in the briars, and a very familiar face. Telemark straightened in surprise.

"Put down your axe, old friend," said Jaric. He smiled at the forester's astonishment, then crossed the expanse of stripped earth at a run.

Though stronger and broader of shoulder than the boy who had wintered in Seitforest, Jaric still moved with care, as if at any moment the soil might rise up and trip him; but a glimpse of his eyes showed that such diffidence was long outgrown. The man who returned to embrace his former mentor owned power enough to shape the very stones for his feet.

Telemark returned the greeting, then stepped clear, his axe rested helve downward in the moss. Sweat streaked his wrists like gilt in the torchlight, and black-and-white hair hung matted with ash. "The Llondelei foretold with truth," he observed, his welcome subdued by grief for his ruined wildlands. "Seitforest burns."

Jaric considered the churned dirt, the swath of razed greenery that love and desperation had accomplished. "I think I can help."

As if a weapon could achieve the impossible, he moved back and drew his sword. Telemark recognized the blade. But what once had been ordinary steel brightened with the triple halo of a Firelord's defense wards.

The forester dropped his axe in amazement. "Great Fires! *You're* the heir of Ivain?"

Jaric gave no answer. Eyes closed, sword upraised, he engaged his mastery and summoned. The fire that raged through Seitforest responded as if alive. Treetops tossed and rattled, twisted by violent drafts. Telemark braced against a beech trunk, as, whipped by terrible energies, the darkness over his head roiled and broke, transformed to a red-gold sheet of inferno. In a magnificent display of power, the conflagration that had devastated leagues of dry woodland coalesced like a whirlpool to the Firelord's bidding. The air shimmered, tortured into heat waves by a vast wheel of incandescence.

Still the fires gathered. Flame melted into flame, until Jaric stood drowned in light. Telemark shielded his face, overawed by a reality foretold by Llondian vision nearly two years past. Pride and emotion stopped his breath. Had he known at the time whom he recovered from the predations of forest bandits, he might never have found the courage to offer the shelter that had succored the heir of Ivain.

Yet even such breadth of revelation could not eclipse Seitforest's need. Telemark squinted and bent and groped after his axe. That moment, a chilly fall of rain pattered over his shoulders. A glance at the sky did not dispel the miracle. The drought had broken; clouds blanketed a sky that only moments before had been harsh with heat haze and smoke. The forester shouted in relief. "Son of Ivain!"

"Go home and rest." Jaric's voice sounded distant through the thunderous snap of flame. "The Stormwarden of Elrinfaer will drown the last cinders and see your forest safe."

Abruptly conscious of a bone-deep ache of fatigue, Telemark straightened before the heat of the Firelord's presence. "What will you do?"

The face in the conflagration smiled. "These flames may be needed in Corlin's defense." And sensing a dry watercourse beneath the ground that sloped conveniently toward the river, Jaric stepped into earth and vanished.

The unbearable brilliance of fire went with him. Blinking in commonplace lanternlight, Telemark retrieved his axe. The sting of his blistered hands woke him as if from a dream. Grateful for solitude, he wept unabashedly while around him the rains beat drum rolls of salvation over green trees, and brush, and acres of seared earth.

The storm gained force at Anskiere's bidding. White torrents poured over the burned expanse of Seitforest, and embers extinguished into hissing plumes of ash and steam; but no rain fell on the south side of the river. Taen, the Stormwarden, and Corlin's contingent of nervous cavalry continued their ride on dry ground. The horses accepted the novelty with equanimity. After the first jigging steps, they trotted willingly forward, hooves lifting spurts of chalky dust from the road. But the soldiers assigned as escort muttered and hung back from the Stormwarden's presence.

"Jaric waits for us ahead," Taen informed Anskiere. Taxed by the need to ride and ply her talents simultaneously, she gripped her reins like the life lines on a boat. "Corlin's main army is driven into retreat. The Kielmark knows. He's gone in ahead of the reserve garrison to take command. We'll meet him with the rear guard, about half a league from the Redwater."

"The enemy lines are that close?" Spurred by concern, the Stormwarden put his mount to a canter.

Light flared suddenly ahead. Leaping, distorted shadows fanned from the forms of brush and riders. Around the next bend in the trail, a figure lined in brilliance blocked the way. The Firelord sat astride his plunging, quivering mare, his sword raised over his head; above the blade towered sixty-foot sheets of flame, drawn from Seitforest, and bound by sorcery to a nexus of biddable force. Glare burnished the ground like beaten metal for yards in each direction, and the trees on either side of the trail rippled with heat waves.

As Anskiere and Taen drew rein, their trailing escort at last caught up.

"Kor!" The sergeant in command covered fear with nervous speech. "Pity the river's too deep for fording. On the other side that fire could spare some lives."

Busy murmuring encouragements to his mount, the Stormwarden flicked sweat-soaked reins. When his animal ceased trying to sidle and bolt, he said, "That's exactly what Jaric intends." He added a bitten syllable. The staff over his head flared purple. An eerie note of power thrummed on the air, followed by a crack like breaking crockery. Every soldier from Corlin cried out as the mighty span of the Redwater glazed over and froze.

"Ride!" shouted the Stormwarden. He kicked his mount to a gallop and reined headlong down the bank. The animal landed on current chilled hard as black glass. Ice chips scattered from its hooves as it slid and careened to keep balance.

Better accustomed to goats than horses, Taen grasped mane in both hands and clung as her bay scrambled after. The animal stumbled. Banged face first into its neck, she cursed, and clutched, and somehow kept her seat. Her mount skated wildly beneath her. It regained stride, only to slip again down the hardened falls of a rapids. Taen dropped the reins and grabbed saddle leather. The thrust of the horse's shoulders pinched her knuckles. Then the beast was across, and galloping up the embankment to the roadway on the far side. Bruised in places she winced to contemplate, Taen fumbled after her reins. She dared a breathless look back. Jaric followed with a frown intent as his father's, his sword point streaming like a fire beacon.

The riders sent as escort still milled in confusion on the far bank. Neither sorcerers nor enchantress paid them further heed. Thankful for the lapse, two score stalwart men at arms abandoned duty and permitted their mounts to bolt in panic toward Corlin.

A mile farther on, the Stormwarden slowed to allow the horses to breathe. Hooves clanged on the wheel-scarred slate of the roadway; that and the gusty roar of flame effectively foiled speech. Taen snatched the interval to gauge the battle's progress.

The outlook proved discouraging. Corlin's troops were hardpressed, with the Duke forced to issue another command to withdraw. Dismayed by this development, Stormwarden and Firelord wheeled their mounts from the roadway.

They continued at a gallop across tilled fields and pastures, until the stone walls of a sheep fold obstructed the way. Anskiere launched his horse in stride and leaped over. But Jaric had not been raised a prince with the finest of blooded horses at his disposal; he summoned Earthmastery and dissolved the barrier into a spattering rain of sparks. Taen followed him through the gap, grateful because her knees galled her. The bay dropped back to a walk.

The defending ranks of Corlin's army were now overwhelmingly close, and losing ground steadily. Just beyond the next rise, shouts and the clangor of weapons tangled with the screams of maimed soldiers. A horn winded close by. The wail of a whistle arrow signaled the recall, answered by the thunder of a cavalry charge to give faltering knots of foot soldiers a second's space to regroup.

"If they get pinned against the river, they're lost," Jaric shouted.

Anskiere gestured in bleak agreement. He reached the crest of the hill, drew rein, and faced forward, stunned speechless by the vista that met his eyes.

Taen and Jaric stopped their mounts at his side, equally appalled. The sight below affronted human dignity. Fires burned, red and raw as wounds across the valley. Outlined in hellish light, two armies struggled, one composed of staunch but frightened men, and the other of bones of the dead, laced clatteringly together by dried strings of tendon. Men, women, even children had not been spared service to Shadowfane's minion. They fought through no will of their own, skeletons animated to grisly purpose. Gut and soft tissues had long since been chewed away by scavengers. The shriveled gristle of the faces exposed jawbones and teeth, and eye sockets scraped clean by beetles; but the bony hands of thousands swung weapons.

Their blows wrought tireless slaughter upon the living. Taen saw a handsome young swordsman get his skull half cloven by an axe. Blood fountained as he stumbled; yet he collapsed no farther than his knees. In horror, the Dreamweaver watched him rise, turn, and slash, killing the shield mate who fought at his side. The soldier died with a look of agonized surprise.

Men slain on the field only augmented the ranks of Maelgrim's atrocities. Taen dismounted. Devastated that such malice should be engineered by one she had known as her brother, she stumbled against Jaric's knee.

Ivainson leaned over his horse's withers and offered comfort. The heat of his fires enfolded her. Taen clung as if she might faint, but no space remained for weakness. As Anskiere called an impatient query, Jaric reluctantly touched her hair. "Little witch?"

Taen straightened with a nod that was dogged bravado; inside, she wanted badly to weep. But her talents could not be spared. Without words, she handed the reins of her gelding to Jaric. Then she settled in the damp grass and gathered her awareness into trance, to assess the strength of the Dark-dreamer whose influence they must overcome, or else surrender the kingdom of Hallowild to Lord Scait and Shadowfane.

The battlefield looked different to the inward eye. In dreamsense, the spirit glow of living flesh outshone the flash of swords and steel-headed lances. At the far flank of the fighting, the flare and sparkle of spells showed where the Duke of Corlin's conjurer bolstered the offensive with wizardry.

But if the army of defenders was visible as light, the enemy they engaged and died to obstruct was darkness, black and featureless as chaos before creation. The shadow that animated the dead arose out of Morbrith. Like tide it swirled and pressed south, tireless enough to engulf the domains of Corlin and Dunmoreland in turn. Cautiously Taen extended her awareness. She probed the edges of the Dark-dreamer's powers, and encountered the singing of Gierj.

Far above the limits of normal hearing, the note that enabled the demons to meld and generate energy dashed against her Dreamweaver's probe. Resonance pierced Taen's defenses, tore gaps in her concentration wide enough to defeat her.

She slammed back with a cry of pain. Her trance broke, awareness wrenched without transition into night and screams and the clash of thousands of weapons. Gasping and confused, she felt someone's arms encircle her from behind; the solicitude was Jaric's. Light thrown off by his fires played in patterns over her lap.

Reluctantly Taen raised her eyes. The fighting was perilously near at hand. By now the Kielmark had overtaken the rear lines; his great shout lifted above the din and exhorted panicked men to hold their shield wall. "Belly-crawling lizards, stand firm! If another of you spins and runs, by Kor, I'll have your gizzards out and bleeding on the lances of the relief garrison."

His imprecations ceased, drowned out by the batter of weaponry as Maelgrim's horrors pressed the attack.

Against smoke and flame glow and night sky, Anskiere sat his horse like a stone image, his hand clenched taut on the reins. "If they stand, they're just going to die that much quicker." Sickened by the killing, the maiming, and the madness that ruined good men without letup, he turned from the battle and saw the Dreamweaver had aroused from trance. The starkness of her features caused his manner to ease just a little. "Can you tell us what we face, little witch?"

Taen shook off the discomfort that lingered from her probe. As Jaric loosened his embrace, she straightened and attempted a report. "Maelgrim directs his assault from Morbrith keep. His source to animate the dead is drawn direct from Gierjlings. I don't know how many, except this time their numbers are too great. I cannot unbind the demons' link. Nor can I break the Dark-dreamer's control so long as his Gierj-circle remains active."

Tortured by the need for clarity, the Dreamweaver delivered the last of her message in image. Through dream-touch, Stormwarden and Firelord understood that Maelgrim's demons generated harmonics forceful enough to strip her defenseless. Unless the melding of his Gierjlings was disrupted, she could do nothing; and plainly Maelgrim intended no surcease until the last of Corlin's inhabitants were annihilated.

Anskiere dismounted. Grim and preoccupied, he tossed his reins over his horse's head, then glanced in apology to Jaric. "I had hoped to avoid the use of force. Now the necessity can no longer be denied."

Ivainson Firelord flinched taut in anguish. He had never wanted a sorcerer's powers. Since the day he undertook mastery, he had prayed beyond hope never to engage his Vaerish powers in the cause of war. All too easily the hurt and the hatred inspired by his father's madness might find new focus in him.

Taen sensed Jaric's conflict. Though closest to his heart, even she could not offer solace. Always Ivainson tried, yet failed, to bend the wind; his destiny inevitably was too great for any mortal to alter.

Sick with shared grief, the Dreamweaver stumbled to her feet. The man she had come to love rose at her back and bore up. Inscrutable now as his father, Jaric gathered the reins of his own mount, and the bay, and finally Anskiere's gelding. He laced the leather gently through Taen's hands, while the Stormwarden delivered instructions.

"The horses must be led clear. We've no time for niceties. The effects of raw power can't help but spook them."

His decision was in no way premature. Shadowfane's army of horrors advanced relentlessly. The cries of wounded men and the horns of the officers sounded almost at the foot of the hilltop where the Vaere-trained prepared their defense. Fighting surged like current dragged through shallows. The foremost line of defenders was spearheaded still by the Kielmark and his scythe of a broadsword. Predictable as death, he shouted insults; and as if by arcane inspiration the strongest men rallied in support.

Yet this once the Lord of Cliffhaven's ferocious penchant for command invited disaster. As the ranks on either side turned toward safety, he and his cadre of fighters were left without support. Already the vanguard of Shadowfane's corpses threatened to surround his flank.

Anskiere stepped to Jaric's side. "Act quickly. Another minute, and we'll have no choice but to slaughter some of our own with the enemy."

Taen overheard. Rein leather crushed in her sweating hands as she tuned her concentration to warn the bravest defenders of their peril. She found the Kielmark and the men he led lost utterly in the clash and chime of weaponry. Her dream-touch itself became a hazard; one careless thought, and she would deflect the fighters' concentration, or disrupt the critical timing of parry and riposte. During crisis perfect concentration proved impossible. Any attempt at precision became overturned by the terrible wail of the Gierj. The convergence of power through Maelgrim's focus frayed Taen's talent until the battlefield below became form and movement without meaning, a nightmare afflicting a mind that did not seem her own.

Stressed to distraction, she had no choice but to abandon her efforts. If she persisted, her meddling might earn the imperiled soldiers a quicker end on the swords of Maelgrim's apparitions. The horses were her assigned responsibility. Firmly Taen took them in hand, to lead them away from the tumult before the powers of Stormwarden and Firelord joined the battle. She managed a scant dozen paces before Anskiere's staff flared active at the crest of the rise.

Light stabbed forth amid chaos. Wards surged and crackled into readiness and triple purple halos scattered ghost glints amid the dew. Storm wind followed, whipping droplets like sparks into darkness.

The horses balked. Intimidated by their huge strength, Taen stroked the sweat-sheened tautness of their necks and coaxed, without success. That moment, Ivainson Firelord engaged his mastery. He built the blaze gathered from Seitforest higher and hotter, until flames ripped skyward with a roar that deafened thought.

The big gelding reared. Wrenched off her feet, Taen shouted, but could not bring it down. Her own mount and Jaric's mare wheeled together. Rather than suffer dismemberment, she let the reins burn through her fingers. The knots at the ends broke her grip with a jerk. As the horses shied and thundered wildly off into the night, Jaric and Anskiere joined forces. The combined intensity of their powers lit the heavens, and burned a baleful, fiery glow over the battlefield beneath.

Taen scarcely noticed. Tumbled in a heap on damp grass, she cursed like a fishwife and sucked skinned knuckles. Above her, the directives of two sorcerers merged. A screaming cyclone of wind wrapped itself in fire, then ripped downslope to the destruction of the risen dead.

The energy struck with the immediacy of a lightning flash. Cavalry bolted in panic. Live men broke ranks and fled before the conflagration; the Kielmark's band wheeled and fell back along with them. But the demon-possessed marched yet, blindly oblivious to ruin. Fires overtook them with a roar like storm surf.

Bones danced an instant in silhouette; whirled like sticks into tangles, thousands of corpses ignited and burned. Rickety fists clenched weapons that heated white, then splashed molten to the earth. Trees exploded into torches. Skulls bounced and rolled over the ground, eye sockets streaming cinders.

The fire seared forth, utterly without discrimination, and razed all in its path. Wounded men and disabled horses screamed and died in agony. The flames raged and cracked and licked outward until the entire valley west of the Redwater lay mantled in scarlet and gold.

Only then did the onslaught cease; between one breath and the next, the fury of sorcery died.

Flame flicked out as if snuffed by darkness. The ground where Maelgrim's atrocities had marched lay black as a pall of death. Charred weeds and bushes tasseled with embers rimmed a field veiled heavily in smoke; feathers of ash sifted earthward. At a price terrible to behold, no bones remained to rise and kill. The song of the Gierj that had animated Shadowfane's army was disrupted at last to ragged and impotent disharmony.

At the brow of the hill, Anskiere quenched his staff and glanced over his shoulder. "Now, Taen!"

Below him, the men at arms left living cheered with hysterical relief. Some banged swords on their shields, but the Dream-weaver could not share in the victory. Called to sever the Dark-dreamer's link with his Gierj, she flung herself deep into trance.

* * *

Dream-sense showed Taen a place of damp, cold stone, and a sensation of dizzy height. Chills touched her, as awareness embraced Maelgrim's lair in the watchtower at Morbrith. The sense of evil lurking inside made her quail. Torches in wrought-iron brackets licked the walls with orange light. Over dissonant eddies of Gierj-whistle she heard a clink of wire; that small sound became her guide.

The Dark-dreamer of Shadowfane leaned by the south-facing window, flicking silver bracelets with his thumb. Night sky framed a face more finely drawn than Taen recalled. Under level brows his eyes shone enormous, depthless as smoke, and entirely devoid of humanity.

"Well met, my sister." Maelgrim bowed in the high style learned in Kisburn's court. "Though I'd say your rescue of Corlin was flamboyantly overdone."

Taen ignored the jeer. A secretive attempt to read the entity that inhabited the flesh of her brother yielded a barrage of viewpoints, as if he perceived his surroundings through multiple sets of eyes. The experience left her queasy and disoriented. The task of separating the minds of demon from host lay beyond her abilities; Maelgrim's mind was *other*, transformed by Gierj contact to the point where even his thoughts were alien. But Stormwarden and Firelord had engaged desperate measures to gain this opening. For their sake, for Corlin's, and for the fact that this atrocity sent from Shadowfane had once been her sibling, Taen had to try.

"The boy you called Emien was pathetic, frightened of everyone and most of all himself." Maelgrim smiled, and the familiarity of the expression wrenched his sister's heart.

"I have no brother." Wary of his malice, Taen probed for a weakness. Maelgrim permitted her search. That in itself offered warning. Her powers were useless here; if she lingered, she risked more than her life.

"You guard the wrong front, my sister." Maelgrim lowered his arm. Bracelets jangled around the heel of his hand, and as if the gesture signaled attack, the Gierj-song's pitch leveled out.

The Dreamweaver never registered their recovery. Demon power crested too swiftly for thought, battering against her senses and threatening her identity with chaos.

Belatedly, Taen strove to rally. In the instant before retreat became necessity, she hammered her query home, and confirmed her worst suspicion. Maelgrim struck now to wound more than human soldiers. The arm and the instrument of Shadowfane, he moved to cut down the only living resource capable of marring the demons' plans of conquest. His target now was Anskiere of Elrinfaer, and after, the Firelord, Ivainson Jaric.

"No!" Taen understood her position was futile. She challenged anyway.

Maelgrim retaliated. His power lanced her mind, cast her away as an ox might shudder off an offending fly. Taen knew darkness. Hedged in by the dagger prick of her brother's desire to see her broken in defeat, she raised a stinging lattice of wards. Yet Maelgrim only toyed with her. His laughter filled her ears, and contact with Morbrith sundered in a ripping flash of pain.

Hurled to her knees on stony ground, Taen twisted to avoid a fall. A hand caught her, Jaric's, red-lit by the aura of his drawn sword. He stood alone on the hilltop, amid weeds and rocks and a windy expanse of night sky.

The Dreamweaver drew breath in alarm. "Where's Anskiere?"

"Down there." Jaric inclined his head toward the valley where, by the dying flicker of fires, men at arms converged around the tall presence of the Stormwarden. "He went to advise the troop captains."

Tiny with distance, the army looked like an array of toy figurines; except that the weapons were sharp enough to kill, and the blood on the surcoats had not been painted on for effect. "Signal the Stormwarden back." Shrill with dread, Taen qualified. "He's in danger."

Before she could finish, the Dark-dreamer struck. Taen engaged her talent to ward, but Maelgrim foiled her. His thrust was not shaped against Anskiere himself. Instead, Shadowfane's minion attacked the undefended mind of the man at the sorcerer's back.

Gierj-power overran the victim's will in an instant. Enslaved utterly by enemy compulsion, the soldier drew his dagger and lunged to stab the Stormwarden from behind.

Taen cried out. Panic constricted her talents. She closed her eyes, strove frantically to recover control enough to warn before treachery struck Anskiere down. But her attempt to establish rapport opened a buffeting channel of sensations. Savaged by a flare of cruel heat, she heard the ringing scream of a man in his final agony.

Surely the possessed man's dagger had found its mark. Crushed by grief and failure, the Dreamweaver looked to find the Stormwarden unharmed within a cordon of stupefied men at arms.

The possessed man who had attempted murder writhed in

flame at Anskiere's feet, felled by Ivainson's conjuring. A senior officer sprang to end the traitor's suffering. As his sword rang from his scabbard, Taen sensed echoes of laughter through the Gierj-song. Before she could rally, the Dark-dreamer struck again.

The officer on the field completed his mercy stroke. With no break in motion, he turned his fouled blade and lunged to murder the sorcerer beside him.

On the hilltop, Jaric gasped as if he had been hit. Again he summoned fire. Dazzled by glare from the backlash, Taen perceived her brother's diabolical design. Maelgrim intended to continue, forcing one man after another to raise arms. Anyone in the field might turn assassin at his command. Taen's talents could never extend far enough to secure the minds of an entire war host. If the Stormwarden was to be saved, Jaric might be forced to massacre every living ally from Corlin.

The night seemed suddenly cold beyond bearing. Taen shivered miserably in dew-drenched weeds, arms clenched around her knees. Her spirit reeled in the throes of bleakest despair. She dared not think of the Firelord, whose distaste for violence could not be reconciled with killing, even to defend the Stormwarden's life.

Yet power rose again at Jaric's bidding. Through empathy compelled by love, Taen suffered equally as the death screams of Maelgrim's victims cut her man to the marrow; she shared guilt and the tearing effort of each successive counterstrike.

"This has to end!" Jaric cried at last.

Below, the Kielmark had perceived Anskiere's peril. Heedless of complications, the sovereign of Cliffhaven gathered his men and stormed recklessly through the ranks toward the center of conflict. His loyalty only courted tragedy; the killing intensity of his fury would make a ready tool for Maelgrim's Gierj.

Jaric closed his fists in an agony of helplessness. Hoarse with self-loathing, racked by the possibility he might be forced to cut down a friend, he appealed in desperation to his Dreamweaver. "Can't you fashion a ward that the Gierj-crazed can't pass?"

Taen lifted her head. The Firelord awaited her reply, desperate as the time he had first scaled the ice cliffs to answer Anskiere's summons. Haunted and horrified and self-betrayed, he fought to thwart the demon-possessed, while she herself had withdrawn, disheartened. Such passivity from her was wrong in a way that defied reason. Jaric regarded her with sudden clear-eyed concern. "Little witch, what's amiss?"

His words sparked revelation. Abruptly aware of outside interference, Taen perceived with damning clarity that her emotions
themselves had become the tool of Maelgrim's design. Snared
during her sally in the tower, she had apparently fallen victim to
his control.

❦ XIII ❦

The Reaving

Before Taen could sound her inner depths to assess the extent of Maelgrim's stay-spell, Anskiere raised the powers of his staff.

In the valley, sorcery shattered darkness as the auras of his weather wards sprang active. Purple glare lit the nightmare reality of another man drawing steel under Maelgrim's influence. Anskiere slapped his attacker off balance with a gust. The man fell heavily upon his back, winded, but struggling still to raise his sword.

Jaric could no longer spare Taen his concern. Determined to avert another killing, he engaged Earthmastery from the hilltop. At his bidding the grasses whipped into rope and bound the assassin's body at feet and wrists. The measure was stopgap, an inadequate diversion that could last no more than a minute.

Struggling still to recover her initiative, Taen caught the echo of Maelgrim's amusement. His laughter mocked her efforts, and cast a veil of confusion over the disciplines of her craft. Still helpless, she felt the Dark-dreamer counter Jaric's ward by releasing control of his victim's mind.

The officer under demon influence recovered self-awareness instantaneously. Denied any memory of his assault upon Anskiere, he discovered himself shackled by earth sorcery. The bodies of slaughtered companions smoldered in the weeds nearby. Over them loomed Anskiere of Elrinfaer, his eyes like chipped ice, and his staff charged with energy like a storm front.

The officer screamed in terror. "Kor's Fires! We're betrayed like the folk of Tierl Enneth!"

Only those men who were closest had seen the attempted assassination. Blocked by the press, the ranks behind knew only that the situation seemed suddenly, dangerously wrong; already traumatized by sorcery on a scale that defied understanding, their commanders shouted orders.

The army raised weapons. Light from the Stormwarden's spells spangled a steely hedge of swords, halberds, and axes with edges angled to charge; archers reached to string bows, and lancers took to horse.

Anskiere raised his staff. Hair whipped back from his face as he bound his waxing powers into whirlwind, to be turned in self-defense against enemies that were human.

But these men were misguided, not possessed. The Stormwarden poised to destroy could not know that his attackers acted outside the Dark-dreamer's influence. Taen stiffened her back. Though she wrestled yet to disengage Maelgrim's restraint, more ordinary means remained to stem the rush of the army.

"Frighten them," she cried to Jaric. "They're not deprived of wits, and they'll run." The tactic might work; certainly panic would make the men at arms more difficult for Maelgrim and his Gierj to manipulate.

Yet sorcery did not answer immediately. On the ridge, the Firelord stood like rock, his face tipped toward a sky pinpricked with stars. His expression seemed strange and remote as he slowly raised his sword.

Light slashed the darkness. Dazzled by an overwhelming discharge of power, the Dreamweaver glimpsed gold-barred feathers. Above her, the light-falcon which once had summoned her to the Isle of the Vaere unfolded wings that spanned the breadth of the heavens. The bird screamed. Its crested head swiveled, eyes of burning yellow surveying the army massed to kill in the valley. Jaric spoke a word. Air hissed between spread pinions; then, with awesome and terrible grace, the focused manifestation of his power sprang aloft. It swooped down upon the ranks of Anskiere's attackers, trailing a wake of crackling flame.

Maelgrim Dark-dreamer sensed the rising flux of power. Pressed by the threat raised by Jaric, his attention shifted; and in that instant, Taen cut through his block and broke free. The crippling despair lifted from her, just as the effects of the Ivainson's conjury reached the valley.

The light-falcon's flight cut the night like a blade heated red from the forge. Scalded by wind off its wings, men looked up, their shouts of alarm transformed to a chorus of terror. No

weapon would avail against the unleashed projection of a Firelord's anger. Most men broke formation and fled. But maddened
by the appearance of certain doom, others leveled weapons and
charged vengefully upon the sorcerer who still stood vulnerable
in their midst.

Yet the Stormwarden stayed his hand. Whirlwinds shrieked in
check in response to Taen's plea for time to engage her dream-
sense. This time Maelgrim's meddling did not cripple her. She
magnified fear into a weapon, striking panic into hostile minds
until, in a rush, the last men broke and ran.

Alone in the wash of light from his staff, Anskiere damped the
winds of his conjuring. Wrapped in smoke and a drifting fall of
ash, he bent his head in sorrow for the dead heaped grotesquely at
his feet.

On the hilltop, stillness reigned. Jaric sheathed his sword. All
expression erased from his face as he said, "We'd better go
down."

Taen sensed the emotions he held in check, even under cover
of darkness. She ached to touch him, but sympathy could not
comfort. The survivors of Corlin's army might flee safely to town
walls and their Duke; but the measure of Maelgrim's victory remained. Word of the sorcery that had unhinged this war host's
manhood would travel the breadth of Keithland. Folk would believe that the malice of Ivain Firelord had been reborn in his heir.
Hereafter, Jaric could expect locked doors, and welcome at no
man's hearth.

Taen shared the chill of that rejection. She averted her face, as
the sacrifices forced upon a man of gentle nature opened a wound
near-impossible to bear. But sorrow, even bitterness, was a reaction too costly to indulge. The crisis was not over. Even now
Maelgrim whipped up his Gierj for a second attack. Too likely
this time his targeted victims would be innocents, the women,
children, and elders who sheltered within Corlin's walls.

"The Dark-dreamer will be stopped," said Jaric, his voice a
reflection of Taen's fear. "If we have to rip down the fortress of
Morbrith to achieve it, your brother will never again wield
Gierj." Hands clenched on his sword hilt, he strode forward to
join Anskiere.

The Dreamweaver followed, bitterly silent. The rending of
Morbrith's battlements could help nothing. Maelgrim and his
demons had grown too powerful to stop by force of arms. Only
sorcery remained, and there the Vaere-trained had run out of resource. A Dreamweaver's gifts by themselves were not enough,

and with horses the fastest means of travel, distance prevented Stormwarden and Firelord from launching an assault in time to spare disaster.

Taen was not alone in her assessment. Ivainson reached the boundary of a farmer's pasture and paused with his hands on board fence. "What about the relief garrison from Corlin? After this, we'd be fools to order an army north to Morbrith."

The Dreamweaver tried to match his restraint, and failed. Her voice shook. "I've warned the Kielmark. The companies raised at his command already return to their Duke. But the King of Pirates insisted on coming himself." At Jaric's unspoken protest, she shrugged. "I can ward the man's mind from Maelgrim's Gierj more easily than I could stop him, I think."

Jaric caught her close. "Little witch," he murmured into her hair. "I'm sorry."

His clothing smelled of cinders and sweat. Pressed against him, Taen felt fine tremors wrack his body. Powerless to ease his distress, or the slightest bit of her own, she made a stilted effort at humor. "I'd rather be here than wait out the conflict at Cliffhaven. Do you suppose Corley's got a blade left that isn't sharpened down to a needle?"

Jaric raised her in his arms and perched her on top of the fence. "I doubt that. The Kielmark has steel enough in his armory to choke the channel through Mainstrait. And look, he's reached Anskiere before us."

Taen twisted around to see a broad-shouldered figure with blood-stained gauntlets striding toward the Stormwarden. The sovereign Lord of Cliffhaven had taken charge with his usual impetuous initiative; with reins gripped in both fists, he towed four shying horses by main force over the scorched and corpse-strewn field.

"Kor," said the Dreamweaver. Strain broke at last before laughter. "Did he have to anticipate the possibility we wouldn't be mounted? Put me in the saddle again, and I swear by Kor's fires, I'll die of a fall."

"Do that and I'll jump after you." The Firelord vaulted the fence and raised his hands to lift her down. "Some things are more important to me than Keithland. Now will you walk, or because there are horses, must I drag you?"

The Stormwarden paced the ravaged earth of the battlefield. Except for the Kielmark's presence, he walked alone, a dark figure against a darker expanse of seared and trampled landscape.

His clothing was silted with ash, and his features were like flint from suppressing sorrow and exhaustion. "The Gierj still sing," he observed as Jaric and the Dreamweaver arrived. His voice showed all of his concern.

Enchantress and Firelord were equally weary and soiled. Jaric had thrown off his fine tunic. Clad in the singed linen of his shirt and hose, he looked haunted by the sorrows of the damned. Taen's robes were crumpled from her sitting unprotected in the dew. Her spirits seemed little better. She halted well clear of the Kielmark's horses and called answer to Anskiere over the restive stamp of hooves. "I couldn't stop the Gierj. Maelgrim has grown too strong. Perhaps if we rode to Morbrith . . ."

The Stormwarden stopped abruptly. "We dare not. With Gierjlings still active, to go closer would invite failure and Corlin's certain doom. Taen, the Firelord and I must lend your mastery support. If we can channel our powers through your gift, you must try again to break your brother's link with the Gierj."

Yet the risks of that suggestion were surely too perilous to contemplate. Had the ground not been littered everywhere with the charred bones of corpses, Taen would have gone to her knees and pleaded to be quit of the Stormwarden's request. No need in Keithland could be great enough to demand such responsibility of her. She controlled but a single Sathid crystal, where Anskiere and Jaric each held mastery of two. For the Dreamweaver to merge minds with them offered the doubled effects of an exponential increase in power. That Taen by herself should trust her lesser discipline to wield the combined might of Stormwarden and Firelord was unthinkable, a transgression of natural limits no desperation would sanction.

"I dare not," she protested.

Jaric steadied her from behind, yet he offered no further encouragement. Anskiere remained silent also, his eyes impenetrable as sheet silver. Neither Stormwarden nor Firelord would compel her to attempt this most dangerous of undertakings. Nor would the sorcerers badger her if she lacked enough courage to try.

The Kielmark had no such scruples. "Girl, you must." He stood like an anchor against the drag and plunge of the horses. "What end could be worse than conquest by Shadowfane's compact?"

"If I failed," Taen said, so softly her voice became lost in the empty landscape. Only a sorcerer bonded to Sathid might understand the consequences. The smallest mistake would bring backlash, an uncontrolled burst of power capable of unleashing cataclysm. The disasters at Tierl Enneth and Elrinfaer would seem but a pittance before the ruin courted by stakes such as these. First among thousands of casualties would be the same Vaere-trained defenders who upheld mankind's last hope of survival.

The choice was one Taen begged to avoid; could time turn backward, she would have asked her lame leg back, and her talents left latent, to unsay Anskiere's words. Not least was the anguish of chancing such unprincipled power to destroy one born as her brother.

Alone of them all, Jaric seemed to recall this; he gathered her firmly against his shoulder. "Maelgrim's death need not be on your hands, little witch. Confine his Gierj-powers under ward, and Anskiere or I will wield the sword."

"Or I," the Kielmark said quickly. "I've not forgotten the oath of debt I swore to the Dreamweaver who spared Cliffhaven from invasion."

But in the end, the support of friends and Firelord did not help. Taen was forced to decision as her brother whipped up his Gierj for renewed assault upon humanity. Even as she deliberated, demonsong resonated against her awareness, invasive enough to paralyze thought. Reflexively Taen cast wards about her dream-sense, yet this time no precaution sufficed. Maelgrim's forces built, and coiled, and beat against her mind, prying to gain entry. The horses milled against the Kielmark's restraint as if crazed, and the very earth went still as the Dark-dreamer marshaled his powers to destroy.

Compelled by a greater fear than failure, Taen slipped clear of Jaric's embrace. She encompassed both sorcerers and the Kielmark with a look that was poignant to acknowledge. In the heat of crisis, how easy it had been to overlook the fact that the Dreamweaver was younger in actual years than her body appeared.

Yet when she spoke, her voice was steady. "By Kor's divine mercy, act swiftly."

"Jaric!" Anskiere spoke sharply.

The Firelord wrested his gaze from the Dreamweaver's. Concern for Taen might inhibit an expedient that might endanger her; though he could be trusted to find his equilibrium in the face of Keithland's need, the slightest delay might cripple their chance to stop Maelgrim. Anskiere took no risk, but raised the powers of his staff at once.

The wards flared active with a crackling explosion of light. To merge with him, Jaric must match the force with conjury of equal and opposite intensity. Blank-faced, he drew his sword. Less fluid than Anskiere, but growing daily more proficient at his craft, he wove sorcery until the halos surrounding staff and sword stood configured in mirror image.

The orange-red light of Firemastery merged gradually into the blue-white glare of storm sorcery. With trepidation, Taen readied herself for what no training offered by the Vaere had prepared her for; as the auras of both sorcerers joined into a halo of incandescent brilliance, she had but a second to brace her will. Then Stormwarden and Firelord caught her into the link.

A hammer wall of force slammed Taen's mind. Utterly overwhelmed, her senses became sundered from reality as a torrent like white-heated magma coursed across her dream-sense. The channels of her awareness burned raw under the pressure. Heightened sensitivities escaped control, and she felt as if her spirit were blasted headlong into the void before creation.

Colors streamed past her inward eye. Her ears were buffeted by unidentifiable sound. Taen struggled to orient, to bridle the forces raging wild within her. Yet even the most basic discipline of her craft failed. As she reached for mastery, her awareness imploded to a pinpoint focus that threatened to pierce her very being. Power that tore with the cataclysmic force of the tides unexpectedly responded to a feather-light touch.

The irony daunted; Taen faltered, directionless in the flood. Afraid to grapple for command lest she misjudge and destroy herself, she knew if she held herself passive she would be equally lost.

"Imagine you could balance a boulder on the shaft of a needle." The voice was Jaric's, and the encouragement an observation gained from his recent initiation to the handling of shared power.

The Firelord's advice seemed simple. Taen fought to embrace the forces that ravaged her inner self, but found them too potent. Her awareness could not encompass such depths, or the dizzy breadth of vision that great power required. Brought to her knees by the scope of her own inadequacy, she struggled through other channels to grasp the subtleties that Jaric had striven to impart.

The knowledge she required was inherent in the minds of the sorcerers who shared their access to power; but the key to true partnership, the path of Jaric's new learning, lay twined through skeins of association. Taen reached forth and became entangled in memories whose vividness shattered thought.

Anskiere's past touched her first. Through him, Taen relived an earlier backlash, the result of a stolen wardspell that brought destruction upon Tierl Enneth. The Dreamweaver felt the rumble of the wave that had arisen to rip homes and men and all their children, wives, and livestock from the shores. She heard the suck and boom of the waters, the splintering of wood. Droves of people fled with their mouths opened wide with screaming.

Yet no mortal could outrace the sea. The cries of the doomed became buried amid tumbling masonry, the falling, grinding crash as an entire generation met its end by drowning. Spray fountained like jewels over the collapsing tiles of the rooftops, then cascaded into waters congested with flotsam. The terrible wave receded, dragging dark swirls of current through a city's ruined beauty; the agony afterward became unbearable. Taen recoiled in an anguish only partly the Stormwarden's: too easily, Tierl Enneth's misfortune might become Hallowild's.

She voiced an unthinking protest. *'Having failed Tierl Enneth, how could you ask this trial of me?'*

Anskiere fielded her accusation with equanimity. *'I made no choice without discretion. Should a Vaere-trained Dreamweaver be compared with a thief enslaved by demons? Merya Tathagres was driven by the greed of the compact. She had no understanding of the powers she stole and tampered with. But if I am wrong, Taen, and my judgment stands in error, better that Keithland's north shore comes to ruin through backlash than fall in malice to the Dark-dreamer. As one born and trained to rule, I say this risk is justified.'* Here the sorcerer who had once been heir to Elrinfaer's crown paused. All the years of his sorrows rang through the nets that bound three Vaere-trained minds together. *'Never did I claim to welcome such a choice.'*

Humility leached away Taen's fury. Power ripped at her senses, made her body ache for a refusal that now was too late to sanction. Jaric had risked his father's madness; Anskiere had seen Tierl Enneth destroyed and before that the ruin of his own fair kingdom of Elrinfaer. Neither man had abjured either sorcery or responsibility. Could she do less and find peace anywhere in Keithland? Cold to the heart, and ridden with doubt, Taen imagined that she balanced a boulder on the shaft of a needle. She immersed herself within the terrible nexus of powers and somehow achieved a response

Dream-sense answered, but not in any familiar manner. Taen

experienced her native talent with a scope and intensity incomprehensibly wide. Her awareness engaged fully with the powers of Stormwarden and Firelord, and the margin of safety narrowed to a thread. If her touch was too bold, she would upset the balance of the link; and if she acted too timidly, Maelgrim's attack would sweep her defenses away before any ward could be conceived to restrain him.

The Dreamweaver focused and gained a vision of Morbrith castle that dizzied in its clarity. The view lay silvered in moonlight, the stone of tower and barbican slashed with ink-deep shadow. Where normally the initial probe would encompass visuals alone, the added talents of Firelord and Stormwarden colored the result; Morbrith rang with emptiness, a queer, brooding presence like coming storm. Breezes soughed through fields overgrown with weeds. Grasses habitually grazed short by livestock waved tasseled heads in the pastures. Dream-sense blended with glimmers of an Earthmaster's perception, of soil leached by unharvested crops and unclipped hedgerows. Stone itself spoke through the link, alive with the glint of mica and the captive heat of sunlight.

Taen was in no way tempted to explore this rich influx of sensation. Her borrowed powers encompassed the city of Morbrith from flag spires to dungeons in a fraction of an instant; amid the wonders of nature and the varied invention of man, the pervasive presence of Maelgrim and his Gierj stood out like rot in the heart of a flower. Even as the Dreamweaver recognized the enemy, Shadowfane's Dark-dreamer sensed her presence.

He struck with the speed of a snake.

Taen had no time to consider consequences, but only to react as energy arose like a whirlwind to crush her. The counterward she crafted sprang up with the brilliance of lightning flash, combining the strengths of three Vaere-trained masters. Stonework seared, and the air flashed fire. Maelgrim howled curses in surprise.

He emerged unscathed. Vexed mightily, and aware that Stormwarden and Firelord had joined their talents to bring him down, he rallied his Gierj. Taen felt his hatred as a storm wind of malice and murder that threatened to smother her defense. She fought an influx of nightmare; if she succumbed, Maelgrim and his demons would rend her mind. They would take their pleasure and hideously dismember her body before she died. The Dreamweaver retained her grip against a wave of stark horror. Maelgrim was too strong. Unless she acted instantly, the combined powers of Stormwarden and Firelord would not be sufficient to thwart the evil her brother had become. Scared to defensive desperation, Taen seized the powers of the link. Heedless of peril, she wove energy into bands that crackled and burned, then forged the result into a barrier to imprison.

The walls of Morbrith defined her outer bastion. To stone and mortar and the metal of lock and drawbridge she added bindings fashioned of sorcery. As the patterns of her labors bloomed in light over postern and gate towers, she felt other forces twine with hers. Finely spun as spider silk, but stronger than drawn wire, Stormwarden and Firelord joined their own spells through the link. Anskiere's long years of experience at confining demon-kind made his handiwork practiced and swift. Before Maelgrim could raise counterwards, the lattice of Taen's prison became anchored by spells wrought of air and weather. Jaric joined in, adding stay-spells rooted like knotwork through the heart rock of earth and stone.

Maelgrim immediately divined his predicament. Gierj-song shivered the air, and his counterthrust shot sparks against the shimmer of the wardspells. Yet the barrier deflected his sally in a pulse of blinding light. Morbrith keep remained unbreached. The Dark-dreamer's cry of rage and frustration echoed among deserted towers, then diminished. Before his last hope of freedom could be sealed, Maelgrim resorted to guile.

Gierj-song breached Taen's shield. In an image keen as a knife slash, she saw her brother, cruelly exploited by demons and pleading a sister's forbearance. Let her hand turn from redress to mercy, let the smallest measure of forgiveness be granted, and Marlson Emien vowed to turn coat on his demon masters. Morbrith's fate might be shared by Shadowfane, and mankind's survival be assured.

"No!" Taen's denial echoed over towers whose occupants were dead beyond redemption. Inured to loss as were her fisherman forebears, she locked sorrow and grief in an iron heart. The boy Emien had chosen his own course; the betrayals that had brought him to his transformation at Shadowfane had revoked any right of reprieve. Yet even as Taen Dreamweaver held equilibrium, the powers of Stormwarden and Firelord faltered. In horror she saw that Maelgrim had breached the link.

The images he inflicted were personal and poisonously cruel. Anskiere of Elrinfaer saw his royal sister, who had died with her kingdom under the depredations of the Mharg. Young, alone, she sat weeping with a crown she had never wanted pressed hopelessly between her hands. Over and over she cursed her brother, for leaving his inheritance to her in his pursuit of Vaerish knowledge. For all his sorcerer's mastery, the Stormwarden was not present to intercede when creatures out of nightmare dropped from the sky and slaughtered Elrinfaer's citizens in the street.

The intensity of the princess's grief was too detailed to be anything other than real. Taen saw that demons had garnered this moment through Mharg-memory, then saved it as a weapon against just such a moment as this. The impact caused guilt enough to shatter Anskiere's poise.

'Free me,' Maelgrim begged. *'Let my powers avenge your beloved sister who died of Shadowfane's designs.'*

Taen did not linger to know how the Stormwarden would resolve his trial of grief and guilt. Worried for Jaric, she reached through the link and found him racked by his own vision of hell. This image was recent, and Maelgrim's own, and vicious enough to stun. For Jaric, Morbrith bailey danced to a bloody flare of light. There, bound with wire to a horse hitch, the master scribe who had championed his cause as a boy writhed in a pyre of flame. Fuel for Iveg's torment was a cache of books and scrolls, the scholarly achievements of a lifetime kindled to roast his flesh.

While Stormwarden and Firelord were diverted, the wards over Morbrith stood in jeopardy. The Dreamweaver acted out of reflex, driven by anger akin to madness. Across Maelgrim's dark dreaming she crafted images of her own, the separate suffering of every soul she had battled to save, and lost, through her months in the borderlands of Morbrith. Children, parents, and elders, she recounted each death distinctly; the agonies of each victim's final minutes distilled to a sorrow overpowering for its cruelty.

As the compact's minion, Maelgrim met her vision of suffering with venomous amusement. But Stormwarden and Firelord screamed with one voice. Reminded of their purpose, they rallied. Power surged back into the link. Now anguish for a tortured scribe and guilt for an abandoned sister became edges honed against a common enemy. Joined in grim purpose, the Vaere-trained of Keithland sealed the wards over Maelgrim's prison. As their combined sorceries fused complete, a shriek of defeat and frustration rang over the wail of the Gierj. The sound was savage enough to daunt the spirit. No mortal could listen, and linger.

The link-born power died out with a snap. Taen relinquished the discipline of trance. Sore to the bone, she opened tired eyes and reoriented her awareness to a battlefield long leagues to the south.

Ashes gritted under her knees. Her hair fell in tangles around her cheeks, tear-soaked, and acrid with the smell of smoke. Taen shook it back. She lifted a face pale with stress to the Stormwarden and Firelord, who stood near, shaken still from the shock of her counterdefense. Shivering herself, Taen drew a difficult breath. She did not voice what all of them already knew: Maelgrim might be mewed up within Morbrith, but his Gierj still sang. Though tired and harrowed to the heart, the three of them had no choice but ride north without delay.

Efficient in all respects, the Kielmark had selected his horseflesh with an unerring eye for the best. Though mounted on a blooded, blaze-faced mare of prized Dunmoreland stock, Taen failed to appreciate the Pirate Lord's expertise. Her knees chafed raw on a saddle intended for a large man, and the animal underneath it pulled like a steer, skinning her fingers on the reins. She cursed and tugged, and barely managed to match pace with the gelding that carried Jaric.

Anskiere rode ahead on a cream stud conscripted at swordpoint from a dandy. Its harness sparkled with a crust of silver and pearls, but threads now trailed where bells had hung from the saddlecloth; in disgust the Stormwarden had ripped the ornaments away. The Kielmark brought up the rear, on a black that snorted with each stride. He sat his saddle with an air of wolfish intensity, one hand poised on his blade.

Yet as the company set off for Morbrith, both silence and vigilance seemed wasted. No travelers fared on the road. Houses by the wayside lay deserted, and the crossroads settlement of Gaire's Main stood abandoned and dark when they stopped to breathe the horses. Spring water trickled mournfully from the stone trough, but livestock no longer drank the run-off. Neglect left holes in thatched roofs, and the inn bulked black by starlight, one door drunkenly ajar.

The Kielmark was quick to remount. Anxious to leave the deserted village, Anskiere and Jaric followed him to horse. No one seemed inclined to speak, since the ordeal of warding Morbrith. Taen swung into the saddle last. Though distracted by the need to review the security of her work, she still remained open to the sensitivities of others. Jaric had passed through Gaire's Main the time he had fled Morbrith on a stolen mount. Now the inept stablemaster who had reshod his horse was dead, along with the young girl who had offered him charity out of pity. Murdered on the brink of womanhood by Shadowfane's possessed, she had neither grave nor kin to remember her. Only chance-met travelers who had passed through Gaire's Main before Maelgrim's devastation might recall that the girl had lived at all.

Weary and sad, Taen let her mount lean into a canter. Gaire's Main fell swiftly behind. The road to Morbrith stretched northward, silver under a haze of ground mist; the mare tried restively to gallop ahead of the others. The Dreamweaver tightened raw fingers and winced as the horse shook its head. It bounced one stride in protest before responding to the rein.

Jaric swerved his gelding to avoid being jostled. "Doesn't that mare know she should be tired by now?"

Taen shook her head. "She smells me for a fisherman's daughter and knows I hate riding."

Only, looking at her, with her brows leveled by an intent frown and her back held straight by something indefinably more than courage, Jaric reflected otherwise. Her childhood in the fishing village of Imrill Kand was behind her now; at no time in life had she ever seemed more like the Vaere-trained enchantress she had become.

Night passed, measured by drumming hoofbeats. The stars to the east paled above the rolling hills of the downs, yet dawn did not lessen the shadow of danger. Each passing league brought the riders nearer to final confrontation with Maelgrim Dark-dreamer. Threat seemed a palpable presence in the air. Unable to shake the hunch that Keithland's defenders rode toward a trap of Shadowfane's design, Taen focused her talents. Braced for the bite of Maelgrim's malice, she cast her dream-sense north to check the security of her brother's prison.

Stillness met her probe. Disturbed, Taen tried another sweep. This time she included the grounds as well as the watch towers at Morbrith. Her effort yielded nothing. Silence deep as windless waters bound the keep's tall battlements; even the pigeons had abandoned their cotes in the falconer's yard. Unnerved by the lifeless air of the place, the Dreamweaver drew a worried breath. She rebalanced her awareness, and only then noticed the absence of the Gierj-whistle. Surprise made her cry out.

Her companions drew rein in the roadway. Stopped in their midst, the Dreamweaver exclaimed in disbelief. "I've lost Maelgrim. The Gierj-whistle's stopped, and I can't track the presence of the enemy."

Anskiere drew breath with a jerk. "The wards are intact?"

Taen started to nod, then froze as she noticed a detail that first had escaped her. A small black hole lay torn through the spells that sealed the main gate. The rift was too small to admit the body of a man, but wide enough, surely, to pass the rope-thin bodies of Gierjlings.

This news raised varied reactions in the gray gloom of dawn; both Firelord and Stormwarden had contributed to the setting of those defenses; the power required to cause a breach overturned their most dire expectation. Jaric raked back hair in need of a trim; his eyes seemed distant with exhaustion under soot-streaked lashes. The Kielmark stilled with a look of rapacious speculation.

Only Anskiere straightened with a glare like frost. His hands braced on his horse's neck, he said simply, "Track the Gierj, then. If Maelgrim's left Morbrith, through whatever means, we have no choice but follow him."

"But the breach is too narrow," Taen protested. "The Dark-dreamer couldn't escape, and he can't have vanished. He shares my blood. Surely I would know if he took his own life." She blinked away rising tears, vaguely aware of Jaric's touch on her arm. The contact failed to steady her.

The creak of the cream's harness filled silence until Jaric intervened. "Kor's grace, can't you see she's upset?"

His plea was ignored. "Taen," the Stormwarden said firmly, "if Maelgrim Dark-dreamer has left Morbrith, we'll have to know at once."

~⌒~⌒~ XIV ~⌒~⌒~

Morbrith

Taen drew an unsteady breath. The surrounding landscape seemed ghostly, a place halfway between dreams and waking where nightmare could transform the ordinary without warning. She disengaged from Jaric's hold. Isolated from his sympathy by the demands of her craft, she rallied and marshaled her talents to trace Maelgrim.

Morbrith's gray walls shouldered through tatters of thinning mist, sealed off by the lacework glimmer of wardspells. Beyond, the houses loomed empty, row upon row of rooftrees outlined coldly in daylight. The Dreamweaver concentrated directly on the palace. Her probe traversed empty corridors and wide, cheerless rooms with hangings moldering on the walls. She swept bed-chambers with mildewed sheets, kitchens where rats chewed the handles of the cutlery. Pantry and granary had been ransacked by insects and mice, while the armory's stock of weaponry rusted in neat, military array.

Taen tried the libraries, and ached for Jaric when she found the door splintered inward. Parquet floors bore the stains of spilled ink flasks; dust layered shelves stripped of books. Burdened by sorrow, the Dreamweaver moved on, past the darkened windows of the guards' barracks and a gate sentry's box whitened with bird droppings. The stables beyond held the rotting carcasses of the manor's equine casualties, from the Earl's niece's pony to war destriers and carriage horses. Only the stair that led to the watchtower was not empty.

Taen found her brother in a windy cranny framed by stone keep and sky.

No Gierj were with him. His Dark-dreamer's presence had diminished to a lusterless spark of his former vitality. Shocked by the change in him, the Dreamweaver brushed his mind. Maelgrim flinched from the contact. Wire chinked as he raised his hands, as though to ward off a blow; the mad, lost light in his eyes bespoke thoughts that were directionless and confused.

Taen retreated without probing deeper. Keeping her awareness well guarded, she listened while wind moaned between Morbrith's empty battlements. Yet nothing untoward arose to challenge her. Maelgrim's condition apparently masked no tricks.

Daylight brightened steadily over pastures whose only yield was weed; the farmsteads beyond the walls lay deserted. The Gierj-demons who had expanded the Dark-dreamer's powers of destruction seemed nowhere to be found. Suspicious of their absence, the Dreamweaver extended her focus over bramble-ridden fields and orchards choked with mist.

If not for the scold of a jay, she might have overlooked the rustle of movement through the valley east of Morbrith. Gierj poured like spiders through the undergrowth, eyes flashing like mirrors filled with moonlight. They ran in silence. Steps coordinated in unison lent the disturbing impression that their movements were controlled by the hand of a mad puppeteer. The sight seeded growing uneasiness. The brother Taen found at Morbrith owned neither presence nor self-command, which meant the Gierj answered now to a new master, one whose summons came direct from Shadowfane.

The Dreamweaver dispelled her trance. Roused to the sting of saddle-galled knees, she stirred under the scrutiny of Stormwarden and Kielmark. Dismounted, Jaric stood at her mare's bridle. He restrained the restive creature with a patience that belied his exhaustion, while the Dreamweaver related her findings concerning Maelgrim, and the apparent desertion of his Gierj-circle.

She finished, feeling drained. Autumn winds whipped the brush by the roadside. The scratch of dry leaves filled silence as her companions considered the implications of an event no man understood.

"Hold the wards firm," said Anskiere. He then issued orders to ride. Jaric released his grip on Taen's reins and set foot in his own stirrup.

"You know this might be a trap!" the Dreamweaver warned. The Stormwarden set spurs to the cream; as his steed leaped to gallop, she shouted after him. "Gierj or no, Maelgrim is still possessed through his Sathid-link with demons. I doubt he's either vulnerable or helpless."

"Belay the talk, woman!" The Kielmark drew his sword and smacked the flat smartly across the mare's hindquarters. He qualified over the ensuing thunder of hooves as both their mounts flattened ears and ran. "We have no choice but go forward. Fool or otherwise, we can't let the Stormwarden ride into danger unsupported."

Blue, fierce eyes reminded that, like the wolf, the Kielmark's loyalties ran deeper than reason. Though few things in life frightened Taen so much as the change she sensed in her brother, she gave the mare rein and galloped.

Leaves scattered, brown and dead, in the wind swirling under the battlements. The bailey beyond lay deserted, the smell of moss and sun-warmed stone glaringly wrong for a keep once filled with the bustle of habitation. No sentry called challenge to the party who rode in with the morning. Silence and the ghost-glimmer of wardspells shrouded a fortress better accustomed to the ring of destriers' hooves, and the shouts of patrols returning from the border. Having loosed their own lathered mounts by the river, Jaric trailed Anskiere through the gates. A thin snap of sound marked his passage as he crossed the boundary of the wards. Taen came after, followed by the Kielmark, whose weapons and mail shirt jingled dissonantly with each stride.

Ivainson emerged from the far shadow of the arch and abruptly stopped.

"Not here." Taen shook off a compulsion to whisper. "We'll find Maelgrim farther on, within the Earl's hall."

But the Firelord gave no response. His first, sweeping survey of the holdfast where he had been born ended at the stone blocks used to hitch horses. Rusted loops of wire dangled from the rings, cruel testimony of a prisoner recently bound there. Breeze blew. The fetters swung, blackened by fire above a flattened circle of ash; amid the debris Taen saw charred leaves of parchment, recognizably the half-burnt remains of books.

The name of Morbrith's master archivist hovered, unuttered, on Jaric's lips. Taen sensed his deep and cutting grief. Although no bones remained, the Firelord beheld proof that his former master had died a tormented victim of demon caprice. "Kor's eternal grace!"

The vehemence of the blasphemy caused Anskiere to pause on the stair, a look of inquiry on his face. "Jaric?"

A shimmer gathered around Ivainson's still form. For a moment raw anger threatened to explode instantaneously into fire. Taen tensed in alarm. But the Kielmark stepped sharply forward and reached Jaric ahead of her.

"I'll skewer the Accursed who did this." The Lord of Cliffhaven wore an expression that chilled. Dangerously still in his silver-trimmed surcoat, he regarded the wire and the ruined parchment, as if to engrave the sight in his memory. Then, with a hand that half steadied, half pushed, he sent Jaric after the Stormwarden. As an afterthought, Taen recalled that the King of Pirates revered books; on Cliffhaven, his archivist was the only hale man not required to bear arms.

Moments later, the party entered the candleless gloom of the keep. Dream-sense overlaid impressions like echoes, as the ruins prompted remembrance of an elegance that now lay wholly desecrated. Backland in location alone, Morbrith's Earls had been gifted with longstanding admiration for the arts. Scrolled cornices above the doorframes had once held porcelain statuary. Liveried retainers and ladies clad in silk and jewels had laughed and listened to music in halls now gritty with the refuse of bats. Unswept stone, and soiled hangings, and the weaponed ring of the Kielmark's tread made that past seem a fanciful dream. Anskiere walked, haunted by memories of other ghosts from Elrinfaer. Harrowed beyond sorrow, for this keep had once been his home, Jaric did not mourn for himself. Instead he ached fiercely for Taen; somewhere within Morbrith waited an enemy who had once been her brother.

A stray shaft of sunlight silvered the Stormwarden's head as he followed the Dreamweaver's lead into a vaulted foyer. Four doors opened into chambers and a corridor swathed with spiderwebs. Dream-sense tugged left. Numbly Taen turned, through bronze portals chased with a hunting scene. The antechamber beyond lay heaped with broken furnishings and the moldered skeleton of a cat. Dampness from the floor chilled through the soles of her shoes. She shivered and kept on, barely aware of Jaric at her side.

"Ahead lies the hall of the High Earl." Echoes blurred the Firelord's words. "An entrance in back leads to the Lord's quarters. Servants used to claim there was a spy closet."

Taen nodded absently. The pressure against her mind grew insistent, and suddenly she knew. The bedchamber and suite of the Lord's quarters lay deserted. The spy closet, if any existed, was empty. Maelgrim Dark-dreamer waited beyond the shut panels of the great hall.

Taen stopped and pointed. Unable to move or speak, she watched Anskiere hook the lion-head door ring and pull. Silent on oiled hinges, the heavy double doors swung wide.

Brushed into motion, a pawn from a fallen chessboard rolled across waxed parquet; it vanished under rucked carpets and a jumble of overturned trestles. A lark cage swung from a scrolled pedestal, the occupant a dead and musty clump of feathers. Taen blinked. Openly trembling, she started as Jaric gathered her close in his arms. The vast chamber was deserted except for the dais, where a man sprawled in the Earl's chair of state. Even before she glimpsed black hair, Taen knew. She confronted the atrocity whose name had once been Marlson Emien.

The Kielmark drew his broadsword. He crossed the threshold like a stalking predator, his step a whisper on wood, his face a mask of controlled fury. For Corley, for the dead scribe of Morbrith, and for six companies of slaughtered men, he was set to kill out of hand. Anskiere flanked him. Rarely impatient, his princely bearing never left him; except a cold glow woke in his staff. His glance carried an edge no mortal ruler could match.

Yet the Dark-dreamer stayed strangely still in his chair. Before the threat of bared steel and sorcery, he lay as if dead.

Taen disengaged from Jaric's embrace. Wide-eyed with distress, she started for the supine form on the dais.

"Don't let her touch him," Anskiere cautioned. Lest sentiment overwhelm her good sense, the Kielmark clasped her shoulder in one mailed fist. With Taen shepherded between them, Keithland's defenders skirted a fallen trestle and mounted the steps to the dais.

Morbrith keep's chair of state jutted like a monument above the table with its seal and documents. The restored rule of the high Earl had been brief enough that he had not finished reviewing his accounts. Struck down with equal lack of warning, his conqueror sprawled with his head cradled on the emerald velvet armrest. Dark hair looped one carved post. Opened eyes shone vacant as sky above cheeks scribed with blood. More scarlet streaked from ears and nose, to pool in rusty stains at his collar. The dread Dark-dreamer of Shadowfane breathed through parted lips like a sleeper; stubble shadowed his chin. Hands that had guided a young sister to the tide pools to collect shells now rested palm upward, as if beseeching mercy. Taen caught her breath in a sob. More than ever, this man seemed the brother she recalled from Imrill Kand, but scarred in places she had not guessed, and lost in clothing too large for his underfed frame.

"When his Gierj deserted him . . ." Taen skirted the edge of breakdown, yet forced herself to qualify. "The effect wounded his mind. He feels like a vessel empty of spirit." Hesitantly she stepped closer.

"Don't touch!" warned Anskiere.

The Dreamweaver seemed not to hear. Near enough for contact, she raised a hand to her brother's shoulder. Yet even as she reached, the Kielmark's hands spun her back, into Jaric's restraining grasp. Taen cried out. Stone walls splintered her grief into echoes, deadened as Cliffhaven's sovereign pushed past. Muscles bunched in his forearm; he raised his sword over the still figure in the chair, blade angled for a mercy stroke.

Taen flinched, then buried her face in Jaric's arms. Even after the massacres at Morbrith and Corlin, and the murder of friends under Corley's command, she could not bear to watch her brother slaughtered.

The blade flashed and fell. Anskiere thrust his staff between. Steel struck brass in a dissonant jangle of sound.

The Kielmark locked eyes with the sorcerer like a wolf whose pack mate had foolishly intervened with his kill. "Are we women, faint at the thought of blood? Kor's Fires, Prince! That's not like you."

Anskiere shook his head. More than compassion tempered his reply. "No. I've not abandoned reason for mercy. For Keithland's sake, we must understand what's happened here. I very much doubt that the Dark-dreamer's collapse was anything planned by Shadowfane."

The Kielmark lowered his sword, point rested with dangerous care against the floor. "Just how will we accomplish that? Taen's not fit to sound the mind of a mouse. If you ask any more of her, I'll stop you."

Anskiere sighed with weary resignation. "I'd thought to contact the Morbrith burrow of Llondelei." The light in his staff faded slowly as he added, "Now, please, would you sheath that weapon? Gierj can't build power in the presence of steel. Between you and Jaric, we've swords enough to safeguard a garrison."

The chamber in the north spire of Shadowfane was curtained, walls and windows, with drapes of woven wool. Yet drafts still seeped through the cracks when wind swept across the fells. A swirl of chilly air teased the flame in the red-shuttered lantern. The wick guttered, thinned to a spark as Scait Demon Lord stepped through the door, into stillness and shadows.

"The Morrigierj stirs," rasped a voice from the chamber's dimmest corner. It spoke a language unknown to men, and used by demons only when contention for dominance made the sharing of thoughts an unavoidable challenge.

Scait stopped. "You say?" He narrowed sultry eyes and waited.

The voice resumed, dry over the moan of the wind beyond the drapes. "I know. Maelgrim's Gierj have deserted. The call of their true master drew them while he was engaged in mind-link. The damage caused then is irreparable. Your Dark-dreamer lies dying and Shadowfane itself is endangered."

The gust ended. Icy air mantled Scait's ankles, and the flame in the lantern brightened, throwing ruddy light over the chamber. On a reed pallet by the wall, a young Thienz with turquoise markings lay ill and gasping for air. Scait recognized the one who had bonded the Sathid that once had controlled the witch Tathagres; when Marlson Emien had stolen that matrix, the process of cross-link had inseparably paired the boy's life with that of the Thienz. The elder who attended the sick one crouched on pillows in the corner, its flesh wrinkled and hideous, and its gillflaps yellowed with age. Honor bracelets crusted all four of its limbs, badges of superior status among its fellows. As the Demon Lord crossed the chamber, the creature watched with bead-black eyes and no sign of humility.

Scait read censure in the creature's manner; short hackles prickled at his neck. "Show me."

The old Thienz delayed, implying defiance. By granting the Dark-dreamer a twelve Gierj-circle, the Demon Lord had directly jeopardized the young Thienz whose Sathid base Maelgrim shared. The old one's outrage swelled as draft eddied the lantern, and shadow dimmed the chamber once again.

Scait ruffled his hackles down, disdaining challenge. "Yes, your kind have grown few in number. But no life has passed to memory in vain. Firelord, Stormwarden, and Dreamweaver, and also the Thienz-murderer called Kielmark, are presently in Maelgrim's presence, true?"

The old Thienz pinched its lips in acquiescence.

Scait gestured. "So, then. Our control of Maelgrim will last so

long as life remains. Let us work together and arrange the downfall of enemies."

The elder demon considered and grudgingly yielded. While
the flame in the lantern stretched upright and brightened, it shuffled over to its ailing companion. There it crouched, eyes hooded
by lashless lids. Presently the one on the pallet sighed and stirred
weakly upon the cushions. Scait shifted his weight, impatient,
but the old Thienz would not be hurried. It removed an honor
bracelet and bent the ornament around the supine Thienz' wrist.
The fact that the recipient lacked strength to acknowledge the
accolade gave the Demon Lord pause; Maelgrim must be failing
fast, to have drained a Thienz to the point where it abandoned
indulgence of vanity.

At last the elder raised its head. *'To the death of enemies,'* it
sent, then passed its ludicrously tiny hand before the lantern.
Awareness joined with the underling linked to Maelgrim in
Sathid-bond, and an image shimmered to visibility above the
flame. The Earl's hall at Morbrith became manifest through the
distant eyes of the Dark-dreamer. . . .

Night darkened the high, arched windows there, but no stars
shone. Hedged by deep shadow, fallen trestles and furnishings
bulked like the broken bones of dragons against a solitary gleam
of light, a candle shielded behind panes of violet glass. Tinted
illumination was unnatural for mankind; at least one figure gathered around the stricken form of the Dark-dreamer was not
human. From the shadowy depths of a cloak hood gleamed the
eyes of a Llondian empath.

The Kielmark stood to one side, both fists clasped to his great
sword. Distrustful as he was of strangers at the best of times, the
presence of a demon called in as ally did little to settle him. He
watched with predatory vigilance as the Llondel sat forward and
laid six-fingered hands upon the unconscious form of Maelgrim
Dark-dreamer.

Taen's brother did not flinch from the touch. The tissue of his
brain had suffered massive disruption, and internal bleeding impaired what bodily function remained. After the briefest moment
of rapport, the Llondelei lifted her hands and broke contact. She
turned bleak eyes upon the humans.

*'He dies the Gierj-death, this human enslaved by Shadow-
fane.'* Her thought-image came tinged with anger, a bitterness
indefinably deep. Maelgrim's affliction resulted directly from
manipulation of a Gierj-circle. Demons at Shadowfane well un-

derstood the consequences attached to such power; they ensnared humans in Sathid-bond expressly for the purpose of manipulating Gierj-born forces without sacrificing one of their own. When their victim collapsed from hemorrhage, a replacement could always be created, until the store of stolen matrix was exhausted.

The Llondel ended with a flourish of apology and sorrow. The crystals had come to Keithland with her kind; malicious creatures from Shadowfane had plundered the heritage of the Llondelei young expressly to engineer betrayals such as Emien's, and before him, Merya Tathagres'.

The Kielmark's grip tightened on his weapon. Taen sat with her face in her hands; Jaric's arm tightened around her shoulder.

But the Stormwarden raised a face turned bleak as midwinter. His voice reflected no gentleness. "Why should the Dark-dreamer's Gierj desert, when plainly the plans of Shadowfane's demons were incomplete?"

The Llondel whistled affirmation. Her thought-image qualified, showing a smooth, spherical object that drifted at the height of a man's shoulder. Harder than rock, and defended by deadly nets of force, the thing wakened slowly to sentience. In future time, energies sparked and flared beneath its surface; Gierjlings that were its natural servants banded together and invaded Keithland, to ravage and conquer. Under their rightful overlord, their power for destruction knew no limit. Even the compact at Shadowfane feared the network of forces that Gierj might sing into being. The Llondel finished with a spoken name, Morrigierj, never before mentioned among men.

Anskiere frowned. "Then the Landfast archives are inaccurate, and the Vaere misled. No Morrigierj was ever listed among Kor's Accursed."

The Llondel whistled a minor seventh. *'Surely the records kept by men are limited. Where there are Gierj, a Morrigierj will eventually develop to focus them. But the creature takes many scores of centuries to mature. Perhaps your forebears did not know.'*

The comment met with silence. That a threat might exist more grave than the existing power of the compact was a concept that defeated hope.

Only Taen thought one step further, to a purpose that all but undid her with dread. Pale in her soiled shift, she locked gazes with the glowing eyes of the Llondel. "What if Emien wasn't the only one?" Sick inside, she reviewed Morbrith's dead, the mind of each person ruthlessly sorted before life had been pinched out with the ease of so many candle flames. Taen forced herself to speak. "Suppose Emien was expended because the demons already got what they wanted? Children with latent talent might have been stolen during his conquest of Morbrith. With no parents alive to raise outcry, who would know? Orphans might be held prisoner at Shadowfane to suffer the fate of my brother."

Air hissed over steel as the Kielmark raised his sword. He tossed the blade fiercely from right hand to left and said, "The Dreamweaver's right. And the Stormwarden deserves an apology for my words against him earlier." He gestured to the Llondel, then angled his blade toward the waxy figure of Maelgrim. "Alive, that scum might tell us for certain."

Anskiere nodded acknowledgment. Too enmeshed in concern to be astonished by a word of conciliation from the Kielmark, he spoke a phrase to the Llondel in the creature's own tongue.

The demon returned an image of stream water running uphill; but the adage perhaps held another meaning to those of her kind, for instead of rebuttal, she bent willingly and laid twig-thin fingers once more upon Maelgrim's brow. . . .

In the red-tinged gloom at Shadowfane, anger finally prevailed; the long hackles lifted at Scait's neck, and he swiped a fist through the tenuous image garnered from Maelgrim through the senses of the failing Thienz. Flattened by disturbed air, the lantern flame guttered. The vision of the Earl's hall with its gathering of men and Llondel went dark.

The Demon Lord hissed. "I've seen enough, toad. Hear my orders. Destroy the one who shares Sathid bond with Maelgrim, that the Dark-dreamer perish at once. Better they both die early than have mankind learn more of the Morrigierj and my plot to ruin Keithland."

The ancient Thienz shifted with a jingle of bracelets. It blinked eyes opaque as gimlets and responded with disarming submission. "Your will, Lord Scait."

The Demon Lord spun on his heel. Shadow swept the room as he strode between lantern and pallet, and departed. Then the outer door boomed closed, leaving the soft sigh of drafts, and the labored gasp of the injured Thienz.

The elder stroked the near-departed's gillflaps long after its master's footsteps died off down the corridor. It saw no wisdom in Scait's high-handed command, not when the Vaere-trained of Keithland had already divined the gist of Scait's intentions. Both of the Sathid-bound would be consigned to memory by morning anyway. Until then, the old Thienz chose to maintain its foothold in Maelgrim Dark-dreamer's mind.

Toward dawn, the wind stopped. The red-paned lantern burned low; the chamber at Shadowfane grew stifling with the reek of hot oil as the sickened Thienz breathed its last. Far to the south, the wracked body of Marlson Emien shuddered a final time and stilled; his wax-pale fingers loosened in death. Taen covered her face in her hands and wept.

At Shadowfane, the Thienz elder's awareness of her faded away with the essence of its departed cousin. The demon stirred stiffly from its corner. Layers of honor bracelets jingled as it rose to ungainly feet and closed the eyes of its departed. Then, with a croak of irritation mostly due to aching joints, the old one waddled out to seek Scait. It bore news of much import. Humans and Llondelei had held council during the night. Between them they had determined that demon-controlled atrocities such as Merya Tathagres and Maelgrim Dark-dreamer were a menace too grave to risk again. Even as Taen Dreamweaver mourned by the corpse of her brother, Ivainson Jaric and Kielmark Thienz-murderer mounted horses and turned east, their intent to steal Sathid from Shadowfane.

A grimace that passed for a smile cracked the old Thienz' lips. Humans might know of the Morrigierj; but Shadowfane had gained warning as well. Shortly Ivainson Firelord and the hated sovereign of Cliffhaven would be bait for the taking.

At Morbrith the night seemed to linger without end. Darkness still cloaked the high windows of the Earl's hall when the candle behind its violet glass flickered in a spent pool of wax. Taen arose from her vigil beside her brother's body. She rubbed stiffened and saddle-galled knees, then straightened her crumpled clothing. What remained of Emien, the creature that Shadowfane's demons had named Maelgrim, was gone now. The grief of his passing was not new. For a very long time, Taen had accepted the fact that she had lost a brother. During his final hour of life she had tried to take comfort from the fact that his end had come without need of an execution by the Kielmark. All that remained was to inter his body, and in that she would have the Stormwarden's help. Jaric had used Earthmastery to carve out a grave site, before he departed.

The final details of burial at least would wait till the morning. Exhausted enough that she thought she might sleep, Taen raised the lamp left by the Llondelei healer. She covered her brother's face with a tapestry, then picked her way around ruined furnishings and passed the great doors to the corridor.

Darkness closed about her, dense and musty as old velvet. Taen raised the candle to see better. The flame flickered, then died, quenched in puddled wax. Caught in the midst of a turn, Taen tripped on an edge of crumpled carpet and cursed.

That moment something beyond the keep walls chose to meddle with her wards. The Dreamweaver felt her skin prickle in the dark. She dropped the spent lantern with a crash and strove through weariness and muddled emotions to muster her talents.

Jaric and the Kielmark had ridden out more than an hour ago; unless they met trouble and turned back, no living being should remain in Morbrith to try her defenses. The alternative was daunting in the extreme, that Shadowfane's demons might already have launched an offensive. That the probe was aggressive was never in doubt. Even as Taen sent a call to warn Anskiere, the disruption came again.

She set her focus at once on the main gate. The mist there glowed silver, but not from moonlight. A robed figure stood before the arch. The glow emanated from raised hands that glittered with rings. Taen's wariness eased slightly. This was no visitor from the compact; the meddler who challenged her barrier was none other than the Magelord of Mhored Kara. Whatever cause had brought that ancient to venture from the security of his towers would not be slight. Taen guarded her relief as she dispelled trance and faced the more mundane problem posed by her spent candle.

Her powers were sorely overtaxed. The idea of using dreamsense to guide herself through the castle's darkened corridors made her head ache. Left the undignified alternative of groping, Taen resolutely trailed her fingers along the wall. After two steps she stubbed her toe roundly on a statue. She hopped, cursing irritably, then compounded her difficulties by banging her elbow against a torch bracket. Her yelp of pain drew notice.

Shadow splintered before a harsh glare of sorcery. Dazzled, Taen squinted. She managed to identify the triple halos of the Stormwarden's staff before she tripped on another rucked edge of carpet and stumbled unceremoniously to her knees.

Anskiere caught her arm in time to spare her from a fall full length upon the floor. "I was just coming to look for you." Worry shaded his tone. "Is something wrong?"

"Maybe." Taen took full advantage of the sorcerer's support and pulled herself to her feet. A wry smile bent her lips. She had

to be the first to be rescued from the perils of the dark by powers
better suited to harnessing storms off the Corine Sea. "We've got
a visitor."

Her evident amusement gave Anskiere space to relax. He
damped the intensity of his staff and rested the brass-shod end
against the floor with studied care. "I gather no one dangerous."

"You'd know better than any." Taen's humor fled. "Waiting at
the gate and demanding admittance is His Eminence the Magelord of Mhored Kara. Why would he come here?"

Anskiere's hand tightened upon his staff; his eyes turned icy
with distance. Yet if he resented the captivity set upon him by
conjurers on the isle of Imrill Kand, his words revealed no ran-
cor. "I don't know. But if the Magelord expected to face me at
the end of his road, his reasons for travel won't be pleasant."

"Well," said Taen, her most irrepressible smile creeping
through, "we'd better go and meet him. The defenses won't
admit him without our help, and his tampering is raising merry
hell with the wards."

~ XV ~

Border Wilds

The wards over Morbrith keep crackled and collapsed with a flare of intense light. Anskiere observed with his brows lifted in reproof as orange sparks trailed from the gate towers, to settle and die as they lit on the cobbles beneath.

"We didn't need protection that strong, anyway," Taen said in belated justification. "If demons send anything more against us tonight, they're going to catch me sleeping."

"Just so the work was yours, little witch." The Stormwarden shrugged his creased robe a little straighter and stepped into the bailey. "Right now I've no stomach for facing a Magelord who is capable of arranging an unbinding on that scale."

Taen gestured rudely, a hand-sign the Imrill Kand fishwives used to express withering disdain. "Was there ever any doubt the work was mine?"

"Not much." Anskiere shook his head, amused; as Taen had hoped, he relaxed his inner discipline and finished with his first smile in days.

The break in his composure was the last anyone was likely to see. Beyond the arch, His Eminence the Magelord of Mhored Kara stood with a fixed frown. His mouth gaped open in perplexity, while the incomplete spell he had intended for the purpose of breaking Taen's wards drifted aimlessly over his hands.

"Your mischief has left our visitor somewhat vexed," the Stormwarden observed. Then, discomfited himself by the unanticipated arrival of an adversary, he indulged in a rare display of

191

power, and kindled the wards in his staff to light his steps through the arch.

Blue-violet illumination seared away the dark. Beyond the gate, the Magelord spun around as though slapped. The spell over his hands flashed out. The next instant a force slammed Taen's awareness that was vicious in its intensity. Startled off her guard, she stumbled backward and cried out.

Anskiere caught her. He guided her so that his body shielded her from harm and, with no break in motion, raised his staff. Wind rose at his bidding. It cracked across the cobbles like a living thing, making the Magelord's robes snap with whipcrack reports. The frail old conjurer could not stand upright against the force of the gale. Neither would he abandon dignity and crouch. Forced back one step, two, then three, he ended awkwardly spread-eagled against the gate tower.

Taen spoke the moment she regained her breath. "His Eminence was only testing to see whether I had sent an illusion." But Anskiere's winds snatched her words away.

His face stayed set with anger as he strode from beneath the arch. Once clear of the stone, the ward halos threw etched light across his prisoner's helpless form. The Magelord blinked in discomfort.

Yet as if pity was a stranger, the Stormwarden addressed him. "What discourtesy is this? To wield power in uncalled-for aggression is an act of rank ignorance, and to try the Vaere-trained worse folly still. Taen Dreamweaver this day spared all of Hallowild from suffering the fate of Morbrith. To subject her to truthspells is an abuse you will answer for. Speak quickly, for my patience is spent."

The Magelord raised his chin against the confining pressure of the wind. His eyes stayed hooded, dark with ancient malice, and the sigils tattooed on pale cheeks seemed grotesque as knotted spiders. "Your Dreamweaver sent illusion to our towers. Knowing our beliefs, is that any less a discourtesy?"

Anskiere said nothing. The light from his staff shone steady as a star, but blindingly bright; only the wind relented ever so slightly.

The Magelord's purple robes settled around his thin ankles. As if the effort pained him, he pushed away from the gate tower and querulously yielded. "I have come to propose an alliance."

The Stormwarden allowed the wind to die, but not the wards. He waited without speech for the Magelord to continue, while unspoken between them rose the tension and the memory left by

Anskiere's imprisonment at the hands of Kisburn's conjurers on Imrill Kand.

Taen edged out from behind the Stormwarden to better follow the exchange. The Magelord spared her a glance, but did not apologize for his aggression. Irked that Anskiere expected him to explain himself, he gripped ringed hands about the bag of amulets he wore knotted to his belt. "There have been portents." His voice turned gravelly with annoyance. "The compact at Shadowfane has brewed mischief, with worse yet to come. My seers have foreseen the wholesale destruction of Keithland."

The prescience must have been dire to induce this sour old man to abandon ceremony. Aware of nothing from him beyond bitterness for the Stormwarden's harsh treatment, Taen watched Anskiere shift unadorned hands on the wooden grip of his staff. For a while no sound intruded but the conjurer's quick breaths, and the crickets singing in the weeds beneath the gate towers.

"They could not have acted without your sanction," observed the Stormwarden of Elrinfaer at last. He did not refer to demons. Through dream-sense, Taen knew he spoke of the past, and the contention that remained unresolved since Kisburn's conjurers had tried to coerce Anskiere to free the frostwargs for the purpose of conquest and greed.

The Magelord knew also. He snapped his teeth shut in offense and squared his shoulders. "My conjurers lost their lives. Was their end not enough to redress the mistake?"

Anskiere went very still. "Have you ever seen a frostwarg disemember a town?"

Aware, abruptly, that he was on trial, and that his reply would be judged, the Magelord assumed the defensive. "My successor, Hearvin, was sent to assess Kisburn's ambitions. He was a true master of the seven states of reality, and never a man to approve of rash action."

Again Anskiere said nothing.

The Magelord squinted under the painful glare of the wards; and in a moment of sharpened insight, Taen perceived what Anskiere had suspected all along: jealousy had motivated the Mhored Karan wizards in support of King Kisburn's plot. They knew well the vicious nature of the frostwargs. Secretly they had hoped to arrange Anskiere's downfall. The lengths to which spite had driven them appalled Taen to outrage. She had not guessed, when she had asked the Magelord to send her message to the Kielmark, that she had dealt in confidence with a den of serpents. In retrospect, she saw she had been fortunate to emerge without trouble.

The Magelord did not speak.

Never looking away, the Stormwarden slowly slid his hands over the staff until his knuckles met. "You never considered, did you, that Tathagres would use children in her attempt to force my will. Only one accepted my protection. She stands beside me, much changed, and never again a carefree girl. The brother who felt too threatened to trust me fell to Shadowfane and caused the wasting of Morbrith. Who will answer for him, Kethal? Your last offer of alliance was nothing but a misguided bid for power. The result cost Keithland dearly."

Dawn had begun to silver the mist beyond the ward light cast by Anskiere's staff. A bird twittered sleepily from a treetop, soon joined by a host of its fellows. Yet the keep behind stayed eerily silent and dark, except for the sheen of last night's dew. The Magelord regarded the Stormwarden with bleak antipathy. His ringed hands hung loosely from the gold-banded cuffs of his sleeves; yet now and again the fingers twitched, as if he longed to shape spells.

"You did not have to submit," Kethal finally accused.

And this time Anskiere bent his head. Dream-sense showed Taen his thought, that a man might misjudge many times in the course of a lifetime; but for a sorcerer, mistakes claimed innocent lives. Had he not yielded his powers for Kisburn's conjurers to bind, the villagers of Imrill Kand would have attempted out of loyalty to defend him. They could only have failed. Any man who offered Anskiere protection would have been slaughtered by king's men, not cleanly, but for sport.

The Dreamweaver refused the implication, that Anskiere might be counted guilty for Emien's defection and the larger disaster at Morbrith. Their earlier melding of minds had shown the opposite. Beneath his stern exterior lay a heart incapable of cruelty; his powers and responsibilities as Stormwarden stood in ruthless conflict with his sensitivity. The deaths in his past haunted him past memory of peace, and here the Magelord's envy found endless opportunity to inflict pain.

Taen was driven to interfere. She lashed out with her dream-sense, and caught the Magelord unprepared. Behind his guard in one swift thrust, she recoiled from what she encountered; Kethal's mind was a snarl of thwarted desires and ambition. Through his years he had accumulated layer upon layer of achievement around a core of deepest mistrust. He called no man friend. Altercations with other mages were never settled until he had subjugated any who came against him. Only the Vaere-trained had balked him, and for that, they and every principle they upheld had earned his undying hatred, until now, when the conjury of Mhored Kara's master seer had placed this pretty old man in stark fear of his life. More ruthless than was her wont, Taen peeled away Kethal's framework of excuses and justifications. She made of her talents a mirror and showed the Magelord of Mhored Kara the unadorned image of himself.

He quivered as the import struck him. Rings flashed as he raised his hands, but not to shape conjury. Instead the old wizard covered his face to hide shame. For the first time in life he understood the guilt borne by Anskiere of Elrinfaer.

The effect catalyzed change, marked him too deeply to shelter behind his accustomed mask of lies; no longer could he find solace in spite, or in the belief that the Vaere-trained held arrogant power that deserved to be taught humility. Forever after, even until death, the Magelord would suffer remorse for the fate of Morbrith, and for depriving Keithland, even temporarily, of her most powerful sworn defender.

Taen relented only when the aged ruler of Mhored Kara had bent his stiff back. As he fell to his knees on the dusty cobbles beneath the gate, she addressed him with uncharacteristic acerbity. "If you come here for help, Your Eminence, then ask."

The Magelord lifted a face traced silver with tears. Revealed by brightening daybreak, his purple robes were travel-creased and worn. Left only desperate rags for decorum, he seemed somehow diminished. "You demand difficult terms."

"Fair ones, I think." Anskiere's voice was only slightly unsteady; but his hands clenched white on his staff as he released his defenses. The wards snapped out with the speed of a lighting flash, leaving the gray weariness of his face exposed in the half-light. "Name me your portents, Kethal."

Without asking, Taen stepped forward and helped the ancient wizard to his feet. He spoke then, in dry, measured phrases, and described a course of ruin that made the destruction of Morbrith look petty by comparison.

"Morrigierj," Anskiere concluded when the Magelord completed his account. Neither he nor Taen need question that the conjury of Mhored Kara's seers were accurate.

"The threat is perhaps much closer than our allies the Llondelei expect." The stormwarden's lips thinned grimly, and he nodded to Taen. "Show the old one in, little witch. There seem to be things we'll need to discuss with him after all."

* * *

While Taen, Anskiere, and the Magelord held council to negotiate terms of alliance with the wizards of Mohred Kara, mist settled silver in the hollows east of Morbrith. Jaric eased his horse over rocky ground, cautious of a misstep that might bring lameness and delay. The Kielmark rode ahead with his great sword slung crosswise over his back. The black that bore him walked with its head held low, stockinged legs buried to the hocks in fog. Both horses stumbled with fatigue; neither beasts nor riders had rested since leaving Corlin the night before. Yet the need to travel in haste could not be denied. Shadowfane held the last of the Llondelei Sathid; if children stolen from Morbrith survived to replace the Dark-dreamer, the well-being of humans and Llondelei lay in jeopardy.

Daylight brightened, catching dew like jewels in the grass beneath the horses' hooves. Jaric resisted the need to collapse in sleep on his mount's neck. His knees ached. When he freed his feet to relieve cramped muscles, his stirrups banged painfully into his ankles. That discomfort kept him alert until the Kielmark called a halt at noon. Pausing only long enough to refill the water flasks and eat journey bread and sausage from the stores in the saddlebags, pirate and Firelord rode on until shadows slanted toward late afternoon. Jaric unsaddled his horse, his only comfort the fact that Taen need not share the peril of his journey; in the company of Anskiere, she would return to Cliffhaven on board *Ladywolf*, for the straits offered the only defensible position should a Morrigierj arise and drive its minions to invade Landfast.

The horses were utterly spent; unbridled and turned loose, they grazed without inclination to wander. The Kielmark stretched out with his sword ready at hand. Nearby, cushioned by the damp wool of his saddle blanket, Jaric slept dreamlessly on the grassy verge of a stream.

The following days passed alike, landscape alternating with the reed-choked banks of an uncountable succession of fords. Orchards gave way to wilderness and the terrain grew rough. The appearance of the riders became raffish to match, as they slept in thornbrakes and thickets and once on the dank floor of a cave as rain hammered the earth in angry autumn torrents.

The Kielmark's black threw a shoe. Progress slowed for two days, until they traded fresh mounts from a remote camp of clansfolk. Dunmoreland stock was prized by the hilltribes; formal in a headdress of mules' ears, the chieftain finalized the exchange without spitting on his knife, meaning no vengeance would be exacted if the beasts proved unsound. But his less trusting wife watched the strangers off with an expression like sun-baked clay. Jaric was glad to ride briskly after that.

In forests and moonlight and cloudy dark, Firelord and Kielmark crossed the northern tracts of Hallowild. On a windy morning, they broke through the scrub to dunes, and the wide white beaches of the coast. There they dismounted and cut brush for signal fires until their palms blistered on the hafts of their daggers.

The Kielmark maintained an outpost on the isle of Northsea for provision and repair of his fleet of corsairs. Few beside his captains knew the location, which was healthiest for the peace of mind of Keithland's merchants. The sloop that answered his smoke-fire summons was lean and efficient, and bristling with armed men who easily preferred battle to bedding a wench.

The boatswain at the helm landed singing, until he noticed who waited on the strand; his stanza ended in a curse of embarrassed surprise. He mastered himself with striking aplomb. After loosing the horses to fend for themselves, Kielmark and Firelord boarded with no more than wet boots, despite the heave of strong surf.

Jaric endured a jostling crossing. After weeks in the saddle, with fire-charred fish or the stringy meat of skulk-otters for fare, the smoky shacks that comprised the Northsea garrison seemed the height of luxury. At a scarred board table in the kitchens, he dined on bread and mutton and wine, while the talk of the men swirled around him.

"Cap'n Tamic's in at Cover's Warren." The officer in charge had a broad south isles' accent, but there was nothing lazy about he way he answered the queries of his sovereign. "Shipyards there been aslacking, and he poked in to shake things up."

The Kielmark scratched his mustache, which had grown like wire over the hard line of his mouth. Idly he retrieved the knife from his plate and began to hack at the bristles. "Does Corely know?"

"Oh, aye." The officer grinned. "Said he'd spit the foremen, one after another, if Tamic reported loose ends. Meanwhile the fleet's at sea, sweeping the bay for demon-sign, as ordered. You wantin' a boat to go across?"

The Kielmark stabbed his blade into the boards. "Tomorrow. But we won't put in at the Warren."

"Where, then?" The officer twirled his tankard, sobered and suspecting trouble.

But the Kielmark refused to reveal their destination, even to a trusted captain. Too much stood at risk should Shadowfane gain wind of his purpose. He closed the topic with a banal change of subject, and presently announced his desire to rest.

Bathed, shaved, and for once unmolested by insects, Jaric slept solidly in a bunk in the officers' shack. But respite from the rigors of travel proved brief; a sailhand shook him awake in the gray light of dawn. Feeling muzzy, the Firelord donned breeches, boots, and shirt. He hurried down to the landing by the harbor with his sword belt dangling from the crook of one elbow.

The Kielmark waited, boisterously impatient, his foot braced on the gunwale of a lean gray yawl. "There's hot bread and bacon waiting, if you're quick at setting sails."

Jaric stowed his sword in a locker, eyebrows raised in reproof. "That's no incentive. I could *make* hot bread in a blizzard."

"Oh, sure. Like charcoal," needled the Kielmark. He stepped aboard and reached to cast off docklines.

Jaric clambered into the bow and began to sort hanks on the headsail, more to keep from thinking how much he missed Taen than from any sense of urgency for Keithland. By sunrise the yawl sheered on a reach around the cliff heads of Northsea, toward the shoal-ridden islets of Wrecker's Bay. Beyond lay the borders of Keithland, and Shadowfane itself.

Clouds rolled in by noon, ragged black and swollen with rain. The sea heaved leaden and dark, knifed to leaping spray by a series of rocky promontories. Gusts hissed in from two directions, battering the yawl like fists, and tearing at Jaric's clothing as he rose to reef sail.

The Kielmark shouted over the slap of canvas. "Leave her be. There's no room to run in this pocket. We're safer on the beach if it squalls."

Jaric eased sheets for a run, then sat and braced against the mast. Outlined by storm sky, the Kielmark's profile seemed hammered out of rock. Muscles bulged under his sleeves as he manhandled the tiller to hold course toward land.

The centerboard banged up in its casing, and the yawl grounded on gravel with a lurch. Jaric freed the sheets and leaped into a boil of foam. Icy water poured into his boots. Then the sky opened, deluging rain. Half-blind in the torrent, the Kielmark wrestled the sails down. Together the two men dragged their boat onto the strand. Behind them, the channel became a smoking cauldron of spindrift as the squall struck full force.

Escarpments of broken rock offered scant protection from the fury of wind and water. Soaked already, and uninterested in standing while the Kielmark wrapped his sword steel in oiled rags, Jaric wandered the beachhead. Rain spattered the ground. Pebbles and small stones tumbled in the run-off, to be battered in turn by surf. The Firelord squinted through the storm and made out the jagged outline of a cliff face; wild and untenanted though that shoreline was, something about the place seemed familiar. As a gust momentarily parted the curtains of rain, he realized why. This was the site of Anskiere's curse against Ivain, following the destruction of Elrinfaer by the Mharg.

Jaric listened, but heard only the voice of the storm. Wind here no longer repeated the curse Anskiere had pronounced against his betrayer. Perhaps the completion of the geas' terms had unbound the spell; or maybe the words on the wind had been nothing more than a tale invented by sailors. Shivering in the cold, Jaric stepped into the lee of a ledge that jutted beyond the tide mark. Barnacles crusted the stone, white as old bone where the waves threw feathers of spray. Saw grass clung in those cracks not swept clean by weather, except in one place. Once a sorcerer had marked the cliff, to leave a message straight and bitter as vengeance. Ivainson blinked droplets from his eyes and beheld the inscription his father had left scribed in rock.

'Summon me, sorcerer, and know sorrow. Be sure I will leave nothing of value for your use, even should my offspring inherit.'

Jaric knew a moment of paralyzing cold. The mad malice of his father seemed to emanate from the stone, choking breath from his lungs, sapping life from his body. Wounded by hatred and spite, the son stumbled backward, into the cleansing fall of the rain. He stood for an interval, shuddering, his eyes stinging with water and tears. Then he stirred and lifted his hand. Alone in rainy twilight, he raised Earthmastery and smoothed the letters from the surface of the cliff.

Surf slammed unabated against the headland, and rain still whipped the strand. Yet somehow the squall seemed less savage, the landscape not so forsaken under the crazed onslaught of elements. Jaric made peace with the memory of his father and turned back toward the beach. He had one goal for comfort: should he and the Kielmark succeed at Shadowfane, mankind might survive to discover an answer to the threat posed by demons. Then Keithland would have no further need for sorcerers, and the agonies of the Cycle of Fire might be abandoned forever.

The crossing of the northern Corine Sea passed smoothly after Northsea, with brisk winds and fair sky seldom interrupted by squalls. The yawl sailed more handily than *Callinde*, which was well, for the waters off the coast of Felwaithe were a maze of shoals and islets that few mariners dared to navigate. Jaric learned more than he cared to know about charts and current as the yawl threaded the hazardous channels across Wrecker's Bay.

Twice their presence was challenged by corsairs flying the red wolf of Cliffhaven. The Kielmark kept the north coast under vigilant patrol, to dissuade merchant ships who thought to evade tribute by avoiding Mainstrait. Captains under his banner carried standing orders to plunder and sink any ship found bearing cargo; but often such tactics proved unnecessary. The reef-ridden channels between islands offered no sea room to fight, and many a hapless merchanter found ruin on hard rock instead. While searching the beaches for firewood, Jaric found rigging among the tide wrack, and the weather-bleached timbers of ships.

Autumn's warmth waned; the sky turned overcast and silvery as a fish's underbelly. On an afternoon that threatened rain the Kielmark beached the yawl on the farmost point of Felwaithe. Chilled in his wet boots, Jaric wondered as he stowed sails whether the two of them would survive to need the small boat again.

"My captains will spot her on the beach," the Kielmark said, as if answering the Firelord's thought. "One or another will pick her up." He did not belabor the fact that such a contingency would be necessary only if they failed to return; instead, he squinted at clouds, adjusted his sword belt, and turned his back to the sea.

Jaric followed, his fine hair stiff with salt crystals, and a knapsack of provisions slung across his shoulders. Since the fells north of Keithland sustained neither forests for cover nor forage for horses, the final leagues to Shadowfane must be crossed on foot. Kielmark and Firelord pressed forward through spiky stands of scrub pine, crosshatched patches of briar, and ravines of loose shale that crumbled and slid underfoot. By sundown, both thorns and pines thinned to isolated thickets. The soil became poor and sandy, pierced by sharp tongues of rock, and knee-high clumps of saw grass and fern. A fine drizzle began to fall. Grimly set on his purpose, the Kielmark seemed inured to the damp, though moisture matted his hair and soaked patches in the calves of his leggings.

Jaric walked alongside with less confidence. Troubled by foreboding, and yearning for Taen's company, he felt every icy drop that slipped off the pack and rolled down his collar. The warded sword at his side chafed his hip like common steel, and boots blistered his heels after weeks of barefoot comfort at sea. Still, he continued without voicing his fears. Day wore gradually into night, and fog cloaked what little visibility remained. Between one step and another, ferny hummocks gave way to stone crusted with lichen. Beyond that point, as if a knife had divided the land, wind moaned over hills unbroken by any living thing.

"We've reached the borders of Keithland." The Lord of Cliffhaven paused and rested his back against a table of black rock. "Sailors say the whole of this world is barren, except for Keithland. I've seen oceans grow strange fish away from inhabited coasts."

Jaric slung off his pack. Inside he scrounged a hardened loaf of bread, which he hacked in two with his knife; he passed half to his companion, who seemed to be listening to the wind. Explanations for Keithland's existence were many. Kor's priesthood claimed the Divine Fires had seeded lands for men to raise crops, and country folk said forests, meadows, and wildlife were the magical gifts of the Vaere. Whichever philosophy a man chose to believe, none who beheld the edge of the growing earth ever felt less than a shiver of dread.

Mist and rain overhung the rock like a shroud. The bread grew soggy in Jaric's hand; in disgust he tossed the last bit away, then dragged the pack onto tired shoulders with a muttered curse at the weather.

"Sky'll be clear before midnight." The Kielmark adjusted his sword sheath, and shook his head. "You'll wish for dirty weather then. We'll stand out on these fells like fleas on a whore's sheets, and Shadowfane's watchtowers are manned by creatures with eyes on both sides of their heads."

Jaric received this comment with a skeptical expression, wasted, because of the dark. "You've been there?"

The Kielmark's teeth gleamed in a brief grin. "Never. But the fellow who told me was sober."

"My sword to a bootlace he wasn't." Jaric shook water out of his hair. "No sailor ever enters your presence who isn't full of beer to bolster his courage. You've the reputation of a shearfish, all teeth and bite."

"And a good thing that will be, if we meet Scait's four-eyed beasties in a fight." The Kielmark pushed to his feet. Spoilingly impatient, he said, "Are you ready?"

They proceeded, and the air grew colder. The breeze shifted northwest. Rain and clouds gave way to a star-spiked arch of sky. The rock of the fells extended in all directions, windswept and deserted, except for a single gleam of scarlet near the horizon. The sight raised chills on Jaric's flesh; a stronghold arose as if chiseled from a hilltop, all angled battlements, with silhouettes of spindled towers bleak and black against the indigo of the heavens.

"Shadowfane, sure's frost." Grimly the Kielmark loosed the lashing on the tip of his scabbard, that his sword might be ready for action.

Ivainson Firelord had no words for the occasion. No longer the scribe who had apprenticed at Morbrith, nor the boy who had trapped ice otter in Seitforest, he bowed his head. His hands glowed blue in the darkness as he summoned Earthmastery to sound the stone underfoot. From the images drawn from Dreamweaver and Llondelei, he knew that a chain of caverns riddled the ground beneath Shadowfane. Through them, a combination of sorcery and sailor's luck might permit entry into Shadowfane unobserved.

Far south, drizzle still cloaked a fortress under a red wolf banner. A sentry paced restlessly, his beat altered slightly to avoid a rumpled figure in Dreamweaver's robes of silver-gray. Taen sat with her head cradled on her forearms, her shoulders framed by the rough stone sill of Cliffhaven's watchtower. She had drifted into sleep while tracing Jaric's progress northward through Felwaithe, but her rest was troubled.

She dreamed of a chamber floored in dark marble where redpaned lanterns burned. There a Thienz in green beads and armbands bowed before a throne built of stuffed human limbs. "Lord-mightiest, the Firelord and his companion have crawled beneath the earth. My kind can no longer track them, but their intent is plain. They will emerge within the dungeons of Shadowfane, to the sorrow of us all."

The figure stirred on the throne, silencing the toadlike creature on the rug. Yellow eyes opened, evil and narrow and set like a snake's; razor rows of teeth gleamed in shadow as the Demon Lord responded. "No sorrow, but the humans', for Shadowfane is prepared for them. Firelord and Kielmark walk into an ambush.

If we introduce a third Sathid to Ivainson's body, how long do you suppose he can maintain control? Very soon his powers shall be ours to command."

Scait added in mind-speak that through Jaric even the Morrigierj might be managed. He hissed with laughter, and his sultry gaze seemed to focus directly upon the watchtower at Cliffhaven where Taen wakened, screaming.

The sentry gripped her shoulders in mail-clad fists, vainly trying to comfort. Shivering, chilled by more than cold, Taen shook him off. "Fetch Anskiere. Tell him we must abandon the children held captive at Shadowfane. Scait has learned of our plan to steal the Sathid."

The sentry hesitated, scarred features pinched in a frown.

"Hurry!" Taen wasted no more words, but snapped her talents into focus and sent north, to warn. Her probe coursed rocky fells, windy and empty of life. The man she loved and the tempestuous King of Pirates had already entered the caverns. Since dreamsearch could not reach through solid stone, disaster was unavoidable. Firelord and Kielmark would walk into a demon trap ready and armed against them.

ᥱᥩ XVI ᥱᥩ

Stalkers

Fading enchantments lent rock walls the fleeting glimmer of faery gold; then darkness fell, in a swirl of cold air. Ivainson Jaric stepped through an archway still hot from the shaping of his Earthmastery. Sweating from the warmth thrown off by the rock, he took a deep breath. The passage he entered smelled muddy and damp. Underground springs trickled over channels worn smooth by erosion, the echoes like whispers in the dark; all else was still. No living creature inhabited the cave.

"There's still rock dividing us from Shadowfane's dungeon." Reverberation splintered the Firelord's words into multiple voices as he concluded. "This is the last sealed cavern we'll cross if you want to enter through the lowest level." He lifted his hands, and controlled flame speared the air above his fingers.

The illumination sparked mad glints in the Kielmark's eyes. Black, unruly hair bound back with a twist of linen lent Keithland's most powerful sovereign the appearance of a brute peasant. "Just so there's headroom. Can't swing a blade while grubbing along on my belly."

Metal whined in shadow as he cleared his sword from his scabbard. "On, then."

Jaric started forward, more like a scribe caught out of his element than the Vaere-trained sorcerer Keithland's survival depended upon. He fretted at the hazard presented by his companion, who might stumble on the rough footing and slice him through with three spans of unsheathed steel. But as always, the Kielmark moved like a cat. Except for his weapon, he might have been enjoying a holiday procession in Kor's temple, so blithely did he keep pace at Jaric's shoulder.

Ahead, the cavern loomed dark as a grave. Ivainson adjusted his mastery, and flames flared brighter from his fist. The passage crooked through buttresses of stone and widened into a troll forest of stalagmites, colored bone and ocher, and sleeked like slag with run-off. A black maw opened underfoot, where streams carved into the unknown deeps of the earth. Jaric jumped the crevice. His heels grated on sand as he strode to the far wall and applied his Earthmaster's touch. The fingertips of both hands flared blue as he traced an area encrusted with limestone. Sathid-born powers resonated through the cavern. Ivainson's features tightened, and the hotter fires that leaped above his knuckles suddenly extinguished.

"You play havoc with a man's night sight that way," carped the Kielmark. His boots scraped over stone as he closed the last stride by touch, disoriented only slightly by the sudden dark.

Jaric disregarded the complaint. "Beyond this barrier lies Shadowfane." Harrowed by sudden uncertainty, he lowered his arms to his sides. Anskiere's distrust, Taen's love; all that he strove to change or cherish in his life within Keithland seemed remote as the lushness of spring when snows lay deep over the land.

Air winnowed, sliced by steel as the Kielmark raised his sword. "Nothing to gain by waiting, sorcerer. Either you make spells, or I shove you aside and start chipping rock."

The ruthless arrogance in the words startled like a blow, until Jaric recalled the six companies of Cliffhaven's men who had perished with Morbrith. The Kielmark's grudges inevitably resolved in bloody vengeance; whether the offenders were human or demon made no whit of difference.

Jaric raised hands that once had penned copy for the archives of an Earl's library; those pages were ash, now, and mourned not at all, unless by the ghost of the master scribe tortured to his death in Morbrith's bailey. With more sorrow than anger, Ivainson Firelord marshaled his powers. He touched, and where his fingers passed, a livid red line seared the stone.

Fumes scoured his nostrils. Jaric directed his Earthmastery through the sheen of tear-blurred vision. Presently the line parted, frayed into light like the edge of a smoldering parchment. Draft rushed through the gap. Ivainson shielded his face behind one arm, his cheek whipped by the laces of his cuff. The Kielmark sweated impatiently; heated air sang across his swordblade as the stone dividing Shadowfane from the wild caves of the fells crumpled away under the influence of sorcery.

A corridor gaped beyond, still as old dust; the one visible wall was patterned in hexagonal brick, pierced by a lintel streaked with rust from a torch bracket. No cresset blazed in the socket. Not even water drops disturbed the quiet. Jaric's enchantment fizzled into sparks, then darkness. Firelord and Kielmark paused, unbreathing, but no outcry arose; no lantern flared to expose the presence of intruders and no sentry leaped forth to make outcry. Though all but a few demons avoided the confining properties of stone, the absence of security in the dungeons under Shadowfane came as a profound relief. Fortune perhaps had seen two humans through the vulnerable moment of entry.

Jaric shifted his weight, but found his step prevented by a crushing grip on his shoulder.

The Kielmark whispered softly as a breath in his ear. "Let me go first."

Startled by an expression of trust, Ivainson conceded. Other than Corley, he had never known the Kielmark to tolerate an armed man behind him.

"Go left, then." Jaric let his Earthmastery range a short way ahead. "You'll pass a row of cells with studded doors, then a stairway. If there's a sentry, we'll probably find him on the first landing." Distressed that he still felt unequal to whatever perils might await, the Firelord summoned a spark to guide the way into Shadowfane's deepest dungeons.

"Belay the light. I'd best go on by touch." The Kielmark pushed past, his sword a flash that vanished as the Firelord closed his fist to muffle his spell.

Jaric crossed the gap on the heels of his companion. As his boot sole scuffed blindly against brick on the far side, contact touched off an explosion of energy in his mind. Evidently the passage was warded. Jaric's hand hardened instantly on his sword hilt. He groped to restrain the Kielmark, but his companion had already passed beyond reach. To call aloud might bring demons. Left no better alternative, Ivainson Firelord crossed quickly into the passage.

The air grew palpably dense, as if shadow had somehow gained substance. Jaric strained to breathe. Left in no doubt that he had triggered defenses conjured by demons, he opened his fingers. Weakened to a dull gleam of red, the spark's thin glimmer revealed a corridor choked with mist. The Kielmark was nowhere to be seen.

Mortally afraid, his body slicked with sweat, Jaric attempted another step. Sorcery rippled around him. The fog vanished in the space of a stride, and darkness thinned to normal. The simple spell in his hand brightened like a beacon star. In the sudden splash of light, Jaric sighted the Kielmark. Vital, indomitable, the sovereign Lord of Cliffhaven poised beneath the stair with his sword raised en garde. On the landing above, rank upon rank, lurked a clawed and hideous pack of demons. The fact they carried no weapon did not reassure; like the Llondelei, their ability to manipulate the mind could be lethal.

The Kielmark reflexively back-stepped. Braced against the wall to avoid being surrounded and struck down from behind, he shouted orders. "Jaric! Leave these to me."

But retreat was already useless. Thienz were telepaths; what one saw, all demons within the fortress would share in the space of a thought. The Kielmark must know that enemy reinforcements could be expected at any moment. Jaric decided their only chance of escape lay through his powers of Earthmastery. He strode forward and drew his sword.

The wards flared active and rinsed the corridor with orange light. "Fall back!" the Firelord called to his companion. In another moment the fullness of his powers could be focused. Jaric fused his awareness with the stone, prepared to seal the passage against the enemy.

But the Kielmark paid no heed. Sword angled at the ready, he beckoned to the Theinz on the stair. "C'mon, spawn of malformed lizards. In remembrance of Corley's companies, it's time to visit the butcher."

Jaric felt the hair prickle at the nape of his neck. Demons would attack the mind before they closed with the perils of steel, and against telepathic compulsion, none but Taen Dreamweaver could offer any protection. Urgently he shouted to the Kielmark, "My Lord, stand clear."

The sovereign of Cliffhaven turned a deaf ear. Since the demons could not be provoked into rushing him, he advanced instead upon the stair.

"No!" Jaric's warning echoed the length of the corridor. The wards of his sword point flared red, available for instantaneous defense, yet all of his Vaerish training availed nothing; he could not strike with a friend blocking him from the enemy. Left no other alternative, he cursed the Kielmark's belligerence and started forward himself.

The Thienz attacked.

One instant, the Kielmark filled his lungs to bellow as he charged. The next, the Thienz invaded his mind in force and damped the fury of his assault. His great sword clanged down, the edge shearing sparks against the granite stair. His hands lost their power to grip and his body to move. As if in slow motion, Jaric saw the Kielmark's stride falter. His knees buckled. Then, snarling, the Thienz of Shadowfane fell upon him.

Running now, Jaric leveled his own sword. He loosed his mastery, and fire stabbed forth, a needle of killing force that seared the air as it passed. The nearest of the Pirate Lord's attackers flared up in a flash of flame. It recoiled and rolled over and over down the stair while its companion squalled in reaction to its pain. Jaric leaped over its dying struggles. Other demons whirled at his approach. Gimlet eyes flashed in the ward light. Frog-wide mouths gaped open and exposed wicked, back-curving fangs glistening with drops of black venom; Jaric felt the sting of Thienz hatred, still more dangerous than poison, permeate his thoughts. Already the demons centered upon his mind. In a second, he would share the Kielmark's fate, as the enemy grappled his awareness with the insane compulsion to collapse the protection of his wards.

Failure was certain. Braced against hope to resist, Jaric squinted through the glare of his sorceries. Past the struggling knot of Thienz, he strove to locate the Kilemark. Not a glimpse of clothing met his search. Through wheeling shadows and the close-packed bodies of enemies, he saw no trace of a living human.

Despair sparked an anger that knew no limit. Jaric raised his sword. He would incinerate Thienz to white ashes. Yet before he could act, a bull bellow emerged from the thick of the fray. The attacking demons heaved up, and a glistening red line cleaved their midst. A gilled head rolled and bounced down the stair, followed immediately by the flopping corpse of its owner. Another body tumbled, nearly severed in half, and then another, cleaved through shoulder and neck. Jaric heard a sailor's blasphemy. Then the struggling Thienz parted like knotwork before the stroke of the Kielmark's sword.

Jaric jumped also to avoid that singing edge. No enemy lunged to strike him. Surprise momentarily left the demons without any wits to act. Perhaps the Firelord's sorcery had distracted their concentration enough to create an opening; or maybe their victim's will had never been entirely subdued. Taen Dreamweaver had found the Kielmark's mind a chaos of unbiddable madness when he indulged in his killing rages. For the Thienz, the mistake proved fatal. The sword cut left, right, and left again, leaving a wake of carnage. In retaliation for the companies destroyed with Corley's brigantine, *Moonless*, the Kielmark was bent on slaughter. Even as the demons realized their quarry could not be managed, half their number lay fallen, bloody and dying.

The ringleader squealed in panic. It and its fellows spun to quit the stair, but Jaric blocked their retreat. From both directions, the Thienz charged headlong into a wall of living flame. Their screams deafened thought as they burned. Smoke choked the corridor, foul with the reek of charred flesh. The Firelord bent coughing over the hot white metal of his sword.

The flames died swiftly. Jaric straightened, blinking stinging eyes. Through the smoke-dimmed glimmer of his wards he saw his companion cast about for more enemies. Nothing stirred in the passage but the twitching of a dozen butchered corpses; the Kielmark's teeth flashed in a grin of satisfaction. He raised his huge sword, pinched the blade in the crook of his elbow, and drew the steel clean on his shirt sleeve.

"Damned toads." He kicked a smoking corpse from underfoot, then moved to rejoin Jaric.

The irrepressible swagger in his stride touched off overwhelming relief. The Firelord resisted a week-kneed impulse to sit down. As his companion reached his side, he said, "You're a madman." His hands shook as he damped the wards, then rammed his own sword home in its scabbard. "No good would be gained if you got yourself killed."

The Kielmark's smile died like a doused candle. "The stinking reptiles are dead, aren't they?"

Speechless, Jaric wiped his palms. Quite wisely he chose not to belabor the point that every Thienz cousin within mind-reach would shortly descend upon Shadowfane's dungeons, maddened as a stirred swarm of wasps. Rather than precipitate trouble, he touched the Kielmark's wrist and indicated the nearest of the iron-barred doors that opened on both sides of the passage.

The Kielmark balked with a sound of contempt. "You mean to hole us up in a prison cell? That's bad strategy, sorcerer. Where do you think you'll steer us next when the head jailer shows up with the key?"

Jaric never paused, but pressed his hands to the iron face of the door lock. "I'll tunnel through rock, if I must. Have you a better suggestion?" He frowned. His fingers flared blue; there followed a click, then the grate of a tumbler turning.

The Kielmark set his shoulder to wood studded and reinforced with strips of corroded steel. "None. Unless your spell-working could conjure me a flask of spirits?"

"Spirits?" Jaric shook his head in astonishment; and the Kielmark heaved. The hinges groaned and gave with a pattering of rust flakes. The panel swung inward, tearing through dusty nets of cobweb. Jaric sneezed violently. He peered into the darkness beyond, then distastefully crossed the threshold. "You always go drinking after battles, is that it?"

The Kielmark raised his brows. Drily he said, "This time I intended the stuff for medicine."

Jaric paused, aware by earth-sense that a stairway lay ahead. It wound upward, doubled, and let onto a pillared gallery where fetters dangled over moldering heaps of bones. The Firelord's blood ran cold, not only for the human wretches who had died of Shadowfane's unnamed tortures. As his companion's laconic phrase fully registered, he said, "You didn't get yourself Thienz-bitten, did you?"

"No. Just clawed and stuck like a lady's pincushion." The Kielmark pulled the door to and paused. A minute passed while both of them listened. Sounds of running feet echoed through the grille from the corridor they had just left. Already more demons came hunting.

Jaric spun around without comment. He slipped past his companion and set hands to wood, steel, and the rust-marked stone of the lintel. Faint halos traced his form as he engaged Earthmastery and sealed the doorway.

"We still might get visitors from the rear," observed the Kielmark.

"We shouldn't." Jaric batted cobwebs from his hair. "I've checked. This stairway leads to a cul-de-sac."

Blank-faced, the Lord of Cliffhaven sheathed his great sword. "I see." He blotted at a cut on his jaw. "From the fireside, and straight into the soup. We're fair put to swimming now."

Earthmastery could carve a retreat, create a passageway to any place in Shadowfane's dungeons that Jaric might choose. Yet no time remained to discuss options. A gabble arose in the corridor, most likely in lament for the slaughtered Thienz. Seconds later, illumination speared through the crack beneath the door, cast by a lantern shuttered with scarlet glass. Evidently more than Thienz came hunting. Seldom did they carry lights; with their poor eye-sight, they relied more on scent to find their way.

The Kielmark held motionless by instinct, the breath stopped in his throat. Jaric waited, sweating, until the light spun away and faded. Even then he held his mind blank, and prayed his companion had insight enough to do the same. The demons of

Shadowfane held advantage over human trackers; they could locate a man by his thoughts.

Minutes passed. No further disturbance arose beyond the door. Jaric touched the Kielmark's shoulder, sticky with blood that might as easily be an enemy's as discharge from an open wound. Forced by priority to defer his concern, the Firelord delivered the gentlest of tugs and started forward. Silent, wary of every movement, the fugitives retreated toward the stair. Earthsense guided Jaric's steps; he led the Kielmark as he would the blind, picking the easiest path and directing the man's feet by touch. All the while he kept his awareness tuned on the corridor beyond the sealed door, where the faintest vibrations through stone warned that a sentry still paced. One sound, a single chance blunder in the dark, and pursuit would be upon them.

For the Kielmark, who owned no sorcerer's awareness, the ascent of the stair seemed interminable. The landings switched back, or turned in convolutions without pattern; no logic dictated the distances in between. At the top, Jaric had to tap his companion twice, to assure that no further levels remained.

At least now they might have light without risk of discovery. Jaric conjured fire and set it adrift to reveal their surroundings. They stood in a gallery. Pillars carved in the shapes of malformed animals supported a ceiling cut from the natural rock of the cavern. The walls were undressed stone, strangely in contrast to floors checkered with squares of polished agate.

"Looks like a Telshire whorehouse," observed the Kielmark. But the rusted sets of fetters robbed his remark of humor. Affixed by chains heavy enough to moor ships, each pair dangled from rings pinned immovably to the pillars. Heaped beneath lay pathetic clutters of human remains, most bearing marks of abuse. "Funny place to keep captives, I say."

The dead victims of demons had not been disturbed by rats, nor had beetles nested among the half-rotted remnants of clothing. For no reason the Firelord could name, the absence of natural scavengers made his flesh creep. He ended his survey only when doubly assured that the gallery contained no exits, or so much as a spyhole in the wall.

Jaric chose not to voice apprehension, but faced his companion, and with steady eyes assessed the wounds inflicted by the Thienz. The Kielmark's linen shirt lay in shreds, stiffened and dark with blood. Between the rents were long, shallow gashes that had barely begun to clot. Gauntlets had protected his forearms; his boots and leggings had suffered scars, but the flesh beneath was unharmed.

"No bites," Jaric concluded, relieved the damage had not been worse. "You're lucky." Once he had suffered from Thienz venom. The experience was a horror he wished he could forget.

The Kielmark shrugged somewhat stiffly and changed the subject. "Luck won't recover the advantage. What did you have in mind?"

Jaric looked down, and noticed that somewhere through the ascent of the stair he had bloodied his own knuckles. The scrape was minor; but it stung with a fierceness out of all proportion to reality just when his attention was needed for planning. The Firelord drew a forced breath. "First let me set safeguards."

He had none of Taen's ability to shield the mind directly from attack. But as Earthmaster he could fashion illusion, cloak their living presence with the ponderous essence of stone, or the still dark of soil without life. Carefully Jaric wrought wards, that demons who hunted human thoughts might sense only the empty deeps, and pass onward without pause for investigation.

Once the defenses about the gallery were stabilized, Jaric and the Kielmark attended the unfortunates who had died of demon cruelty. In wordless accord, they burned the bones, and whatever pathetic rags remained to differentiate between individuals, not because the gallery lacked warmth or light, but to restore some dignity to the dead. The smoke of the pyre stung their eyes and made them cough, but neither one offered complaint. They rinsed their mouths from the water flask in the pack, but drank sparingly, for the chamber had no amenities. After that, both sorcerer and Kielmark chose to rest before moving on. Now the demon pursuit would be hottest. Later, when Shadowfane's sentries were weary, and the hunters forced to extend their search over a wider area, the chance of stealing forth unseen might be improved.

There followed an interval in which Jaric tried to sleep, but suffered miserably from nightmares. Not far from him, the Kielmark sat with his back to a corbel, methodically heating his dagger in the mage-fire left burning for light. To prevent infection, he pressed the hot steel to one wound at a time, and in the process acquired a frown that even Corley would not have challenged. If his hand trembled by the time he finished, throughout his doctoring he had uttered no word except an imprecation against sorcerers who achieved mastery without learning to conjure spirits. "Nicer by far on the nerves, and a swallow or two goes a helluva long way toward knocking the edge off the pain."

Jaric made no reply. Having been rebuffed at dagger point earlier when he offered to cleanse the wounds with Firemastery, he pretended to doze with closed eyes. The Kielmark charred his blade clean in the fire, then spat on the steel until it cooled enough to sheath. Too uncomfortable to lie down, the sovereign Lord of Cliffhaven eventually slept where he sat, his head tipped back against stone, and his knuckles loose on his sword hilt.

The next time Jaric checked with his earth-sense, the sun had arisen over the fells. Winds made brisk by autumn frost moaned around the spires of Shadowfane, sharply in contrast to the air within the gallery, which hung still as a sealed tomb. The Firelord ignored the hunger that cramped his belly. He struggled to contain the deeper longing left by a certain Dreamweaver whose path took her leagues to the south. Love for Taen could do nothing but make him ache, with demons quartering every cranny of the dungeons for the humans who had invaded their stronghold. Earth-sense could occasionally discern the pattern of the search, here by the slap of webbed feet as a party of scouting Thienz turned a corner, and there by the boom of a grate grounding against bedrock.

The demons persisted with a thoroughness that was both alien and frightening. Unable to know how readily his awareness might be traced through the stone that he probed, Jaric used sorcery with caution. He explored only caverns and stairs that seemed empty, while, with laborious precision, the Kielmark used ash to map his findings on a square of linen shirt garnered at need from their pack.

Their makeshift floor plan of the dungeons stood barely half-complete when Jaric encountered what he sought, a cell with living prisoners whose limbs were chained to rock. Though unable to divine awareness, as Taen did, his mastery could differentiate subtleties with great detail. Steel set to use as fetters absorbed the warmth of the body, and the stone floor immediately beneath sang with the queer, crystalline resonance of Sathid in the process of bonding.

"I've found them," Jaric announced. He opened his eyes, to a look from the Kielmark that made his flesh prickle. The man sat coiled, a hairsbreadth removed from unbiddable violence. Gently the Firelord tapped the map. "Here. The children stolen by Shadowfane's compact have been closed in a cell by this vent shaft." He paused and carefully added, "There appear to be six of them. I fear we're too late for rescue."

"We can end their misery, then." Single-mindedly impatient, the Kielmark consulted his chart. "And we can be sure no others

suffer the same abuse, but we have to get there first. Can you
guess where demons might store the Llondelei Sathid?"

Jaric forced speech. The fetters sensed through his mastery
had been fashioned for wrists that were heartbreakingly small.
"On the level below the cell confining the children, there's a
double-sealed door that appears to secure an apothecary. I sensed
shelves of wood, and rows of things stored in stoppered glass;
drugs, mostly, and minerals. But among them I found a rack
woven out of vines that never grew in Keithland's soil, with
sealed containers inside. That's where I'd look for the Sathid."

The Kielmark nodded. As he folded his charcoal chart, his
blue eyes flicked up to meet Jaric's. "Can you get us there?"

"I'll have to." The Firelord dusted ash from his fingers and rose
swiftly. Trouble was imminent. The dull sense of pain beginning at
the back of his head was not the effect of fatigue. Shadowfane's
demons had discovered the sealed cell. As they sounded the
chamber beyond for intruders, the touch of their probe against his
wards caused an ache that mounted with each passing minute.

"We have visitors." Jaric motioned the Kielmark to his feet,
then strode across the gallery and placed his palms against the far
wall. "Set your hands on my shoulders," he instructed. "Whatever happens, keep them there. If you lose your grip, you'll end
up entombed in solid rock."

The Kielmark complied without visible hesitation. "Better thank
Kor for the fact I don't get jumpy in tunnels." Yet this once his
bluster hid bravado. When he took hold of the Firelord, his fingers
bit deeply into fabric, and his breathing went shallow and fast.

Whether the Lord of Pirates' unease stemmed from the confinement about to be imposed by earth sorcery, or the fact that,
with both hands occupied, he could carry no unsheathed sword,
Jaric dared not ask. Compelled by a rising sense of urgency, he
engaged his mastery at once.

The air around him seemed to shimmer. Light struck the stone
wall with a flash like reflection off mirror glass. The Kielmark
squinted against the glare, and felt Jaric move under his hands.

He stepped forward, braced instinctively for a collision that
never came. Though his senses insisted that he walked into solid
rock, no barrier obstructed his body. Pirate King and Firelord
moved unimpeded into a gap fashioned spontaneously by sorcery.
A blister of air moved with them, charged with dry heat like
storm winds swept across desert.

The Kielmark stole a look back. Behind, the gallery had vanished, replaced by a stone face that showed neither flaw nor fis-

sure. Veins of quartz and the flash of mica flowed together at his heels, as if at each stride the sorcerer who led him traversed through matter in the midst of a moving bubble. The effort required to achieve such a wonder belied understanding.

Newly aware of the sweat that dampened the shirt beneath his grip, the Kielmark looked nervously upon the sorcerer responsible. "You know where you're going?"

Jaric did not answer. Absorbed in the workings of his art, he moved one foot, then the next, in carefully unbroken rhythm. Light flared from his raised palms, and at his command the rock parted, smoothly, soundlessly, insubstantial as a lifting curtain.

Though the effect might seem effortless, passage through the deeps of Shadowfane did not come without cost. In time, the air grew stale. The Kielmark noticed a quiver in the flesh beneath his hands. Until now mechanically even, Jaric's step became unsteady and slow; the rock gave way before him sluggishly as syrup thickened by cold. Still the Firelord pressed on. His skin grew clammy with exertion. The power discharged from his person grew uneven, flaring like wind-torn candles into searing spatters of sparks.

At length Jaric stopped entirely. The stone before him rippled into solidity, hard and impenetrable as always, leaving the two of them within a sealed compartment of air. He rubbed his face with his hands and, in a voice muffled through his fingers, said, "You can let go."

The Kielmark allowed his hands to fall. Sweating in the closeness of the stone, he gripped his sword and grimly awaited admission of trouble. The Firelord seemed taxed more than sorcery alone should warrant.

Jaric spun around quite suddenly. "We're being flanked." By the fire glow he maintained for illumination, exhaustion lay printed like bruises beneath his lashes. His hair curled damp at his temples, and his eyes shone fever-bright. "I've found demons waiting each place I've tried to emerge. Maybe they sense the currents of my conjuring. The reason doesn't matter. Quite soon we're going to run out of air."

"Overextend your resources, and we'll be trapped." The Kielmark fingered his blade. "I'd rather go fighting than get trapped like a fossil."

Jaric closed his eyes. He pulled himself together with painfully visible effort, and did not add that the working of his Earthmastery seemed strangely difficult in this place. Whether that complication was also the work of demons, only Anskiere with his years of experience might have told. Shaking in fear of final failure, the

Firelord strove for steadiness. "Getting cut to ribbons by Thienz won't spare the children, or recover the Llondelei Sathid."

"Neither will suffocating in what amounts to a bubble of rock." Vexed, and disturbed by the first warning signs of dizziness, Cliffhaven's Lord jerked his head at the stone that sealed them in. "Bring us out, and quickly. Debate will do nothing but weaken our chances."

In the eerie glow of the mage fire, the Kielmark showed spirit unblunted by regret or apprehension. His hair in its linen band hung limp with sweat. He had discarded his ruined shirt; long, scabbed gashes from yesterday's battle grooved his shoulders. Still he seemed a wolf on a fresh scent, vengeance for his slaughtered companies a thorn that needled him endlessly to action. His ice-pale eyes gleamed with an anger only killing could assuage.

Jaric regarded his hands, shaking now with weariness and nerves. Never a fighter, and a sorcerer only with reluctance, he found his own wants more complex. Taen and the Cycle of Fire had taught him the value of perseverance, and Tamlin of the Vaere had sworn him to a service not lightly put aside. He was not ready yet, to settle on a recourse that could only end in death. Though weariness dragged at his nerves, and his powers as Firelord seemed less than adequate for the task, he tuned his awareness to rock and sent forth another probe.

The cell that confined the children was guarded now; Jaric knew by the whisper of air currents that eddied over stone as demon sentries paced through their term of watch. The apothcary beneath had been rigged as a snare, for the wooden shelves there resonated like sounding boards with the queer vibrations of wardspells. In every corridor, every likely cranny his earth-sense could detect, Ivainson Firelord read movement against the earth, the restless steps of scores of prowling enemies.

Desperate, he turned downwared, toward the natural caverns that riddled the strata beneath Shadowfane. Most lay too far to be of use; but deep, at the end of a narrow tunnel, he encountered stillness. There lay a grotto submerged in silence so profound he could sense the settling of dust. No trace of demon presence lurked in wait to trap them. Resolutely Jaric focused his mastery. He bade the Kielmark to set hands to his shoulders once more. Then the heir of Ivain Firelord mustered his will and bored downward into earth on the chance the two of them might reach a haven to recover strength and regroup.

ᔕᓂ XVII ᔕᓂ

Ambush

The stone dissolved in a rain of sparks. Too spent to arrange an entry with more finesse, Jaric stumbled into the narrow passage which sloped downward toward the grotto. A half-step on his heels came the Kielmark. Dizzy and starved for air, at first the two of them could do nothing but stoop and gasp awkwardly for breath.

No demons appeared to challenge them. The place was dark and smelled of dust, to all appearances empty. Yet as equilibrium returned, Jaric felt the hair on his arms prickle with uneasiness. He could not escape the feeling that somehow their presence had been noted.

The Kielmark's instincts were aroused also. "Kor damn me for a fool if we aren't being watched." Quiet as a threat, he eased his great sword from the scabbard and rested the point against the floor.

Jaric damped his breathing with an effort. He sounded the dark with his Earthmastery, but encountered nothing untoward. The emptiness that had seemed a promise of safety now rasped at his nerves like dissonance. A feeling that waxed more insistent by the minute urged him not to linger. "We can't stay here."

The Kielmark shifted his weight to a soft grate of steel on granite. "Are you thinking of turning tail and holing up in the wild caves? If so, your reasons better be grand, sorcerer. Backtracking sticks in my craw, and no toad-faced pack of demons is enough to sweeten cowardice."

Striving for Corley's casual exasperation, Jaric raised his

brows. "Every toad-faced pack of demons between you and those captive children is hoping you'll think just that. Do you always seek thrills by dangling your hide out as bait?"

A chuckle echoed drily through the passage. "Sorcerer, until demons learn not to murder Cliffhaven's companies, I'll split lizard heads until my dying moment. By the sword my mother forged, I swear I'll have your balls before I go belly down through more rock to avoid them."

"Your *mother* made that sword?" Jaric grinned in disbelief. "My ears hurt."

"You saying I'm a liar?" But the rest of the Kielmark's rejoinder died unspoken. From the hole left by Jaric's conjuring came the sound of furtive scraping.

The Kielmark recoiled from the wall. His steel whined through air as he whirled to face the disturbance. "Mothers bedamned, sorcerer, you'd better make me a light to fight by."

Fire bloomed against blackness. Jaric raised his palm, and lit the passage in a spill of raw gold. Shadows danced grotesquely over walls of water-smoothed stone. Against the natural contours, the depression left over from their retreat by Earthmastery gleamed smooth as the inner dome of an egg.

"It's still sealed," said the Firelord.

"For how long?" The Kielmark flexed his upper arms and shoulders, and shifted to the balls of his toes.

The scraping grew louder. Like sand grains before an avalanche, part of the spell-smoothed surface crumbled away. A fissure parted in the rock.

"Back," cried the Kielmark. He slammed Jaric clear with his forearm and, in wildly wheeling light, raised his sword. "Fires alone know how, but Kor's Accursed have followed us."

"Through *stone?*" The achievement should have been impossible. Bruised from the blow that had spun him toward safety, Jaric raised Earthmastery. Even as he tried to probe the nature of the breach, more sand rattled from the crack; there followed a bouncing rain of pebbles. A claw pried through. Beyond the opening rose bloodthirsty howls of impatience.

Pressed to the wall, the Kielmark braced himself at the ready. His eyes went feral with eagerness.

Jaric felt his hackles rise. He set his mind to seal the stone, or, if that failed, to sear the opening with fire and trap the enemy inside. But this time he did not face routine sentries. The fissure widened. A demon that was narrow and spined like a lizard thrust its head through the gap. As a force more dangerous than Thienz compulsion slammed Jaric's mind, he perceived the scope of his peril. This creature he faced had somehow fathomed his mastery; while he had cut his escape portal from the gallery, the adepts of Shadowfane's compact had tapped his unguarded thoughts and managed to draw from his resources, even past the shielding properties of stone. Purloined power had enabled them to replicate earth-sense and track him.

The demons' grasp upon the principles of Vaerish sorceries was shallow, yet if they found means to build upon the rudiments of rock-shifting, they might achieve the release of both frostwargs and Mharg. Keithland's dangers now lay redoubled.

"We're in trouble," Jaric whispered.

The Kielmark acknowledged with a slight jerk of his head. Then the lead demon leered in triumph. The last of the barrier crumbled away as dust. As the creature leapt through, a murder-bent horde of followers pressed toward the breach.

Jaric dared not strike. Though he held the full command of his Firemastery coiled to engage in defense, demons had tapped his talents for their own use. Until he divined how, and took precautions, the chance existed that Shadowfane's minions might also rip power from his mind, turning his own energies against him, even as they had the earth-powers that had enabled his passage through rock.

The Kielmark understood the complications. Savage as a cornered beast, he roared out to the Firelord behind. "Go back! Close the stone as you leave!" His sword never wavered. Light splintered on the edge angled to slash the attackers who charged in waves down the corridor.

The moment held all the horror of nightmare, yet retreat offered no recourse. Jaric sounded his inner self, frantic with fear, and saw that the demons' first efforts at borrowing upon the effects of his Earthmastery were crudely managed. They had succeeded only because he had been unaware.

Guarded now, he raised a ward against invasion, then jerked enchanted steel from his scabbard. The triplicate aura of his Firelord's defenses burnished the passage with glare, far too late to escape. Even had he been willing to abandon the Kielmark to peril, in the lighted entrance to the grotto at his back lurked row upon row of glowing eyes. Jaric made out the spidery forms of Gerij, ink against darkness, and pressing slowly toward him.

Their whistle rose painfully shrill in the enclosed space. Trusting the presence of steel to foil their attack, Jaric ignored them in favor of the demons who threatened his companion.

The Kielmark jerked a knife from his boot top. "Save yourself, sorcerer! Flee!" His shoulders bunched, as demons of every shape and description launched at him from the gap.

An Earthmaster could engage power, mesh his own being inseparably with the matrix of the rock; this might foil the enemy indefinitely, but only another sorcerer capable of mind-link could partner such a course. The Kielmark would be doomed. Uncomplaisant, Jaric raised fire.

The Kielmark felt heat stripe his side as he slashed. His sword bit deep into flesh. The demon in the lead tumbled against his boot, sliced nearly in half. Blood streaked the Kielmark's leggings and splashed lurid spatters on the wall. As he kicked the floundering corpse into the press of living adversaries, a fireball screamed past his elbow. In the moment while demon flesh charred, he glanced back and saw Jaric had disregarded his instructions. He also noticed the Gierj pack, whose whistle shrilled toward the upper registers where their power normally peaked. The presence of steel no longer appeared to deter them; even if Jaric sealed off the gap, attack might continue from behind.

Anger suffused the Kielmark's features. "Kor curse your loyalty, boy! *Get clear of this!* Taen asked that I keep you safe, and I swore her an oath of debt."

In the passage, demons hurdled the bones of charred comrades. Cliffhaven's sovereign spun to meet their charge. The blades in his hands arced around and gutted the front ranks. Spiny lizard forms tumbled and writhed in their death agonies. Those Thienz mixed among them collapsed, scrabbling webbed hands and screaming. Ones behind tried to grapple the Kielmark's mind to keep him from killing. Their attempt tangled ineffectively in fear and rage, and crazed determination. They might sooner stay a cyclone with threads than apply compulsion against madness.

The Kielmark glanced aside and again saw that Jaric had not fled. His exasperated curse became lost in the snarls of enemies. In a decision that could be neither predicted nor reversed, he abandoned the security of the wall. He leaped the bodies of the slain like a berserker who craved death, and plunged slashing into the horde of assailants in the passage.

Jaric shouted. "No! Kor's grace, no!" Then despair canceled speech. To summon fire would sear friend and foe alike. Helpless, Ivainson watched the sword rise once, then twice, steel drenched crimson with blood. Then the black hair with its simple twist of linen disappeared, pulled under by claws and ravening fangs.

Jaric swore. Grief could not eclipse understanding; the Kielmark had made no pointless gesture of braggadocio. He had bought his own destruction deliberately, his purpose to sever the Firelord's responsibility for his life. Beyond the horrid tearing of flesh, and the resonant whistle of the Gierj, his words seemed yet to ring through the caverns of Shadowfane: *"Taen asked that I keep you safe, and I swore her an oath of debt."*

Wild with sorrow, Jaric could not believe that the imposing vitality of the man was quenched forever; that scarred and toughened captains would sweat no more under the scrutiny of blue eyes whose keen perception could measure merit and shortcomings at a glance. The Firelord raised his powers, but not to seek refuge within earth. Instead, in a single discharge, he unleashed the latent forces of his sword.

Sorcery screamed forth, indomitable as volcanic eruption. The hordes of Kor's Accursed had no chance to react. Fire flashed, blinding-bright, and blasted stone instantaneously to lava. The gap in the passage crumpled with a roar like hurricane surf. Snared in a holocaust, the murdering horde of demons flared incandescent as lint. Bone, flesh, and sinew, they and the corpse of their victim became immolated within the space of a second. Through a spill of uncontrollable tears, Jaric beheld the brief white outline of a sword. Then the arched ceiling of the passage collapsed. Gripping the charred twist of metal his own blade had become, he evoked mastery to shift earth.

But no powers answered. Force lashed out of nowhere, and pinched off his talents like so many flickering candles. Jaric spun, seeking fresh targets. He found himself surrounded by Gierj. With a horrid, jolting shock, he realized his steel no longer worked to inhibit their powers. In the grotto beyond, the circle of silence he had mistaken for emptiness in fact masked Shadowfane's ultimate peril. Too late, he perceived the stillness for what it actually was: he had stumbled unwittingly upon the warded lair of the Morrigierj. No opportunity remained to flee before the whistle of its Gierjlings crested and sundered thought. Mortal consciousness crumpled before a venomous onslaught of pain, and Jaric tumbled downward into dark.

Ivainson Firelord slowly recovered awareness, to hurt and guttural syllables of speech. Too stupefied to distinguish words, he stirred. The sour chink of fetters shocked him fully awake. Memory returned, of a passage where the Kielmark had leaped to his death. Jaric flinched. Harrowed by loss, he opened his eyes to a bloody wash of light.

The voice continued, echoing within stone walls. "Look you, he is moving. Did I not say the Morrigierj and its minions struck him lightly?"

Jaric blinked, unable to distinguish the speaker from the shadows. The bonds of his wrists were forged, not of metal, but of a substance of glassy hardness that shimmered with ward-spells. Glare prevented his pupils from adjusting.

A hiss like a stoppered kettle sounded from the opposite side. "Foolish toad! Only that ruined lump of sword steel spared his life. Had the Morrigierj's defense reflex killed, all plans would have been spoiled."

Jaric realized with a chill that the language was unfamiliar; comprehension arose from the demons' touch within his mind. Close proximity apparently forced a link with his captors similar to Taen's dream-sense. At present Ivainson had no strength to resist. His flesh stung with abrasions; Kor's Accursed had dragged him, perhaps by the cutting edges of his fetters, for his wrists burned unmercifully. Worse, his Firemastery would not answer; somehow demons had impaired his powers of sorcery. A furious attempt to force the ward restricting him brought pain that stopped his breath.

"Your manling grows restless," observed the first demon. "Best you subdue him while he is disoriented and plaint, or he may do as his companion, and destroy his own life to keep honor."

The second demon laughed. Claws scratched lightly over stone, and a spurred foot prodded the prone body of the Firelord. "You speak as if he is a threat! And what harm could he do, even to himself, with his limbs bound and his powers under ward? Still, get him up. Then summon the Thienz pawns who will cross-link the Firelord's Sathid-bond."

Jaric recovered his wind with a hoarse cry. He made a deter-mined effort, and managed to prop himself on one elbow before blurred vision overcame him. Clinging to consciousness, he heard a rattling clank of metal. Drafts raked his body, followed by the slap of many feet on stone. Small, tough hands grasped his tunic and hauled him upright before a trestle topped with a mar-ble slab.

Relieved from the blinding effects of his fetters, Jaric viewed a chamber packed with the squat forms of Thienz, and other demons whose shapes he did not recognize. A lantern dangled from a length of chain overhead; at the boundary of light and shadow sat the reptilian Scait, resplendent in gems set in wire and a mantle of purple plumes. Jaric was startled by his size, for the Lord of Shadowfane rose no more than shoulder-high to a grown man. Yet he poised himself with the muscled quickness of a lizard. Hungry eyes searched his captive, while spurred fingers stroked the handle of a short, sharp knife over and over, as a lover might caress a woman.

"How very timely of you to summon fire so near the chamber that grows the Morrigierj," said Scait in the tongue of Keithland. His tone held honeyed satisfaction. The most promising talent among the human children had died that morning, too frail and too young to endure the rigors of Sathid-bond. But in Jaric the compact had acquired a better victim. The Demon Lord bared teeth, and qualified. "That made your downfall swift, and inevitable. But you were doomed long before you trespassed within Shadowfane. Like Marlson Emien, and before him Merya Tathagres, you have been chosen to serve."

Jaric searched for response, but defeat sapped the nerve for defiance. No words came to mind; only the image of Taen weeping over the ravaged body of her brother. Dizzied, numb, and sick with weakness, he caught the trestle for support. Stone jarred his fingers. He barely felt the shove as packs of Thienz forced him upright.

Demon speech came and went in his ears. Through fragmented phrases, bits of thought-image, and ragged patches of vision, Jaric saw a Thienz hand Scait a dark chunk of crystal. He recognized the same matrix that was the foundation of a Sathidmaster's powers, and suddenly divined Shadowfane's intent. Dread made him blurt his horror aloud. "You mean to impose a demon-controlled Sathid upon me, and overthrow my mastery of fire and earth?" Outrage cleared his senses; he straightened in his singed tunic, and glared at the Demon Lord's scaled visage.

Scait smiled, his plumes dancing with magenta highlights in the red-paned light of the lantern. Thienz rustled in the corners, impatient for the moment when one of their own would partner the Firelord's overthrow.

Hotly Jaric protested. "You'll never control the result. Tamlin of the Vaere already tried to train men to mastery of tripled Sathid crystals. Each time he created a monster."

Scait rasped serrated teeth and tossed the contaminated matrix from palm to palm. "Monster? If by that your mythical name for

Set-Nav defined a creature dedicated to destruction, nothing less would suit the compact's purpose. Our method is assured. The human mind fares poorly in multiple bonding because it is isolated. But the Thienz whose crystal cross-links with yours can achieve dominance without harm, since thousands of Sathid-free siblings will shelter its psyche from madness."

Jaric took a firmer grip on the table. Blond hair slipped forward, veiling the fury in his eyes. He heard Scait's premise and felt cold, for his fate at the hands of demons now redoubled the threat to those children left living in captivity. If the secrets of his masteries provided the final key to their survival as demon pawns, Keithland's destruction could no longer be prevented. Eyes closed in the agony of failure, the Firelord hoped the Thienz who pressed at his sides mistook his trembling for weakness. In a useless effort to buy time, he grasped after a tangent. "Set-Nav? You claim the Vaere hides a machine?"

Scait fielded the crystal, set it gently down on marble, then laced spurred fingers over his knife. "Shortly you will verify that. But the spoils of your discovery shall benefit Shadowfane."

Mute as he considered implications, Jaric wished he had obeyed the Kielmark's directive to flee while the chance had existed. Now escape of any sort was impossible. The chamber's only entrance was secured by a studded door and a clumsy mechanism of counterweights and chain.

The Demon Lord rose. Feathers rustled like whispers as he swung the hook suspending the lantern closer to the wall. Shadows shifted to reveal shelves jammed with bottled elixirs and tins of dried herbs. Among them rested a row of flasks, filled with clear fluid and cradled in a rack of woven vine. Jaric recognized the intricate craftwork of the Llondelei; and irony stung like a thorn. The very Sathid he had entered Shadowfane to steal would engineer his doom and Keithland's final conquest. Jaric drew an angry breath and bore down on the support of the Thienz until the pair of them squealed in complaint.

"Lord-mightiest, he faints!"

Scait hissed his displeasure. "Conscious or not, hold him upright." The Demon Lord selected the nearest of the flasks and released the hook. The lantern swung in drunken circles overhead; alternately flicked by shadow and light, he set his blade to the seal and slashed. Yellow eyes flashed briefly at Jaric. Then Scait took the slave crystal from the trestle and dropped it in the flask with a click. The contents churned as if alive, and a Thienz huddled in the pack cried out.

Jaric swayed. Desperate in his weakness, he watched the liquid in the flask settle and darken to amber. The change recalled a Llondelei thought-image shared on the night he and the Kielmark had set off for Shadowfane from Morbrith: *'You will know pure matrix from that enslaved by demons, for bonding turns the color like wine.'* The matrix within the flask had now melded inseparably with the Thienz-dominated crystal. A single drop in the bloodstream would initiate cross-link, and slavery more ruinous than Emien's.

Scait dipped the dagger to the hilt in the flask and waspishly addressed his underlings. "Hold him. Misery to you all if your hold slips."

The Thienz seemed small, even laughably ungainly; but their strength proved more than a man's. They caught Jaric's fetters and pinioned his arms against the marble. The vulnerable lines of human tendon and bone stood exposed in scarlet light. The blade poised above, dripping and deadly with Sathid solution already under demon domination.

Scait struck downward to cut.

"No!" Jaric twisted; fetters flashed like sparks as he jerked aside. The dagger missed flesh by a hairsbreadth and screeched across stone. Scait cursed, even as the Firelord slammed against the trestle. The flask overturned, splashing the floor with amber liquid. Wooden bracing chattered across tile as the ponderous slabtop slid and rammed the Demon Lord's midriff against hard edges of shelving behind. Tins and crockery rocked while Scait rebounded in rage. Jaric ducked the spurred swipe of the demon's fist. He dove for the elixir untouched in the rack behind, his intent to end the misuse of the Llondelei crystals forever.

Thienz sprang to restrain. Toad fingers snatched at linen and broke the impetus of Jaric's lunge. He sprawled sideways, hand outstretched. Sickness and the interference of his captors caused him to miscalculate; instead of sweeping the flasks from the shelf, to topple and spill and maybe contaminate the Thienz whose solution already puddled the tile, the Firelord crashed headlong in their midst. Glassware shattered. Edges like razors cut deep into his hands, and wrists, and forearms. Fluid deadly with unbonded Sathid seeped into open wounds.

Jaric screamed. Tamlin's care had spared him the pain of first contact through the cycle of bonding on the Isle of the Vaere. At Shadowfane, alone, he endured an excruciating tingle of nerves as multiple Sathid coursed through his flesh. His senses blurred, smell, and sound, and light milled under by fiery agony. Jaric

heard snatches of a Thienz' hysterial screech; then Scait, in cold
fury, calling out, "Don't touch! He'll cross-link, you father-lick-
ing fools! The wards binding his Firemastery will give way
through multiple bonding and wild Sathid could overwhelm you
all."

Chain rattled, followed by the boom of a door. Jaric thrashed
on cold stone. His features gleamed, sweating in the glow of
enchanted fetters, while two score untamed Sathid threaded rapidly through his consciousness. He began vividly to dream.

But where the progression of Vaere-trained masteries had been
orderly, a logical sequence of images as Sathid assimilated experiences from infancy to adulthood, the present experience was
chaotic. Each entity had a separate will, and all sought dominance over the others; Jaric felt his mind torn to fragments as
Sathid awareness ransacked memory, fighting to establish parallel
consciousness with the being whose body they invaded. Scenes
formed, only to splinter, overturned by a bewildering and irrational succession of images. Jaric saw snowfall in Seitforest,
beeches and evergreens cloaked in mantles of purest white; in a
hollow between two deadfalls, Telemark shook ice from his cape
and knelt to set snares for fox. The scene had scarcely stabilized
when winter vanished. Fire and wind ripped the trees without
warning, and sparks blew like driven lines through darkness. The
forester swung his axe; sweat and grit and tears marred features
racked by grief, but there memory distorted. Telemark checked in
mid-swing, breaking the precision of his stroke. His blade bit
earth with a thud, and fire faded before the scent of living greenery.

"Jaric?" Cleansed of tears and filth, Telemark's face furrowed
with worry. "Jaric, are you all right?"

This query was not borrowed from the past. The words
echoed, as if the forester spoke in the very chamber where his
former apprentice lay stricken. Even as Ivainson framed answer,
the Sathid jostled his mind. Telemark's presence ripped cruelly
out of reach. Gale winds screamed and slashed whitecaps into
spindrift. The stormy roar of breakers filled Jaric's ears. *Callinde*'s steering oar yanked blistered hands, even as Anskiere's
geas tore his heart and mind toward madness; salt spray drenched
his shoulders and salt tears wet his face. Then, like glass frosted
with moisture, that image also faded, overlaid by the ward-bound
silence of the ice cliffs.

The Stormwarden of Elrinfaer called out of darkness, his tone
terrible with command. "Ivainson Jaric! What's happened?"

But that voice became lost as a great sword rose, sheened with blood in the shadowy deeps of Shadowfane. Helplessly the Firelord watched the blade fall, never to rise again. Cliffhaven's Kielmark whispered, his anger subdued to purest sorrow. *"Taen asked that I keep you safe, and I swore her an oath of debt."*

Grief caught Jaric like a blow. He wept, and the image buckled, replaced by the smoky vista of stars once revealed by the Llondelei in dreams; but this time the velvet dark where the probe ship *Corinne Dane* had sailed was slashed by fiery lines of lettering. Words that once had been strange and meaningless now were uncannily clear: *"With the Veriset-Nav unit lost in the crash, no ship can find the way back to Starhope.... Will our children's children ever know their forefathers ruled the stars?"*

Jaric wondered who would leave such a message, hidden in the spine of a book for a scribe to find generations afterward; as if at his command the writing faded, replaced by the face of a man with tired eyes and close-cropped gray hair. His clothing was blue, trimmed with silver in the fashion of Kordane's priests, but cut from no cloth woven on Keithland. As Ivainson puzzled over the anomaly, the image vanished. Multiple Sathid scrambled to displace their fellows, and for a moment no entity dominated.

Jaric gasped for breath. He assimilated the reality of sweat-stung eyes and muscles knotted from contortions before dreams overwhelmed him once again. Colors swirled through his mind, overlaid by light that pooled and focused. He found himself helpless under the malevolent glare of Scait Demon Lord. A Firelord in captivity repeated a phrase he had uttered only minutes before coherency left him: *'Set-Nav? You claim the Vaere hides a machine?'*

Prone on cold tile, his cheek pressed into the hard edges of his fetters, Jaric poised on the brink of vital revelation. But the crazed turmoil of the Sathid left no interval for thought or interpretation. Drowned in a flux of memory, he stepped barefoot onto sand. Sunlight warmed his body like a lover, and the spicy scent of cedar filled the air. Ivainson blinked. Touched by awe, he recognized a place whose uncanny perfection never failed to move him.

Bells jingled, merrily at odds with a voice raised in reprimand. "Ivainson Jaric! Firelord's heir! Stand and face me."

Shocked as if plunged in cold water, Jaric whirled and met Tamlin of the Vaere. This encounter was no memory; the clamor of the Sathid receded as cleanly as a knife pulled through cloth.

Drawn into stillness beyond human understanding, Jaric lost his last hope of rescue.

The gaze of the Vaere bored into him as if fey eyes could murder. "Young Master, you've transgressed mortal limits. That's trouble. No resource of mine, nor any endowment of *Corrine Dane*'s can spare you now."

Whipped by a shiver beyond his means to subdue, Jaric regarded his teacher across the boundaries of dream. "I had no choice."

The Vaere stamped as though vexed. Poignant sorrow touched his face, half-glimpsed as he turned away. "Then understand me, Firelord's heir. I, too, have no choice. Remember that, when you face the consequences."

The querulous, leather-clad being wavered, its origin traced by an Earthmaster's perception to a form that defied all belief. Buried beneath soil and sand, Jaric saw an angular engine crafted of metal. The structure of its surface was scarred, as if from terrible impact; and energies cycled endlessly on the inside, marked by blinking patterns of light. *'I am the master of space and time,'* whispered Tamlin's voice from the past. Llondelei references aligned with other words spoken by demons, to reveal a terrible truth. Jaric identified the engine as the source of Tamlin's identity: Veriset-Nav, the lost guidance system of *Corrine Dane*. With a jolt of wonder and fear, he realized he had disclosed the secret of the Vaere; but so, also, had demons. The heritage of mankind stood in jeopardy as never before.

Light danced as Jaric fought his fetters. Cut by the glassy stuff of spells, his wrists bled, and he cursed. The image of the machine reshaped, became a white square of parchment upon which he practiced letters. Ink stained his knuckles. The draft through the rickety north casement raised chills on his back as, sharply attentive, Morbrith's master scribe reviewed his work.

"You know the smiths thought me too stupid to keep accounts," said a younger, more diffident boy. "Why did you take me in?"

Master Iveg peered over his spectacles, his large-knuckled hands hooked loosely over his knees. "Sure, I don't know, Jaric." He grinned, affectionate as an old hound. "Your butt's so skinny, I doubt you can even warm the bench for me, come winter. Now fix those *T*'s. They lean like a hillman's tent poles."

The kindliness of his criticism had made Jaric smile on the day he began study under the archivist. But now, with the bonds of Shadowfane constricting his flesh, and his mind lashed to delirium by wild Sathid, he cried out. Library and copy table vanished. The old scribe's voice broke into screams of agony; aged limbs jerked against wire as demons roasted him alive in a furnace of flaming books.

Jaric thrashed, retching, his wrists pressed hard to his ears. Discrepancy pricked through his torment. He coughed, tearblinded, and remembered: he had not been present when Iveg died. The scene he currently witnessed was drawn not from past recollection but from the altered awareness of the Sathid-link itself. Ivainson explored, and discovered his perception expanded to awesome proportions. The events of past, present, and a multiple array of futures were accessible to him simultaneously. Revelation followed, bright with new hope. Mastery of fire and earth might be shackled by demon wards, but resources acquired through bonding with two score wild crystals were not. Possibly a blow could be struck against Shadowfane before the cycle of the Sathid destroyed his will.

Jaric marshaled his stiffened body. With a grasp of tortured effort, he rolled onto his back. Sweat dripped like tears down his temples, trickled through hair to pool in his ears. Dizziness flooded his mind. Queasy and whimpering and hounded by fragments of nightmare, he glimpsed Taen's distraught and weeping face. The image of her sorrow shattered thought, just as the door to the chamber boomed open.

Footsteps and voices approached, deafeningly immediate after the dream-whirl of images.

". . . must be destroyed," hissed Scait in a monotone. Spurs grated horribly against metal. "His powers are useless to us now. Even the Watcher cannot predict what befalls when wild Sathid conquer a mind that has mastered the Cycleof Fire."

Through eyes muddled by fever, Jaric saw a sword flash red by lanternlight. Rage stung him. He would be killed with no more resistance than a beast raised for slaughter; in the moment the blade sliced downward, two score Sathid shared his perception of threat. Their competitive tumult ceased, instantaneously melded to focused and biddable force. Jaric recovered power to act, even as steel stabbed a searing line of agony through his chest.

᚛XVIII᚜

Shadowfane

Black tents clustered like clumped mushrooms upon the slopes between the town and the inner fortress of Cliffhaven. As dusk fell, lanterns flickered and swung from the twisted limbs of the almond trees, while dark-robed conjurers conferred in groups beneath. To Taen, who overlooked the scene from the harborside battlement, the gathering looked like a hill tribes' summerfair gone eerily silent without music. The arrival of the Mhored Karan wizards had been her doing, and Anskiere's; despite the fact that the conclave's differences of ability had just place in the scheme of Keithland's defense, she looked upon her accomplishment and felt no confidence.

The presence of the conjurers made itself felt in strange ways. The wards they established to enforce the reality that formed the foundation for their creed ran counter to Vaerish sorcery. Proximity to their encampment tended to inhibit the workings of dreamsense; still, Taen sensed that something, somewhere, went amiss. Against all logic, the feeling persisted. The spells of the Mhored Karan conjurers were no part of the cause, but only the foil for an apprehension Taen had no name for.

The air above Mainstrait hung unnaturally still. Over the crack of shipwrights' mallets, the Dreamweaver heard footsteps approaching from the postern. She lifted her head and saw Deison Corley stride toward her, his hair tangled with pitch and his brows leveled in an uncharacteristic frown.

"You know," he said as he drew alongside, "I'm going to get spitted on a shark gaff for this." He gestured toward the tents, and

Taen understood he referred to the Kielmark's vociferous hatred of the wizards and their secretive conjury. The subject had sparked wild speculation among the men; wagers were on that Corley would lose his command, at the least, and just as likely, his head.

The Dreamweaver returned a sympathetic smile. "You speak as if you had a choice in the matter. You didn't, as I remember, unless you wanted to watch Anskiere call storm and scuttle every brigantine in the harbor."

Corley leaned on the battlement beside her. "Threats cut no cloth with the Pirate Lord." He paused, irritable, and rubbed to ease the unfamiliar weight of the torc at his neck. Below, boys in the gray robes of acolytes continued to kindle lanterns until the trees glittered like an opium eater's dream of exotic, night-blooming flowers. Yet the captain left in command at Cliffhaven found no beauty in the sight. "To the Kielmark, wizards are trouble, the sort that invariably leads to bloodshed."

His remark brought no reply. A herd of goats bleated in the shadow below the wall, and afterglow shed light as flat as beaten metal on the waters of the harbor. The sounds and the view seemed oddly, inappropriately ordinary. Taen stared unseeing into distance. As if hooked by a crosscurrent of thought, she murmured something concerning an oath of debt that was too quiet to be quite understood.

Corley's hackles prickled. "What?"

"He won't be shedding any man's blood. Not ever again." And as if slapped into waking awareness, Taen suddenly flinched. Her face drained utterly of color. "Kor's grace, it's Shadowfane. The Kielmark—" Her eyes widened in shock.

Corley caught her hard by the shoulders. "What about the Kielmark?" His fingers bit, unwittingly harsh, and wrinkled her linen robe.

Taen shivered. "He's dead." Her words seemed unreal. The event they described should have been beyond the pale of any Dreamweaver's insight. The Kielmark's demise had happened in the dungeons of Shadowfane, deep under rock where no Vaere-trained talent should reach. Chilled through, Taen knew of no natural way she could pick up echoes of the tragedy.

Yet the vision had come to her, hard-edged in its clarity. Taen had no chance to fear, that an absolute of Vaerish law had been unequivocally overturned. The immediacy of Corely's grief overwhelmed her sensitivity and canceled the contact.

The captain drew Taen close to offer comfort. The act became motion without meaning. The weight of the ruby torc bore heavily as a curse about his neck. He fumbled after words to ask what had happened, but his mind refused acceptance. Deprived the challenge of the Kielmark's explosive character, the future seemed brotherless and empty.

Below the walls, the lanterns of the wizards tossed gently in the wind. Corley shut his eyes as their lights splintered to rainbows through his tears. "Bad luck," he said thickly. "Any sailor knows. Talk about storms at sea, and they come. I should never have agreed when the man left his rubies on the table."

The captain's voice seemed almost detached, but Taen Dreamweaver heard beyond control to a core of blighting anguish. "Your Lord always intended to come back."

A man stopped the Kielmark at his peril, once his mind had been set; Deison Corley knew this, and was silent. His hands convulsed upon the cloth of Taen's shift. The wizards' lamps shone too bright beneath the walls. To escape their brilliance, the captain raised his gaze to the ship's masts in the harbor. "Just tell me one thing. For the sake of his final peace, and the lives lost at Morbrith, did the great foolish hero take any demons with him?"

Beyond speech, Taen Dreamweaver managed a nod.

Corley's fingers slackened slightly, though the tension coiled within him gave not at all. "My Lord would have cursed like a cheated whore, but after twisting the tail of the compact, he'd have to agree. Shadowfane's vengeance is bound to be brutal and swift. I was right to let wizards ashore on Cliffhaven."

Taen had nothing to add. She regarded the camp of the wizards, terrified to fathom the source that had touched her. All too likely, through some dangerous and unseen turn of events, the vision had come through the man who lay dearest to her heart. The son of Ivain Firelord would now be alone, and in immeasurable peril.

Night deepened over the harbor, and the air took on a bite that warned of winter. Deison Corley stirred, finally, and guided Taen firmly from the wall. "Let us go in out of the darkness. Anskiere will need to be told."

"He already knows." The Dreamweaver struggled to explain what should never have happened; her powers by themselves held no means to breach stone. Whatever force had lent her news of the Kielmark's end boded no good. Suddenly her body stiffened. Without warning she doubled over with a harrowing scream, her hands pressed tight to her chest.

Corley caught her. "Taen?" She gave no sign she had heard. "Taen, answer—is it Jaric?"

The Dreamweaver's eyes clenched shut with agony. Though her lungs felt transfixed by pain, she managed a tortured affirmation.

Corley cradled her against his chest, then sprang at once to a run. Foreboding lodged like sheared metal in his gut. He dispatched the nearest guard to fetch the Stormwarden to the Kielmark's study. Then, as an afterthought, he shouted back over the wall and demanded the presence of the Magelord of Mhored Kara. If that ancient and crotchety person did not hurry his old bones to share counsel, the successor to the Kielmark's command swore under his breath that he'd spit the old conjurer on a shark gaff.

Jaric screamed, a high-pitched cry of shock and despair that did not quite mask the scrape of blade against bone, nor the grate of steel on stone as the sword pierced through his flesh and jarred unyieldingly into tile. A flood of warm fluid gagged his throat. *Dying,* he thought resentfully; pain left no space for fear. Yellow eyes flared in darkness as Scait Demon Lord flexed his wrists to clear his blade.

Jaric coughed in agony. His hands spasmed in their fetters. Beyond the reflexes of mortal pain, he knew fury so focused his vision seemed seared with light. Unaffected by the wards blocking his Firemastery, the Sathid entities within him retaliated. Skeins of energy ripped up the swordblade and exploded with a terrible cracking flash. Scait was flung backward, spurred fingers clenched to his weapon. The steel pulled free with a horrible, sucking jerk. Jaric arched, mouth opened to scream. But ruined flesh framed no sound; his awareness splintered into a thousand spangles of fire. Scait collapsed on the floor beside him, cut down without chance for a death-dream.

Yet the Demon Lord's end did not satiate. The rage-roused tide of wild Sathid reached around the torment of Jaric's chest wound and ransacked his memories for facts. In a flash their awareness encompassed the massacres that had decimated Elrinfaer, Tierl Enneth, and Morbrith. Polarized to immediate revelation, the crystalline entities perceived the demon compact as a threat. Their clamorous bid for survival meshed with Jaric's own cry for vengeance, not least for the theft of human young and the entrapment that had destroyed Marlson Emien.

Even as Ivanison Jaric thrashed in the throes of dying, hysterical packs of Thienz sensed the stir of wild Sathid within his mind. They backed away from the corpse of their overlord, and stampeded in terror from the chamber. However frantically they barred the door, neither flight nor steel locks could save them. The fading spark of the Firelord's awareness charged two score Sathid to a rage like unleashed chaos. Jaric allowed the current to take him. Even as death dimmed his thoughts, power more intense than any he had initiated as Firelord surged forth. The Thienz who scuttled through the corridor were obliterated in a searing flash. No outcry marked their passing. Neither did the Sathid subside.

Instead they fused with his hatred. One terrible instant showed Jaric the passions that had twisted and ruined his father. He discovered in full measure the lust in his desire to destroy. Capacity for power touched off a heady joy. His enemies would fear him as they perished. One breath ahead of oblivion, Jaric embraced the poisonous euphoria of vengeance. The Sathid within him responded.

Dizzied by a rush of expanded perception, Ivainson sensed the citadel of Shadowfane in its entirety, every warren and passageway and convulted maze of stairwells; lightning-swift, cruel with excitement, the killing powers of his anger coursed outward. From deepest dungeon to the spindled eaves of the keeps, every cranny became seared with unbearable light. All that lived perished instantly. The eggs of Karas shape-changers scorched to dust in their sacs, and Thienz died wailing. The great hall of the council chamber entombed Scait's advisors, favorites and enemies alike immolated to drifts of ash; between one moment and the next, the mirror pool reflected an empty throne, and a sooty arch of vaulting.

Deep beneath the storerooms, in a grotto that opened onto a corridor of fire-slagged stone, a warded circle of stillness remained untouched. Alone of the demons of Shadowfane, the Morrigierj and its underlings escaped the Sathid's cyclone of destruction. Jaric could do nothing in remedy. Bleeding, cold, and abandoned, he had no resource left. His last thread of self-awareness slipped inexorably downward into night, as he battled, and failed, and lost consciousness. Motionless alongside a corpse whose spurred fingers clamped the grip of a bloody sword, Ivainson Firelord stopped breathing.

Yet the bindings of his spirit did not loosen.

Alien energies coursed through his body, pinching off blood flow to ease his labored heart, and mending with speed and sureness no surgeon could have matched. Being self-aware and psionic, the will of the combined Sathid could unriddle the mysteries of nature in an instant. While the damage inflicted by sword steel sapped life, their collective awareness diverted to the knitting of bone and sinew and organs.

One Sathid, two, even three could not have cheated death; but Jaric bore the seeds of two score entities. Each one constituted an exponential increase in power, the sum of which approached the infinite. The echoing clangor of the chain and counterweights that dead Thienz had used to secure his tomb had scarcely faded from hearing when his chest shuddered into motion. Breath wheezed through torn tissues. Life endured, precarious as candle flame winnowed by draft.

Hours flowed into days; Jaric drifted on the borderline of death. At times, his skin glimmered blue, as the resources of crystalline entities lent him energy to survive. Later, fever raged, and he thrashed in delirium. Dreams gave rise to nightmare as, inescapably, the cycle of bonding continued.

Days became weeks. Jaric's condition stabilized. Sathid attended the needs of his body and mind, and at length encountered the wards restraining his mastery of fire and earth. The crystals challenged, displacing the patterns of the spells. Enchanted fetters flickered on lax wrists. Dimmed as coals in ashes, the bindings of sorcery faded; and two score wild Sathid encountered the quiescent presence of their own kind. Innate obsession for dominance drove them to meld.

As their energies roused and interlocked with the crystals of Vaerish origin, the cycle granted an interval of reprieve. Jaric opened his eyes to darkness thick as felt. He shuddered and breathed, and immediately choked, overpowered by the stench of corrupted flesh. Dizzied, he wet his lips with his tongue; then he flinched, recalling Scait and the sword that should have ended his life. A frown marred his brow. He raised scabbed wrists, and by the absence of illumination recognized the collapse of the demons' wards. Though Firemastery might answer his will once more, he dared raise no light. On that point, Tamlin's teaching had been explicit. To engage Sathid-based sorcery while bonding additional crystals could only hasten disaster.

Jaric sat up. His own rasping breath and the chink of spent bonds echoed loudly in the dark as he crossed his hands on his knees. His mind seemed suspiciously lucid. Certain the passive state of the Sathid could not last, Jaric tightened the muscles of his forearms and jerked. The links connecting the cuffs of his fetters gave way with a sound like breaking glass. Grateful for even that small freedom, Ivainson rubbed his abraded skin. Then a presence touched his mind, insistent, familiar, and gentle enough to break his heart.

'Jaric?'

The Firelord stiffened. Wary and alone in his misery, he presumed the call was illusion; the chamber of his prison was still sealed, and no Vaere-trained Dreamweaver could breach the barrier of stone. Well might the Sathid indulge in such tricks to torment him. But the touch came again. Undone by longing, he surrendered himself. The reality of Taen's presence embraced him, warm and immediate as sunlight. Yet the reunion yielded little joy; wild Sathid coiled to observe, patient and deadly as a nest of adders. The Dreamweaver sensed their presence with a cry of dismay. *'Ivainson, beloved, what have they done?'*

Defenses parted. Jaric beheld a cherished face framed in black hair. He tried words. But the knotty mass of scar tissue left by Scait's sword obstructed his voice, and he barely managed to croak. "Little witch, if life were just, I should have died before you found me."

'Sathid, Jaric. Demons infected you with crystals?'

"Not exactly." He qualified with incriminating brevity. "Scait tried to place my mastery in bondage through a matrix cross-linked to a Thienz. I avoided the same fate as Emien, but only by contaminating myself to the point where Kor's Accursed dared not meddle." Ivainson swallowed painfully and finished. "Scait perished. The compact died with him, but the Llondelei should know. Their store of stolen matrix can never be recovered."

A disturbance eddied the dream-link. Taen's image diminished, and the sealed chamber at Shadowfane seemed suddenly, intolerably desolate. Jaric sensed echoes. Shivering, his eyes flooded shamelessly with tears, he waited while the Dreamweaver pleaded with someone far distant. Then, poignant with distress, she sent an abbreviated farewell. *'Jaric, I love you. Never, ever forget.'*

Her warmth faded sharply away. Savaged by loss, Jaric struggled to recover composure, even as a voice of uncompromising command snapped across the dream-link. *'Ivainson Jaric!'* Wind eddied the chamber, fresh as frost amid the miasma of decay; through discomfort and despair slashed the presence of Anskiere of Elrinfaer.

Unnerved by failure, Jaric shrank but could not evade contact. The Stormwarden appeared, straight and tall before the wind-swept arch of Cliffhaven's watchtower. Cloaked in cloud-gray velvet, he stood with his staff propped in the crook of one elbow; breeze off the sea ruffled his white hair. His eyes were lowered, sorrowfully regarding a pair of amber crystals in his palm. Chilled to the heart, Jaric recognized the jewels that founded his mastery of fire and earth.

Brass-shod wood grated gently on stone as the Stormwarden turned. *'You are doomed.'* He gazed into the haze of the horizon; so long had Jaric known darkness that the vision of ocean and sky and sunlight that filled his mind seemed unreal. At length Anskiere qualified. *'Tamlin of the Vaere warned you. No help and no hope remain. Have you strength enough to keep loyalty to your race, or do you need assistance?'*

The gravity of the plea overshadowed all else; for the safety of Keithland, the Stormwarden required Jaric to take his life before wild Sathid overturned his mastery and brought disaster upon mankind. The request was not made lightly. The crystals cupped in Anskiere's hand were no longer coldly neutral but warmed by conflicting energies. Even as the Stormwarden awaited answer, wild Sathid sensed threat to their numbers. In a flash of shared awareness, they stirred their bonded counterparts toward rebellion.

Ivainson needed no urging to perceive the gravity of his predicament. He laced scarred fingers together, tightening his grip until his knuckles went numb. He had effectively died once. A second time should not prove unendurable, except that Scait's fatality thwarted all hope of simplicity. Impeded by scars and uncertainty, Jaric strove to relate how intervention by wild Sathid had healed a sword wound of fatal proportions. He might take courage into his hands, run himself through with a blade, yet still survive the result. Words would not come. The dizzy whirl of Sathid-sickness defeated concentration, and his struggle to frame speech went unnoticed.

Anskiere spun from the window with his brows forbiddingly lowered. *'Firelord! You swore me an oath, that day beneath the ice cliffs. Dare you break faith?'*

The accusation cut like a lash. Jaric knew pain, then anger, that his sincerity still stood in question. He ignored the suspicion that wild Sathid tuned his emotions for their own gain, and returned a look wholly his father's. "Do you doubt my word?"

Anskiere did not speak, but lifted his hand so Jaric could see; the crystals he held glowed red. Provoked by the rigors of bonding, their surface flared hot enough to blister. Yet the Stormwarden's least concern was the pain. At any moment the structure of the matrix would collapse, unleashing hostile energies no human could withstand. Before then, for the safety of humanity, the man who had mastered them must die.

Sweat sprang at Jaric's temples. His anger transformed to raw desperation, for steel no longer held power to kill him. If he consented to the grace of a mercy stroke, even one fashioned by sorcery, disaster might follow. His executioner might provoke wild Sathid to the same defensive reaction that had slain Scait and every demon in the compact. Ivainson forced his ruined throat to frame speech. "Your Grace, there is danger in my death."

'More than this?' Anskiere opened his fist. Ruby light speared

the chamber; with a sudden, searing spark, the crystals burst raggedly into flame.

Powerless to bridle the blaze of his own mastery, Jaric shouted frantic affirmation. No chance remained to explain. Wild Sathid whirled his thoughts like wind devils. Through rising curtains of fire, he saw Anskiere tumble both crystals of mastery across the sill. Unseen to one side, Taen shouted a useless plea concerning conjury and the wizards of Mhored Kara. The Stormwarden returned a look of anguish. Sorrowfully he shook his head. No magic in Keithland could spare the life of her love. Pitiless as an autumn storm front, Anskiere of Elrinfaer caught his staff in blistered fingers. Defense wards activated with a blinding shimmer of light.

"No!" Ivainson raised his hands, as if the gesture might somehow span ocean and avert the staff's descent; by Vaerish law, the destruction of a sorcerer's matrix would kill with swift finality. The wild Sathid were aware. Jaric cried warning, not for himself, but in agonized concern for the lands and the people under the Stormwarden's protection. "Prince, you and all you defend are in danger!"

The protest emerged as a whisper that had no chance to be heard.

Isolated by brightening veils of power, Anskiere prepared to obliterate the crystals on the sill. Necessity compelled him to wall away sympathy for the boy he had called from Morbrith keep, who had suffered the Cycle of Fire and won a Stormwarden's freedom from the ice cliffs, only to be judged and slain in the comfortless dark of Shadowfane. No sorcerer held power to change destiny or reverse the command of the Vaere. For the sake of mankind's survival, the Stormwarden repressed awareness of private tragedy, the impact of which was cruel enough to deter him. Later, when Keithland's safety was secured, the ghost of Ivainson Jaric would join the dead of Elrinfaer, and Morbrith, and Corlin, until one day the sorrows of guilt and responsibility became too heavy to endure.

Jaric screamed in a rage of futility.

And the staff struck.

A note parted the air like a slashed harpstring. Jaric suffered a blow that rocked the seat of his being. He crashed on his back, winded, paralyzed, blind, and deafened, while the fires in the crystals at Cliffhaven extinguished like water-drowned sparks. All mastery of power sundered instantly.

Yet like a curse, life endured.

"No," Jaric whispered. His body seemed a husk sucked hollow by torrents of wind as two score wild Sathid marshaled force to retaliate.

In vain he tried to resist, to smother the cataclysm of ruin that earlier had destroyed the demons. His effort was swept aside by pain that thrilled and a joy that sickened him to experience. An insatiable lust for cruelty was now permanently instilled in the Sathid's collective memory. No act of reprisal could unmake the forces his rejection of principle had created. Jaric cried out in agonized recognition. Too well he understood the downfall of Marlson Emien; too late he begged for remission. His plea might as easily have reversed the flood of the tides.

Anskiere sensed the surge as power aligned against him. Undone by memory of a second betrayal, he cried out, "Ivain! By Kor's grace, not again!" White with recognition, he angled his staff toward the window, as if some miracle wrested from the sea might save him.

No evasion could bridle the untamed Sathid's attack. Energy cracked forth, virulent as summer lightning, and hammered against the Stormwarden's defense.

For an astonishing moment, he held out. Jaric sensed a reflection of the stresses Anskiere withstood through long years of experience and a persistence born of ruthless desperation. Yet courage could not avert the inevitable. The pressure of the wild Sathid lashed sparks from the wards. The Stormwarden called warning to Taen, then slammed his staff horizontal. Energies snapped and sang. His defenses crumpled, instantaneously obliterated by a shattering explosion of light. The powers of the Sathid whirled away Jaric's view of Stormwarden, tower, and ocean in a blazing coruscation of energy no sorcerer could hope to survive.

Jaric howled denial. The enormity of the wild Sathid's retaliation inflicted a burden too terrible to bear. As the rage of crytalline entities milled the last of his reason to slivers, he thought he heard Taen weeping. The sound pierced his soul. If the cycle of destruction took her life, her Dreamweaver's intuition might never unlock understanding that he had never intended betrayal of Keithland for Shadowfane when the Sathid's powers of defense struck Anskiere down.

The backlash did not end with the Stormwarden's fall. Worse than the darkest nightmare, Sathid entities redoubled their ferocity. Utterly helpless to intervene, Jaric thrashed as surge after surge of force arose from the depths of his being. Blame could not be attributed to the crystals' willful nature. They had melded with his mind, molded their earliest awareness from him. Jaric's own passion for vengeance had schooled the Sathid to murder. That humanity might share the fate of Shadowfane's compact as a result left guilt that could never be assuaged. No ward ever raised by Tamlin's masters could thwart such fury from destruction; the heir of Ivain Firelord could do nothing but endure through the evil his weakness had created until the storm of the backlash was exhausted.

In time the riptide of cataclysm faded; like spent ripples on the surface of a pond, all settled finally to stillness. The Sathid entities retired, their focus of fearful energies centered once more upon the drive to mature and dominate.

Ivainson Jaric was left to the prison of his thoughts, and horror too grievous to escape. Firelord no longer, he raged, broken and damned by fate. Misery acquired new meaning, and its edge cut deep; still braceleted with the husks of Scait's fetters, he smashed his fists into stone. Over and over in his mind he saw his view of the Stormwarden cut off by energies no sorcerer could withstand. Hope perished also. A forester's wisdom, an old fisherman's gift of a boat, and a master scribe's kindness no longer held power to inspire. Jaric covered his face with bleeding fingers. Possessed by despair near to madness, he wept in understanding of the father he had never met.

Ivain Firelord had inflicted ruin as wanton as this. Gone to the Vaere a laughing, generous man, his hope of serving Keithland fresh as morning, he had suffered the Cycle of Fire, then yielded up integrity to survive. He also had seen all that he valued come to grief. Finally, poisoned by self-loathing, torment, and loneliness, he had died by his own hand.

Abandoned in confinement at Shadowfane, Jaric drew a shuddering breath. Like the tortured soul who had sired him, he had nothing left in Keithland to lose. Close by, the corpse of the Demon Lord lay with a sword still clenched in its fist. Jaric rolled onto his side, fingers outstretched and groping. But two score Sathid divined his intent. Secure in their bid for conquest, they lashed out collectively to prevent him.

Pain mauled his body, more intense than anything he had endured through the Cycle of Fire. Jaric convulsed, whimpering until his lungs emptied. Wretched with agony, he sought refuge within his mind. But the flare and spark of alien energies pursued him even there and denied him sanctuary. Sathid arose in force to break his spirit, swiftly, violently, and forever. No vestige of will would survive their final assault. Death itself would become irrevocably beyond reach.

Jaric reacted on reflex. Although the foundations of Fire- and

Earthmastery were destroyed, exhaustive hours of training left their mark. Experience handling Sathid forces had long since fused with primal instinct; and rage lent the strength of a beast snared in a trap. Ivainson twisted, and slashed, and boldly singled one entity from the composite mass of its fellows. The move touched off an avalanche of reaction.

In instantaneous awakening, Jaric shared every scrap of knowledge gleaned and stored by the matrix. His mind expanded, assimilating web upon web of structured information. He perceived the workings of his physical body in minute detail, comprehended a miraculous capacity to heal; perception doubled, then doubled again in the dizzy change of a moment. Beyond muscle and bone and organs, he saw the helical chains of matter that encoded the secrets of life. The web work of energies that comprised mastery and emotion stood revealed, and he saw in himself nearly limitless reserves he had never tapped.

Jarred by revelation, Jaric pushed to his knees. The Sathid possessed keys to the riddles of fire and earth, taken intact from memory. The entity that emerged supreme after bonding could re-create every aspect of his Vaere-trained talents, but with near-infinite power.

Wakened as never before to the perils of possibility, Ivainson saw in himself a potential more ruthless than any mad quirk of his father's. Anskiere's death had taught him remorse; now his matrix-born potential for evil canceled temptation to engage in a struggle no mortal could win. On the chance, however slim, that isolated humans might survive, the judgment of the Vaere must stand. Even as Sathid-force poised to smash his will to oblivion, Ivainson delved inward. Inspired by new knowledge, he seized the spark of awareness that was his life and, in defiance of the wild crystals' sovereignty, claimed the initiative to unbind the threads of his existence. Warp and weft, he found a way to negate the fabric of his spirit as thoroughly as if he had never been born.

His strike caught the Sathid unprepared. The primary mortal instincts of survival had conditioned the assumption he would not violate selfhood and seek immolation from within; no healing of the body could stave off such a death. In a flurry of desperation, the Sathid pried at his resolve. Force proved counterproductive; Jaric's grip could be loosened only by precipitating the very end he desired. Nonbeing offered defeat more final than dominance. The Sathid floundered. Incapable of jeopardizing their own survival, there remained no further option. Jaric committed his will. As the spark of his selfhood flickered, the crystals reacted.

Enraged in defeat, they yielded control, utterly, finally, and with a viciousness that ceded to Jaric a burgeoning nexus of power. The influx burned his senses beyond tolerance, and broke the progression of negation he had sacrificed all to achieve.

He screamed. Ripped into chaos in the shattering space of an instant, he struggled to cope; but crosscurrents of resonance flayed body and mind to tatters. Like a swimmer battered by undertow, Jaric strove to recover his wits. His eyes stung with light. Nerves sundered from bone and muscle, agonized by forces never meant for mortal endurance. No discipline taught by the Vaere could assimilate such a flux of energy; one after another the bastions of reason gave way.

Harrowed to the brink of madness, Jaric was driven to innovate. His Sathid-born inheritance superseded every former limit. The expanded prescience of his mind sorted futures and the branching avenues of event each possibility might take. From a million projections of disaster, Ivainson Jaric found and seized the one safe recourse left open to him. He resorted, in the end, to sorcery that violated every known law of creation.

Consciousness altered by Sathid recombined the basic patterns of matter; like metal smelted and reborn in the spark-shot heat of the forge, Jaric underwent change. No longer the sickly scribe from Morbrith, nor the Firelord taken captive at Shadowfane, he wove the composite energies of two score Sathid through the living essence of his body. He himself became the instrument that gathered, contained, and warded the near-infinite energies of new mastery. The result married flesh to a legacy of unimaginable power.

Victory left him exhausted. Sapped by sorrow and grief, and aching for Taen's lost trust, Ivainson Firelord cradled his head on crossed wrists. Too beaten to examine the miracle of his accomplishment, he closed swollen eyes and slept.

∽∾XIX∾∽

Starhope

Jaric woke to a golden blaze of light. He gasped. Certain that
Thienz with lanterns had unsealed the chamber to do him harm,
he pushed in panic to his feet. Movement brought vertigo. Braced
unsteadily in one corner, the Firelord blinked and sought his enemies.

The trestle where Scait had threatened him canted against
shelving; boxes and flasks and spilled bundles of herbs lay jumbled in dusty disarray. The lantern hung dark on its hook. On the
floor, amid an eggshell sparkle of smashed flasks, the sprawled
skeleton of the Demon Lord leered in death. Spurred and bony
fingers still clenched the rusted grip of a sword. The doorway
beyond stood sealed, its mechanism webbed over by spiders.

Jaric shut his eyes. He forced trembling muscles to relax, then
carefully traced the illumination to its source. Power discharged
from his body in a steady corona of light. The patterns in the aura
were similar to those of a sorcerer's staff, but brighter, more
intense, and complex beyond mortal comprehension. Jarred as if
bedrock had shifted under his feet, Jaric recoiled against cold
stone; the surrounding brilliance slivered through a blur of anguished tears.

He had changed. Only time would determine whether he had
traded humanity for survival. Unwilling to sort ramifications, and
afraid above all to contemplate the fate that had befallen Taen,
Jaric immersed himself in the immediate.

Measured by dust and the decomposed stage of Scait's corpse,
his mastery of the wild Sathid had spanned considerable time. Yet

Ivainson knew neither thirst nor hunger. He surveyed his hands, found his wrists reduced to tendon and bone within the slack husks of his fetters. A white webwork of scars marred flesh that was pale, yet supple with health. Hunger, even thirst, had not touched him. Against all odds, he had survived; he wondered whether the folk of Keithland had fared as well.

The thought provoked a surge of clairvoyance; Jaric felt his mind turn like a mirror, reflecting a dizzy succession of images. Fallow after harvest, the fields at Felwaithe showed a herring-bone stubble of cut corn; hill clanswomen beat clothes in the spume of Cael's Falls, and leather-clad herders drove weanling foals to Dunmoreland pastures. Ships offloaded baled wool at Landfast harbor, rigging like ink lines against wintry skies. Enveloped by consciousness of humanity's teeming complexity, Ivainson encountered no trace of Anskiere or Taen. His loss sparked awareness of others; at Cliffhaven, Corley paced the battlements, his black cloak of mourning whipped by changeable winds; at the captain's throat nestled the ruby torque that once had been the Kielmark's. Shared grief snapped the sequence.

Sheened with sweat, Ivainson Jaric gasped for breath in the musty confines of Shadowfane. Anskiere's sacrifice had not, after all, been in vain: to all appearances, Keithland had been spared the rage of the wild Sathid.

The reprieve was unexpected. Ivainson turned his face to the wall. Relief threatened his balance, and flood after flood of tears wet his cheeks. He did not weep only for release. Though his own powers of sorcery had inspired the visions, the scope and intensity of newfound awareness unnerved him. A considerable interval passed before he regained any semblance of control. Still more time elapsed before he dared to explore the source of the miracle that had preserved his land and people from destruction.

Trembling, more than distrustful of powers that bent his thoughts like a prism into focused arrows of force, Jaric directed his sight toward the watchtower at Cliffhaven. He sought the nightmare moment in the past when Anskiere of Elrinfaer had leveled his staff against the combined retaliation of two score wild Sathid.

The scene unfolded with damning clarity. Again the light bloomed with a brightness unendurable to the eyes. Like a stab to the heart, Jaric saw the sorcerer become enveloped by a raging tide of destruction. His Stormwarden's defenses were obliterated; the rough-hewn stone of the tower reddened with heat, then glazed in an explosion of force. Jaric compelled himself to watch as the blaze of the Sathid backlash coursed outward, hungry to destroy. His willpower threatened to fail him. Yet in the moment before he broke, the current turned inward upon itself, caught and twisted in check by the shadowy circle of a wardspell.

Joined in their unfathomable chants, the wizards of Mhored Kara fenced the tower with conjury that negated all resonance of Sathid power. From without they imposed the reality of un-harmed tranquility that the killing backlash could not overwhelm. The wizards' philosophy provided the framework, Jaric saw. But the energies that set peace into harmony were familiar to the point of heartbreak, unmistakably lent by the hand of Taen Dreamweaver.

Keithland had been saved, but at a cost that wounded to be-hold.

In the comfortless dark of Shadowfane, Jaric slammed his fist into stone. Taen had divined the scope of the backlash the Sathid might unleash. Alone, betrayed, cut where love left her vulner-able, still she had mustered courage enough to act. As Anskiere had fallen, she had reached beyond heartache and achieved the salvation of Keithland.

The consequences of her sacrifice could not be escaped. Jaric suffered remorse without reprieve as wave after wave of power broke against the wizards' wards. Some robed figures rocked under the impact, others collapsed soundlessly in death, but the singing of their colleagues never faltered. The adepts of Mhored Kara held firm through the worst onslaught of destruction ever to challenge Keithland. Never once did they break either rhythm or concentration. Their defenses held. When at last the fury of backlash became spent, the watchtower at Cliffhaven remained, a slagged and smoking shell ringed by a charred expanse of paving.

The sorcerer who accounted himself responsible watched numbly while the wizards released their wards. Haggard, singed as scarecrows, the survivors of the conclave bent and tended their fallen. Jaric saw them bind the hurts of their wounded, then wash and bury their dead.

In the town, smoke rose from the chimneys of the craftsmen's shops. Ships rocked at anchor in the quay, and the sky shone an untouched blue; flocks of gulls squabbled undisturbed at the tide mark. From Felwaithe to the Free Isles, Keithland remained whole and in sunlight, as if no disturbance had threatened the continuinty of life. Yet no wizard of Mhored Kara ventured across the blasted stone that marked the boundary of their protec-tion. They did not set foot near the tower.

Neither, for all his awesome power, could Jaric. Pain stripped away his resolve; the memory of Taen's laughter would haunt him to the end of his days. Not miracles, nor breadth of vision, could lend courage enough to search amid the ruins for her remains, or meet the accusation in her eyes if by some twist of fate she had managed to survive. Anguish of spirit could never restore the trust Ivainson had taken oath to preserve. The fate of his father had at last become his own, canceling every hope he had ever dared to foster.

Left in bitterest debt, Jaric raised his face from his hands. He longed for nothing beyond forgetfulness. That being impossible, he buried his shame, abandoning all memory of the watchtower so that he could set his killer's instincts toward preserving what Anskiere had died to keep safe.

The danger posed by demons was not ended. Recalled to the peril of the Morrigierj, the son of Ivain Firelord bent his will away from the fortress at Cliffhaven. Empty with sorrow, he began a systematic review of Felwaithe's north coast, which lay closest to Shadowfane, and most vulnerable to invasion.

At first glance nothing seemed amiss: winds whipped a reed-ridden channel to whitecaps, and a cutter flying the wolf of Cliffhaven scudded with her rail buried in spray. Jaric lingered in appreciation of her captain's bold seamanship, and power bucked his control. A subliminal suggestion of ruin suffused his inward eye, as if the tranquility of the bay with its rugged chain of isles were destined not to last. Jaric shivered. Touched by a clear note of dread, he hesitated; and prescience snapped all restraint. Visions of pending devastation came upon him in a virulence of Sathid-born perception.

The wind changed key. Ivainson heard the suck and thud of breakers fouled with debris. Smoke clogged his nostrils. Stumps thrust like rotted teeth from shores where, moments earlier, stands of pine had notched clean air and sunlight. The view shifted. Sea water scalded his hands, oceans sloshed with scorched fish; neglect laced runners of briar between the bones of cattle and men. South, the land was littered like storm wrack with razed towns. Roadways lay choked with toppled wagons, traces draped like knotwork over the shriveled corpses of oxen. Clansfolk rotted amid the crumpled wreckage of their tents, and the sunken masts of fishing fleets speared through the tide pools at Murieton. Cliffhaven's proud corsairs had smashed like eggshells on shore, and silent, foggy nights blanketed a beacon tower thrown down into rubble.

Sick at heart, Jaric turned to Landfast. Spires there lay tumbled like the sticks of a bird nest abandoned to winter. Waves combed vacant beaches, and the crabbed, uprooted apple trees of Telshire moldered like arthritic skeletons in dusty beds of soil. Spurred by distress, Ivainson quartered the length and breadth of Keithland. Desolation filled his vision. Not a man, woman, or child would survive the devastation to come. He recoiled in horror, hounded by prophecy, of the failure that had shattered him hideously made real. Energy cracked in white sparks around him as he dispersed his focus.

The dusty stillness of Shadowfane seemed suddenly unbearably confining. Ivainson Jaric pressed his cheek against stone and shuddered. The shadowed, sunken sockets of Scait's skull seemed to mock him from the floor. Though the compact itself was obliterated, the Morrigierj would complete the extinction of mankind. No Vaere-trained sorcerer remained for defense; the wizards of Mhored Kara possessed mettle, but little means to ward. Keithland stood open for conquest. Whipped to frenzy by their overlord, the Gierj might ravage and murder at will.

Shadowfane's stillness abruptly acquired overtones of menace. Jaric flexed scarred hands and pushed himself off from the wall. Light flared golden around his person as he pitched the force of his mastery against his prison door. Iron glared briefly red. Wood steamed, and counterweights trembled on their moorings. Then a high-pitched whine sliced the air. Planking and chain ripped apart, solidity scattered to a drifting billow of dust. Too concerned to be unsettled by the violence of his works, Jaric strode through, into a vaulted hallway where gargoyles leered from the cornices.

The light of his presence dissolved shadows from his path. Although the demon fortress was convulted as a maze, expanded perception lent bearings. Jaric moved through passages of checkered agate, and turnings carved with runes. Slim as a wraith, and bathed in power, he sought the uncanny circle of stillness that harbored the source of all danger.

His steps reverberated through empty halls, unchallenged. Beyond a triad of hexagonal portals, he climbed the spiral staircase that pierced the inner core of Shadowfane. No demon emerged to battle him. Jaric heard nothing but the moan of wind through bleak towers; the expanded sensitivity of his mastery detected no life but the scurry of foraging mice.

The great hall of Shadowfane rose high above the level of the fells. Ivainson Firelord strode through the entry where Marlson

Emien had once been dragged by the grasping fists of Thienz. No carpet remained to soften his footfalls. Shadowless amid the natural glow of his wards, he crossed an echoing expanse of marble. The chandeliers over his head hung dark on dusty chains; lancet windows outlined an overcast sky, and cloud light gleamed cold on the floors. The silvered surface of the mirror pool reflected the soaring lines of columns and a vacant expanse of dais. Scait's throne stood tenantless, a knife blade thrust through the leather of a human wrist.

Chilled to a halt by the sight, Jaric took a moment to sort the shadow ghosts of past events and recall the present. Scait Demon Lord could threaten humanity no more. Only dust remained of the compact that had hated and plotted vengeance through the centuries since *Corinne Dane*'s luckless wreck.

Yet through the emotional afterimage left by Kor's Accursed, Jaric's heightened senses picked up resonance of something stirring, the ruthless and alien force that lingered yet in Shadowfane's halls. His mouth went dry. Humans had been pawns in the demons' bid for power, yet the Morrigierj made no distinction. For the transgressions of Emien and Tathagres, who had manipulated and abused the Gierj, the desecration of Keithland would inevitably come to pass.

The Firelord whirled. The flurry of his footsteps rebounded from rock walls as he fled urgently toward the passageway. Once he might have summoned Earthmastery and stepped through stone in his haste. Now the intensity of his powers overwhelmed him to the point where he required the ordinary for reassurance. He ran like the simplest clansman. His breath rasped through scarred lungs as he plunged through the archway leading from the great hall.

The stairway beyond lay dark. Jaric needed no torches. The diffuse glow of his presence rinsed shadows from his path and shed clear, unsettling light over carved and inlaid risers.

Ivainson had not far to descend. The eerie circle of stillness began on the level below; between the posts of the first landing massed a horde of glowing eyes. Gierj gathered like clotted ink in the gloom of the stairwell, barring the way down. Above them drifted a featureless sphere. Its surface was polished ebony, and it spun in midair with a whine like swarming bees.

Jaric jerked to a stop. Sweating, ragged, and winded, he reached reflexively for a sword that was not there. The lapse made him curse. Every principle taught him by the Vaere, every painstaking refinement gleaned from Anskiere's instruction, now failed to apply. No discipline in memory could guide him. The complexities of multiple mastery were too vast to be encompassed, and even the simplest thoughts overreached his intent. Yet against the Morrigierj he had nothing else.

Jaric braced his feet upon the stair. Humanity would perish if he hesitated. Desperately seeking redemption for the lives his illicit mastery had cost, he gathered courage and raised sorcery. The Sathid glow that surrounded him split, singing, into hard-edged halos of force.

Inscrutably spinning, the Morrigierj acknowledged his presence. Ruby light pulsed beneath its surface. The glassy outer shell maintained its rotation, but the glow, like an eye, swiveled and steadied, scanning the nature of the being who trespassed within its lair.

A tingle coursed through Jaric's mind. Warned by impressions of near-infinite force and imminent danger, he attempted a counterward. Sathid-born energy defended with a snap. The alien probe disengaged. Unbalanced by the abruptness of its withdrawal, Jaric recoiled. His heel snagged on a riser, and he stumbled, shoulders rammed against the wrought-iron scroll of the balustrade. Below, like a matched horde of puppets, the Gierj advanced with a scrabble of claws on stone.

The Firelord did not give ground, but straightened and flung tangled hair from his eyes. "Demon!" he called hoarsely. "I challenge! To ravage Keithland, you must first contend with me."

Wary within the golden blaze of his wards, Jaric awaited the nerve-rasping whistle that heralded attack by the Gierj. But no sound arose. The Morrigierj melded its underlings and struck with none of the preliminaries required by Maelgrim or Tathagres.

The air went suddenly brittle. Warned only by a tingle of prescience, Jaric sprang tense. Then a flash of white heat stripped his shields. Had he not owned a Firelord's trained resistance to burns, his flesh would have seared instantaneously to ash. Instead, blinded by a flux of light, he tumbled over backward into eddies of deflected energy.

Risers banged his head, then his back and shoulders. He hooked the rail to brake his fall. Backlash sizzled around him, slagging stone and jagging sparks the length of the balustrade. Cut like a whip across the palm, Jaric cried out. He curled protectively into a crouch and waited for the sally to end. But strength flowed from Gierjling to Morrigierj, there to be channeled into violence with the unassailable surge of the tides; no direct measure could stem the onslaught. The assault raged on without letup.

Driven to act, Ivaison Firelord shaped a defense from the materials nearest to hand.

Earth wisdom answered. Power roared forth with a vehemence never equaled among mortals. Stone exploded; a storm of spinning, knife-edged fragments raked the front ranks of Gierj. Howls tore from the throats of the mortally wounded. The grazed and hale alike screeched in fury, while the Morrigierj zigzagged in the air, its aggression blunted by a fraction.

Ringed by a turbulent corona of light, Jaric struck again. His sorcery wrenched at keystones and pillars, exploding them to vapor with a force that negated sound. Stone rumbled; cracks ripped across vaulted ceilings, and the central edifice of Shadowfane shuddered toward collapse. Sand showered, rattling down the stair, followed by a grinding avalanche of rock and debris.

Yet even as the stone crashed downward, Jaric understood that he would fail. His Sathid-born gift of prescience read the outcome. A split second before reality, he knew the rubble would slow and tumble in the air, arrested in place by the Morrigierj.

The event followed like a double image; Gierjlings scrabbled from beneath tons of suspended stone. As they scuttled like rats toward safety, Jaric gained an instant to regroup. He moved to steal the advantage and, with a Firelord's defensive reflex, blasted the keep to inferno.

The sorcery struck in a white flash of heat. Stone ruptured. Lava dashed airborne with the fountaining force of storm spray. The walls ran red and crumpled. Isolated on an island of stairway, lit scarlet by currents of molten stone, Jaric closed his eyes. Desperate and blistered by heat, he pitched the sum of his vision into the future. There he sorted through meshes of pattern and outcome for a reality that left Keithland safe under sunlight.

His thoughts expanded with a rush that left him dizzied. The space of an instant showed him eons, a thousand times a thousand overviews of destruction. Scoured by the grief of uncounted deaths, he saw cities swept clean of life, whole planets overcrowded and enslaved. He watched great metal ships fire bolts that exploded with eye-searing brilliance against an ocean of darkness and stars. The images spanned all, from the infinite to the infinitesimal.

Houses burned, and forests withered. Stunted, malformed humans scratched crops from dusty furrows. Men in metal armor hunted other humans with nets, then lit cookfires to roast the meat of their skinned and slaughtered quarry; in another sequence, people crawled on all fours, eating roots torn raw from the ground. Their eyes were placid and dull as cattle, and their young grew to maturity without laughter. Jaric perceived all this and a multitude of other futures instantaneously. Hard on the heels of vision, he understood that the Morrigierj itself intervened. Its presence robbed him of inspiration, pinched off all possibilities that offered untrammeled outcomes of life and success.

The Firelord's heir knew anger then, resentment deeper than any experienced by Ivain. Power amplified his emotion, and the entire spired citadel of Shadowfane exploded in a focused discharge of fury. Rock melted and glazed, and the scream of tortured elements jarred on the air like a blow.

Still the battle raged. The circle of stillness that surrounded the Morrigierj stayed unbreached, while Gierjlings danced across lava with complete and terrifying impunity.

The counterstrike came without warning.

One second, Jaric stood juggling for balance against the flux of heat and chaos whipped up by the ferocity of his attack. The next, the whine of the Morrigierj changed pitch.

Reality altered.

Hurled adrift in a dimension beyond grasp of human logic, Jaric strove to recover orientation. Sensation was lost to him. His vision seemed smothered in felt. No awareness of his body remained, and other than the golden haze of his Sathid wards, he retained no concept of self beyond a spark of conscious will.

Energies flashed, blue and violet and ruby. Uncertain how to battle the intangible, Jaric tuned his perception to search for the enemy who stalked to kill. Darkness swallowed his attempt. He blundered, lost, and his uncertainty drew immediate attack.

Malice arose, cruel as the bite of a strangler's cord, and throttled his right to exist.

"No." Jaric steadied his wards.

The Morrigierj pressed a ruthless demand for proof of his worthiness.

Jaric countered by instinct, the shield he raised the constancy of his love for Taen. Too late, he realized his mistake; what had been his innermost strength now reflected his gravest shortfall. The Morrigierj granted no quarter. With a terrible, twisting sense of vertigo, it caused the darkness around Jaric to dissolve: As a man he found himself standing naked and alone on heated stone. Before him rose the ruined watchtower at Cliffhaven.

His breath caught in his throat, then exploded in a scream of anguish. "No!"

Protest changed nothing. Between himself and the tower's seared stairway loomed weakness he could not face: the meanness of spirit that had destroyed Marlson Emien, Merya Tathagres, and, not least, the firelord who had sired him. Behind, blocking retreat, waited the Morrigierj and the threat of humanity's downfall. Jaric must go forward and confront the wreckage of his dearest dream, or bring total devastation upon Keithland.

The conflict beggared pride, left both spirit and dignity in shreds. Having given in once to cowardice, he found the first step a hardship of unbearable proportion. Jaric threw back his head. Tears spilled from his eyes and dampened the hair at his temples. No death or threat of bodily torment seemed worse than the condemnation that loomed beyond the tower's dark entry. The reality was double-edged. Either he would discover himself guilty of Taen's murder, or, worse, he would meet stinging accusation in her eyes, the wholeness of her love poisoned to loathing. More horrible still, she might live, and be piteously maimed.

Sooner would he have endured another trial by Sathid.

No such option existed. The Morrigierj pinned him without quarter. With a cry of unmitigated despair, Jaric regarded the tower. Anskiere and Taen had already suffered for his weakness. The rest of humanity must not be left to share the brunt of the consequences; greater evil could not be imagined. The son of Ivain Firelord renounced his last vestige of pride. He gathered his screaming nerves into something that passed for resolve, and started toward the tower's bleak doorway.

His next step proved no easier than the first. Shadows at the threshold seemed to wring him with sorrow. Stone heated still from the chaos unleashed by the Sathid blistered his soles as he set his feet on the stair. Almost, that pain became welcome, a distraction to blunt the greater wound in his heart. As Jaric climbed, memories arose to haunt him, of Taen's teasing laughter, the warm weight of her as she pressed into his arms. "You worry for three people, Jaric," she had said in her berth aboard *Moonless*. "Keithland won't collapse while you smile."

Yet no joy remained to him now. If he hesitated, the existence and the memory of humanity would be obliterated.

The end of the stairway loomed ahead, wreathed in clearing smoke. Through wrung and twisted lintels lay the chamber where Anskiere of Elrinfaer had raised his staff to end the life of Ivainson Firelord. Now the place seemed to echo the boom of the sea, bounds of Keithland, would reluctantly blaze the path toward the stars. The thought caused him untold sorrow, until a shower of sand struck his ankles.

"Fish-brains! Beloved, you took forever to get here." Two hands plunged through the light of his presence, to lock with fierce strength around his chest.

"Taen," Jaric murmured; he turned and buried his face in black hair. Only the Dreamweaver knew that he wept. She waited, patient in his embrace, as other footsteps approached. The presence of a second sorcerer brushed her awareness. She smiled then, but said nothing. When her Firelord looked up, he would find the Stormwarden of Elrinfaer limping across sand to meet him.

Here ends
The Cycle of Fire